ARRAIGNED

A LEGAL THRILLER

John W. Dennehy

Macabre Tales Publishing

Macabre Tales Publishing
127 Main Street, Suite 1
Nashua, NH 03060

Written by John W. Dennehy
Cover Design by Wendy Saber Core
Edition: Trade Paper

First Printed in the United States of America, 2021.

PROLOGUE

ALL DEBTS eventually come due. Sometimes repayment has a high price, especially when the debt is owed to someone in a powerful position.

Back in the first year of law school, I tended to run around with two classmates. We were in the same section, taking most of the first-year classes together. All three of us were non-traditional students, slightly older than many in our class. We were military veterans.

The night began like many others. I'd hunkered down in the main reading room on the lower level of the library. It resembled an old-fashioned setting, with rows of long wooden tables and chairs. Vintage light fixtures hung from the ceiling. There wasn't any talking allowed in the room, and I preferred it that way.

Leaving the library for the night, I stretched out my long frame. I ran into Jack Delaney by the staircase leading to the next level where the elevators were located. He was average height, muscular, and wore his hair short due to a receding hairline.

"Hey, Dwyer," he said, grinning. "Want to grab a cold one with us?"

Jack was talking about joining him and Brad Wallace for a few rounds at a pub near the law school. This had become a regular Friday night routine, with each of us buying a round.

"Sure," I said, brushing my wavy black hair aside. "Brad going to meet us there?"

"He's down in the lobby. And that's not all…" Jack smirked.

"What?" I wasn't in the mood for games.

"Brad has a few girls who are going to join us."

I shook my head. "He's quite the player."

We ascended the staircase and headed over to the elevators. A gaggle of law students eagerly awaited the lift. We stood quietly as others chatted about their professors and assignments. Everyone appeared ready to put an arduous week of classes behind them. Most would tour the local bars then crash for the evening, wake up late the next morning hung over, and then they'd hit the books until early Saturday evening. Rinse and repeat.

When the elevator doors whisked open, only one student got off the lift. Everyone squeezed inside. Cramping the small space, we'd overloaded the elevator. Nobody volunteered to take the next ride down. All of us were impatient to get out of the building.

The shiny elevator doors whisked opened, and everyone piled off. A few groups pushed ahead of us, while lone students trundled to their lockers, weighed down with knapsacks stuffed full of law books.

We stepped from the elevator bank into a palatial lobby. Doric columns jutted upward for three stories. Then, a circular opening protruded into a fourth floor. Black iron rails, capped with a wooden handrail, traced around the upper opening, so people on the fourth floor could take a gander down into the palatial lobby area below. A pristine school logo was embossed on the limestone tiles of the lobby floor.

Balconies ran around the next two levels, continuing with the iron railings and wooden handrail found in the opening further above. Most of the first-year classes were held on the second and third floors. Many of the classrooms were large, tiered lecture halls, where professors grilled students using the Socratic method.

An immense staircase ran down from the upper floors, and rows of students herded from classrooms around the balconies, down the stairs, and out of the building.

"I'm going to ditch this," I said to Jack, pulling on the strap to my backpack.

He nodded. "Doing the same. I'll meet you and Brad in five."

"Sure."

Cutting across the lobby, I caught a glimpse of Brad and he smiled. "You going with us?" he called to me.

"Yeah." I slipped off my backpack, heading to the lockers.

The girls circled him. One glanced my way, checking to see who'd caught Brad's attention. The rest were glued to him. Unreal.

He was tall, lean, and had sandy blonde hair. Girls seemed to fancy his hazel eyes and square jaw. But I sensed his personality is what captivated them. He flattered people and feigned interest in them, even if a topic bored him. A natural born politician.

I stepped into a room full of lockers, stacked two high. Finding my way through a small maze of students and jogs in the room, I reached my locker and worked the combination lock open. Fortunate to have a top locker, I dumped my pack inside. Then, I perused my wool coat, wondering if it was worth lugging around. We'd just be going to a pub nearby. I decided against it, shut the door, and snapped the lock secure.

I'll come back for it if we head around town, I thought. But I didn't expect to make this a long night. There was too much work to do the next day. Like always, I had fallen behind and needed to study all weekend to get caught up. The workload was intense.

And then, I walked into the lobby, relieved to have another week of classes behind me. It was relaxing to have a breather from school. Looking forward to a few casual beers, I never anticipated what the night had in store for me.

***

MEETING UP WITH THE CREW, I was the last to arrive. Brad led the way, and everyone headed to the front doors. We stepped outside into the frigid night.

An overhang jutted from the building, where a group of students chatted and smoked.

We traipsed past a set of columns, supporting a curved portion of the façade, and walked down the sidewalk. Snow and ice had piled up along the roadside, and traffic buzzed down

Tremont Street. Crossing a side street, the sidewalk became decrepit and broken.

A vacant storefront lingered on the corner, dark, with a ramshackle exterior.

Further along, the neon pub sign hung over the sidewalk at the doorway, near the far side of the establishment. We walked past a plate-glass window; the bar was packed. I questioned whether we should consider another place. Before I could say anything, Brad had already disappeared through the front door. The crew followed him inside, single file.

I pulled up the rear and stepped into a tiny entranceway.

The others cleared out and I stopped at the bouncer. Racket from the barroom echoed a distinct contrast to the still night outside. The bouncer sat on a stool and asked for my identification, frowning as I fished through a pocket for my wallet. Most just let me through, so I hadn't expected to need it.

When I finally got my driver's license out, he didn't even inspect it.

He nodded, and I shoved my wallet away. Then, I pressed through a crush at the bar. I found everyone further down the narrow pub. They were huddled against a small counter opposite the bar. A picture window above the counter overlooked an alley.

People gathered around the bar had spread into the travel area, leaving scant room for anyone trying to get to the bathrooms and pool tables out back.

Some of our group draped their coats over stools. The girls put their handbags on the counter, and we all circled around to catch up. A scent of spilt beer wafted up from the floor.

Jack looked us over and shook his head.

"What?" Brad asked.

"This place is packed. We're not going to get served. And the bartender has his hands full," Jack said, looking disappointed.

The bar was overloaded; there wasn't any room to squeeze in and place an order.

Brad grinned. "You shouldn't doubt me."

Everyone laughed and waited to see what shenanigans he'd pull.

He reached for his wallet and plucked out a crisp hundred-dollar bill. "I'll take care of the first round," Brad said. "Stacey, do you want to help carry the drinks over?"

"Sure." She was lean, blonde, and well dressed, especially for law school.

All four girls were dressed up.

They must have planned on a night out, I figured.

This was probably just a warm-up before they headed out to the trendy bars and nightclubs, after they ditched us, or at least me and Jack.

"What will you girls have?" Brad asked.

They requested cosmopolitans and trendy vodka martinis; top shelf orders.

He didn't ask me or Jack for our order. We kept to the same routine.

Brad turned and meandered through the crowd, walking toward the end of the bar with Stacey in tow. He stopped at the opening where the bartender left drinks for servers. Barbacks ducked underneath the spot to restock the shelves and coolers.

"He knows how to get around," Jack smirked.

Brad leaned over the opening, waving the bill. The bartender frowned at the tactic, until he saw the crisp hundred-dollar note. Then, he quickly finished up an order and headed directly for Brad.

Soon, Brad and Stacey were plying their way back to us, hands full of drinks. Jack stepped over and relieved them of a couple glasses. He handed me a pint of Bass Pale Ale. Everyone ended up getting their drinks and we made introductions. The other girls were Monica, Kristen, and Charlene. All three of them were from another section.

A section is a group of about a hundred law students, who take the required first-year courses together. I wondered how Brad had met them.

Stacey hung on Brad's every word, but Monica seemed actually interested in getting to know me. I told her about my background, having grown up in Hamilton, studying history at the University of New Hampshire, and then serving in the Army. She didn't ask whether I'd gone overseas, and I didn't offer any details about my time in the 82nd Airborne Division.

Brad turned to us and raised his glass. "To the Bass Boys," he said.

The girls giggled. We all clinked our glasses and took a sip.

"And to these lovely ladies," Brad continued.

We repeated the act, then Monica looked at me and snickered. "What's all this… with 'the Bass Boys.'"

"We tend to go out on Fridays and each of us buys a round," I said. "The first night it was three rounds of Bass Ale, so we've continued the tradition."

She frowned. "And you've dubbed yourselves the Bass Boys?"

"Not us." I laughed. "Some folks in our section came up with that one."

"Any other good nicknames I should know about?" Monica said, laughing.

"They have a really good one. Luckily, it's not about us."

"Sounds dicey. What's that one?" she asked.

"The Slick Boys," I whispered to her.

Monica canted her head and grinned. "The Slick Boys? Really?"

"Yup," I said taking a sip of beer.

She shook her head. "There must be a story with that one."

"There is," I said, scanning the bar to see if they were within earshot.

A couple of guys in the group were in my section, so I figured they'd come over to the bar before going clubbing. And I was right. I spotted them huddled near the bar, laughing, and carrying on. They wore suits and business casual attire, despite merely being law students.

Francis Vincent caught my glance, and I nodded to him. Frannie grew up in Hamilton. We'd attended middle school together, then lost contact when he went to a Catholic high school. Now, we were in the same section in law school and didn't really talk much.

"Who's that?" Monica asked.

"A guy from my hometown," I said, turning to her.

"That's cool." Then, she ascertained my dismay. "What's wrong?"

We seemed to be hitting it off. I don't usually connect well with girls. Maybe I'm too reserved. But talking with her came easy. I really didn't want to get into this. My past held some secrets, and a couple people in that group brushed up against it.

"Just don't know why he hangs out with that crowd," I finally said. "It's really not like him… at least the guy I knew growing up."

"So, what's the deal with them?" Monica pressed closer.

"The two thinner guys are in my section. And the chubbier one is a year ahead of us. Thinks he's a big deal because he's made it past first year. He's dating the girl next to him. Those two are on the moot court team, and everyone is talking about how they'll get married and become a Boston power couple."

"You're not jealous…?"

"Nothing like that." I shook my head. "They're known for going clubbing, and the one on the end chases after girls, who are well below the drinking age. There are rumors…"

"Yeah, what kind?" She canted her head, concerned.

"Rumors of cocaine use."

Monica inhaled. Then, she suddenly jounced forward, her eyes wide. Alarmed.

"What?" I didn't understand what happened.

Jack Delaney leaned towards us. "Did what I think just happen?"

Monica nodded. "Let's not make a big deal of it."

"What?" I was confused.

"Someone nearby just groped her," Jack said.

"Really?" I couldn't believe it. My blood boiled.

"Forget it," Monica said, then she began stepping further away from the travel lane, trying to avoid a repeat encounter.

Her eyes lit up again.

Looking down, I caught a glimpse of a hand slipping off her behind. Then, I spotted the offender. "It was him," I stammered, pointing.

A burley group of men had moved closer to us. They resembled union workers, who likely knocked off late in the afternoon from a jobsite and had gotten an early start drinking. The culprit was in his mid-forties, with a barrel chest and thick arms. He had a beer gut and glassy eyes.

His crew egged him on, laughing at his antics. And he smiled, pleased with himself.

Jack stepped between Monica and the crew. "That's enough."

"What are you going to do about it?" the offender said. He made a groping motion with his hand. All his friends laughed, and Jack stewed.

A Marine veteran, Jack could probably take the guy, but none of them seemed to appreciate it. This really pissed me off. Just because you're clean cut, they think you're a chump. All too often, guys like this were cowards when they're alone. Most of them never served in the military. Just a bunch of obnoxious barroom brawlers. Bullies who preyed on the weak.

Although she was out of reach, the guy gestured like he was grabbing at Monica. Jokingly, he made repeated groping actions with his hands. He laughed and looked to his friends for encouragement. The man riled me.

He stepped closer and meant to actually do it again, perhaps touch her close up. Like we didn't matter. As if we weren't even there.

Without a conscious thought, my hand shot out and struck him in the chest. I hit something solid, but the force of my arm was incredible.

He stumbled backward. A confused look crossed his face.

"Hey!" he yelled, regaining his balance.

All his friends stood idly by, appearing shocked that someone had stood up to them.

I expected from their reaction that nobody would throw in with him.

He seemed to know it too. "I'll handle this," he said to them.

I waited for his next move. Everyone around us had grown quiet.

Adjusting himself, the man was furious. He regained composure after I'd humiliated him in front of his friends. He stepped toward me. Floorboards squeaked under his weight. "You and me… are going to step outside and have ourselves a little talk."

"Fine with me," I said.

"Ken, it's not worth it," Brad said.

Monica grabbed my arm. "It's okay. Let it go."

"He's a brick shithouse," Jack said. "Forget about it."

They didn't think I could take him. My pulse pounded with indignation. I set my beer down and shook my head. Then, I followed the bruiser out of the bar.

Chilly air whapped into my cheeks, but the rest of my body didn't feel the frigid weather.

We meandered into the alley, footsteps crunching over crusty snow.

He turned around and grunted. Then, he ducked his head down and charged, trying to wrap his arms around me in a bear hug.

I stepped to the side and punched him in the head as he ran past.

He stood up and shook his head, trying to regain composure.

Now, he was really embarrassed. Fury raged him on. He came at me swinging wildly. A punch hit me in the jaw, knocking my head sideways. I didn't feel any pain, but the blow me.

Then, I stepped towards him, and everything went black.

When I came to my senses, Jack and Brad were pulling me off the man. The snow was covered in blood. His blood.

He lay strewn on the ground, groaning in agony.

I looked up and saw Frannie staring at me through the picture window. His mouth agape, he looked at me awestruck. Monica was in shock; disappointment registered on her face. I knew that I'd blown it with her.

Jack led me back down the alley.

Police cruisers halted on the street, tires screeching. Blue lights flashed, illuminating the night. Boots smacked the ground. Everything seemed surreal, as if moving in slow motion. My mind drifted, like it was outside of myself. My body felt numb.

Officers quickly discerned the situation. They handcuffed me and took me into custody.

Down at the precinct, Brad arrived and acted on my behalf. A lawyer in a fancy suit and wool overcoat showed up. He was a high-priced attorney, and a friend of Brad's father. The desk sergeant knew the other guy. Apparently, the culprit had a long rap sheet, including a couple resisting arrest charges. The cops didn't like him.

Frannie showed up and gave a statement, along with Brad and Jack. Somehow, Brad was able to make the whole thing just go away. I wasn't even booked.

Walking out of the station, I turned to him. "Thanks."

"You owe me," he replied coolly.

I smiled. "Sure."

He didn't smile back. This wasn't just a saying. Brad really meant that I owed him big time, and I understood someday he'd seek payment on the debt. I just never expected it would have such a high price.

FIFTEEN YEARS LATER

PART ONE

A DEATH

ONE

THE CALL CAME during the late evening hours. I'd finished up after a long day at the office and driven my aging Porsche over to the condominium on Revere Street. After circling the block a few times, I finally found a parking space.

Entering my unit, the warm, cozy place helped shake off the winter chill. A picture window caught a view of the Boston skyline. Lights from office buildings reflected through the glass.

The place was basically a long rectangle, with a living room adjacent to a dining area and kitchen. There was a master bedroom off the living room, and a spare room that I used as a study was connected to the kitchen. The place was furnished with mid-century furniture. A gray sofa with chaise took up much of the living area. It was complemented by an orange swivel chair and oval coffee table.

I slipped off my overcoat and suit jacket. Then, I loosened my tie, rolled up my sleeves, and went to work preparing a gin and tonic. I'd earned a Thursday nightcap.

Just as I slid the green bottle of Tanqueray to the backsplash, I heard my cellphone buzz. It was set on the coffee table in the living area.

I grabbed my drink and strolled over to check the message.

Taking a seat on the sofa, I unlaced my shoes, kicked them off, and peered at my phone. It was Alyson. My ex-fiancé had texted: *Call me. Urgent.*

She'd broken off our engagement over a year ago. We had gotten together a few times, feeling the waters. But we hadn't spoken in months. I took a sip of my drink, then set it down and picked up my phone, my interest piqued.

A call came through before I could respond to Alyson. Brad Wallace, an old law school buddy, was trying to reach me. He only contacted me when he wanted something. Often, it was a request to help someone out. He'd moved up the ladder in state politics, holding the Senate minority leader position. There was talk of him running for governor one day.

I answered his call. "Ken Dwyer."

"Ken, glad I caught you," Brad said, breathing deeply. He didn't sound like his typical cheery self.

"What's up?" I wondered what was going on.

"Afraid I'm in a bit of a pickle."

"You'll work it out." I chuckled. "Always do."

"This could be serious," he said, voice quivering.

"What's going on?" I grabbed my drink, sat back, and took a long sip.

Expecting to hear about some shenanigans, I wondered if his wife had finally had enough. He'd gotten himself a reputation for flirting with women. Nobody knew how far he'd taken it, but I suspected he'd crossed the line occasionally. Brad had met his wife Harper in prep school. They were the ultimate power couple, dating on and off for a number of years before he finally popped the question after law school.

"It's not like that," he said, as if reading my mind.

"What is it, then?" I was tired and wanted to cut to the chase.

He huffed for air. "Can you just come over here? I'll explain it all when you get here."

"Brad, it's kind of late on a working night. Can't we just talk now?"

"You *owe* me," he snapped.

And there it was. He'd finally called in the debt after all these years. I was taken aback. Then it occurred to me that something big had gone down.

"Sorry," he said after a moment. "I just *need* you to get over here. *Please*?"

"Okay, relax," I said, standing up. "I'll be there in a few minutes."

He ended the call before I could say anything else.

Dressing quickly, I slipped on my shoes, and threw on my overcoat. Then, I stepped into the hallway and took the elevator down to the lobby. I grabbed my phone and hit the Uber app.

A few minutes later, a car rolled up in front of the building. I stepped outside into the cold night and hurried over to the rear door. He was double-parked.

Opening the door, the driver turned to me. "You Ken?" he said.

"Yeah." I slid inside.

"Let's see, you're headed over to the posh side of town." He shook his head grinning.

The driver pulled away and soon we were cutting through traffic, maneuvering towards the high-end homes on Beacon Hill. We drove through the aging city, past old limestone office buildings and historic landmarks. My mind raced with thoughts of Brad's predicament. It wasn't like him to engage in histrionics.

Approaching Brad's brownstone, police cruisers had cordoned off the street. A couple of them had blue lights flashing. Crowds pressed against police officers, trying to hold them back. Some of them looked like reporters.

"Man, wonder what's goin' on here," the driver said, shaking his head, baffled.

"Don't know," I said, wondering how bad it was for Brad.

The car came to a stop, gridlocked in heavy traffic.

"You can just let me out here," I said, opening the door.

"Sure thing." He laughed. "You know the drill. Automatic pay. I hope you give me a nice review. And there's always an opportunity for a *gratuity.*"

"You've got it."

"You're a nice man. I hope…"

Shutting the door, I cut off the rest of his comment. I didn't mean to be rude, but the commotion was distracting. And I was growing concerned about Brad, wondering what had gone down. This wasn't just a domestic squabble about an office flirtation.

Hoofing it over to Brad's place, I spotted a crime scene van parked at the curb. *This isn't good*, I thought, heading up the brick stairs.

A uniformed officer stood post outside the front door. "Sir, I can't let you in there."

"I'm a friend," I said.

"No dice." He smirked.

"Listen, I'm the homeowner's lawyer," I barked. "Now, let me in."

He grimaced, then reached for the microphone attached to his body armor. "Got a guy out here who wants in the house. Says he's the owner's lawyer."

The receiver crackled, but I could hear the command. "Let him in."

Stepping aside, the officer sneered. "Be careful in there. We've got a dead body."

My heart raced. *What the hell was going on?*

TWO

ENTERING THE HOUSE, it was crammed with police officers scrambling everywhere. I pushed through the hallway, trying to find Brad. The tumultuous scene left me disoriented.

The house was an old brownstone, with high ceilings, plaster walls, and crown moldings. Hardwood floors ran throughout. It was opulent, with antique furnishings; oil paintings hung on the walls, and oriental rugs covered the wooden floors.

A scent of perspiration and stale odors accompanied the officers, who crowded the house, working the case at the end of a long shift. It was a drastic change from the usual scent of fresh cut flowers mixed with spicy air fresheners.

People chatted down in the kitchen, and footsteps traipsed around upstairs. The place was chaotic.

Peering into the living room, I spotted Brad on a Chippendale sofa. Harper sat beside him, with her long, chestnut hair draped around a rather somber face. A female, plainclothes officer sat in a wingback chair across from them. She was stocky, but attractive, with suspicious eyes. Patrolmen were positioned around the room.

Stepping through the open double doors, I strode onto an oriental rug and stood before a mahogany coffee table. They all looked at me. "What is the meaning of this?" I said to the plainclothes officer.

"We're just having a discussion," she replied. "I'm Detective Sergeant Kara Malloy."

"A custodial interrogation?" I pressed.

"Just a discussion," another person broke into the discussion. The response came from the other wingback chair. A familiar voice.

Turning, I found Alyson seated with her legs crossed. She wore a black pantsuit, and her taut body accentuated the outfit well. Her black hair was cut in a bob style. She smiled, and her dark eyes flickered. She looked good, and I wondered who she was dating now.

"What are you doing here?" I demanded.

She shrugged. "Kenny, I tried to get you to call me."

Then, I remembered the text she'd sent.

"We're just trying to get some investigation done. Brad's not a suspect at this time."

At this time, I thought. Just like a typical lawyer, she'd qualified her response.

Shaking my head in dismay, I turned to Detective Sergeant Malloy. "Have you read him his rights?"

"He's not a suspect at this time. We are merely asking basic questions."

"Give us the room," I said, waving for them to leave.

Everyone stood still, as if not sure what to do. Nobody offered an objection.

"Now!" I snapped, completely annoyed.

Alyson stood. "Come on, let's give them a moment."

The police and prosecutor cleared the room.

Pulling a wingback chair closer to Brad, I then sat down.

He shrugged, as if not sure what to say.

Harper looked at me with sorrowful eyes.

"I'm sorry," I said to Harper. "But I must speak to Brad alone."

"She can stay," Brad insisted.

"I'm not entirely sure that attorney/client privilege will apply to this discussion, if she stays in the room."

"What about marital privilege?" asked Brad.

An attorney, Brad knew there were protections for communications between husband and wife. I doubted the privilege would come into play here.

"That privilege is not absolute," I replied. "And you don't hold all the rights relative to a potential waiver. I'm sorry, but she needs to step out."

Brad looked at her and nodded.

"Okay," Harper said, rising to leave.

She walked into the hallway. Then, she pulled the French pocket doors closed behind her. She stood on the other side for a moment, peering through the glass, and looked at me askance. After a moment, she headed down the hallway, likely to check on their daughter, Hailey.

Turning to Brad, I said, "Tell me what's going on."

"You'll never believe it," he said with a sigh. "My aide, Audrey Martin… is dead. It happened right here at this house."

"Dead?" I muttered. "How?"

"Don't know." Brad shook his head, seeming genuinely perplexed.

"What *do* you know?"

He looked distraught, as if he were about to cry. I'd never seen him lose composure during the entire time I'd known him. Brad's good looks were complemented by an iron will. This disconcerted aspect was entirely unfamiliar territory for him.

"All I know," he said, gathering himself. "I came home, and she wasn't here—"

"Wait," I interrupted. "She had access to your house?"

He nodded. "Both my aides have a key to the house. We work out of the study on the second floor. It's no big thing."

I frowned.

"Listen, it's not like that. One is a guy. And I'm pretty sure… the two were dating. This was just work. Nothing to worry about."

"Then why are the police questioning you?"

"Because I have a dead body at my house." He spread his hands, palms up.

"I get the feeling they suspect you."

Brad shook his head. "They always suspect a politician."

"Okay, walk me through this… one step at a time."

"There isn't much to tell," he said. "I came home, and the house was quiet. Threw my coat over a living room chair, then I went to the kitchen and grabbed a bottle of water. I went upstairs and headed into the study. She wasn't there. But the computer was on, so I figured she was around. Maybe went to the bathroom."

I watched him pause, and he leaned back into the sofa. Then, he covered his face in his hands, as if reliving something. "Brad, what happened next?"

"Then, I went up to my bedroom on the third level," he said. "I took off my shoes and suit coat."

"And?"

"There was a draft. I checked the windows, then I found the balcony door ajar…"

"What happened next?"

"I went to close it. And… I saw footprints in the snow. There was snow at the edge of the balcony, near the railing."

"Did you see anything else?"

He nodded and started to cry.

"What did you see Brad?"

"Her."

"Where?"

"On the brick patio below." He sat forward and put his head between his legs, crying like someone who just learned a close relative had died.

The scene came to mind. I'd been given a tour of the house on my first visit. A three-story brownstone, the master suite was on the third floor. It had hardwood floors, a poster bed, and wooden chests of drawers. A balcony overlooked the small backyard. Below was a brick patio with planters, outdoor furniture in the nicer weather, and a small grassy patch of lawn. Stockade fencing enclosed the entire yard, and Harper had planted flower gardens and shrubs along the fences.

I pictured it in wintertime, with the patio furniture put away and snow blanketing the backyard. Cold and desolate.

A serene spot in the spring and summer. But a terrible place to die in winter.

"What did you do after noticing her?" I said.

"I rushed downstairs," he said. "Then, I went out to check on her."

"Did you touch the body?" I asked.

His reaction was normal. An innocent person is inclined to help someone in distress. But doing so can leave traces of evidence at the scene. It was risky and could lead to inferences that are later used against a suspect.

"I was careful just to touch her wrist, checking her pulse. I suspected she was dead." He looked glum. "Afraid that I was right."

"Tell me what happened next?"

"I called the police."

"What did you do after calling the police?"

"I called Harper."

"Then, what?"

He shrugged. "I came in here. Haven't left since."

I took a deep breath. "When you called me, were the police already here?"

He nodded. "The detective and a few others."

Taking a moment to think about the situation, I said, "Did you do anything else? Call anyone else?"

"I called my other aide. Phillip Danforth."

"The guy dating the girl that died?"

He nodded, then began to sob. "Didn't take it well."

"Where's he now?"

"At his apartment. Over in the back bay."

"Okay, you sit tight," I said, inhaling to settle my nerves. "I've got to check on a few things. Don't talk to anyone."

Standing up, I walked over to the pocket doors and slid one open. Then, I headed into the hall and found Harper. She explained that she'd arranged for their daughter to stay with a friend, and they were instructed not to watch the news.

I told her to sit with Brad, but they weren't permitted to talk about the situation.

She went into the living room and closed the door behind her.

At this time, we only knew there had been a death. It could have resulted from a freak accident, or suicide. We didn't know if it was murder.

Police officers were crawling all over the house. A few officers piled up parts to a computer in the hallway. Others seemed to be ransacking the place.

Making my way through the crowd, I headed towards the kitchen hoping to find the lead detective. I needed to check on the scope of the warrant. Something told me they were going way beyond the extent of search authorized by the judge.

Detective Sergeant Malloy stood by the marble-topped kitchen island. She was talking with Alyson. Cherry cabinets lined a couple walls, and stainless-steel appliances were located about the room.

They both stopped talking and looked at me as I approached.

"Can I speak to you?" I said to Malloy.

"Sure, counselor," she replied. "What do you need?"

"I'd like to see the warrant?"

She looked at Alyson and exhaled. Then, she looked back at me. Malloy reluctantly dug a document out of her coat pocket. "Here you go," she said, handing it over.

Perusing the warrant, I gleaned that it had only recently been issued. My guess, when I pinned down the timeline, was they had begun the search while waiting for the judge to sign it. He had limited the search to the second-floor study, master bedroom, balcony, and patio. And he had authorized confiscation and forensic examination of the computer from the study.

I'd seen officers rummaging through closets. One had even gone through Harper's pocketbook. Shaking my head, peeved, I then looked at Alyson. "You people have gone way beyond the scope of this warrant."

"Kenny…" Alyson pled.

"Don't Kenny, *me*."

"I'm just trying to say—"

"Enough," I snapped. "This ends now."

Alyson and Kara Malloy were taken aback. They glanced at each other, dismayed.

"Everyone listen up," I called through the house. "Unless you're in the study, master bedroom, on the balcony, or the patio. Stop what you are doing… and get the hell out!"

The din from officers searching came to an abrupt halt. Whispering followed, as if some of them were asking who had made the announcement. The place turned still.

I motioned for Alyson to instruct them.

"You heard him," she called out.

Then, the sound of footsteps echoed throughout the house. Boots trod down the staircases, and officers traipsed across the hardwood floors. Many exited the building, while a few moved to the authorized areas.

"Happy?" Alyson said.

"Not in the least." I shook my head. "You shouldn't even be on this case."

"Why not?" She frowned. "It's not like we were married."

Trying to ignore her, I turned to Malloy. "Is this my copy?" I said, waving the search warrant.

"You can keep that one," she replied. "I've got another."

Putting it down on the marble countertop, I straightened out the edges. Then, I folded the document and shoved it into my pocket. Just as I stowed it away, a few officers standing out on the patio shifted their position. This provided a clear line of sight through the patio doors.

The body of Audrey Martin came into view. She was young, attractive, and a pool of blood had congealed on the bricks around her delicate face. With a cheek resting on the frozen surface, her lifeless eyes stared at me, as if fixed in the moment of death, resonating shock.

Something in the gaze confirmed this wasn't an accident. The girl had been murdered.

THREE

KARA MALLOY watched how the lawyer handled the situation. At this point, they merely had a dead body. There wasn't any concrete evidence of murder. Yet, he'd chosen to take the damage control route, instead of playing ball and working with them to get to the bottom of this.

Sure, it was a cautious route, and she couldn't entirely blame him. Kara might have done the same if she was a defense lawyer. Still, she wondered what the lawyer knew about his friend to make him react so defensively.

Ken Dwyer headed back to the living room. Then, Kara turned to Alyson Sheehan. "I'm going to trace through the scene."

Alyson nodded. "Sure, I'll check in with the crime scene folks."

Considering the information she'd extracted from Bradford Wallace, Kara decided to follow the likely path of the decedent. She went to the front door, then she turned around and scanned the vantagepoint from the entryway.

The hallway ran past the living room, back to the kitchen. A staircase led to a landing at the top. The study was immediately off the landing. Then, a second staircase ascended to the third floor.

What would be the first thing the girl would have done? She pondered the situation thoughtfully.

Given the frigid weather, she might have waited a moment before removing her coat. In fact, she recalled it being found in the study, so the decedent didn't likely go into the living room. Audrey Martin could have gone to the kitchen for something to drink, like Wallace had done. Kara decided to ascend the steps and check for any sign of a drink up there.

Reaching the landing, she stood near the study door. A couple officers were finishing up in the room. "Did you find any drinks in there?" Kara asked.

An officer held up a plastic bag with a water bottle in it. It was half empty. "Yup."

Kara nodded. "Anything else?"

"There was an empty coffee mug on the desk," he said.

"Any signs of how long it had been there?"

He shook his head. "No telling. Could have been from when she got here, or it could have been put on the desk days ago. It was empty. The inside was dry."

"Okay."

"We've secured the desktop computer," he said.

"Did she have a laptop?" Most young professionals don't go anywhere without one.

He grinned. "We found a tablet in her bag."

She considered the find. "Good work."

The officer grabbed a few bagged items of evidence, then he headed downstairs, carrying everything out to the van.

Kara perused the room. It had high ceilings and minimal furniture, so two or three people could easily work in the space. But it was smaller than she'd have guessed. She could see the slick politician getting cozy with a young aide.

So, the girl came into the house. Likely got some water out of the refrigerator, then she headed up to the study. Officers reported the computer was still on when they first entered the room. Kara noticed a coffee maker on the credenza, along with a few mugs. Martin must have come right upstairs and made a coffee, alternating java with the water. The house was too tidy for Kara to believe the mug had sat around for days. Martin must have worked for quite some time. Long enough to drink a cup of coffee.

There wasn't anything else significant about the study. No sign of a struggle.

She stepped onto the landing, then headed around and climbed the staircase to the upper floor. Kara glanced down the hallway. Typical, it had doors leading to bedrooms.

The master bedroom was spacious, with a large poster bed against one wall. Across the room were French doors leading to a small balcony. Kara took stock of the dressers and furniture in the room. A small armoire didn't match the rest of the items.

She walked over and pulled a handle. A rectangular door swung downward, latched by a couple hinges, revealing what she'd expected: an upstairs bar cabinet.

Only the rich, she thought.

Inside, there were two glasses standing upright, set near a bottle of Macallan 25 Year Scotch, VS. Kara knew the stuff went for over a grand a bottle. She leaned over, careful not to touch anything, and sniffed each glass. A residue of potent liquor floated into her nostrils.

Somebody was celebrating something big, she figured. *Or they are filthy rich.*

Kara glanced at the bed; it was neatly made.

Stepping to the doors leading to the balcony, she carefully opened one and inspected the scene. Wrought-iron railings about three feet high ran around the edge. There were patches of snow, which traced along the balcony under the railings. The snow was only disturbed in one spot. Along the left-hand side, there were footprints. Both prints were entirely on the inside of the railing. The girl hadn't likely climbed over, stood on the edge, and jumped off.

The railing appeared too high for someone to merely have fallen over. And the bottle of scotch had only recently been cracked open. It was almost full.

Kara suspected there wasn't much alcohol in Martin's blood. No drunken mishap.

She went back inside and walked over to the bed. Lifting up the comforter, she'd found the blanket and sheet weren't tucked in. It could have been hastily made that morning by someone rushing off to work.

Then, she considered Harper, and decided the woman was too uptight to leave it that way. *Maybe the bed had been used that evening?*

Stepping into the study, she instructed a crime scene investigator to bag and tag the bottle of scotch and both glasses. She told them to take the bedcovers and sheets too.

Then, she headed downstairs, through the hallway, and into the kitchen.

Outside, she found Detective Chandler supervising a couple crime scene folks. He was an old-school detective a few years older than her, who spoke with a thick Boston accent. Chandler had skipped college and spent time with the military police in the Army. They appeared to be wrapping up.

"Find anything?" she asked.

He nodded. "There was some skin under the fingernails of her right hand."

"Any blood?"

"Nope." He shook his head, doubtfully. "Wasn't much skin."

Kara knew what he meant. It could have been anything. Martin could have scratched an itch. They'd have to wait for the forensic examination results. "What else?"

"This is better." He pointed to her left shin.

There was a tear in her pantyhose. A scrape ran along her shin.

Kara glanced up at the balcony. The body rest a short distance from the overhang. It wasn't far enough to conclude that she hadn't just dropped from above, but it wasn't a straight shot down, either. The location and the scraped shin suggested that she'd had been forced over the edge.

This was shaping up like a murder.

FOUR

STANDING NEAR BRAD and Harper, I was surprised when the police and prosecution burst into the living room.

I stepped between the intruders and my client. Harper stood up and peered over my shoulder at them. Some development had excited them. The officers appeared edgy, and Alyson's eyes were intense.

"What is the meaning of this?" I demanded.

"Kenny, we're going to need to speak with Brad further," Alyson said.

"Are you arresting him?"

Alyson and Malloy glanced at each other. Malloy frowned and shook her head. Turning toward me, Alyson paused. Then, she said, "Not at this time."

"So, he's a suspect?"

"We need your help, here," Alyson said. "Some things could point to him, but if he answers our questions and we're satisfied, then we can cross him off the list."

"No way." I shook my head. "Especially not tonight."

"We've been through a lot," Harper chimed in.

I motioned for Harper to stop talking. "Listen," I said to Alyson. "We understand you have a job to do, but I seriously doubt you found anything substantial pointing to Brad. Otherwise, you'd arrest him. This is just a fishing expedition."

Alyson crossed her arms. "It could help eliminate him as a suspect."

"You can go ahead with your forensics. Tell me what you've found, then I'll decide whether Brad will speak to you."

"Kenny, it doesn't work that way. And you know it."

Officers trudged down the hallway with plastic bags filled with evidence. It seemed like they were finishing up their crime scene investigation. At this point, I just wanted them out of the house. We needed some breathing room to settle things down. I also wanted Brad to level his emotions and get some rest, so I could delve into this further before we made a decision about speaking to the police.

"Are you almost through?" I asked Malloy.

She nodded. "We're wrapping up now."

"Then, I'll have to ask you all to leave," I said, turning away.

"Kenny…" Alyson persisted.

I shook my head. "We'll follow up on this in the morning."

"Mr. Dwyer," Malloy said. "We photographed the study, master bedroom, and the patio area before the search and again afterward. We've taped off an area around the patio. And we're sealing the study and master bedroom. They cannot go back in there… at least not now."

Harper stood up. "How will I get my things?"

Malloy shrugged. "The two of you can go grab a few items right now to get you through the next few days. Officer Kendrick will accompany you. Then the rooms will be sealed."

She was referring to a taped seal the police utilize to keep people from entering and disrupting crime scenes. There simply isn't any way to get through a door without breaking the seal, and you cannot repair a broken seal. It helps deter nosy people.

"Thank you," Harper said.

"You can only go in the master bathroom and closet."

"I'd need to get into my bureau," Brad said.

"Straight to your chest of drawers and her dresser will be fine." Malloy motioned for them to proceed.

Brad stood up. He placed his hand in the small of Harper's back, then they walked out of the living room. They followed Officer Kendrick and ascended the stairs. Harper didn't have any affectation, like she was in shock. Brad seemed nervous, really nervous.

"Is all this necessary?" I said to Alyson.

"We might have to come back for follow-up. You know the drill." She forced a smile. "I'll put a rush on this, so they might be able to get back in relatively soon."

I'd seen them lock people out of apartments for months. There was no telling when Brad and Harper would get back to normalcy. Perhaps never.

"We're going to get out of here," Alyson said, canting her head.

I suspected Alyson wanted to hug me, kiss me on the cheek. Now, we were adversaries, and we couldn't fall back on our usual pleasantries. Things definitely would be different between us going forward.

They cleared the room. I took a seat in a wingback chair and waited for Brad and Harper to return. I'd been thrust into a maelstrom and hadn't taken time to digest the situation. Everything that occurred since I rolled up in the Uber had merely been done on instinct.

Later, Brad and Harper stepped back into the living room. "We packed a few bags," she said. "Enough to last a week. They're in the spare room."

"That's good," I said, forcing a smile.

She sat down on the sofa across from me, and Brad walked off. We sat idle and I wondered what she was thinking. *Does she suspect Brad of anything?* I thought.

Brad returned with a stiff drink. He sat down and took a swig. "Hits the spot," he said.

"I can't blame you," I said. "After a night like this."

"So, what's next?" Harper asked. "Do we stay here, go to a hotel, or head off to the cape house?"

Brad shook his head. "It's too late to head down to the cape."

They were talking about their second house in Chatham, Massachusetts. I'd been there a few times for clam bakes. A small bungalow style house with cedar shake siding, the property had been in Brad's family for decades. It was nestled in the sand dunes.

I sat up. "We need to meet tomorrow. And we can't get to work with you out of town. You should either stay in the spare room or check into a hotel."

"I'd rather go to a hotel," Harper said. "I feel funny with that girl dying here."

"She died outside," Brad scoffed. "Let's just use the spare room. I'm bushed."

His remark was curt and insensitive. It made me wonder if all the emotion I'd seen earlier in the night was more about him possibly getting into trouble than the loss of a colleague.

How deep does this go? I wondered.

Shrugging at his comment, Harper's countenance reflected dismay. She clearly objected to Brad's suggestion. But her response demonstrated she didn't want to fight about it. "Not sure I'll get much sleep if we stay here," Harper finally said.

"Pour yourself one of these," Brad said, lifting his drink.

She frowned. "Don't think that will help."

"Why don't you guys try to get some rest," I said. "We can pick this up in the morning."

Brad stood up. He took Harper's hand and helped her rise from the sofa. The look in his eyes was kind, as though he held some regret about what she was being put through. They walked towards the hallway.

Harper turned back. "Ken, are you all set?"

Nodding, I replied, "Sure. I'll show myself out, and I'll lock the door."

She nodded, then she followed Brad upstairs.

A few EMTs rolled a stretcher down the hallway with a sheet covering the decedent. Brownstones in Boston often do not have a means to exit the backyard. They exited the premises through the front door. Then, a police officer walked past the living room. He nodded to me, then he stepped outside and closed the door.

The house grew quiet. All the first responders had cleared out.

Glancing out the front window, the crowds had dispersed. I wondered what the morning news would report about the event. If we were lucky, the police would just provide a press release that the department was investigating a death. Somebody in the precinct might divulge that Brad was a suspect in a murder, though. People liked to talk out of school about big cases. I could only hold my breath and wait to see whether we'd dodge a bullet.

Retracing the events of the evening, I couldn't think of any mistakes I'd made. The primary goal was to shield the client from police questioning. Next, you try to extract information without revealing anything yourself. We hadn't gotten much, but we hadn't given up anything since my arrival, either. I did have concerns about what Brad and Harper had told the police before I'd gotten there. And the way the police had rushed into the room demanding a further statement was revealing. This suggested they had found something, or they had observed a clue that made them feel a crime had been committed.

The police weren't pursuing this as an accident or suicide. They were looking at Brad for murder. My stomach dropped at the thought of it.

Was Brad capable of killing someone?

FIVE

THE NEXT MORNING, I hit the snooze button on my alarm clock a few times before getting out of bed. Luckily, I didn't have court, or a deposition scheduled. Fridays were often spent on pleadings and paperwork.

My head felt dazed, like after a long night of drinking, even though I hadn't finished my first cocktail. The events of the night were surreal, like recollecting a bad dream.

A call came through on my cell. I answered. It was Jack Delaney, wanting to meet at his office and debrief everything that had gone down. He represented Brad in political and civil matters. I reluctantly agreed to do so.

After a shower and a shave, I found myself in an Uber headed to the glitzy Seaport District, located in South Boston. The area was just a bunch of fishing piers when I was a kid, but it had grown into a modern little city of its own. High-rise office buildings, hotels, restaurants, coffee shops, and a movie theater had sprung up everywhere. Many of the offices had picturesque views of Boston Harbor.

The Uber meandered through the district, braking for sundry pedestrians and numerous lights. Eventually, we hooked a right and the car rolled up in front of the East Seaport Tower. I hopped out and treaded through a revolving door into a luxurious lobby. It was three or four stories high with limestone tile floors.

I checked in with security then walked over to the elevator bank. It was lined with five or six elevators on each side; the doors were reflective chrome. Hitting the up button, I waited with a few professionals for a lift. A light illuminated and a bell dinged, then a set of shiny doors whisked open.

We piled inside and I smacked the button for the tenth floor.

Moments later, I stepped onto the floor of Jack's fancy law firm. A set of glass doors lay ahead with the firm name frosted across them. Swinging a door open, I walked into the office and an older woman glanced up from the reception desk. My heels clicked on marble tiles, and the place had a scent of pine cleaner. Behind reception were conference rooms with glass doors and walls. Large windows ran along the outside walls of the conference rooms, with panoramic views of the nearby office buildings.

I checked in and stepped over to the waiting area. Taking a seat on a trendy leather sofa, I reached for one of the morning newspapers resting on an oval, modern coffee table. A picture of Brad's brownstone was plastered on the cover. The headline read: Police Investigate Death of Political Aide.

Perusing the article, I didn't see any mention of Brad being implicated in a crime. Then, I looked over the other two papers, spreading them out on the table. One hadn't even run the story, and the other had similar coverage to the first. I felt relieved.

Footsteps squeaked over the tile floor, then Jack's mug popped out from behind an interior trellis. He'd lost more hair since law school, but still maintained a muscular physique.

Jack approached with a friendly smile. "Ken, glad to see you," he said, holding out a hand.

"Jack, good to see you." I stood. "Too bad it's under these circumstances."

We shook hands, then he led me through the office.

I'd expected to meet in one of the conference rooms out front, but he plied through the workspace. Large partner offices lined the outer walls, and smaller associate offices were tucked along the interior space. Cubicles filled the spaces between them. Everyone was busy at work. It was quiet, like an insurance company office.

We passed a small kitchenette, then we cut through some workstations, heading towards a door on an outer wall.

Stepping inside, I found myself in a spacious conference room. Brad and Harper sat next to each other on the far side of the table. Large windows ran along two sides of the room. It was situated on the corner of the building with views of Boston Harbor. Choppy waves rippled across the surface, an undulating motion. I almost felt my balance let go. My legs turned rubbery, and my head spun, like standing on a sailboat. Tugboats churned and pushed an oil tanker. Sailboats whipped across the harbor, and fishing boats churned out to sea.

The scene was crystal clear and appeared so close, it felt like I was watching the surroundings from aboard a nearby ship, rather than an office building.

Jack pointed to a chair across from Brad and Harper. "Take a seat," he said.

I sat down and set my briefcase on the floor, then reached inside for the file.

Shutting the door gently, Jack then took a seat at the head of the table. He had a proud smile on his face, as though feeling pompous for landing a position at a decent firm with opulent surroundings.

Sliding a notepad from the redwell, I waited for Jack to take the lead with the discussion.

My notepad had Dwyer & Associates embossed in gold, directly in the center of the black tape, running across the top. The redwell had the name of my firm printed in black on the outside. Many lawyers were awed by this, but attorneys in bigger firms all had similar accoutrements. They didn't opt for notepads from discount chain stores. Jack wasn't impressed. In fact, we were supposed to be dazzled by his showy conference room and spectacular harbor views.

He sat there smiling, as if waiting for a compliment before getting started.

Brad remained the consummate politician. "Jack has done quite well for himself," Brad said, trying to provide the reinforcement Jack was seeking.

"Nice digs," I finally said.

"Thanks," Jack replied. He shifted in his chair and reached for a notepad.

"He's going to make partner soon," Brad added.

Harper just sat quietly by his side, appearing slightly miffed by the display.

We weren't here to discuss a real estate closing, so the situation didn't call for a law school reunion. Jack nodded, as if understanding the need to plow ahead.

"You're probably wondering why I called this meeting," Jack said.

I nodded. "It helps to set an agenda."

"My firm is representing Brad relative to campaign legal consulting," Jack said. "We were already onboard before the recent development."

"He already holds office. What's this about?" I asked.

Jack looked at Brad and Harper. Brad nodded for him to divulge something to me.

"Brad is planning a run for governor," Jack said.

"I don't recall hearing that announced."

"Ken, there's a lot of planning that goes into it before you announce," Brad offered. "We don't want this getting out just yet."

Jack nodded. "We need you to keep it close to your vest."

"Okay, sure."

This development was something we were all expecting in the future. But hearing them reveal the strategy made me realize something had accelerated the run for governor. I suspected a serious contender had confided he won't run in the next election, paving the way for Brad to get his party's nomination.

"Don't worry," Jack continued after a moment. "You're still lead counsel in the criminal matter. Brad insists that you handle it."

Lead? I thought, not liking where this was going at all.

You can't defend a criminal case with a civil lawyer looking over your shoulder.

Jack was a decent guy, and he was a tough litigator, but criminal defense wasn't his forte. And I began to question his objectivity. He was a senior associate in an upscale firm and looking to make partner. Jack was on the fast track. Brad was a major client, with plenty of billable hours and political connections. Surely, any event that would serve to harm Brad could derail Jack's future, or at least significantly disrupt it. I anticipated Jack would do almost anything to preserve Brad's reputation.

"Nobody is going to step on your toes," Jack said, as if reading my mind.

"What gives, then?" I sat back and looked Jack in the eye.

"You will run out the criminal aspect of this case. I'll monitor and help with damage control and public relations."

"How far will this case go?" Harper interjected.

The comment caused me to consider the potential exposure of having her in the room.

"We should consider the protections of this discussion before we go any further," I said. "Brad and my firm have not even executed an engagement agreement yet."

"Relax," Jack said. "We've got this covered. My firm drew up a joint defense agreement for Brad and Harper this morning. This discussion is protected. Plus, we have grounds through a marital privilege—"

"This isn't a civil case," I snapped and shook my head, perturbed.

Everyone was taken aback by my outburst. They stared at me, waiting for the explanation.

"You need to understand how these things can *possibly* play out," I said.

"We're listening," Jack said, holding a pen ready to take notes.

"First, you have to think of potential conflicts." I sat back. "The police could find some evidence pointing to Harper. They could arrest *her*. Such a situation is not likely, but it is possible. That would create a conflict of interest. Second, the joint defense agreements used in civil cases do not tend to apply in criminal cases. Defendants often aren't represented by the same lawyer due to conflicts that arise during plea deals. The police could arrest both of them. It would likely call for two separate criminal defense teams."

"So, you don't think a joint defense agreement would apply?" Brad asked.

"I seriously doubt it. And you'd have to contend with Harper knowing defense theories."

"What do you suggest?" Jack said.

"She can join in basic public relations strategy sessions. But when it comes to conversations about handling a criminal defense, if the matter even comes to it, she needs to clear out of the room."

Harper looked dismayed.

Jack turned to Brad and Harper. "I think we have to trust Kenny on this."

Brad grabbed his wife's hand. Looked solemnly into her eyes, then said, "We need to listen to the expert."

She nodded, then stood up.

"I'll have my assistant take you to another conference room," Jack said.

They stepped out of the room.

Brad shook his head.

"What?" I said.

"Do you really think all these precautions are necessary?" He sounded sincerely interested, rather than peeved or questioning the approach.

"Quite frankly, I do."

"Why is that?"

"The minute an attorney starts relaxing his approach to a case, a bunch of issues arise that create problems." I shook my head. "Trust me. As soon as you let your guard down, the Commonwealth steps in and takes advantage of any mistakes."

He nodded. "I know you are just doing your job. And you take it seriously."

"That about sums it up."

"Well, I appreciate your looking out for me."

Jack returned and sat down.

"We'll get you an engagement letter today," I said.

"How much is the retainer?" Jack asked.

"We charge a 5,000-dollar retainer for handling a police investigation matter," I said. "Our approach is to use phased retainers. If there is an arrest, the retainer goes up to 25,000 dollars."

"I'll just cut you a check for the twenty-five grand now," Brad said, reaching into his suitcoat for a checkbook.

Jack raised his eyebrows, as if impressed with Brad's ability to write such a large check on the spot. He looked at me and grinned.

I wasn't as impressed. Brad's decision made me wonder what I was missing. It seemed like he anticipated an arrest.

He finished writing out the check, then he slid it across the table.

Fetching it, I slid it into the file without perusing it. "Now, let's get started," I said.

"Before we do anything further," Jack said. "I want to thank you for taking the damage control approach. The two phased retainer demonstrates that you try to short circuit cases to avoid an arrest from the very beginning."

"That's what we usually try to do. Whenever possible."

"Well, I think that I speak for everyone," Jack continued, "when I say we really need this to go away. Brad cannot afford to be arrested and arraigned. It would be a political disaster."

"That's what we strive to avoid."

"We don't just need a good effort," Brad said, harshly. "We need a successful result."

Glancing from Brad to Jack, I got the feeling he had told Jack something I didn't know. They were intense, worried about where this might go, and they wanted it snuffed out quickly. Criminal defense lawyers aren't miracle workers, however.

"Let's have it," I said. "Tell me everything about that day, and don't forget the part you two would prefer to keep from me."

Jack shrugged. Then, he nodded to Brad, who gave me the lowdown for that entire day.

After hearing everything, I was left thinking this matter had some serious hurdles to overcome, if the police got wind of all the angles. I still doubted they had told me everything, too.

Walking out of Jack's office, I wondered if Brad had killed his aide.

SIX

KARA STOOD by the coffeemaker in her precinct thinking about the new case. An aroma of hazelnut drifted through the air. The place was timeworn with tiled concrete floors, cinderblock walls, and aging desks and chairs. Much of the furniture was past its useful life.

She heard heels clacking and turned. Alyson approached with a friendly smile.

"What brings you here?" Kara asked, holding a cup of black coffee.

"Just wanted to stop by and see how things were going." Alyson poured herself a cup and didn't add cream or sugar. She wore a wool overcoat and had likely just come indoors.

Kara held up her coffee. "You take it the same as me. I like that."

Alyson smiled. "Who has time for condiments?"

They laughed and stood there, sipping coffee quietly for a moment.

Several officers checked Alyson out as they walked past. Alyson attracted attention.

Kara came from a long line of Boston police officers. She obtained a degree in criminal justice from Saint Anslem's College up in New Hampshire. After working patrol, she rose through the ranks quickly, acing the detective and sergeant examinations. She moved past officers who had more time on the job, which created a little resentment. But many officers pulled for her. She'd earned her way, but the family name helped keep people off her back.

Alyson was attractive, but she had some tough qualities Kara admired. "So, what brings you by?" Kara asked again.

"Like I was saying," Alyson said. "I just wanted to check in."

"We don't usually get in-person visits from prosecutors the next day."

"Something tells me all these people are going to lawyer up. Then, they'll clam up." Alyson said, shaking her head. "We'll be left with an upward battle."

Kara smiled. "We've got a witness interview about to start. Care to watch?"

"Who is it?" Alyson smiled, her interest piqued.

"The other aide."

Alyson looked at her amazed. "Well done. Does he have a lawyer?"

Kara shook her head and grinned. "Nope."

"Very well done, then." Alyson seemed genuinely impressed.

"I'm heading down there now. You can watch from the observation room."

"Great," Alyson said, walking alongside Kara.

They meandered down busy corridors and stepped through a few metal doors, which snapped shut after them. Eventually, they entered a secure area, where the floors were scuffed, and the walls were painted battleship gray.

Kara opened a door to a small, dark observation room. Detective Chandler stood inside with his arms crossed, peering through a one-way mirror into an interview room. A nerdy man with a beard and thick glasses sat at a table on the other side, staring at the glass, like he knew he was being observed.

"Here you go," she said to Alyson.

Alyson stepped past Kara and entered the room. She took a position next to Chandler and sipped her coffee, like she'd done this countless times. Maybe she had.

Then, Kara gently closed the door, walked down the hallway a short distance and opened another door. She entered the interrogation room. It was dingier than the rest of the building. Suspects had bled on the walls, puked on the floor, and banged up the table and chairs.

Overhead lights hung from the high ceiling and cast a fluorescent glare over the dull room. There weren't any outside windows. The brightness caused Kara to pause, allowing her eyes to adjust before entering the room. A musty smell topped off the dismal room.

Taking a seat, she addressed the man. "Do you mind if I record our discussion?"

"Go ahead," he said, sitting back.

"Just so you know, this is not a custodial interrogation. We merely asked you to come down to help us straighten out some facts."

He shrugged. "I understand."

Kara went over some preliminaries to get his name and permission for the interview fully on the record. Then, she asked him some background questions. Phillip Danforth graduated from Williams College with dual degrees in political science and English literature. He then went on to earn advanced degrees in law and government form Harvard. Over the last few years, he'd worked as a lawyer and political consultant for a number of high-level political campaigns.

"You currently work as an aide for Bradford Wallace?" Kara asked.

He adjusted his glasses, poking the bridge. Then, he nodded. "That is correct."

"How long have you held that position?"

"Ten months."

"Exactly?"

"Precisely. Almost to the day."

Danforth's responses reflected he wasn't intellectually lazy. He paused and gave consideration, then provided succinct and definite answers. She wondered if he'd been coached by an experienced lawyer.

"Is that a full-time position?"

"Yes."

She wondered how a state senator could afford someone like Danforth. He was young, but not a kid right out of college. His beard and glasses made him appear older. "What is your role?"

"I'm afraid that's confidential."

Kara nodded. "Let's go over your routine for yesterday."

"That's what I'm here for," he said, forcing a smile. His tone was condescending.

"What time did you get up yesterday morning?"

"About 9:30."

She looked at him surprised.

"We do a lot of work in the evening due to Brad's schedule, so it's sometimes a late start."

"Tell me what you did when you got up."

"Let's see," he said, stroking his beard. "I had a bowl of cereal, watched the news, and drank some coffee while reading the morning papers online."

"Papers?"

"Sure. In my business, you peruse the local newspapers and the major national outlets." He grinned. "The *Times*, *Post*, *USA Today*. Occasionally, I check the papers out of London and Paris, too."

Kara couldn't imagine having the time to read so many newspapers. "How long did that take?"

"I wasn't in a rush. I'd say about an hour and a half."

"Really, seems like a lot of reading." She sought to warm him up with a compliment, so he'd let down his guard. Stroking the ego can sometimes lead a witness to say too much.

"I've got it down so that I can get through the meat of an article pretty quick."

"What did you do afterward?"

Danforth stroked his beard again. "I went to the gym."

"For how long?"

"Maybe another hour and a half, if you include walking there and back," he said. "Give or take fifteen minutes."

"Then what?"

"Lunch." He smiled.

This guy really has the life, she thought.

"I had a turkey sandwich, pickle, and grapefruit. Figured you'd ask."

"About what time did you finish up?"

He glanced at the ceiling, as if considering. "Maybe one o'clock."

"Did you make any calls or exchange text messages from the time you got up until 1:00 P.M.?" Kara stared at him to see if he was telling the truth.

"Nothing of any consequence," he said.

"What did you do from there?"

"I worked all afternoon. From home, logged into my computer."

"Can we look at your computer?"

He shook his head. "It's all confidential. And I doubt it would shed any light on your investigation."

"That would be for us to decide."

"You'd have to get a warrant."

She was dealing with a lawyer who seemed to know his rights. Kara wondered how a guy working on the consultant side of things could have such a solid grasp on criminal procedure. Sipping her coffee, she wondered if he was highly intelligent. "Did you leave your apartment that afternoon?"

He nodded. "Yes. I went out for a coffee."

"What time?"

"I'm not sure. Probably before 3:00 P.M."

"Did you meet anyone?"

He shook his head. "No."

"Did you communicate with anyone?"

"Sure. I always use that time to check in with people."

"Who did you check in with?"

"Audrey for one. And Brad… possibly a few others."

"What was the gist of your communications with Audrey?"

"I was just seeing how she was coming along with her end of a project that we were working on together. And I wanted to know what time we'd meet that evening."

"What time did you plan to meet?"

"At 10:30 P.M."

"Where?"

"Brad's house." He adjusted his glasses again.

"Tell me about your communications with Brad that afternoon."

"Just that we would meet for a drink before circling up with Audrey."

"What time?"

"I don't know." Danforth shrugged. "I think we planned for about 8:00 P.M. But I can't be certain if the time was set during my coffee break."

"Did you meet at that time?"

He nodded. "Yes."

"What did you do from the time you grabbed a coffee in the afternoon until you met up with Brad?"

"Just went back to my place and worked the rest of the afternoon."

He glanced up at the lights and squinted. Then, he perused the mirror and smirked, as if amused at the thought of someone standing on the other side watching them. Kara noted his grandiose demeanor; she wondered if he relished attention.

"Did you have dinner before seeing Brad?"

"No. I might have grabbed a snack," he said. "But I figured I'd get something while we were out."

Now, the discussion was leading up to the key timeframe. Kara wondered how much detail she could extract from him.

"Where did you plan to meet Brad?"

"Scollay Square. At the bar."

A pricey restaurant in the heart of Beacon Hill close to the Massachusetts State House. She wondered how much money Brad's campaign was floating on meals and expenses. This seemed like it could prove to be a romance gone bad situation, but she began wondering if there were other possible angles. Maybe campaign funding violations.

"How did you get there?"

"Uber."

"Did you go directly there?"

He nodded. "Sure."

"What time did you arrive?"

"I'm not positive, but the Uber receipt would show it." Danforth pulled his phone out of a pocket. He pressed a couple buttons. "Appears I probably got there ten minutes early."

"So, you arrived at 7:50?"

"Correct."

"Was Brad there?"

"No."

"What did you do when you got there?"

"Just walked in and smiled to the hostess," he said. "Then I made my way to the bar and took a seat."

"You didn't talk to anyone? The hostess?"

"I might have told her that I didn't need a table, or I'm heading to the bar," he replied, stroking his beard. "We go there all the time. They know us. And we hardly ever get a table."

"Anything else?"

"I may have nodded to the manager. And I probably said hello to a few of the regulars."

"Can you recall who you might have seen?"

"Afraid not."

She looked at him, disbelievingly.

"Look, this was just another night at that time. It sort of blends in with many others."

"What time did Brad arrive?"

"He was late. As usual."

"How late?"

Danforth hiked his shoulders. "Maybe fifteen minutes. Hard to say for certain because it appears I was a little early. So, he was five to fifteen minutes late. I'd guess he was there by 8:15 at the latest."

"Do you know where he'd come from?"

"The State House, I assume."

"We don't want you to assume. Do you know where exactly?"

"No."

"Why did you think it was the State House?"

"We were meeting late at Scollay Square. I figured he'd come over from the State House. But it's possible he met with someone first."

"At another restaurant?"

"That's how these things usually roll."

"Did he appear to have been drinking?"

"Brad?" Danforth smiled, amused.

"Yes."

Danforth chuckled. "Heavens no. Brad drinks soda water most of the time, and he nurses his drinks. A politician can't afford to have loose lips. Besides, he tries to stay lean."

Kara shook her head. *Image.* That's a major consideration for these people. Bradford Wallace would take every precaution to protect his precious image. She wondered if he was meeting with a team of lawyers and political consultants at that very moment.

"Okay, what did you guys talk about?"

"All business. He doesn't waste any time on small talk."

"Only business?"

"There are the usual pleasantries… asking how you're doing. And a comment on the Patriots or the Celtics. Then, we get right to business."

"How long did you discuss business?"

"Until he left."

"What time did he leave?"

Danforth shrugged. "I didn't notice."

"Well, estimate."

"You told me not to guess. He probably left about half an hour before me." Danforth's voice quivered, like this line of questioning had made him nervous.

She paused before asking another question.

He looked away and poked the bridge of his glasses, apprehensively.

"What time did you leave?" she finally asked.

"Not sure."

She frowned. He was dodging her attempt to establish a timeline.

"I can check," Danforth said, sheepishly. He pulled out his wallet and fished out a receipt. "I paid the tab at 11:20."

"So, that's when you left?"

"No." He shook his head. "I'd say ten or fifteen minutes later."

"Why the delay?"

"I'd ordered something to eat and was finishing it up. And I had a glass of Merlot to polish off." His tone was condescending again. She figured he was back on sure ground with the rest of the questioning.

"Then, what did you do?"

"I went home."

"You went home?" she repeated. "I don't follow."

"You asked what I did. I went home."

"What time did you get there?"

Danforth looked at his phone. "The Uber receipt says 11:45."

"I thought you were going to meet with Brad and Audrey?"

"He called and told me what had happened."

"When was the call?"

"After I cashed out." He glanced at the phone and pressed a few buttons. "He called me at 11:34."

"Why did he leave without you?"

Danforth furrowed his brows. "Afraid I don't understand."

"You told me the two of you planned to meet with Audrey at 10:30. But apparently you were still at the restaurant an hour later… without Bradford Wallace."

He shrugged. "Our plans get changed all the time. He texted Audrey we were running late."

"Do you know where Brad went after he left you at the restaurant?"

He shook his head.

"Why didn't the two of you head over there together?" Kara was getting miffed. It seemed like Danforth was jerking her around.

"He told me that he needed a half hour or so."

"To meet with Audrey alone?"

Danforth shook his head. "Remember, you told me not to guess. But I got the feeling that he was making another stop along the way."

"What made you think this?"

"He got a text and left shortly afterward."

"Could it have been Audrey?"

"Perhaps. But I doubt it."

"Why?"

"She's not the type to hound the boss," he said. "Audrey had plenty of work to do. Time slips by when you're busy. I'd expect she got to the office and just plowed ahead."

The witness had cooperated enough for them to develop a chronology of events, but he was careful not to pin everything down to an exact timeframe. Danforth had described a window of time as to when Wallace had left the restaurant. It could have been anywhere from 10:50 to 11:10.

Kara wondered if Bradford Wallace had prepared this witness, or someone working on his behalf.

"Did anyone know you were meeting at Brad's house that evening?" she asked.

Danforth shrugged. "Not from me."

"How often did you meet there?" She thought it unusual to work out of a home, especially where Bradford Wallace seemed to have enough money to pay two aides. Then, she really didn't know too much about the inside workings of politics.

"A couple times a week. Usually, we'd meet earlier in the week."

"Why?"

"Thursdays are typically for drinks on the town." He cracked a smile. "We meet people socially at the end of the week."

"Why not work out of an office?"

He canted his head. "It's not unusual to put your resources into staff and keep the overhead low, especially at the state level."

A lull fell over the discussion. Kara got the point.

"So, what's your best estimate as to when Brad left the restaurant?" she finally said.

He inhaled. "I'd say about a half hour to an hour before me."

"Up to an hour?" She was surprised by the admission.

"Yes. But I cannot be certain."

"That would be about the time you were both supposed to meet Audrey Martin, right?"

"Sure. But like I said. I'm fairly sure he went somewhere else first."

Where the hell did he go? Kara wondered. She knew from her experience that finding this out would be a major break in the case.

SEVEN

CLIMBING FROM the Uber in the financial district, I headed over to my regular coffee shop on the corner of Broad and Milk Street.

Wind gusted and pelted me with harsh, cold temperatures. I hurried up the steps and yanked open the door, which was set at an angle to the intersection.

Treading across hardwood floors, I reached the counter and ordered a medium Columbian blend. Reflecting on the meeting at Jack's office, I wondered if the two were playing me. I couldn't shake the feeling they were holding something back.

The server brought over a steaming cup of coffee and put it on the counter. She snapped on the plastic lid. After paying for the coffee, I set my briefcase down on a café stool near a counter overlooking the sidewalk.

Late morning, the place was dead. I preferred it that way.

The coffee shop had high, open ceilings with exposed ducts for heating and cooling, painted dark brown. Walls were exposed brick mixed with sections of balsam paneling. Behind the counter, freshly brewed coffee flowed into pots.

An alluring aroma wafted through the shop.

I walked over to a condiment stand and tossed in some raw sugar. Then, I stepped over to the counter near my bag and fished out my cellphone. Checking messages, there was a text from Brad asking me to call him.

I pressed a couple buttons, and the phone rang.

He answered straightaway. "Brad Wallace."

"Ken Dwyer here. You wanted to talk."

"Sure. Thanks for calling." He sounded cheery, but his tone seemed forced. This situation had to be the worst thing he'd faced in his entire life.

I'd normally wait for a client to get to the gist, but I had lingering concerns about confidentiality being pierced. "Are you alone?"

A pause. "I'm by myself in the conference room at Jack's firm."

"Where are the others?"

"Jack walked Harper to the restroom."

"What's going on?"

"We've known each other a long time," he said. "The topic never came up. But I wanted to let you know that I'm innocent, Ken. If anything happened to that girl… it wasn't me." His voice cracked and he sounded contrite.

I didn't take the bait. Most criminal defendants say they are innocent. Keep them all guessing, including the lawyer, and maybe you'll show reasonable doubt. Although he came across as quite sincere, many guilty defendants in the past had professed their innocence even more convincingly.

"You believe me, don't you, Ken?"

"Brad, it's my job to zealously represent you," I said. "But I have to stay objective and consider the evidence. A criminal defense attorney only has so much time and limited resources to defend a matter. The Commonwealth has unlimited resources to put into something like this. So, while I would like to believe you, I have to consider everything before deciding upon next steps."

"Meaning?"

"If the evidence points at you, then we defend by chipping away at their case. We show there's reasonable doubt."

"And if I am truly innocent?"

"We might open an investigation into who actually committed the crime."

"That's what I want to do," Brad said firmly.

"You can't rush into something like this." I looked around to make sure nobody was within earshot. "We cannot obstruct a police investigation—"

"I'm not asking…"

"Let me finish," I said. "Just hear me out. What if we start investigating and something the police never would have come up with points to you?"

"Would we have to turn it over?"

"Depends."

"I see. Not everything you do is protected."

"Most things are. But when you start going around kicking things up. Well, you can't control where the dust goes."

"People that might have stayed quiet… start talking?" he asked.

"Pretty much."

A lull fell over our discussion. Waiting for him to respond, I glanced at the abstract prints hanging on the paneled walls of the coffee shop.

Customers shuffled into the café from the cold. A young woman smiled at me. She wore a long Canadian Goose jacket and insulated boots from L.L. Bean. I wasn't as prepared for the drop in temperature and didn't look forward to going back outside.

"Listen, I'm squeaky clean," Brad finally said. "We hire good lawyers, accountants, and political consultants. Nothing resulting from an investigation will turn up anything on me. I didn't kill her."

The comment took me aback. He kept protesting his innocence, but the police still hadn't even declared the death a crime. It was like he knew a crime had been committed; a murder would likely be announced soon.

"I'm not saying you did," I replied after a moment.

"Okay, so we're on the same page."

"What is it you want me to do?"

"Find out who killed her. That's the cleanest way out for me."

"This is going to cost you."

"Don't worry about expenses, I've got you covered."

"We'll need to start with a list of people and organizations that have it in for you," I said. "And we are going to need the same for Audrey Martin."

"The first part is easy. I'm a politician, so it's going to be a lengthy list."

"And the second part?"

"I really didn't know her that well…"

“Get as much together as you can, and I’ll follow up with you this afternoon.”

“I might need to check with my other aide, Phillip Danforth. He could help find out more about her,” Brad offered.

“You just do what you can. I don’t want you speaking with anyone,” I said, then took a sip of coffee. “We’ll handle any follow-up inquires.”

We ended the call. Now, I started to believe Brad might actually be innocent.

He was smooth and I could see him shacking up with a young aide. But he tended to rely on flattery even more than his good looks to win people over. The comment about not knowing her all that well sounded sincere. It made me think he’d never bothered to know her well enough to charm her.

So, who killed her, then? I wondered, growing more intrigued.

EIGHT

LEAVING THE COFFEE SHOP, I stepped into the cold New England winter and trekked towards my office. It dawned on me that we had just taken on a case with high publicity and nobody in the firm knew the details.

Crossing the street, I looked over my right shoulder for oncoming traffic. The Custom House towered in the distance. State Street was one-way, and cars tended to whip onto it from Atlantic Avenue and rush down the roadway.

A car stopped and the driver waved for me to proceed.

I darted for the decrepit sidewalk across the street and stepped through a curb cutout near the Insurance Library Association building. Turning up the sidewalk, a number of high-rise buildings came into view. The Old State House lingered in the center of an island. Ahead, the sidewalk spread out near a glitzy office building. But I wouldn't make it that far.

Stopping at 100 State Street, I opened the plate-glass door and stepped into a small, one-story lobby. My heels clacked on marble tiles, heading to the elevators in the back right. Hitting the up button, the doors rattled open.

A moment later, I alighted onto the fourth floor; my firm took up the entire level.

Anne sat behind the reception counter. "Good morning, Ken," she said, with a cheerful smile.

"So, it's still morning." I huffed.

"Been that long of a day already?" She grinned.

"You could say so."

The wall behind her was painted taupe, with the firm logo displayed in silver letters: Dwyer & Associates. A conference room was nestled to the left. Peeking in, I found my senior associate, Joey Argenziano hunched over a pile of documents.

Joey was a portly lawyer with thinning hair. He tended to buy his clothes from outlet stores and wore the same manner of dress almost every day: blue pleated pants, a blue checked Brooks Brothers shirt, and maroon Johnston & Murphy shoes. In the colder months, he opted for orange Syracuse University ball caps and knit hats.

He sat with his back to the wall adorned with plaques of newspaper articles about our major victories. Opposite the door was a large picture window overlooking State Street.

Law books were stacked around him, like a soldier in a fighting hole.

"How's it going?" I said.

Looking up, he shook his head. "Giving it my best. But they've made a few good arguments."

"You'll develop the best response possible."

He was working on the response brief to an appeal filed in a wrongful death case. It involved a matter with a lot of complex legal issues. The case had garnered some attention in the press.

Given the technical legal issues, we were facing an uphill battle. Now, there was a separate lawsuit pending over the insurance coverage. The case was dragging on and I wasn't sure we'd ever collect.

While contemplating telling Joey about the new case, Barbara Garrity approached us. She carried a stack of law books, a notepad, and held a cup of coffee in one hand. Everything was jumbled in her hands and appeared ready to topple. I couldn't assist her out of fear that removing a book would cause something else to tumble free.

"Barbara," I said kindly, moving aside, so she could enter the room.

"Ken, nice to see you." She gave me a slight nod and quickly slid the books onto the table. Then, she set the coffee cup down and took a seat with her back to the wall of case books.

Barbara had come to the legal profession later in life after earning a PhD in history. She had shoulder-length graying hair and the unkempt demeanor of a college professor. In the past, I'd had issues with her chatting in the office, and poor productivity. But lately she'd been more focused and hadn't been distracting the other lawyers and staff. This was likely because I had assigned her to work on the appeal with Joey, which held a great deal of intellectual curiosity for her. Keeping her busy helped deter her from office banter.

"Well, I'll leave you two alone," I said.

Turning from the conference room, I headed down the hallway. Joey's office was the first one and I found the door wide open. His office was a mess, with stacks of files spread out on his desk and credenza. I preferred that he kept the door slightly ajar in case any clients walked past.

Next, came the office of our youngest associate, Nate Tomlinson. He was athletic and polished with an incredible work ethic. Nate had already won four jury trials and we expected remarkable things from him. Active in the Massachusetts Black Lawyers Association, he was making a good name for himself among lawyers and the bench.

He was busy at work as usual, so I only popped my head in the door. "How's it going?" I said.

"Good. I'm crafting a motion to dismiss," he said, smiling. "I'll send it your way before the end of the day."

"Nice. Keep up the great work."

After greeting Nate, I moved down the hall.

The next office belonged to Courtney Richardson. She was my second chair trial attorney for most big cases that came our way. We'd once had a spark between us, but we had decided to let that settle down until things had sufficiently cooled off between me and Alyson.

The two of them had been friends in high school and gone to Boston College Law School together. I'd met Alyson through Courtney, back when I was finishing up at the Suffolk County prosecutor's office and Courtney was starting there. Alyson ended up becoming a prosecutor and Courtney eventually left for private practice and went to work with me. Maintaining their relationship was important, so I had backed off pursing a relationship with Courtney. Yet, I still wondered if we might have a chance someday.

Courtney's office was empty, so I continued on.

Stepping into the corner office, I set my briefcase on the UNH captain's chair, and I placed the coffee cup on my desk. A Suffolk Law chair was loaded with a Bankers Box from a recent trial. Then, I took off my overcoat, and I hung it on the back of the door.

A large wall in my office had windows with a view of State Street. The other outside wall had windows overlooking an alley. You could see into the building across the way, so I opted to keep those blinds partly closed. One interior wall had plaques from my days in the Army. The other held my sheepskins.

I walked into the hallway to fetch a cup of water.

Rounding the corner was Barbara's office, followed by an empty office we used as a war room for bigger trials. The back corner office was for our administrator, Emily. She was young and not long out of college, but she maintained focus and helped keep our books together. Across from them was a bullpen, with cubicles for assistants. The area also housed the copy machines and a small kitchen area with a watercooler.

My assistant Pat was at her desk. She'd been with me for a decade and had worked in the business for at least thirty years. Pat knew more about the profession than many lawyers.

Stepping to her ledge, she looked up cheerfully. "Hi, Ken."

"Hey, Pat. How are you doing today?"

"Great. What's up?"

"I'm going to email you an engagement letter to review and print out," I said. "It will come over shortly. I don't want it sitting on the printer. And don't mention it to anyone just yet."

She smiled, curiously. "What's going on?"

"Just a new case. I want to talk to everyone about it."

"They won't hear about it from me." She grinned, then returned to her work.

I headed back to the watercooler and ran into Courtney.

She was standing in the galley with a steaming cup of coffee in hand. Wearing a button-down blouse and fitted skirt, she looked like a model from an Ann Taylor catalog. "Hey, Ken," she said, appearing concerned for me. "How you holding up?"

"What do mean?" I said, reaching for a cup.

"I've seen the news. Your friend Brad had a rough night."

I filled the cup with coffee, then faced her. "How do you know about Brad?"

She frowned and shook her head. "Really?"

Her response made me ponder how much Courtney had gotten to know about my personal life. It was something I tried to keep separate from the office. But when you work closely with people over long nights and stressful times, things tend to get divulged.

"Well, the situation is a little more complicated… than merely having a friend suffering an unfortunate event."

"So, what's going on?" She furrowed her brows.

"We're opening a new case. Let's head to my office to discuss it further."

***

CLOSING THE DOOR, I then moved my briefcase and motioned for her to take a seat in the UNH captain's chair. She nestled into the chair, and I walked behind my desk and sat down.

"So, what's this about?" Courtney looked at me, interested.

"We are taking on a new matter. This office will be representing Brad Wallace."

She leaned forward. "Has he been charged?"

"Not at this time."

"Do you think they are going to charge him?" Courtney sat back, as though running it through her mind before I could even answer. "The press hasn't even reported this as a crime yet."

I nodded. "We're just taking precautionary measures."

"You think they'll charge him," she said. "Right?"

"There's no telling what they'll do." I shrugged.

She crossed her slender legs and glanced around the room. Then, she looked me in the eyes. "But you think it's likely they will charge him?"

I sighed. "Listen, I don't like to make predictions in matters like this."

"Okay. What do you need?"

"You'll have to step up as second chair counsel," I said. "We're going to need Nate to help run out a number of balls, including starting our own investigation."

"So, he says that he's innocent?"

"You catch on quick."

"Aren't you worried an investigation could hurt us?"

"The client understands the risks. He wants it done this way."

"What else?"

"This matter needs to be kept under wraps. Nobody in the office can talk about it, or even disclose our representation."

"Understood."

"I need you to round everyone up in the conference room, while I get the engagement letter together. We have to get that out and make this official."

Courtney nodded, then rose and left the room.

Swinging around to my desktop, I pulled up our electronic filing system and found a recent engagement agreement used in a criminal matter. I made edits and changed it over to reflect representation for Brad, including a 25,000-dollar retainer.

I emailed the letter to Pat, so she could print it when the copy machine was clear. Then, I took a sip of coffee. Grabbing the retainer check from my briefcase, I then headed to Pat's workstation.

By the time I got there, Pat had taken the engagement letter off the printer. She came over and placed it on her shelf. I signed the document. "Scan it," I said. "And email it to Brad Wallace. His contact information is in the system. Then, please join us in the conference room."

I stepped over to Emily's office and put the check on her desk.

Walking down the hallway, I ran through my mind what I'd tell them. Less was more in circumstances like this, but I needed to inform them enough to make the message sink in: they shouldn't talk about the case outside the office.

I entered the conference room, and everyone stared at me, nervous.

These types of meetings didn't happen often.

"Look, I want to begin by saying this meeting has nothing to do with the firm." I closed the door and perused them. Everyone relaxed.

"What's it about, then?" Joey asked.

"This is about a new case."

Nate grinned and a few of the staff shook their heads.

"You might have heard in the news about the death of a political aide on Beacon Hill," I continued.

"That state senator friend of yours…" Joey muttered.

"Yes." I nodded. "We're taking on this case."

Everyone appeared curious as to why hold a meeting for this. Barbara canted her head.

"I've called this meeting because nobody has been charged with a crime," I said. "Our representation itself is extremely confidential. This means that you cannot talk about the facts of this case with anyone. And you can't even mention that we represent him."

"Won't that get out pretty quick?" Joey said.

"Not from us," I barked.

My tone caused a few of them to recoil. I snapped at him because managing lawyers can often be like herding cats. As professionals, they are difficult people to control. You sometimes have to be forceful to make a point stick. Pausing, I gave them a moment to reflect on how serious I was taking the situation.

"This isn't the time for talking out of school about a case," I added. "No discussions with lawyers, friends, or even family."

Joey raised his eyebrows.

"I mean it, Joey."

"Understood," he said. "But family… I can understand lawyers and friends."

I shook my head. "This client's political career is at stake. We can't afford any mistakes."

"Fine." Joey took a deep breath. "All I was saying is… families usually talk about major news events, and we'll have to sit there pretending we don't know anything."

"It won't kill you to keep quiet for a few nights. Are we clear on this?"

Everyone nodded in agreement.

Then, I dismissed everyone, except Courtney and Nate. After the others funneled out of the room, I spoke to the team for this case. "The three of us will begin the legwork on this matter," I said. "We'll start by getting a private investigator onboard."

Nate nodded. "So, you want to prove he's innocent before the police arrest him?"

I shook my head, while grinning at the question. "You people really know me."

They both laughed. "Sure do," Courtney said.

"What if that doesn't go our way?" Nate continued.

His comment caught me off guard. It was one thing for Courtney to mention our own investigation going south, but two attorneys having the same reservations caused me to pause and reconsider the approach. There were risks, but the client understood them and wanted to go in this direction.

"Okay, I'll manage the initial investigation," I said. This would be handled in a manner to avoid creating a paper trail in case we dug up something on Brad. Very little would be committed to writing.

NINE

BACK AT MY DESK, I called Brad and obtained information about his political enemies. He really hadn't undergone much drama in his life, so we couldn't pinpoint anyone who might wish him or Harper any harm strictly for personal reasons.

Audrey Martin was another story altogether. Brad knew little about her.

I tried calling the other aide, Phillip Danforth, but couldn't get through. Leaving a message, I was surprised when hours later I still hadn't gotten a call back. My thought was people like him were at someone's disposal around the clock. *Why the delay?*

After making a couple more attempts without success, I reached out to Brad and asked him to get Danforth to contact me. This was against my better judgment. You make every effort to insulate a client from contact with others in this type of case. Even a casual call with a friend could lead to a slip of the tongue.

Danforth had been out of pocket for some time, and I began worrying the police had him in custody. This caused a great deal of concern. He could say anything.

Brad speculated that Martin and Danforth might have been in a relationship. Detectives would seek to question a boyfriend. If the police contacted Danforth to come in for questioning, he should have reached out to Brad. We could have helped him obtain counsel. An attorney, Danforth should have known better about talking to the police. My evidence professor at Suffolk Law told us we'd have to return our law degrees if we ever spoke to the police.

Maybe he had information pointing at Brad and didn't want to tip us off, I considered.

Picking up the phone, I hit the extension for the conference room.

"Hello," Barbara answered.

"This is Ken."

"I got that."

"Is Joey still in there?"

"He's right here with me."

"Do me a favor and put him on the line," I said.

The phone crackled and echoed a loud thud, as she handed it over to Joey. It had likely taken a bounce off the conference room table. A moment later, Joey came on the line. "What's up?" he said.

"Tell me you still have a cousin down at the precinct?"

"Sure." He paused. "But we only play that card for something big. He could get into trouble giving information to me."

"They talk to the press and friends all the time."

"But they see me as a criminal defense attorney. The bad guy."

"You mostly do civil work."

"Not to them."

"Okay, but this is big."

"What's going on?"

I told him about my suspicions with Danforth. Then, I asked him to find out if the police had pulled the aide in for questioning. Joey agreed to do so.

Gathering as much information as possible, I then called a private investigator. Paul Beckerman was a former Green Beret and knew how to run things out and keep his mouth shut. And he was responsive. He answered on the second ring. "Hello?"

"Paul, this is Ken Dwyer," I said.

"How you doing, Ken?"

"Good. Listen, I've got an assignment for you," I said. "Has to be confidential. We don't even want you speaking to an assistant about it."

"Understood. What do you need?"

I explained the situation and he expressed reservations. "Not saying that I don't want the work, but this could lead in a number of directions. Many will be dead ends," he said. "The cost will run quite high."

"You let me worry about the cost," I said. "Call me when you find anything."

"Sure. I'm on it."

"Paul…" I hesitated.

"Yeah."

"Nothing in writing."

***

THE AFTERNOON DRAGGED ON without any developments in the new matter. Police and prosecution were likely running out the forensics from the scene. Nobody contacted me with another request for Brad to give a statement. This reflected they were digging into every angle, then hoped to get a statement and catch him in a lie.

We had plenty to do around the office, so I busied myself revising motions and catching up on various cases. I also had the task of ensuring we had enough funds to cover payroll. It was Friday and direct deposits hit that night.

Looking up from my desk, snow flurries whisked past the windows. The flakes were large and plentiful, and you could hardly see the building across the street.

The place had quieted down, and I expected most everyone had already left for the weekend.

I packed up, then put on my coat and headed for the elevators.

Most of the lights were out and all the offices between me and the door were empty. Courtney stood by the elevator bank waiting for one. "Where are you off to for the night?" she asked.

"Just heading out early. It's been a long week."

"Not going anywhere special?" She smiled mischievously.

"I have no idea what you're getting at," I replied. And I didn't.

"Figured you'd have a hot date planned."

I frowned. "When would I have time to make a date?"

Courtney giggled. "Right. You tend to just go for a girl in the office."

The elevator doors rattled open, and we stepped into the lift. She was talking about the interaction we'd had about a year ago. A quick physical encounter that hadn't led to us sleeping together. Nothing had happened since.

"What about you?" I said, changing the subject.

"I've got nothing," she said, shrugging.

"Want to grab a quick drink?" I said.

She looked at me quizzically. "Business or pleasure?"

"Maybe a little bit of both." I grinned, playing along with her game.

"Sure. Where do you want to go?"

The doors opened and we stepped into the lobby.

"Across the street," I said, opening the door; I held it for her. We turned left on the sidewalk.

"So, this isn't a Clarke's night?" she said, catching up.

"No this is more of a gin and tonic night."

Traffic was at a standstill, gridlocked with commuters trying to get out of the city. Snow cascaded downward, quickly covering everything in sight. We meandered across the street, darting between cars. Squeaking windshield wipers reverberated all around us.

We made it to the other side unscathed, as traffic jostled forward.

Standing on the corner by a Dunkins, we waited for a line of cars turning onto State Street. The light turned red with automobiles stopped in the crosswalk. We again dashed around traffic at a standstill. Reaching the opposite side of the street, I pushed a set of oak double-doors open.

We stepped inside the upscale restaurant, and I felt a reprieve from the elements.

Courtney smiled playfully. "That was interesting."

"Sure," I said. "Like playing Frogger."

The hostess stepped over and asked if we needed a table.

"We're just going to sit at the bar," I said.

"This place is packed," Courtney said, tugging my arm.

She directed me to an open spot on the righthand side of the restaurant. As we stepped over, the rest of the place came into focus. Somehow, she'd sized up the entire situation and spotted open seats before I could even assess the place.

We took off our coats and draped them over a couple plush barstools. Then, we climbed on them and hunkered down at the bar. A Celtics game was broadcasting on a flatscreen.

"This was a great find," I said, impressed.

"A few minutes longer and we'd been left standing the whole night."

We laughed. Then, a bartender approached, and she took our drink orders.

Courtney perused the menu, trying to decide upon the perfect appetizer to go with her chardonnay. She gave me the feeling this wouldn't be an early night.

Glancing around the bar, I tried to spot any lawyers who might overhear our discussion. A group of attorneys and politicians sat at a table across the room. Michael Flannigan was surrounded by an eclectic crew: lawyers, politicians, businesspeople, and likely a union boss or two. He generally chummed with well-heeled folks who covered the tabs.

He wore an expensive wool suit and had a full head of gray hair; the consummate Irish politician, who hailed from South Boston.

Flannigan was a partner at a midsized firm. He also held a position on the Boston City Council and had unsuccessfully run for mayor. A well-connected guy, I nodded to him when he looked my way. Always a gentleman, he hoisted a glass and smiled at me.

"Who's that?" Courtney asked.

"Michael Flannigan?"

"The guy who ran for mayor?"

"Yup. That's him."

"Do you know everyone in Boston?"

"It's a small town."

The bartender returned and placed our drinks in front of us. She smiled and asked if we planned to stay for dinner.

I looked at Courtney to gauge her reaction.

"Don't look at me," she said. "I don't have any plans, and I'm not one to refuse a free dinner."

"Guess we're staying then," I said to the bartender.

Courtney ordered appetizers, while I nursed my drink.

As the bartender stepped away, Courtney looked at me and grinned.

"What?" I said, befuddled.

"Her approach was better than just asking if we wanted something to eat." Courtney took a sip of wine. "She forced us to broach a subject that neither of us wanted to raise. Quite perceptive."

"Not sure that I follow."

"We're dancing around the prospect of dating. She picked up on it."

"I'm not sure how you get all of that out of a business dinner. I mean—"

"Ken, this is a date." She smirked. "You're paying."

I was taken aback by her comment. Although we'd had clear romantic interests, it hadn't gone anywhere. This just seemed like two colleagues going out after work. Innocent. "Not sure that I agree."

"Would you ever be sitting here with Joey on a Friday night?"

"He's married with two little kids…"

"Nate?"

"Well, I've been out with Nate for a drink every now and then. He's a lot of fun"

"But?"

"He's a little younger than us. He's got better things to do."

Courtney's eyes narrowed. I thought she was going to yell at me. Instead, she threw her head back and laughed.

"What's so funny?"

"You make it seem like we're a couple of spinsters killing time together."

I chuckled. "You said it, not me."

The bartender returned. She slid a bowl of shrimp cocktail in front of us and a plate of potato skins. Taking a step back, she smiled and looked us over. "Need anything else?"

"Not at the moment," Courtney said, answering for both of us.

We were beginning to comport ourselves like an old married couple.

Digging into the food, my thoughts turned to the situation with Brad. I gave Courtney all the details and she wasn't surprised by anything. We had our work cut out for us. This wasn't going to be an easy case.

She looked at me in earnest. "Do you think he's innocent?"

"Frankly, I don't know what to think," I said.

"Won't a lot of evidence point to him? It happened at his house."

This was the likely consideration of police detectives. I expected they would focus on Brad, but it wouldn't be that easy. "That's what makes it next to the perfect crime."

"I don't follow." She shrugged and took a sip of wine.

"The perfect crime is when a person disappears. No body. No murder weapon."

"And the second-best crime?"

"That's when the person dies in your house."

"But the forensics will point to the homeowner…"

"Yeah," I said. "But the homeowner is expected to leave traces of his presence in his own home. Makes application of the Locard Exchange Principle extremely difficult."

"What's that?"

"The principle speaks to the notion that forensic evidence is left behind at a crime scene." I ate a potato skin, then washed it down with a swig of gin.

"Won't they find forensics pointing to Brad?"

"Sure. But that just proves he'd been at the crime scene, which can be explained away because it's his house. Most of the time, forensics are used to show someone was at the crime scene, and so you use the evidence to prove the person was there and capable of committing the crime. Often, they don't have a reason for being there."

Courtney nodded, understanding. "Shouldn't they find evidence pointing to someone else if he didn't commit the crime?"

"Maybe. But the killer could have been careful. And a lot of people go into that house."

"So, you definitely think she was murdered?"

"Very likely."

"And the police will make an arrest?"

I nodded. "Most likely."

"Do you think Brad's a suspect?"

"Yes."

"And he'll be the one they arrest?"

Reflecting on the discussion at Jack Delaney's office, I considered Brad's arrest the most probable move by the police. I nodded.

Then, a meaty hand smacked my shoulder. It shoved me forward on the barstool.

When I turned to ascertain the offender, a large man stood beside me. He was burly and wore a tweed jacket. His eyes were fierce and glassy from drinking.

A rush of adrenaline shot up my spine. "What?"

He cracked a smile. "Had you there for a minute, counselor."

I didn't recognize the man. He'd spoken with a thick Boston accent.

He glanced over his shoulder at Michael Flannigan's crew. They all laughed at my expense. Flannigan raised his glass to me and took a sip. Then, the beast of a man gently placed his hand on my shoulder. "Michael tells me you are a good man," he said.

"Some people might disagree," I replied.

He laughed. "You're funny. I'm Patrick O'Sullivan."

"With the Teamsters?"

"You know your stuff," he said.

"What can I do for you?"

"Not looking for anything. Just stopped by to say hello." He paused. "There used to be a time when everyone got together in this town, made sure things kept running. We used to help *control* outcomes. These are different times, but not *quite* so different."

"Not sure that I follow," I said.

"That itself reflects a problem." He smiled. "Let me tell you a story. I'm head of the local Teamsters. Before me, my father was head of the Teamsters. We had someone who planned to snitch to the police back in the day. This rat was a patient at the Holy Family Hospital up in Methuen. He'd gone in for a bleeding ulcer."

"I'm familiar with the place."

"That's right. Michael reminded me that you're originally from the suburbs." His tone reflected disapproval.

"Hamilton," I said, expecting it would rub salt in the wound.

O'Sullivan flashed a knowing smile. "But not always, right?" He laughed.

He'd struck a chord. I didn't talk about my background with anyone. My birth parents had a house in Lynn, Massachusetts. It was a rough working-class town just north of Boston. There had been a few rough years when my parents had gotten divorced. My late-brother and I had lived in a foster home in Saugus. His comment reflected he knew some details of my life that weren't well known.

"Not always," I finally said.

He clapped his hand on my shoulder again. "This is what makes you tough."

"You were talking about a snitch," I said, refocusing the discussion.

O'Sullivan looked at me, then he glanced at Courtney. He nodded, as though understanding he shouldn't get into my personal life in front of her. "This is true," he said, directing his attention on me again.

"Up in Methuen," I said.

"This man was going to speak against the union. Rat people out to the police," he continued. "Hard working family people would suffer. So, my father dressed up like a nun and went into the hospital. Walking down a corridor to the rat's room, my father grabbed a fire extinguisher."

I watched him closely. He seemed to believe the story.

"My father entered the rat's room, stood by the bed, and pulled the curtain back." O'Sullivan had a mad gleam in his eyes. He then raised his arms, like hoisting an imaginary fire extinguisher. "My father lifted the fire extinguisher and told the rat that if he ever spoke to anyone, my father would cave his skull in."

"What happened?" I asked.

"The man found the good sense that God gave him. And he kept quiet."

"Couldn't the rat have gotten police protection?" I said.

O'Sullivan grinned and stepped back, spreading his arms. "We are the police," he said, motioning to Flannigan and the others.

I nodded, understanding.

He shook his head, disappointed that I hadn't completely caught on. "Besides," he said, "if my father had been dimed out and picked up, the task would have fallen to someone else. The rat wouldn't have lived a week."

"Think I get the picture," I said, taking a sip of gin.

"Do you?" he said, leaning close to me.

"Sure."

O'Sullivan looked me in the eyes. He stood poised, just inches away. A primal fury percolated beneath his calm. "If you get my drift, then you won't have someone looking into things where his nose doesn't belong."

His comment caught me off guard. That was twice he'd surprised me.

Then, he eased back, and clapped me on the shoulder. "You take care," he said, and headed towards the bathroom.

I watched him walk away. Then, I glanced over at Flannigan's table.

The city councilman had taken it all in. He didn't smile or hoist a drink. Instead, he turned back to his meal, like threatening a local lawyer was an everyday event. I wondered what our private investigator had stirred up and how they had found out so fast.

PART TWO

UNEXPECTED TURN

TEN

TUESDAY MORNING, Kara Malloy found herself at the Medical Examiner's office, looking over the slain young woman's body, turned hard from rigor mortis. The aide's beautiful skin had turned gray from death. She lay on a narrow, stainless-steel table.

Leaning over the prostrate body, the M.E. busied herself like an archeologist perusing the skeletal remains found at a dig site. Dr. Chenoweth wore her gray hair pulled back and tucked under a shower cap. Glasses sat askew on the end of her long nose, and she peered through bifocal lenses while inspecting the body. She had a professorial demeanor and utilized a pair of tweezers to pluck fibers and other physical evidence from the decedent.

The dank room was cold, and Kara felt a chill run up her spine as she took in the examination. Cinder block walls and tile floors, the spacc should have resembled a police station or public school. Yet, somehow, it held a grimmer milieu, as though a setting from a macabre film.

A wall was lined with steel lockers, which held dead bodies. Another wall housed a counter and cabinets, overflowing with medical supplies. Everything was worn, dingy, and the steel surfaces were dull, like they hadn't been cleaned in years. The scent of ammonia or formaldehyde hung in the air, piercing her nostrils.

Dr. Chenoweth had rolled a stainless-steel tray near the deceased; she used it to store evidence removed from the corpse. Plastic bags were laid out in a row, with a sharpie nearby. Every time she extracted something useful, she deposited it into a bag, sealed the baggie, and wrote a number on the outside. A few items were stored in paper bags. Closed bags were piling up.

Finally, Dr. Chenoweth paused and looked over at Kara, while slipping off her latex gloves. "We'll need to get these back from the lab before I can finalize my opinion," she said, pointing to the evidence bagged on the tray.

"What's your preliminary finding?" Kara stepped closer to the doctor.

"Thought you'd ask," Dr. Chenoweth replied, shaking her head.

"I'm just looking for your thoughts. Nothing formal," Kara said, trying to coax her.

Dr. Chenoweth looked Kara over, as though wanting to chastise the officer for insulting her intelligence. An educated woman with a long professional history, she obviously couldn't be cajoled into talking out of school.

"Come step over here," Dr. Chenoweth finally said, motioning for Kara to observe something on the lower torso.

Kara took this as the doctor cooperating on her own terms.

"See here," Dr. Chenoweth said, pointing.

"Yes." Kara glanced at scrapes on both shins.

"There was a wrought-iron railing at the scene, right?"

Kara nodded. "Yes."

"So, you probably gathered that the victim scraped her shins, either being pushed up over the railing, or hurling herself over it. Am I right?"

"That's what we figured," Kara said.

The M.E. pointed to bruising on the upper thighs. "This is consistent with your theories. See, the bruising on the thighs reflects pressure against the top of the railing."

Kara hadn't seen the bruising before. But it didn't clarify anything.

"You're still unsure?" asked Dr. Chenoweth, like speaking to a student.

"The bruising doesn't resolve the matter," Kara admitted.

"Why don't you come around here?" The M.E. gestured for Kara to join her.

Kara stepped around the table and took up a position alongside the Medical Examiner. "What have you got?" Kara asked.

Dr. Chenoweth pointed. Fingernail scrapes ran along one thigh.

Kara gasped. "Somebody scratched her, while trying to hoist her over the railing."

Dr. Chenoweth looked at Kara with a knowing smile. "Would seem so."

Audrey Martin's death wasn't accidental, or the result of suicide. Somebody had murdered her. And the only sign of a struggle were the few scrapes on her body. Nothing had been disturbed in the house.

Kara surmised the victim may have known the murderer.

ELEVEN

WRAPPING UP at the office mid-afternoon, I left for a meeting with Paul Beckerman. We planned for a verbal debriefing at an upscale cocktail lounge located in a posh hotel on Tremont Street. The clientele of The Last Hurrah wouldn't recognize him. Hiding in plain sight is often a suitable method to converse with a private detective.

I hoofed it over there from my office. Sun reflected off the snowbanks and blinded my eyes. After cutting through the packed Downtown Crossing shopping district, I headed over to School Street. Trudging up a steep hill, I finally reached Tremont Street and the sidewalk levelled off. Traffic buzzed down the busy one-way street. Exhaust fumes choked the winter air.

Although there was a side door off School Street, I preferred arriving through the main entrance. The exterior commercial level of the building was comprised of obsidian tiles. Windows and features along the front of the first story were trimmed and etched in gold; an art deco flair of the 1920s resounded from the lower façade. The remainder of the fourteen-story building was comprised of aging limestone. A marquee jutted from above the entryway with the words Omni Parker House plastered across the front.

Waving to the bellhop, I stepped under the awning. Then, I pushed through the revolving door into a hotel lobby with paneled walls from top to bottom. The cocktail lounge was to my left, with two swinging doors propped open.

I stepped inside and my eyes took a moment to adjust to the dim lighting.

The place was quiet. Early afternoon on a Tuesday wasn't typically for cocktails. Jazz played lightly in the background. Leather chairs and sofas were situated about the place. Oriental rugs covered the floor and oil paintings and portraits hung on the walls. A bar ran along the interior wall, while plate-glass windows overlooked Tremont Street on the front and School Street on the side.

Beckerman waited for me at the bar with a glass of whiskey in hand. He wore an insulated trench coat, unbuttoned, with lapels and a belt.

A host approached me. "Do you care for a table, or a seat at the bar?" he asked.

"I'll take a table," I said, pointing to one in the corner. I didn't want the sensitive discussion overheard. Then, I waved for Beckerman to join me.

We removed our coats and sat down at a small table with narrow leather chairs, situated by the window surveying the side street. King's Chapel sat on the corner across the way. An independent church, King's Chapel had a portico with Corinthian columns supporting it. Still in operation, the church dated back prior to the revolution.

Beckerman sat with his back to Tremont; gold leaf lettering, identifying the cocktail lounge, adorned the window near his left shoulder.

"What would you like to drink?" the host said, sliding a cocktail menu onto the table.

Glancing at Beckerman, I said, "What are you having?"

"Blanton's." He smirked. "Neat."

Being more of a gin and tonic man, I wasn't much of a bourbon drinker. The place was known as a whiskey bar, so I decided to have at it. "I'll go with a glass of Buffalo Trace," I said. "On the rocks."

"Excellent choice." The host grinned. "I'll be right back."

The host gave me the feeling that he'd pegged me for a lightweight. When Beckerman cracked a smile, my suspicions were confirmed. Shaking my head, I said, "If I drank that stuff, neat, at this time of the day, it would go straight to my head."

"Not having a drinking problem, isn't a problem at all." He chuckled.

His comment caught me off guard. "Never thought of you as having a drinking problem."

Beckerman shrugged. "I'm not dysfunctional…"

"You're not the slightest overweight."

"Some of us handle it better than others," he said. "All I'm saying is that being a controlled drinker isn't something to be ashamed of."

"Understood."

A server came by with my order. He placed a few coasters on the table and set the drink down. Then, he placed a complimentary glass bottle of Evian beside it. He slid a tin of peanuts in front of us. "Anything else?" he asked, straightening his vest.

Glancing at Beckerman, I sought to see if he was all set; he shrugged.

"That will be all," I said.

As the server stepped away, I scanned the room. There were a few gentlemen seated at the bar. They looked like lawyers and politicians. None were within earshot. A family of five had taken up seating on a couple of the sofas. They were clearly tourists or in town for a wedding. A professionally dressed duo were seated in leather chairs about ten feet away. The woman wore a black suit and pearls, while the man donned a blue pinstriped suit with a red power tie. I took them for corporate lawyers, hashing out a deal.

The famed cocktail lounge was once connected with old-time Boston graft. Politicians greased the skids for public projects in exchange for payoffs. The details were handled in the elegant leather seating of the barroom, while the bribes were transacted in the lavatory located on the second floor. Now, it was just a place to conduct business.

"What do you have for me?" I finally asked.

He grinned. "Quite a bit."

"Let's start with the political end. Then we'll discuss personal."

He explained how Brad had backstabbed a couple of state senators in order to obtain the minority leader seat. Somehow, he'd dug up dirt on two of them. He'd threatened to use it against them if they didn't support him. Beckerman had the general background, but he didn't know the information Brad had used for leverage.

"Doesn't sound like the dirt ever got out," I said.

"We couldn't find it, so I doubt others have."

"This sounds like serious enemies, but it reeks of people that want to keep things quiet," I said, taking a sip of my drink. "Anything else?"

"All the unions hate him."

"What's the deal?"

"Brad has started a movement to get rid of the unions in Massachusetts."

"Good luck with that," I said.

Beckerman shook his head. "They aren't taking it lightly."

"Come on," I said, frowning.

"Massachusetts has taken a hit over the last decade. Businesses that consider locating here end up going south or to the Midwest due to overhead and tax concerns."

"What has that got to do with the unions?"

"Everything costs more here."

"Fine." I took another sip of bourbon.

"You're not convinced?"

"The point is taken. But I don't see how they could have a meaningful concern. Unions aren't going away. Nobody should take this issue seriously."

"Well, they do." He shifted in his chair.

I glanced at him askance.

"Brad's campaign is bursting with money. A lot of businesses are backing him. Everyone gets tired of the expense and bureaucracy. The costs of construction in this city are enormous. You go just a few miles north to New Hampshire and it's drastically less. No unions up there. Christ, you have to hire union workers to move a chair into your office in Boston. You can't carry it in yourself."

"All right." I shrugged, conceding the union issue caused friction.

"You want to know about the money?"

I nodded. "Campaign funding could be an issue."

"A staffer gave me the lowdown. Brad is expected to generate a record number of contributions shortly after announcing."

"What about now?"

"He's spending on meals and entertainment like a drunken sailor."

The comment made me pause. An aide might have a grasp on a campaign spending issue. Such a problem could cause Brad to take drastic measures to protect himself. Someone close to him could go too far to keep things quiet, too. But murder seemed unlikely. Most people with knowledge of wrongdoing can be bought, especially in the political arena. He also had layers of people between him and the funding, so Brad could claim ignorance.

"Anything else on the political front?" I asked.

"Yeah," he said. Reaching for his coat, he pulled a manilla folder from a deep pocket.

"Hey, this is supposed to be a verbal report. Nothing in writing."

"Relax." Beckerman shook his head. "This is just some items to help facilitate our discussion. Everything here is fairly accessible."

"So, what did you find?" I didn't plan to take anything from him.

Beckerman opened the folder, and a picture of Audrey Martin was plastered to the first page. It appeared to have been ripped from her driver's license. He'd accessed the Registry of Motor Vehicles. She looked young and vibrant in the photograph. Alive.

"She was from an affluent family down in Connecticut," he said. "Went to prep school, college, then law school. Played lacrosse while at Trinity College. Father was a local politician and lawyer. Mother an architect."

This was the type of background I'd expected. "Anything shedding light on why she died? Who might have an axe to grind?"

He shook his head. "Afraid this girl was squeaky clean."

Taking another sip of bourbon, I noticed the place had quieted down. I scanned the room. The family of tourists had left and a few guys in suits had taken their place. Nestled in the plush leather sofas, they sat near a window, as snow flurries whisked around outside. Likely politicians grabbing a drink after spending time in the State House on Beacon Hill, they spoke in hushed tones and didn't seem interested in anyone else.

Beckerman turned the page. Another driver's license photograph came into view. It depicted a younger man with a beard and arrogant countenance.

"Phillip Danforth?" I asked.

He nodded. "That's him."

"Did you find any proof that he was seeing Audrey Martin?"

"No." Beckerman smiled as if amused.

"What am I missing?"

He flipped the page. This time it was a mugshot.

"Arrested? For what?"

"Lude behavior." He shrugged. "Happened four years ago in Raleigh, North Carolina outside a gay bar. Danforth wasn't seeing Martin. He was seeing a guy who lives in the South End."

The comment took me off guard. Surely, they would have done some background research on Danforth before bringing him onto the campaign. Brad's people should have known about the arrest.

So, why would he tell me the two aides had been seeing each other? I pondered.

"I didn't find anything to suggest Martin was seeing anyone," he added.

This turn of events was bizarre, but it wasn't leading anywhere. "What did you find on a personal level?"

Beckerman smirked.

"You've got something?"

He nodded. Flipping the page, there was a driver's license photograph of a young kid; he was maybe twenty years old. Beckerman turned the page. A mugshot. Then another. The kid stared into the camera with dark, penetrating eyes.

"Who's this?" I said.

"Keith Evers."

The name didn't ring a bell. "What's his deal?"

"A troubled kid," he said. "The usual rap sheet. In and out of trouble. Drugs. Petty crimes. Kid's got a temper. He's got a few assault and battery charges to his name."

"How does he fit in?"

"Harper Wallace has done volunteer work. Some of it concerned a halfway house. Evers met her there. He became obsessed with her."

"Anything physical between them?" I said.

Beckerman paused before answering, like he wanted to choose his words carefully. "Nothing conclusive," he said.

"So, there were rumors?" I couldn't believe it.

"There were rumors." He took a sip of bourbon.

His comment hung in the air, and the thought of her betrayal had stung me personally. I'd known her for years. She always presented as the perfect woman, untainted by the drama and throes of modern life. Even as a young woman, she carried herself as someone above the fray, untouchable. I'd attributed a lot of Brad's success to her.

Reaching for my drink, I took another sip and glanced out the plate-glass window. The snow had picked up and reduced visibility. I could barely discern the pedestrians across School Street. A young man stepped into the crosswalk, heading toward the Omni Parker House. He stared at the ground, watching his footing on the slippery roadway.

Something blurred in the corner of my right eye. Turning my head, a dilapidated blue van sped up School Street. It was going too fast for the conditions.

The vehicle had to stop for the pedestrian and the intersection with Tremont Street.

My body tightened, expecting the van to skid when the driver hit the brakes. But he didn't brake at all. The ramshackle van plowed headlong into the kid, striking the lad with a menacing thud. A pair of glasses flew off.

The kid's head smashed into the windshield and cracked it. A spiderweb of fractured glass shot outward from the impact.

The van raced ahead, and the young man slipped down towards the grille. Then, he dropped out of sight. As the vehicle rushed along, it jounced into the air, as a couple of tires rolled over the kid, who was too dazed to scream.

A moment later, the van whipped onto Tremont Street and blasted out of sight.

I stood and ran out of the building with Beckerman on my heels. By the time I reached the prostrate body, people had begun to circle around him.

"Step back!" I said, pushing through the bystanders.

"What?" someone muttered.

"I'm a veteran, with first-aid training," I said, kneeling beside the kid.

A light dusting of snow covered the roadway, and the flakes were slowly turning crimson, like a cherry snow cone. Perusing the victim, I sought to determine the points of impact.

Stop the bleeding, start the breathing, dress the wounds, and treat for shock, ran through my mind.

The kid stared up at me, with his eyes locked in a state of fright and shock.

Slipping my hand behind his head, I felt the warm flow of blood ooze from a gaping wound. This was the injury that needed the stop of blood flow.

Most gunshot wounds are associated with a pressure point, which you can tie off to stop the blood loss. Headwounds don't afford the option for a torniquet. The impact appeared to have cracked the kid's skull.

Tearing off my dress shirt, I wrapped it around his head, trying to impede the bleeding. I tightened the makeshift dressing utilizing my tie.

Just as I leaned forward to begin CPR, a hand clamped on my shoulder. Looking over, Beckerman had the kid's wrist, taking a pulse. He shook his head.

Glancing back into the young man's eyes, they were glazed over in a state of death. The kid was gone. He looked familiar. A trim beard outlined his face. Then, it hit me. Phillip Danforth lay on the street before me.

TWELVE

STEPPING AWAY from the body, I fished my phone out of my pants pocket and called 911. By the time a cruiser arrived, the crowd had grown quite large.

A young officer approached me, and I explained what happened.

He wanted to lay out the scene and got me to show him where the impact occurred, which was slightly downhill from where Danforth lay in the road. His partner checked on the decedent.

"Wouldn't the impact have been further down the road?" the young officer asked.

"No. It happed right here," I said, pointing.

"But the impact would have tossed the body…"

I'd handled countless pedestrian cases, as a prosecutor and for personal injury matters. The body moves toward the impact, folding into the force being applied to it. Many times, a strike from a speeding car will cause the person to corkscrew into the air, while other times, the body gets pushed under the car. Sometimes, a pedestrian is struck at an angle or near the corner of the car, and the body gets tossed to the side.

Most people think the force would send the person hurling away from the point of impact, but it just doesn't work that way. The van had struck Danforth and he went underneath it. Then, he was dragged a few feet up the road.

"Listen, I have explained what happened and pointed it out to you. Maybe you should speak to the traffic accident investigator when he arrives on scene."

The officer was about to snap at me when his older partner grabbed his arm. "We need to move the crowd back," he said.

"Okay." The younger officer glowered at me, then stepped to the crowd with his partner.

My phone buzzed. It was Joey Argenziano. "What's going on?" I answered.

"You told me to check on that Danforth fella. I spoke to my cousin."

"And what did you find?" He had my interest piqued.

"The police had him in for questioning this morning. Without a lawyer."

This was a disturbing development, considering the hit and run we had just witnessed. "Well, now he's strewn in the street. Dead."

"You're kidding me?" Joey sounded alarmed.

"Nope."

"This is getting really weird," he said. "I don't like it."

"We're stuck in the middle of it."

Another cruiser pulled up School Street and blocked off traffic from Downtown Crossing. I ended the call with Joey, as an ambulance rolled up to the scene. "A little late for that," I said to Beckerman, pointing at the ambulance.

He shook his head in dismay.

We stood there for a moment, and I shivered from the cold. Now, I only wore a t-shirt and trousers. My dress shoes were soaking up the slush from the wet snow in the street. Danforth lay in the roadway with the life gone out of him. I wondered why he would have spoken to the police without reporting to us.

The traffic investigator pulled up in an old squad car and started unloading his gear: a wheel for measuring distances, a tape measure, and aerosol paint cans.

He approached and asked us to report what we'd seen.

Beckerman gave him the details.

"Thanks," he said, nodding.

Then, the traffic investigator went to work. His experience apparently led him to understand that we had provided an accurate report. He started laying out the scene, taking measurements and marking key spots with paint on the roadway.

The cold was getting to me, and I wanted to head back to the lounge and warm up. Spotting the older officer, I started walking towards him. I planned to inform him that I was going inside.

An unmarked cruiser rolled up. The front passenger door opened, and Alyson climbed out of the car. She wore an overcoat. Snowflakes collected in her black hair, as she walked up to me. "Trouble seems to find you," she said, without cracking a smile.

I shook my head, not wanting to get into it with her. "I'll be inside."

She looked me over, taking in the wet shirt, then cracked a smile.

Now, the t-shirt was completely soaked; I'd begun shivering uncontrollably.

"Okay," she said. "Just stay put. We'll come find you."

I nodded. Then, I started for the cocktail lounge. Beckerman stayed behind to walk her through the events. I'd made it a short distance, then someone ran up behind me.

Beckerman smacked my shoulder and pointed.

Following his gesture, I peered through the window. A man in a three-piece suit stood by our table, flipping through the manilla investigation folder.

THIRTEEN

KARA SET THE FORESENICS report down on her desk and leaned back in her chair. Glancing over to the next workstation, she checked to see if Chandler had arrived while she was engrossed in reviewing the latest findings. He wasn't in.

She got up and headed over to the kitchenette. It was a basic arrangement with a few cabinets, small counter, sink, and a white refrigerator. Pouring herself a cup of coffee, she took a sip and turned around.

Detective Davis had sidled up and made his way for the coffeemaker. "You take it black, like your old man," he said, jokingly.

"Learned this from my mother," Kara said, lifting the cup. "Dad wasn't around much."

"Where do you think *she* got it from?" He laughed again.

Davis was an old-school detective, who never bothered to take the sergeant's examination. He wore a frayed tweed jacket, shirt, and tie. He liked to run out the leads. Resembling a basset hound, with drooping jowls, and double-chinned, he was known as a hound dog for sniffing out clues to a crime.

"All I know," she said, "is that it hits the spot."

"You can say that again. The life juice for any good cop."

Kara nodded in agreement.

"How you doing on the new celebrity murder case?"

She shrugged. "Not sure."

"Forensics back?"

"Yup."

"Take you anywhere you weren't expecting?" He reached for a doughnut from a box on the counter and dipped it in his coffee. Then, he stared at her expectantly.

Kara thought about the dismal results. The injuries on the victim's thighs, shins, and the scratches on her leg reflected a murder. The whiskey bottle had come up clean. One glass had fingerprints, but the prints didn't belong to the victim, and they weren't in the system. The other glass had been wiped clean, like the person didn't want to risk being connected with the house. A scrap of skin found under the victim's fingernails did not match the victim's DNA. They had run tests on the scrap of skin. That wasn't in the system either.

There was another wrinkle. She considered the results further. "We found evidence that could put another person at the house," Kara finally said.

"Unconnected with the family?"

She nodded. "Yes."

"These matters come down to love, revenge, or money. And mostly it's about money."

"Meaning?"

"Whoever killed that girl knew her."

Chandler approached. "Didn't know we were having a party."

"That's because you weren't invited," Davis said.

"Find anything on the security system?" Kara asked Chandler.

"Sure did." He fetched himself a cup of coffee.

His mustache disappeared behind the mug as he took a long swig. Kara waited for him to get settled and thought he'd look better without it. The facial hair had a bit of a 1970s feel.

Chandler leaned his lanky frame against the counter. "Appears the *vic* arrived at 10:15 P.M. She deactivated the security system. Didn't reset it. Probably expected the others to show up right away. The system doesn't have any video. And without the alarm being reset, we don't know what time the next person entered the house."

"I thought you had something to report?" Kara was annoyed.

"Just hold on." He reached for a doughnut and ate half of it in one bite.

"Any day," she said.

He held up a hand, while gulping down more coffee.

"Geez," Davis said. "You'd think he hadn't eaten today."

"Okay," Chandler said, smiling at them. "What time does the M.E. think the *vic* died?"

Kara shrugged. "Time of death is estimated between 10:30 P.M. to 11:30 P.M."

"There you have it," he said, grinning.

"Have what?"

He wolfed down the rest of the doughnut, and held up a finger, while taking another long swig of coffee. The cup was probably empty now. "The answer to your question," he finally said.

"What question?"

"Yeah," Davis joined in. "You're not making any sense."

"Maybe you're getting senile," Chandler said to Davis. "Getting a little long in the tooth."

"Hey," Davis snapped. "I'm the one who trained you. Just remember… I taught *you* everything you know, but not everything that *I* know."

"Okay, enough," Kara interrupted. "Answer to what question?"

"You've got this idea of some tryst due to the bed covers…"

"Yeah. So, how does this fit?"

"We know it wasn't her fooling around because she died shortly after she got there." He shrugged, like it explained something.

Kara shook her head. "There was time for sex if she was killed closer to 11:30."

"Maybe." Chandler shrugged. "But I think she died soon after she got there."

"Why do you say that?" This from Davis, who appeared interested.

"The email and text results."

"What about them?" Kara asked.

Chandler refreshed his cup of coffee. "Boy, you college girls really don't look at the details. It's all in the memo on the technical reports."

"And?"

"She's reported to be a workaholic."

"And?"

"She didn't send any emails or texts after 10:30 P.M. The initial computer forensics reflects Audrey Martin had stopped all internet searches at that time."

"This shows—"

"She was dead shortly after 10:30 P.M.," said Davis, finishing the thought.

"But if she *was* fooling around," Kara said, "there wouldn't have been any text messages or emails, either…"

Chandler looked chagrined. It was the kind of position officers take and a good defense attorney shoots down. She was often amazed at how Chandler didn't see a theory through to the end. The case needed a lot more investigation.

Kara thought about the empty coffee cup, then wondered if Audrey Martin had been working on something. The aide could have been typing a report or reviewing documents. A person doesn't have to send emails and text messages to be at work. There was a possibility the victim hadn't been engaged in sexual relations right before her death.

***

KARA AND CHANDLER headed over to Audrey Martin's apartment. It was a studio in South Boston, comprising of a single room.

A bed was neatly made and pushed against the largest wall. There was a small seating area with a love seat and television, which was adjacent to a kitchen with a counter and two stools. A desk was propped against a wall in the seating area. They found a desktop computer on it and a Kindle reader. The place was bereft of wall coverings.

Chandler flipped on the computer and started clicking the mouse.

"We should just take that and let the forensics peeps do their thing," Kara said.

He waved her off. "I'm in." A few more clicks and he grinned.

"What?"

"Passwords automatically saved." He shook his head. "Look at this. She wasn't even connected to Wallace on Facebook."

Kara leaned over his shoulder as he perused messages. Some were a few weeks old. None were with Bradford Wallace.

"Something tells me an affair angle won't pan out," said Kara.

"I'm not so sure. These politicians crave the power."

"And?"

"Well, sex and dirty dealings go right along with it."

He clicked into her email and got in.

Kara watched as he found Wallace in her contacts. Chandler went into her mail history and found various emails back and forth with Wallace. They spent a few minutes reading various emails. Bradford Wallace was a little complimentary at times, which could be taken as flirtations. But there wasn't anything revealing an affair. No plans to meet alone. Nothing to indicate they had anything more than a cozy work relationship.

"Not much," Kara said.

"Maybe she deleted the juicy stuff," Chandler said hopefully.

"We're going to have to leave this to forensics."

Kara's phone vibrated. She pulled it from her pocket and glanced at the screen. Alyson Sheehan was trying to reach her. "I've got to take this," she said to Chandler.

"Sure, go ahead." Chandler sat still, eavesdropping on the conversation.

"This is Malloy," Kara said, stepping away.

"Alyson here."

"What's up?"

"Phillip Danforth is dead. Killed by a hit and run." The call had static, and the sound of traffic and a gust of wind resonated on the line. Kara expected Alyson was calling from the accident scene.

"Are you serious?" Kara said after a moment.

"Very serious."

"When?"

"About thirty-five minutes ago."

"Where?"

"Corner of Tremont and School Street."

"We'll be right there." She ended the call and looked over at Chandler. "We've got to get going."

"What's the deal?"

"The other aide was just killed," Kara said.

FOURTEEN

RETURNING to the cocktail lounge, the place felt warm. My t-shirt was soaked, and I'd been trembling. The respite from the cold and snow was a welcomed relief.

I scanned the room for the man in the three-piece suit. He was seated with a crew of politicians in deep sofas. A blocky woman shared a couch with him.

Approaching, I accosted him, "What were you doing going through my things?"

The man just sat there and smiled at me condescendingly. Gray eyebrow hairs jutted in sundry directions. He resembled the gent from the old British Airways television commercials. I waited a moment, and he still didn't answer. The man just locked glances with me, seething in anger from my disrespect. He clearly wasn't accustomed to getting called out on his behavior, even when he'd done something flagrant.

"Do you know to whom you're speaking?" the woman snapped.

All the others just sat there, dazed, staring at me.

Then, it registered. *The Speaker of the House*, I thought.

He grinned. "See. Now he gets it," the Speaker said.

"Listen, I don't care who you are. You don't have any right going through confidential material."

A waiter came over after hearing the commotion. He looked around at everyone, unsure who was acting inappropriately. "I'm afraid that I am going to have to ask you all to quiet down," he finally said, addressing everyone.

"Talk to him," the Speaker calmly said, pointing at me.

"He was riffling through my papers," I complained.

The Speaker shook his head, dismissively. "I walked over to the window to check on the accident. This brave fellow had run outside to help. A folder of materials lay open on the table.

I closed them up. Many of us patrons deal in delicate matters. I was merely trying to help."

The waiter grimaced, as though he didn't buy the explanation. But it was one you couldn't argue with. "Let's settle down and get back to our seats," he said.

The Speaker grinned and nodded an adieu.

I headed over to my table and sat down. Taking a sip of bourbon, the ice had melted and took a bit of the zip off. Then, I glanced out the window and watched the crime scene investigator busy at work.

Beckerman remained outside, talking with the police, giving a statement. He was probably trying to avoid my involvement. The aide was loosely connected with my case. Beckerman had enough sense to shield me from potentially being a witness.

Lawyers often hire private investigators to obtain statements from witnesses merely to avoid having the lawyer conflicted out due to becoming a witness in the lawyer's own case. If a witness recanted, an investigator could be used to impeach the witness, without involving the attorney directly. Otherwise, the lawyer might need to appear as a witness in the case, which could conflict him out of handling the trial. Beckerman clearly understood all this.

A moment later, Beckerman headed inside and sat down at our table. He took a belt of whiskey and shifted in his chair. "Did the best I could," he said. "But they're going to come in here to speak with you."

***

THE DEVELOPMENT with Danforth's death caused me to call Brad for an update. He was in shock at the news. Brad couldn't provide any insight into the event. To be honest, I wasn't sure if the hit and run was a freak accident or a carefully planned execution.

Just as I ended the call, Alyson stormed into the lounge. She strode up to me with Detective Malloy in tow. A few plainclothes officers trailed behind them.

"We need to talk," Alyson demanded.

Her voice was loud and cut across the hushed din of the cocktail lounge.

Everyone stopped talking at once and listened to our quarrel. The Speaker smirked at me.

There wasn't anyone at the bar, and it was located further away from the seating area. I knew Alyson couldn't keep her voice down. She tended to get loud when she grew frustrated, and it didn't take much to make her angry.

"Let's step over to the bar, so we don't annoy people," I said, thinking about my earlier encounter with the politician. I also didn't want anyone eavesdropping on the discussion.

We all walked over to the bar. I'd left my drink on the table, but Beckerman carried his over and polished it off before we even got started. He placed the empty glass on the bar, then raised his index finger to the bartender, ordering himself another round.

"Are you planning on giving a statement?" Alyson said.

"No." I shrugged coolly. "You already got a statement from Beckerman. We basically saw the same thing."

"So, you're not going to talk to me?" Alyson shook her head, miffed.

"Not about this," I said, waving toward the window and the scene outside.

"This is tantamount to obstruction of justice."

"No. It's not."

"You won't give a statement."

"I'm not required to give a statement."

"We'd like you to give one."

"Why? So you can compromise my case?" I shook my head. This was getting old, and it felt like I was being bullied.

Alyson looked confused. "I don't see why you won't cooperate."

"Really?" I was surprised. "Don't they teach you about conflicts of interest at Boston College Law School?"

She still didn't understand.

"Look, the decedent outside was a potential witness in my case. If I talk to you, I could end up a witness in my own case about these events. I'd be conflicted out."

"I don't see how this is connected. Besides, we haven't charged anyone yet."

"But my client is a suspect in Audrey Martin's death, right?"

Alyson didn't answer. So, I had my answer.

She looked me over. Taking in my wet t-shirt, cinched tightly around my lean torso, she appeared impressed. Her pupils dilated. Despite the intense situation and our adversarial roles, her interest in me piqued. I wondered if we still had a chance when all this was over.

Malloy stepped closer. "We think your client should come in for questioning."

"At this point, I don't think that's a good idea." My approach was to give a vague response, rather than a flat denial, hoping they would reveal something while trying to convince me. The tactic often resulted in police divulging too much.

"We have two dead aides," Alyson cut in. She was hot under the collar.

"No dice." The development gave us more reason to keep Brad quiet.

"You might force us to do something that could be avoided," Alyson said. "Your boy comes in and explains himself, then we cross him off the list."

"Tell me what you have to date."

"You know we can't do that. Bring him by the station. He's got nothing to lose if he's innocent."

Unlike many lawyers who opt to never talk with the police, we sometimes engage in risk management measures. If you prepare the client well, you can sometimes speak to the police and avoid an arrest. Brad couldn't afford an arrest. And a public arraignment might kill his political career. Yet, I had serious reservations about letting him talk to them.

"Let me think about it," I finally said, uncommitted.

FIFTEEN

LATER, KARA STOOD in the observation room with Alyson beside her. They watched Chandler sizing up the witness, putting his years of interrogation experience to use.

She had decided to let him run this interview by himself. He was better suited to getting something out of this witness, and he was more vested in this one. Kara doubted they would even get anything from the interview.

Chandler leaned forward, placing his elbows on the table. He crowded the witness's personal space.

Harper Wallace sat poised, but she appeared uncomfortable with the surroundings. Bright lights caused her to blink. The grimy room may have been unsettling to her. Counsel didn't seem familiar with the dismal interrogation room either. A civil litigator, Jack Delaney wasn't accustomed to police stations and jailhouses. Kara hoped to use his inexperience against him.

"Tell me where you were on the evening of Audrey Martin's death," Chandler said.

Harper Wallace stared at him for a moment. "I was working in my non-profit."

"Until what time?" Chandler stared her down.

"I believe that I worked late and was there when Brad called me to come home." She carefully qualified her responses.

"What time did he call?" Chandler asked.

"I'm not certain. Maybe 11:30."

"Do you make it a habit of working that late?" Chandler sat back and observed her.

Harper shrugged. "No. But I was putting in for a grant and the paperwork had to get done."

"There's an electronic filing on that," the attorney blurted.

Jack Delaney was dressed in a fancy suit, and Kara wondered how much he charged an hour. Couldn't be cheap. He'd likely go to no end to protect them. Although he seemed like a fish out of water, Jack Delaney maintained a smug demeanor.

"What did your husband say when he called?" Chandler said.

"Just to come home."

"He didn't tell you about the death?"

She shook her head. "No."

"What did you make of that… after you got home?"

"Nothing. I expect he didn't want to alarm me."

"Some things are better said in person?" asked Chandler.

"Yes. Something along those lines."

"What did you talk about when you got home?" Chandler was fishing around and not coming up with much.

"He told me that Audrey had died. He didn't know how."

"Anything else?"

"Just that the police were on their way."

"What else did you discuss?"

"Not much. We were kind of in shock."

"What did you do before the police got there?"

"Nothing. We waited in the living room."

"Can you tell me which rooms you went in from the time that you got home, until the time the police arrived?"

She nodded. "Brad met me in the hallway when I walked in. He led me into the living room and told me what had happened. We waited there until the police came."

"Did he make any calls?"

"He called Ken Dwyer. But that was after the police arrived."

The lawyer shot up. "I think we're getting into some attorney/client privilege area, here. You're also treading on marital privilege."

"Come on," Chandler griped. "These are softball questions."

"You can continue. But I may instruct her not to answer."

"That's your prerogative," Chandler said, then he turned back to the witness. "Are you aware of Brad making any other calls that evening, aside from you and the lawyer?"

Harper canted her head, thinking. "I believe he called the other aide. Phillip."

"Were you present when he made that call?"

"No." She shook her head.

"How do you know he made the call?"

"I think when I got home, he told me he'd called the police and Phillip."

"Why call Phillip Danforth?"

Chandler was obviously trying to determine whether Bradford Wallace had taken steps to formulate an alibi. A call to a confidant right away might have been made to compare and contrive stories. Kara thought back to Danforth's interview. The guy went to great lengths to leave some wiggle room for Wallace's actions.

Harper Wallace didn't appear overly nervous. She presented like the usual helpful witness.

She shrugged. "Brad had a notion the two might have been involved," Harper finally said. "He probably wanted to break the news himself."

"Were the two involved?" asked Chandler.

"Heavens no."

"Do you know why your husband thought so?"

"I presume he thought she was an attractive young woman. They were both single. And they spent a lot of time together. Working late. Dinners."

"Sounds like a romance to me."

"It wasn't."

"You sound sure."

"I am."

"Care to explain?"

"You'd have to ask him."

"Phillip?"

Alyson broke silence. "Oh my. She doesn't know he's dead."

Harper looked towards the mirror, as though she'd heard something from the observation room. The room was soundproof. But it was old and likely compromised. "Keep it down," Kara whispered.

Alyson nodded and turned back to the interview.

"Yes," Harper finally said.

Kara watched her detective. He clearly was trying to decide whether or not to divulge the latest event. Then, his face leveled; he'd decided against it.

"What time did you get to your office on the day of Audrey Martin's death?"

"About 9:30 A.M."

"Did you leave for lunch or any meetings out of the office?"

"I took a lunch break."

"What time?"

"About 1:30 P.M."

"Did you leave for anything else?"

"No. I don't believe so."

Chandler sat back and grinned like a Cheshire cat. "Thank you," he said, abruptly ending the meeting.

"I could have stepped out to the bank," Harper offered, anxiously.

"That'll be all." Chandler stood. "Thank you, ma'am. Counselor. You're both free to go."

They rose from their chairs, looking confused.

All of them filed out of the interrogation room. Kara wondered what Chandler had learned but hadn't disclosed to her.

SIXTEEN

THE COCKTAIL LOUNGE turned into a madhouse with patrons spilling out of the chairs and crowding the bar. Happy hour had begun in full force. I'd planned to meet Brad for a drink and a debriefing session, then changed the location to my office. Leaving Beckerman at the bar nursing another bourbon, I hoofed it over to my office.

Stepping outside, the snow had tapered off. I meandered around the crowd, still lingering about, observing the accident scene. Then, I strode down School Street.

I cut through Downtown Crossing and treaded up Washington Street. Working my way over to State Street, a gaggle of tourists blocked the way. A man dressed as a colonial patriot, with a triangular hat, stood near the Old State House. He explained tidbits about the American Revolution. Bypassing the crowd, I shot across the busy street and headed down the sidewalk towards my office building. The familiar din of city traffic accompanied me the entire way.

Entering the lobby, I considered how to break the news about another death to our attorneys and staff. Only Joey knew of the new development. The elevator doors rattled open on my floor, and I found the reception station empty. I headed for my office to unload my overcoat. Dumping the coat into a captain's chair, I pulled a dress shirt out from my lateral filing cabinet. I kept a few shirts and ties around in case of an emergency. After putting on the shirt, I wriggled into my suitcoat and stepped out to fetch a glass of water.

Before I could get far down the side hallway, someone called out from behind me. I turned and headed back. Joey stood in the doorway to the conference room.

"What's up?" I called to him.

"You better step in here."

Hurrying to the conference room, I found Courtney seated at the table. The local news was broadcasting on the small flatscreen television we had mounted to the wall. She didn't acknowledge me and sat glued to the news.

I glanced up and saw a reporter standing at the scene of the accident on the corner of Tremont and School Street. A picture of Brad was located in the upper righthand corner of the screen. She was describing the hit and run fatality of the Senate Minority Leader's aide. I couldn't believe how fast the story had broken.

"That's not all," Joey said. "They had a shot of you walking out of The Last Hurrah."

Courtney cleared her throat. "They've mentioned Audrey Martin's death, too."

"Jesus!" All the air left my lungs.

A lull settled over the room, with the reporter yammering on about repetitive facts. Nobody knew what to say next. The firm was looking for me to lead them. But this level of media attention was new ground, and I required a moment to think it through.

"We need to keep quiet," I finally said. "Contain this as much as possible."

They both nodded in agreement. Yet, a doubtful look crossed Joey's face.

Reaching into my coat pocket, I groped around for my cellphone. I needed to call Brad and update him on the developments. And I wanted him to be careful entering my office. He had to avoid being seen.

Joey stared at me with a stern look in his eyes.

"What?" I snapped, finding purchase on my phone.

"That's not all," he said.

Pressing a few buttons, I had Brad's contact information open, ready to make the call. "What else do you have?"

"My cousin called again…"

"And?"

"The police interviewed Brad's wife. And Jack Delaney was there."

My heart skipped a beat. *What the hell was going on?*

"You didn't know about this?" Joey said.

I shook my head. "No."

"That's what I figured," Joey replied.

"What's going on?" asked Courtney.

"That's what I want to know," I muttered.

All the air left the room. I managed a shrug. It was my case, and I didn't have the slightest idea how two police interviews went down without me knowing about them.

SEVENTEEN

BRAD ANSWERED on the second ring. "Have you seen the news?" I said.

"Just catching it now," he replied. His tone was calm.

"How can you be so relaxed?" I pressed.

"Goes with the territory. At this point, they have two tragic deaths." He paused. "Nothing has been tied to me. There's sadness for my team."

"You're not going to issue a press release, are you?"

"Thinking about it. Need to run it by legal counsel first."

"And you haven't been able to reach him yet?"

"How did you know?" He sounded miffed.

I thought about briefing him on the latest developments. Brad's comment demonstrated that he probably didn't know about Harper's interview. Delaney had kept it from us. It was better to discuss this in person. Things were getting out of hand.

"Listen, you need to get over here as soon as possible," I said.

"On my way right now."

"You should take care not to get noticed, too."

A gust of wind reverberated through the phone. The clamor of street traffic buzzed over the call, and I figured his driver had let him out in front of our building.

"Too late," he said. "A group of people just pointed at me."

He must have stepped through the front door, because the sound of street noise abruptly ceased. I ended the call and asked Joey to give us the room.

Stepping to the elevators, I greeted Brad when he walked onto the floor. Then, I directed him into the conference room.

Courtney stood and shook his hand. "Nice to meet you," she said.

"The pleasure is all mine." Brad flashed a sly grin.

His world was crumbling around him, and he had the gall to flirt with his counsel. I considered whether he suffered any personality defects that I hadn't noticed before.

Maybe he's narcissistic, I wondered.

Brad slid out of his overcoat and took a seat across from Courtney; I shut the door.

Sitting down at the head of the table, I observed him closely. Brad appeared composed. We discussed the recent media blast and talked about how the deaths had gone public and were tied to him. Brad insisted the connection only related to their employment for his political team, and news sources had not disclosed him as a potential suspect. He seemed to feel that was an excellent development.

"People can draw connections," I said.

"Listen, you're an excellent lawyer, Kenny." Brad spread his palms. "That's why I hired you. But running political interference isn't your thing. Let's leave all this to Jack."

The comment brought me back to other important business. But I decided to lean into Brad with some questions before divulging the latest. "Did you know where Phillip Danforth was going at the time of his death?"

Brad shrugged. "Beats me."

"I thought you had these people on a short leash. At your beck and call."

"We usually do." He sat back and relaxed a bit. "But since this business with Audrey, I haven't asked much of him."

"He lives in the Back Bay?"

"Right."

"Any reason why he'd be walking down Tremont Street?"

Brad shook his head. "Afraid I don't know what he was doing."

"Do you know he recently spoke to the police?"

Brad's eyes widened. He inhaled deeply. "No," he said, shaking his head. His reaction appeared genuine. Brad was either proving to be a sociopath, or he was telling the truth.

I let my question and his answer hang in the air for a moment.

"Why would he do that?" he muttered aloud.

"Not sure."

"Well, he didn't tell me about it. Kind of burns my ass."

Another misplaced comment. Danforth was a subordinate, who talked out of school, but now the man was dead. The statement made Brad appear to be preoccupied with his own self-interest. However, the comment wasn't tied to his self-preservation in the criminal matter, which might be understandable. It arose solely from ego about not being consulted on the issue.

He seemed to read my dismay. "What's wrong, Ken? You're not starting to think I had anything to do with these deaths?"

"No." I sat back and stared him in the eyes.

"So, what's the deal?"

"You have a close aide, who goes and meets with the police. And we don't even know about it… at least not from him."

"Maybe he told Jack about it. I'm sure it's all right."

"First, how could you be sure?"

"Because I haven't done anything wrong. What could he say?"

"Okay." I leaned into the table. "And if he told Jack, why wouldn't Jack tell you?"

Brad shrugged. "I'm not going to get into dubious theories. He has my trust. As do you. Let's just ask him."

"There's something else to ask him about."

"What?" Brad canted his head, confused. "You're holding something back."

I nodded. "Yup."

"What?"

"Harper was interviewed by the police today. And Jack was with her."

"That can't be!" He shook his head, refusing to accept it.

"We heard it from a reliable source."

"There must be some mistake." Brad reached for his coat and dug a hand into a pocket, like he was fishing around for his phone.

"I don't suggest you call her right now."

"She's my wife for Christ's sake!"

Now, Brad was losing his cool, which was uncharacteristic of him. He hadn't shown the least bit of concern when the deaths of two aides ran as breaking news. Blindsided by this issue with Harper, he revealed the panic associated with betrayal. We see a lot of duplicity in this business. I suspected he had misgivings about his political future if Harper decided to turn on him.

This latest development caused me to ponder whether she was working an angle against him.

Perhaps the police interview was a prelude to a divorce? I couldn't rule it out.

EIGHTEEN

LATER, we settled back into the conference room after taking a short break. I called Jack and asked him to drop everything and join us.

"What's the urgency?" Jack said, trying to sound aloof. But his voice appeared nervous, fidgety. It wasn't like him. A Marine combat veteran, he was usually cool, tough.

Jack wasn't stupid. He knew the jig was up, and he likely expected me to bring the hammer down. He probably worried it would cause a riff in his relationship with Brad. I didn't want to reveal my cards until I could do it face-to-face. I preferred to get a read on people.

"We can talk when you get here," I finally said.

"Fine." He ended the call without further comment.

"How long is he going to take?" Brad asked.

"Not sure. He ended the call before I could ask."

Brad shook his head. He clenched his teeth, and his jaw muscles flexed. I'd never seen him so angry, like he wanted to belt Jack in the face. I fetched coffee for everyone to help distract him. We didn't need an outburst from Brad before I could assess the damage.

"Just let me handle the discussion," I said to Brad.

"Sure." But he didn't sound convincing. I wondered if he could hold back.

"We know you're upset, but I need to do this."

Brad canted his head. "You think there's something going on here?"

"I'm not sure."

Courtney took a sip of coffee, then put her cup down. "Ken's good at extracting information from people."

Brad nodded. "I can see that."

The two of them chuckled.

I couldn't join in the comic relief. The day was slipping into late afternoon, and I had too many loose ends. Lack of control in a murder case can lead to mistakes. We had witnesses from our team volunteering to speak to the police when they shouldn't be talking at all. Either someone thought they could outsmart the police and game the system to cover for Brad, thinking they could put the police off, or someone was setting Brad up for a big fall.

About fifteen minutes after my call to Jack, the elevator doors rattled open.

"We're in here," I called out to Jack.

He stepped into the conference room and looked around with a meek expression. Jack obviously knew he was being taken to the woodshed.

"You can sit right over there," I said, pointing to a spot next to Courtney. I wanted to force him to look Brad in the eye when he gave us his explanation.

Jack sat down with his back to the wall of bookcases. He wriggled out of his overcoat, then perused the wall behind Brad, which was covered in plaques of newspaper articles featuring our firm's major victories. "Nice and cozy," he said after a moment.

I wasn't in the mood for big firm snobbery. Jack's comment was the standard approach used by bigger firm lawyers: they make a comment that appears like a compliment, but beneath the remark the person notes the disparity between large firms and smaller firms. Typically, lawyers from bigger firms turn their noses up at attorneys practicing in smaller firms. Sometimes, even a tough lawyer with a lot of trial victories under his or her belt will feel embarrassed from the condescension. Other times, you respond with aggressive lawyering.

Today, I wasn't having any nonsense. The best way to address snooty comments was to ignore them altogether. I decided not to respond. "Let's cut the small talk," I said.

"Sure. What's up?" Jack glanced at Brad as if trying to read him. Then, Jack turned to me, waiting to see what happened next.

Brad shook his head, dismayed. But he held his tongue.

"There's no way to sugarcoat this," I said. "We know that you and Harper went to see the police today."

Jack sat back and exhaled, like an ex-con picked up on a parole violation.

Brad leaned forward. "Is that all you have to say for yourself?" Brad snapped.

"Look," Jack said to Brad. "I was just—"

I held up my hand to silence them both. "Listen, the both of you. My office is handling the criminal investigation. I'll lead this meeting. Understood?"

They both nodded. Brad looked a little chagrined.

"Now, why did you decide to meet with the police?" I said.

"They contacted Harper," Jack explained. "She called me because you made such a fuss about keeping things separate. I called the detective and she just wanted Harper to come in to explain what she'd done that day. Said it would help clear her as a suspect."

"So, you decided to go forward with a custodial interview without informing us?"

Jack shrugged. "I didn't see it that way."

"Why didn't you tell us?" I barked.

"You'd made such a big deal about keeping everything separate. I figured you'd defend Brad, and I would take care of Harper."

The explanation sounded reasonable on its face, but I had reservations. "You could have told us your plans for an interview without divulging attorney/client privileged information."

Now, he looked mortified. Jack's expression reflected that he hadn't considered what I just proposed. It never ceased to amaze me how many lawyers went into things with blinders on. They approached cases like mechanized infantry, checking off steps and following a predefined playbook. You have to problem solve each obstacle and consider all possibilities. I began pondering if this was just a blunder by a civil litigator unaccustomed to criminal matters.

"Okay, tell us what happened during the interview." I said, sitting back to listen.

Jack seemed to relax. He took us through the details of the interrogation. Everything he told us appeared innocuous.

"Appears we may have dodged a bullet," I said when he was through.

Brad had sat quiet since I'd intervened at the beginning of the meeting. Now, he was fuming and ready to blow. "Are you really going to sit there and say this was okay?" he shouted at me.

"Brad—" I tried to placate him.

"And you," Brad said, pointing at Jack.

"Look, I'm sorry," Jack said, sounding contrite. "I didn't think any harm would come of it."

"What else is going on?" Brad stammered, eyes wide. A suspicious rage boiled to the surface. He leaned into the table, staring Jack down.

"Nothing," Jack said. "What else could there possibly be?"

This time he didn't sound so convincing, and I wondered what else he'd done. Danforth going out of pocket and undergoing a police interview came to mind. I also considered why the aide was walking down Tremont Street when he was hit by the van.

Jack was definitely hiding something. What exactly, I couldn't be sure.

NINETEEN

KARA GRABBED a cup of coffee then walked into the war room. The detective unit had established a conference room at the precinct for investigations into the two dead aides.

They had set up a whiteboard and two corkboards. The corks were plastered with mugshots, scene photographs, and pictures of key evidence, as well as a sketch of the crime scene; the whiteboard had squares and rectangles with the names of people and places written in each box. Arrows connected certain players and locations.

She took a seat at the head of the table, alongside the lieutenant. Lieutenant Johnson was in phenomenal shape after being on the job for almost twenty years. She wore dress pants and a tightfitting dress shirt. Chandler and Alyson sat on one side of the table, and Davis and his partner were opposite them. Detective Nguyen had been partners with Davis since before Kara had become a police officer. He was a tall, lean Air Force veteran and liked to work the streets. A few plainclothes officers huddled at the far end of the table.

The lieutenant had decided to split up the investigations: Kara and Chandler were assigned to the Audrey Martin death; Davis and Nguyen were assigned to the Danforth hit and run. Lieutenant Johnson felt that if the hit and run wasn't connected to the Martin death, then leads on that matter could be run out without interruption. And if the deaths were connected, the additional personnel could help.

"Who wants to roll this out?" Johnson asked the group.

Chandler raised his hand and started to rise.

"Hold on," Johnson said. "Kara why don't you go first."

Kara stood up and walked over to the corkboards. "All set?"

"Let's hear what you've got," Johnson said.

Kara cleared her throat. "We know that Martin died between 10:30 P.M. and 11:30 P.M. She was likely tossed over the balcony railing and fell to her death."

"What's the evidence of murder?" asked Johnson.

"Martin had bruises on her thighs, indicating that she was pressed against the railing." Kara pointed to photographs of the victim. "The railing was used for support to heave her up and over. There were scrapes along her shins, which demonstrate that she was hurled over the railing and scraped them in the process. If she had jumped, there wouldn't likely be symmetrical scrapes on both legs."

"Anything else?"

Kara nodded, then took a sip of coffee. "We found scratches on her left thigh." She pointed to another photograph. "They appear to have been made while someone was trying to hoist her over the railing."

Johnson nodded. Then, she smiled proudly. "Good work."

"We also have a scrap of skin from under her fingernail," Kara added. "But the DNA does not match anyone in the system."

"Usually doesn't in cases like this," Johnson said. "Anything else?"

"We ran out fingerprints and the usual forensics without any significant hits."

Johnson nodded, as though understanding it was hard to point out evidence if the killer was someone connected with the house.

"There was one wrinkle," Kara offered.

"What?" Johnson said, anxiously.

"There was a print on the front door. It belonged to someone in the system."

"Who?"

"A Keith Evers. He apparently had an obsession issue with Harper Wallace. They had to take out a restraining order on him. Evers has spent time in juvenile detention. Has a history of substance abuse. Some violent tendencies. An arrest for assault and battery."

"Any past sexual abuse crimes?" Johnson said.

"None."

Johnson glanced over at Chandler. "Anything to add on the facts?"

Chandler shook his head. "That about covers it."

"Theories?" Johnson glanced around the room.

Chandler started to rise from his chair, like he had earlier in the meeting.

"Malloy, you start," said Johnson.

Kara walked over to the corkboard with the photos and pointed to Audrey Martin. "She has a squeaky-clean background. We haven't found anything to connect her with the type of conduct that gets someone killed: gambling, drugs, etc."

"What about the campaign?"

"Some potential irregularities, but nothing of consequence so far."

"Continue."

"There is a gap in time unaccounted for in Bradford Wallace's activities. Some of us suspect he went over to the house alone. They had a fling going, and things got out of control."

"What's the motive?" Johnson shook her head. "Why kill her?"

"Afraid we do not have an answer for that right now. Just Wallace had opportunity."

Davis interrupted, "Evidence of a tryst is enough motive for a married man to commit murder, especially a married politician."

"If that's so, then your ex-wife has reason to kill you," Nguyen said.

Everyone burst out laughing. Davis's face turned red, then he chuckled.

"Okay," Johnson said. The room fell silent. "I'm hearing opportunity. Where is the evidence of an affair?"

"Lengthy amounts of text messages," Kara said. "Phone calls."

"That could be two busy people working together. This guy is a state senator. You have to give me something better than that. Anything risqué?"

Kara shook her head. "No."

"So, we need to run out more on this before an arrest can be made." Johnson sat back and took a sip of water from her Hydro Flask. "What about the interviews conducted to date?"

"What about them?" Kara truly didn't understand the question.

"Don't you all find it unusual for people connected to someone so high-profile to agree to questioning?

Everyone nodded in agreement. Kara pondered whether anyone would admit to disagreeing with the lieutenant. She wanted to keep this objective. "One lawyered up. The other was an attorney, who appeared prepped for questioning."

"That goes to my next point. Are we being played by defense counsel?"

Alyson vehemently shook her head. "No way. That's not Ken Dwyer's style."

Johnson considered Alyson closely. "You two have a history."

"Sure. But it doesn't cloud my judgment," Alyson answered. "This isn't him."

"Maybe it's someone else then."

Alyson shrugged. "Perhaps Jack Delaney and Phillip Danforth just aren't very experienced in criminal matters."

"Look, we can speculate on a lot of this. Get me more evidence."

"Got it," Kara said.

Johnson looked at Davis and Nguyen. "Do you have anything on the hit and run?"

Davis nodded, and his jowls and chin shook. "You bet."

"Well, let's not wait all day."

He flashed a broad and satisfied grin. "We have something to connect the van to Bradford Wallace."

TWENTY

WE ADJOURNED THE MEETING and took a break to allow things to settle down. I led Brad into my office, while the others headed back to the kitchenette.

We had installed the small break area as a tenant fit-out at my expense. I'd used a recent case as collateral for a loan, even though I pondered whether we'd ever collect from the defendants.

Closing the door after Brad, I walked over and grabbed my overcoat off the UNH captain's chair and tossed it into the adjacent Suffolk Law chair.

Brad took a seat, as I rested on the corner of my desk.

"How do you think that went?" I asked him.

Brad shrugged. "His rationale makes sense. But…"

"But, what?"

"I don't know." Brad shrugged. "Something gave me the feeling we're not getting the full picture."

Nodding, I said, "I got the same feeling."

Glancing out the window, I noticed the snow had let up. The sky had turned gray and began slipping into night.

"What do you want to do about it?"

"That's entirely dependent on your answer to my next question. Do you still trust him?"

"Not entirely."

His comment made me consider whether Jack might be capable of turning on the young politician. There could be a divorce in play and Jack had sided with Harper. Her family had more money than Brad's family. We just didn't have enough to make a play against Jack. I opted for the least disruptive approach.

"Then we'll keep him in the loop," I finally said. "But we won't clue him in on any important strategy."

"Keep him in the loop?" Brad questioned.

I smiled. "Sure. That way we get him to disclose what he knows and what he's doing. 'Keep your friends close and keep your enemies closer.'"

Brad cracked a smile. "I always liked you, Ken."

"Good to know." I chuckled. "Let's grab a drink."

We got up and headed down the hall. I knocked on Joey's door and told him to join us. Then, I popped into the conference room. "Let's go. We're grabbing a drink."

Jack smiled. He seemed relieved to be out of the hotseat.

"Where we headed?" asked Courtney.

"These two are far too fancy for Clarke's. Figured we'd head across the street." I was talking about the upscale restaurant and bar located on the corner of State and Broad Street.

She smiled. "I just have to grab my coat."

A few minutes later, we were all suited up and headed down in the elevator.

When the doors rattled open, we stepped into the lobby and pandemonium hit us. A blur of people stood on the sidewalk. The mob spread into the street. Police cars and a television news van were blocking traffic. Blue lights illuminated the gray afternoon. Flashing bulbs popped from oversized press cameras.

At first, I figured someone had jumped from a building. It had happened once before with a similar frenzied response. Scores of officers formed a gauntlet, leading from the front door to a parked cruiser with the rear door ajar. I then discerned the situation.

"They're coming for Brad!" I yelled.

"What?" he stammered.

"You have to be kidding me," Jack said.

Joey looked dazed, and Courtney went into high alert. Her eyes darted in various directions, assessing the situation and determining how to respond.

"Brad?" I called.

"Yeah."

"They've come to arrest you. Don't say anything to anyone, except me."

"Okay," he complied. But his face was frozen in shock.

"Courtney, push the door open."

She stepped ahead of us and shoved the plate-glass door open. Cool air drifted into the lobby. Grabbing Brad by the arm, I led him into the fray.

As soon as we hit the sidewalk, officers clamped onto his arms. The senior plainclothes officer informed Brad he was under arrest for conspiracy to commit murder. They handcuffed him and led him towards the patrol car with the door open. Malloy and Alyson trailed behind the prisoner with the detective reciting Brad his rights.

"You could have contacted me," I yelled to Alyson. "I would have turned him in at the station."

She ignored me and kept after Brad. News cameras filmed her taking the senator into custody. The officers stuffed Brad into the cruiser, then piled inside and hit the siren. The police car eased through the throng and headed down the street. An ensemble followed behind, providing a victory motorcade.

Alyson walked toward an unmarked car.

"I can't believe you pulled this stunt," I called to her.

She continued to ignore me. Alyson started to climb into an unmarked car, and a few of the remaining officers formed a line between the masses and the departing prosecutor. I stepped after her, tired of the rebuke.

"Do you hear me?" I bellowed. "This was entirely uncalled for!"

Officers grabbed me and kept me from getting closer.

"You don't have any evidence connecting him to Martin's death," I complained.

She poked her head out the car door and sneered. "This relates to Danforth."

PART THREE

ARRAIGNMENT

TWENTY-ONE

A GUST OF WIND blew frigid air and sent a chill down my spine, as I alighted from an Uber at the precinct in downtown Boston. My mind raced with questions of how they could charge Brad in connection with Danforth's death.

Courtney climbed from the car, then we rushed to the front door.

Entering the police station, we approached a reception station. Our heels smacked the tile floor. Reception was lodged in a wall that separated the precinct from the waiting area. A young female officer sat at a counter behind bulletproof glass. The place smelled moldy.

We asked to see the desk sergeant. She picked up the phone and a few minutes later he stood on the other side of the glass. A tired demeanor consumed the sergeant. His jowls drooped, and wrinkles were etched into his thick skin. We demanded to see our client.

He looked at us dumbfounded. Obviously, the detectives hadn't clued him in on their plans. He didn't seem to know anything about the case. Courtney suggested that he call Malloy. The sergeant told us to take a seat and wait, while he looked into the situation.

We walked away and sat down on filthy plastic chairs, bolted together like an old airport waiting area. The precinct had seen better days. I couldn't believe they had found something to connect Brad to the hit and run, especially in just a few hours. This was extraordinarily quick police work. The development made me consider the possibility that someone was trying to set him up. I really didn't think Brad would kill anyone. And if he had done this, he was too smart and well connected to make a big mistake; he simply wouldn't have done something so easily detectable.

My thoughts turned to the night at the bar when the union boss had paid me a visit. Then, I considered Beckerman's comments about a rift between Brad and people supporting the unions. At first, the idea seemed ludicrous. There wasn't a snowball's chance in hell the unions would be broken up in Massachusetts. Surely, a political agenda that was bound to fail wouldn't be cause for murder. Yet, the thought kept clawing at me. They probably knew the unions weren't going anywhere, but perhaps Brad's campaign might weaken their hold.

Maybe the unions were worried about getting investigated? I wondered.

Courtney elbowed me, then pointed to reception. The sergeant waved for us to come over with a grim countenance. Something was amiss.

We approached. The place was dead silent. Courtney's heels clacked on the floor. The young officer smirked at us. I wondered if she already knew something, or at least anticipated that we were in for bad news.

The sergeant stood beside her; he leaned towards a speaking device lodged in the window. "Counselor, I'm afraid you're not going to be able to see your client right now."

"What's the meaning of this?" I griped.

He shrugged. An older officer nearing retirement, the fight had gone out of him. "Look, that's all I can say."

"When can we see him?" asked Courtney.

"Not sure. They didn't say."

"What did they say?" I demanded.

"Just that he's not available for legal counsel right now."

"You listen here," I said, pointing. "Make sure you tell them that Brad Wallace has counsel, and they are not permitted to question him. You got that?"

He nodded. "Will do."

"Sir," Courtney said. "Did you see him back there?"

"You said it, not me."

"Thanks," I said, then raised a hand, signaling we were through.

The sergeant turned away and returned to some paperwork at his desk, while the young officer stared at us for a moment. Appearing miffed from our contentious questions, she likely was accustomed to people speaking to them with greater deference.

We stepped over to the waiting area and requested an Uber.

"Are you thinking what I'm thinking?" Courtney said.

"Yeah. He's not even here."

TWENTY-TWO

KARA SAT BESIDE ALYSON at a metal table in the grimiest interview room she'd ever encountered. The stench of recent puke and industrial cleaner hung in the air.

Bradford Wallace wore an orange jumpsuit, and he was handcuffed to the table.

Alyson took the lead with the discussion. She had pushed the proverbial envelope, possibly violating Wallace's civil rights, when seeking to interrogate a defendant represented by counsel. They had booked him at the precinct then rushed him over to the county jail. Alyson planned to make Wallace's lawyers go to court and request a bail hearing, which wouldn't happen for another day.

"When can I talk to my attorneys?" Wallace asked.

"You will be allowed a call once we're all settled here," Alyson said. Her tone was calm and slightly patronizing.

He sat back and smirked. "Looks like we're all set now."

"Well, you have a moment with us… if there's something you want to say."

"I know my rights. I'm an attorney."

"Sure. And so you know that you can choose to speak with us, despite saying you want to speak with your counsel. Maybe you can help clear things up."

Wallace shook his head. "You've arrested me. Probably ruined my political career."

"There's the chance that could be salvaged. If you help us clear you quickly."

"You just want to help me?" He shook his head in disbelief.

Kara pondered whether this was a good idea. If the defendant spoke to them, his lawyer would try to get the statement, and any evidence derived from it, kicked from the case. The evidence was flimsy enough. She also worried Alyson might reveal too much, far too soon, while fishing around for information from Wallace.

He was smooth and confident. Wallace didn't have a hair out of place. Grinning at Alyson, he shook his head again, as if her tactics were futile. A slick politician.

"You could help yourself," Alyson said after a moment.

"How?" Now, he seemed to be digging for information from her.

"Tell us your activities the night Audrey Martin died?"

"What's that got to do with this arrest?" Wallace looked confused. "You brought me in here on conspiracy to commit murder… regarding Phillip Danforth's death."

The approach Alyson took was one they used all the time. Bring someone in on a charge and try to get him to talk, revealing information to help support another charge. It was a bullying tactic that worked on dim-witted street thugs and inexperienced criminals. Kara wondered if it could produce results on a high-profile politician with legal training. She doubted it.

"Maybe they're connected?" Alyson finally responded; she sounded like a lawyer, answering a question with a question.

The comment caused Wallace to lean back in his chair, contemplating the situation. The handcuffs made his arms stretch out. He was uncomfortable.

Alyson slid a form across the metal table. "This is a consent form," she said. "You can just sign it and tell us what we need to know. Maybe we can get you out of here. Otherwise, you're going to be here all night until a bail hearing tomorrow, and maybe until you stand trial."

Wallace smiled coolly and shook his head. "You've got nothing on Audrey Martin's death, so you ginned up this conspiracy to murder charge. And if you had anything solid on that one, you would have just charged me with murder. Sorry, but you are not here to help me. You're on a fishing expedition. I'm not talking. I'd like to see my lawyers."

Alyson cringed. She bolted to her feet. "Guard!"

A burly corrections officer entered the room.

"Take this man to his cell."

The officer nodded, then another officer entered the room. Releasing the handcuffs attached to the table, the guards then shackled Wallace for transport to his cellblock.

As the politician shuffled from the room, the chains binding him jingled and dragged on the concrete floor with each half step. He concentrated on ambulating and didn't look back.

Alyson took a step towards him, looking frustrated. "I doubt you'll see your lawyers today."

Wallace turned. His eyes piercing, "What?"

"You heard me. By the time you get situated, visiting hours will be over."

He shook his head; outrage percolated from every fiber of his being.

The door shut and the detective and prosecutor were alone.

Kara faced Alyson. "What do you think he'll do if the investigation points to someone else and we have to release him?"

"He'd sue the department and both of us."

"Maybe his arrest was premature?" Kara muttered.

The comment hung in the air like an ominous portent. It was something that should never have been spoken out loud. A lull in the discussion caused Kara to regret having divulged her thoughts. She knew better than to voice a concern.

Loose lips sink ships, her father always told her.

"No. We have the right man," Alyson said. Her affectation seemed forced; she presented with a disingenuous air. "We're going to have to prosecute him all the way to trial."

TWENTY-THREE

WE STEPPED OUTSIDE the police station and the frigid air smacked my cheeks. Courtney shook her head, annoyed.

"They already took him to Nashua Street, right?" she said.

I nodded. "That's about it."

We were talking about the Nashua Street Jail, which was the jailhouse used by the Suffolk County Sheriff's Department. Cases awaiting trial in Boston have inmates there. Sometimes, on lesser crimes, the police allow bail right from the precinct.

"Guess with a murder charge, they want a bail hearing," Courtney said.

"Sure. But I doubt that's the entire picture." I shook my head. "They moved him too quickly."

"What's their play?" She stepped closer.

"Get him over to the jailhouse. Intimidate him. Make him think he's going to spend the night or months there. Then, entice him to talk so he provides them with an alibi in the hope to go home. They catch him with an inconsistent statement and use it against him."

"Do you think he'll talk?"

"I certainly hope not. But who knows?"

Her question made me consider the way this case had unfolded. Many events had gone down without me being aware, like someone was intentionally keeping me in the dark. I couldn't believe Danforth had spoken to the police without calling someone on Brad's team. Then, he suddenly got run down. The whole matter had my hackles up.

We slid into the Uber and Courtney told the driver to head to the office. The car was clean and smelled of air freshener. As the driver darted through traffic, I dug out my phone and called Joey. "We need to get an update from your cousin," I said.

"I'm way ahead of you..." Joey's comment trailed off.

"What's wrong?"

He paused. "We're not getting anything else from him. Since the arrest, the department has told everyone to keep quiet. There were threats of severe reprimands. He's not going to risk his career to help us. Besides, we weren't representing a criminal defendant when he helped us before. It was just a routine investigation. Things have changed."

"Okay. You did the best you could." There wasn't any sense in pressuring his cousin.

"Appreciate it."

"Anything else going on at the office?"

"Just that you got a call from Jack Delaney. Sounds panicked. Wants you to call him as soon as you can with an update after speaking with Brad. The press is all over this."

His comment cut through me like a knife. All the air went out of the small car. It felt as though the doors and roof were closing in on me. Inhaling deeply, I tried to level myself. For the first time in my career, I was in over my head. We'd handled high-profile cases before, but this one was different. There were higher stakes at play. More than just defending someone's liberty. A man's entire future could implode over one wrong move.

"Okay, I'll call him right now," I said after a moment. "And just one more thing…"

"Yeah."

"Where's Nate? I have a feeling we're going to need him."

"He's finishing up a fender bender trial at the BMC. A two-day case," Joey explained. "I'm not sure he even knows about any of these developments."

"All right. Don't distract him with this. But as soon as he's done, you have him give me a call."

"Sure thing."

"Thanks." I ended the call, then searched for Jack's number in my contacts.

He answered on the first ring, like he was waiting on the edge of his seat for the call. "How did it go?" he asked. "Brad holding up?"

Things were moving fast, so I didn't know how to break it to him. Jack wasn't going to handle this well. I decided to just get it out there. "We didn't get to see him."

"You didn't get to see him! What's going on?"

"They're playing games. I think they've taken him over to Nashua Street."

"Nashua Street?" He sounded confused. "Is that another precinct?"

A civil lawyer, he didn't understand. "No. That's the county jail," I said.

"Why would they do that?" He huffed for breath. "Can't they just let him out on bail?"

"We called the jail, and they wouldn't confirm that he was there. It's a game they are playing, likely trying to delay us from seeing him. They'll say he was still being processed when we called. You should understand, this isn't a shoplifting charge. It's murder."

"So?"

"This is going to require a bail hearing." And I knew that couldn't happen until the next day. Jack would go apeshit about Brad being locked in a cell.

"When?"

"Tomorrow."

A pause. "You mean he has to sit in a cell overnight?" he finally asked.

"That's it exactly."

The line went silent. We were meandering though the city in the Uber. Large limestone buildings jutted into the air, casting shadows on the narrow streets. Sometimes the tall buildings disrupted reception. I thought the call had gotten cut off. "You there?" I asked.

"Yeah. I'm here." He sounded like his entire world was coming unraveled.

"Look, I need to get back to my office and regroup. Do you need anything else from me?"

"Shit, yeah." He suddenly regained his drive.

"What?"

"You need to get over to my office, so we can coordinate with PR and respond to this situation."

"Shouldn't we involve Brad?" Then, it hit me.

Alyson's entire approach was intended to split up our team, throw us off balance. She'd sequestered Brad away from his counsel and public relations firm, making us fend for ourselves. Even with the strong players Brad had in place, he ultimately made the final decisions. And he'd done quite well over the course of his political career. She sought to create a wall between Brad and his people to get an edge with the press.

"We don't have time to wait until they let us see him." Jack said. "How long will it take you to get over here?"

"A few minutes. Just as soon as we get the Uber turned around."

***

AFTER PROVIDING the driver with the new address through the Uber app, I sat back in my seat and gathered myself. The driver cleared the tall buildings of the financial district, then sun reflected off the windshield as we approached Atlantic Avenue. Gray skies had dissipated.

We skirted through the traffic light at the main throughfare, making good time. Crossing the bridge spanning the canal separating South Boston from Boston proper, the Seaport District lay in front of us. New high-rises with sparkling glass facades overlooked Boston Harbor. Coffee shops and stores packed the spaces between the office buildings, and restaurants lined the area. Most of the construction had taken place in the last ten years.

Buildings went up in old parking lots. A few of the staple landmark businesses remained. A James Hook and Co. lobster house sat on one side of the bridge and The Barking Crab on the other. The crab house was fanned by the federal courthouse and The Envoy Hotel. The hotel had a rooftop bar that overlooked the channel with picturesque views of the city's skyline. Now, the district resembled an upscale city, with pedestrians crowding the sidewalks that ran along the boulevard.

Slowing for traffic, the driver shook his head, frustrated. "Man, this guy won't get off my rear."

"Probably late for a meeting," I said, trying to rationalize Boston drivers.

"No. I don't think so." Our driver clenched the wheel, angry.

"What makes you say that?" The driver had me curious.

"This damn fool has been on us since I picked you up. Turned around just like us."

"Maybe he's tailing us," Courtney offered.

"Would be horrible surveillance tactics if that's the case," I said, turning to get a glimpse of the car through the rear window.

It was a Chevrolet sedan, fairly compact. The driver looked rough, but he didn't resemble a street thug, more like an undercover cop or private investigator. The car wasn't equipped with a long antenna or government plates, so I suspected it was a private dick. But you couldn't rule out a cop altogether.

"Who do you think it is?" Courtney asked.

"Probably a P.I.," I said.

"Do you have any idea who hired him?" she said.

Courtney's question was revealing. There were certain parties who might fit into this matter, but many wouldn't have the funds to hire a private investigator. People without deep pockets could be ruled out.

"Somebody with means," I finally answered. "And a serious agenda."

TWENTY-FOUR

WE DROVE PAST the new high-rises, then entered the older part of the district. The Uber whipped by the West Seaport Tower, then the Seaport Hotel. A couple piers jutted into the harbor on the other side of the street. A wooden schooner was tied to a wharf. Waves splashed against the hull.

We finally turned right onto a small lane, leading between the hotel and our destination at the East Seaport Tower. I glanced over my shoulder and watched the Chevrolet continue past. The driver stared at me, and I expected he'd circle the block.

We climbed out of the Uber and Courtney assured the driver he'd get a tip. He smiled and sped away. A breeze blew off the harbor and the scent of brine wafted through the air.

Pressing through a revolving door, we treaded over the fancy tile floor and checked in with security. Once they cleared us, we walked over towards the elevator bank. Our footsteps echoed through the palatial lobby. Courtney stepped over and pressed the button. At this time, in the late afternoon, we were the only ones waiting for a lift.

Courtney frowned. "This is beginning to feel like a risky case."

"How do you mean?" I really didn't follow.

"Getting threatened at the bar," she said. "Now, someone is following us."

"Your point is well taken," I replied.

"But you still think it's safe to stay in this case?"

"There hasn't been cause to be overly alarmed just yet." I hiked my shoulders. "We'll get through this soon enough."

Elevator doors whisked open. We stepped inside and hit the button for Jack's floor.

Back in the conference room with the view of the harbor, we didn't engage in pleasantries. Jack sat at the head of the table like before, with Courtney on one side with her back to the windows and me sitting across from her.

All the pomp and circumstance of the earlier meeting weren't in play. I got the feeling Jack was under tremendous pressure. He simply didn't have the time or energy to put on airs.

"We've got to get a handle on this and do some damage control," he said.

"Jack, we're here to help with your end as much as possible," I replied.

"Good. We need to be on the same page."

He relaxed a bit. I noticed his suit appeared a little wrinkled, like he'd been outside in the foul weather earlier in the day. He might even have spent the night in the office. There was a lot going on that I didn't know about. Now, he planned to grill me for details, while likely withholding information. I wondered what he was holding back.

"Tell us what you need," I said.

He leaned toward me and stared intently. "I need to know all the angles, Kenny."

I shook my head. "You know we can't reveal the strategic aspects of our case. Besides, we really don't know all that much about Danforth's death."

Jack nodded, understanding. "What can you tell me?"

"A van hit him while crossing the street."

"You saw it happen, right?"

"Sure."

"Don't you think that's a little convenient?" He held up his hands, palms towards me.

The comment caught me off guard. Jack sounded suspicious of someone.

Courtney was taken aback. "You don't think *we* had something to do with it?" she said, obviously puzzled by Jack's question.

Jack shook his head. "Heavens no."

"You just think it was planned to coincide with a meeting I was having, right?" I sat back and glanced out the window. Tugboats worked at pushing a large ship in the harbor.

"Something along those lines." He shrugged.

"They'd have to know my schedule and where Danforth was going. We don't even know where Danforth was going."

"Are you sure about that?" Jack shook his head.

"Brad said he didn't…"

Then, it occurred to me. I was supposed to meet Brad at the cocktail lounge when I got through with Beckerman. Brad knew I'd be sitting there. He could have arranged to meet with Danforth at the time of our meeting, which would put the aide in the vicinity of the bar at the time he was run down. But he wouldn't necessarily know what direction the aide would take to get there. Anyone coming from the Back Bay wouldn't likely cross the street near King's Chapel. They'd come from the other direction. The killer knew where Danforth had been.

"What?" Jack sought to probe my thoughts.

I shook my head. "This entire matter leaves more questions than answers."

"What did Brad say?"

"Just that he didn't know why Danforth was there. He hadn't spoken with him."

Jack nodded. "But are you sure about that?"

"Listen, I can't be sure about anything."

"What else do you know?"

"Absolutely nothing."

"Why are they charging him with Danforth's death and not Martin's murder? And why is it a conspiracy to commit murder, rather than just murder?"

The police often make an arrest on a lesser charge in order to obtain search warrants and build out the bigger case. I suspected they had some minor link between Brad and Danforth's death, and they planned to use it to gather evidence into both deaths.

"These are sound questions," I said after a moment. "But we won't know until we see the prosecution's case. I'm afraid I don't like to engage in guessing games and theories without all the facts."

"I thought that's exactly what you do." Jack smirked, disbelievingly.

Sitting up, I looked Jack in the eye. "Not with clients and their lawyers."

"You're holding something back from me," Jack snapped.

"No." I shook my head, annoyed.

"Well, the goal is to keep Brad from being arraigned."

"A little late for that. It's almost a certainty."

"We can still try to run interference. Maybe if he talks to them, they'll cut him loose."

"Jack," I said, shaking my head. "The bail hearing is tomorrow. He'll get arraigned at that time. We're heading into late afternoon. I doubt we could arrange an interview prior to his court appearance tomorrow."

"Okay. But could you at least try?" He looked us both over.

"We'll call the prosecutor and consider it." I didn't want to commit to anything.

Given certain information divulged during our last meeting at Jack's office, I had my concerns about letting Brad talk to the police. There was an issue with the timeline. Now, I worried an interview would lead to Brad's arrest in the Audrey Martin matter.

Courtney watched Jack closely, then she glanced at me. A skeptical glint resonated from her eyes. She'd picked up on something, and I considered taking a break to speak with her.

Jack pulled on his lapels and shifted in his seat, like he was worried about our reaction to the next thing he planned to say. "We need to discuss a press release," he finally said.

"That's your territory," I said, waving him off.

"A statement from you would go a long way. It's a better approach than something just issued from our office."

"My standard approach is to tell the press: No comment."

"Can you make an exception here?" Jack opened a folder and slid a document across the table. "We've been working on this with our public relations firm."

Perusing the press release, it was two short paragraphs. The document contained the usual denials of guilt and assurances of innocence, while noting a trust in the legal system and an expectation of working things out favorably. It was something meant to be published, not spoken on the courthouse steps.

"This really is something better released from you," I said.

"We think it would stand a better chance landing in the news if it came from you."

"I understand your position. But I deal with real world considerations."

"And I don't?" He sounded miffed.

Exhaling, I leveled myself before responding. He was beginning to irritate me. This was just the sort of interference that I'd been concerned about from the start. "We have a standard way of doing things for a reason," I said. "When a politician's office releases a statement, the press tends to print all or most of the statement as written. But when a trial attorney talks to the press on the courthouse steps, they use what is said however they choose, often splicing it and using comments out of context. And the more you say…" I pointed at the proposed release. "The higher the chance it goes awry."

Jack nodded. "You make a good point."

I couldn't believe he had conceded to my being right about something. "But?"

"We prefer that you look this over. And if you get a chance with the press, you could use some of it to help Brad. He's your friend, as well as a client."

And you owe him, I could almost hear Jack thinking.

Jack was present the night Brad had bailed me out in law school. He knew the score and had just played a chip, an important chip. Now, I grew concerned the debt might cloud my professional judgment. It felt like a car skidding on ice. And danger lurked around every corner.

He smiled coolly. "So, you'll consider it then?"

I nodded. "Sure."

"And you'll reach out to the prosecutor about a possible interview?"

"Jack." I shook my head. "Look, I don't think that's a good idea." I held out my hands. "We've got a serious timeline issue. Speaking to the police without a concrete alibi… well, that can be problematic."

He nodded. "Understood. But I think we might be able to explain things."

Jack was talking about the gap in time, between when Brad had left Danforth, and the time he had called the police.

Courtney leaned forward. "How will you explain it, Jack?"

Jack glanced at her, then he looked back to me. "Brad has a bit of a zipper problem."

TWENTY-FIVE

BACK AT THE STATION, Kara went to get a cup of coffee. She knew the caffeine would keep her up that night, but the events of the day had worn her down. Alyson's unorthodox approach left Kara with concerns.

Walking through the detective's open cubicles, most everyone had gone home for the day. She enjoyed getting things done in the evening after the place cleared out. Davis and Nguyen were bickering about something. Otherwise, you could hear a pin drop.

She took the long way around to avoid them. They were engrossed in a heated dispute and didn't seem to notice her.

Kara stepped into the kitchenette and found Chandler rummaging through leftovers. The scent of coffee and old doughnuts hung in the air. "Didn't know you were still here," she said.

"Just grabbing a bite." Chandler turned around with a coffee mug in one hand. And he shoved a plain doughnut into his mouth with the other.

"How do you stay thin eating junk like that all the time?"

Chandler shrugged. "Got a lanky build to begin with. Just don't ask for my cholesterol count."

They both laughed. She stepped past him to get to the lifer juice.

After grabbing a cup of black coffee, Kara turned to face him.

He stood there munching down the doughnut and sipping coffee, acting like he didn't have a care in the world. The guy had been through two divorces and countless breakups with girlfriends. He'd been in the hot seat a few times with the department. A real Teflon man, nothing ever stuck.

"What's eating you?" Chandler said, polishing off his snack.

She was taken aback by his observation.

"Well?" he continued.

Kara glanced around, making sure she wasn't overheard. "I think we rushed to make the arrest. We don't have much evidence. And now it will get harder to collect more."

Chandler nodded, agreeing with her statement.

"What if Bradford Wallace walks free?" she said.

He raised his eyebrows.

"Do *you* think we rushed into this?" asked Kara.

"You bet." He shook his head, dismayed. "I think the prosecutor saw headlines and went after them. She got a big politician in her sights. And she decided to take him down. We still have suspects to clear, like Keith Evers."

"She jumped the gun," Kara agreed.

A lull fell over the discussion, as they contemplated having the same observations. She took a sip of coffee and inhaled, worried about being caught up in a boondoggle down the road. This situation could get even worse. The department could get sued. *She* could get sued.

"Do you want to know the worst part?" Chandler finally said.

"No. What?"

"I'm not even sure Wallace killed Audrey Martin."

Chandler's words cut through the air like a knife. His comment hung there for a moment, as a storm cloud lingers over a summer picnic. The thought of it turned her stomach. She wondered what he was thinking. "Meaning?"

"I think the wife might have done it."

"Why?"

"A couple reasons."

"Care to explain?"

"First, the scratches on the *vic's* thigh. They seem like longer fingernails. A woman." He took another sip of coffee. "Second, I have her on CCTV going to a bank, late in the evening, just prior to the murder. She likely had accessibility to the murder scene."

"What's the motive?"

"Jealously. The *vic* was younger and quite attractive."

Kara shook her head. "I'm not buying it. She mentioned possibly having gone to the bank during her interview. And Bradford Wallace is a politician. Probably gets a manicure. We also don't have any concrete evidence of an affair."

"Aside from the countless texts and phone calls between the two of them?"

"That could be explained from them working together."

Chandler shook his head. "I compared them to Danforth's communications with Wallace. There was three times as much activity with the girl."

"Maybe she was the lead?"

"He was senior to her by a number of years and a few campaigns."

"Then who killed Danforth?"

"Perhaps Danforth was the only one that would know the two were having an affair?"

"So, wouldn't that implicate Bradford Wallace in Danforth's death?"

Chandler shrugged, aloof.

This entire theory left more questions than answers. Kara felt the two murders were connected, but she couldn't see Harper Wallace running someone down in a dilapidated van. In fact, she couldn't picture Harper Wallace climbing into an old van. It was possible Harper Wallace hired someone to run Danforth down. Yet, that seemed like a stretch. The text message information only showed the number of texts and data usage. The actual texts had been deleted. "Why didn't you bring this Harper Wallace angle up during the lieutenant's meeting?"

"I started to mention it," he said. "Remember when I began to weigh in, but the lieutenant wanted you to explain your theories. The lieutenant made it clear she was looking for solid evidence. These are just theories. Hunches. I don't have much to go on. So, I kept quiet."

His theories weren't likely on point. But his line of thinking might be used by a criminal defense attorney. Kara pictured Ken Dwyer in court confusing a jury with potential suspects. This entire case was proving to be a disaster.

She decided they needed to stay late and delve into the investigation further.

They headed to their desks and got back to work. Kara felt like they were trying to dig out of a hole Alyson Sheehan had created, rather than conducting an objective investigation.

A few minutes later, Chandler leaned back in his chair. "We should interview Keith Evers," he said.

"How are we going to do that?" Kara shook her head. "We don't know where he lives."

Chandler nodded. "I've got some plain clothes guys working on it. We might figure it out soon enough."

TWENTY-SIX

WE MET OUR TEAM at the upscale bar near the office. The pressure had increased exponentially. It required a gin and tonic to take the edge off.

Surrounded by the crew, we considered our options. Courtney sat next to me, and Nate took up the stool on the other side. Joey sidled up to Nate. The place was hopping, but nobody paid us any mind. Even though a news broadcast of Danforth's death showed me in the background, patrons of the bar hadn't put it together. People were engrossed in their own lives. No one had noticed me.

The bar was fairly busy for a Tuesday evening. A cacophony of chatter and dinnerware clanging on plates served as protection against eavesdroppers. A scent from seasonings on seafood and steak floated through the restaurant.

"This case is a complete nightmare," I said, polishing off my first drink rather quickly.

"You've seen worse," Joey commented.

"There's a lot of fingers in the pie. It's usually just us against the prosecution."

"What do you mean?" asked Joey.

"He means," Courtney cut in, "we're being micromanaged by a civil litigator. The client is an attorney with his own ideas. A public relations firm is weighing in. And to top it off, we got tailed by some goon this afternoon."

Joey nodded, conceding to the point. "Tailed?"

"Don't worry about it," I said. "Probably someone just keeping tabs on us."

"Well, I don't like the sound of it." Joey chugged his beer.

"Our client's civil counsel might be holding something back," Courtney said. I took this to reflect the consternation she'd revealed during our last meeting.

"About what?" Joey said, stating what the rest of us were likely thinking.

Courtney shrugged. "I don't know."

"Then how can you know he's holding something back?" Joey probed.

She glanced at me. "Just a feeling. Guess I'm picking things up from Kenny."

Everyone laughed. I'd been known to act on intuition.

"So, where do we go from here?" This from Nate, anxious to hear the playbook.

The question was the elephant in the room. We had been reacting to events the entire time, rather than gathering information and getting ahead of things. This case was a moving target with astonishing developments, including a second death. The charge being brought against the client wasn't even the one we were initially hired to address.

"Beats me," I said, ordering another drink.

They all stared at me surprised.

"That's it," Courtney chided me. "You're just going to give up?"

"I'm not saying that. All I'm saying is… we are in the dark, and it's hard to develop a path forward from where we sit."

"Afraid I don't quite follow." Nate said.

"You're speaking for all of us," Joey said to Nate.

"Listen, a lot of federal cases deal with a grand jury indictment. You don't even see the charges coming."

A bartender placed my refill down on the bar.

"You eventually get the government's case," I continued. "Then, you review what they have and plan your defense strategy."

Courtney took a sip of wine. "You're saying let's wait to see what they have."

"Exactly."

"That's not terribly proactive," Joey said, shaking his head.

"Afraid we don't have much to go on right now." I took a long sip of my drink and let the comment sink in. There just wasn't any telling what the police had dug up to substantiate the charges against Brad for Danforth's death.

Courtney shifted in her chair and her thigh brushed against my leg. A scent of her perfume drifted over. My attention on the case shifted into the background for a moment. The feelings I'd suppressed had swiftly bubbled to the surface. My pulse quickened. I inhaled, trying to squelch my feelings. A major case in the works wasn't the time to revitalize a romance.

My phone buzzed.

I'd tried to reach Alyson a few times about an interview with Brad. She hadn't responded to my calls or a text message. Reaching into my suitcoat pocket, I figured she was finally getting back to me. There could still be time for an interview and an opportunity to put this all to rest.

Finding my phone, I glanced at the screen before answering. It wasn't Alyson.

"Ken Dwyer," I said.

"Hey, Ken. It's Paul Beckerman."

"What's up Paul," I said, sliding off my stool.

"Got an update for you."

Stepping away from the din from the restaurant, I found a nook near the restrooms. The crush at the bar and the packed tables didn't bleed over to this side of the place. Without anyone nearby, the clamor tapered off. "What have you got?"

"This is entirely confidential. You didn't hear it from me."

"Understood."

"The police connected the van used to kill Danforth with Brad's campaign."

Such a development shouldn't have come as a surprise, but it shocked me. A dilapidated van was something that I'd associated with the Teamsters.

Now, the conspiracy to commit murder charge made sense. They probably didn't know for certain who was driving the van, but the police linking it to Brad's campaign suggested he'd retained someone to do the hit, if he hadn't done it himself. Killing the other aide was meant to silence him in connection with the Audrey Martin case. A dead man cannot testify.

"How did you learn about this?" I sought to confirm the reliability.

"Counselor, you obviously didn't listen. Heard what?" he said, chuckling.

"Fine." I glanced around to see if anyone was listening. All clear.

"Keep this one close to your vest," Beckerman said. "I cannot afford to lose this source. It didn't come easy."

"Sure. Do have anything else?"

"Afraid not."

"Nothing else on Keith Evers?"

"Not at the moment. I'm working on an angle," Beckerman said. "I'll let you know as soon as anything develops on that end."

"Thanks for taking the time to call tonight."

"No problem. That's why I get paid the big bucks." He chuckled.

"Thanks again." I ended the call, then rejoined the others.

They were hunkered at the bar talking shop. I nudged in beside Courtney, but I didn't climb back on my stool. It was time to make a hasty exit.

"What was that all about?" asked Joey.

I shook my head. "Nothing."

The waiter brought over appetizers and another round for the others, who were trying to catch up with me. I reached over and grabbed my drink. I took a sip. Then, I set the glass down on the bar; it was half full.

"Listen," I said to them. "You guys go ahead and have a nice time."

"Where are you going?" Courtney asked.

Handing her the firm credit card, I slid on my overcoat. "I've got a few things to prepare for tomorrow morning."

Courtney's fingers glided over mine as she took the card. A wry grin crossed her face. I wondered if the wine had gone to her head, or if she was having similar feelings. Sparks happen at the most inopportune times.

"Do you need any help at the office?" Nate said.

Slapping him on the shoulder, I said, "No. I've got this. Have a good time."

They all smiled and appeared ready to engage in office banter with the boss gone.

Leaving the restaurant, I nodded goodbye to the hostess. Then, I pushed the door open and stepped into the frigid night.

Somehow, I suspected Alyson planned to torpedo me with something at the hearing in the morning, even though it was a routine event.

I wanted to spend more time preparing, but I couldn't fathom what she had in store for me.

TWENTY-SEVEN

ON THE WAY TO THE OFFICE, I crossed State Street and headed up the decrepit sidewalk. A small mound of snow ran along the curb. It was turning black from exhaust fumes and grime being splattered by passing cars.

Tall buildings and an overcast sky left the night extremely dark. A cool breeze whipped into my cheeks. I kept my head ducked to ward off the cold.

Our latest development had me lost in thought, as I wandered past a sub shop, which was closed for the evening. The area was desolate, with most people already having left the city. I approached our building, wondering what I could glean from our investigation to help thwart a surprise attack from the prosecution.

Suddenly, I got shoved from behind. Spinning to face the assailant, I met the crude eyes of a husky worker. His face was gaunt and the skin rough and leathery from the outdoors.

Footsteps on the sidewalk behind me revealed a few more people approaching from the alley, which led to the parking lot behind the building. I was quickly surrounded and outnumbered.

We stood in front of the door to my building. They stared at me menacingly.

"Do you plan to attack me, right here on a main street?" I said, waving towards traffic. But only a few cars edged past.

"Who says attack?" The man that shoved spoke in a thick, working-class Boston accent. He feigned a smile.

Another man slapped my shoulder. "How we doing, counselor?"

This one was older and burly; he looked vaguely familiar. I couldn't recall where I'd seen him before. Boston is a small town, where you tend to run into the same people, often without ever really knowing them.

Then, the man that made first contact stepped closer.

I addressed him. "Look, you need to stop touching me, or I'll be forced to retaliate," I said, squaring off to defend myself.

"Oh, you gonna retaliate?" the leader said.

Cars buzzed up State Street, as people headed home late from the office, restaurants, and bars. The light on Atlantic Avenue must have changed color. There was probably a traffic surveillance camera nearby. Something told me this wasn't planned as an attack.

"Let's have it. What do you want?" I demanded.

"We think it's in your best interest to *withdraw* from your new case."

The comment came as a surprise. "What?"

"You heard me. *Withdraaaw.*" He spoke the last part slowly, and the word hung in the air. His stale breath permeated the cold night.

"What good would that do?" I said, trying to reason with thugs.

"Let him hang in the *wind.*" He flashed a sardonic grin.

"He'd just get another lawyer."

"Maybe. But not as good as you. Not as committed."

There was silence for a moment. They'd delivered the message.

"All right." I stood tall. "You've said your piece."

The leader nodded and smirked. "It would be best that you follow our advice. You never know what could happen to one of those pretty girls you cherish."

Stepping towards him, I cringed. A surge of anger rose through my entire body. It took intense focus to restrain myself. I desperately wanted to throw him into the street, crack his head on the pavement. "Are you threatening me?"

He shook his head. "You're a tough guy. That wouldn't work."

"So, what's your angle, then?"

"You need to look out for the ones you care about. They aren't as tough as you."

Before I could respond, he turned and walked into the street. Traffic halted. Cars braked and his crew followed suit, darting between stopped vehicles. They all crossed the street. When they reached the other side, the leader saluted me. Then, the crew turned up Broad Street and disappeared into the shadows.

Once they were gone, I entered my building and took the elevator up to my floor.

Walking back to my office, I wondered how many people wanted to bring Brad Wallace down.

TWENTY-EIGHT

KARA HUNKERED DOWN in the war room with a few members of the investigation team. Davis, Nguyen, and Chandler had all agreed to stay late in hope of ferreting out more evidence to assist with the prosecution.

They combed through CCTV footage and reviewed each piece of evidence again. Bradford Wallace's arrest had led to additional balls being run out. Now, they had his fingerprints, DNA, cellphone, and Danforth's cellphone and laptop, and Audrey Martin's computer.

After a couple hours, Davis pointed at the screen to his laptop and said, "We've got it!"

She walked over to see what he'd found. Davis stood up and made room for the others to get a glimpse of his discovery. Watching the screen, Kara realized it was a remarkable piece of evidence connecting Wallace to the first murder. She checked the timestamp and it helped.

The video had come from a camera located on the outside of a building. And part of the building was occupied by a local news station, located near the State House, which was across the street. "Nice work," she said to Davis.

He smiled proudly. "Can you believe it? It came from the building of a news outlet. A fucking news station."

"This helps a lot," she said. "But we still have to get over a few hurdles."

Despite this recent development, some of the other evidence found at the scene couldn't be traced to Bradford Wallace. Such evidence didn't entirely rule him out as a suspect or change his position as a defendant. But she knew it had to be turned over to the defense. Ken Dwyer would have a field day with this case. She figured the lawyer might even obtain an acquittal.

Chandler watched her closely. "You concerned about something?"

"Yeah." She explained it to him.

"Maybe you should just call the prosecutor."

Reaching for her phone, Kara called Alyson Sheehan expecting to get voicemail. It was after hours and getting late.

Alyson answered on the second ring. "Hello?"

"This is Kara Malloy."

"Understood. It's the only reason why I answered. What's up?"

Kara divulged the latest positive development. Then, she paused. "We have a few items… however, the defense could potentially use them against us at trial."

Alyson quietly listened to her. "We need to bury the problematic material," she finally responded.

"How?"

"You let me handle that. But your team is going to have to gather a bunch of additional evidence before we turn over the prosecution's case materials. You'll need at least ten more statements, additional DNA tests from the victim, and about twenty more fingerprints."

"Won't they just sift through the additional stuff."

"Let me handle that," Alyson said. "Dwyer will probably request a quick trial. Then, we'll send over ten boxes of discovery materials."

"How do you know he'll ask for a quick trial date?"

"A politician will want to move fast hoping to shut down the publicity with a favorable result as soon as possible. Plus, I was engaged to this particular defense lawyer, remember?"

Kara ended the call. She stood there for a minute, questioning the ethics involved. This approach cemented her feelings the arrest had come way too fast. She worried about getting embroiled in the prosecutor's tactics.

Chandler tapped her on the shoulder, taking her out of deep thought. She looked at him.

He grinned. "Got something," he said. "Let's go."

TWENTY-NINE

DIGGING THROUGH OUR FILE, nothing stood out to provide a clue where the prosecution was going during the hearing the next day.

They would arraign Brad and argue bail should be denied. The evidence, as I understood it, was flimsy and shouldn't warrant keeping him behind bars while he awaited trial. Yet, I continued to have a nagging feeling that I was missing something.

My phone buzzed. It was Paul Beckerman. "What's up?" I said.

"Got a new development. Has to do with Keith Evers."

He filled me in on the details, and he headed across town to pick me up. I took the elevator down to the lobby, then stepped out into the cold evening and waited a few minutes for him to arrive. The time gave me a moment to reflect on the matter. It was headed in various directions, and I didn't feel as though we had our hands around the facts. Not even close.

Climbing into his nondescript Ford sedan, I wasn't certain the effort to locate Evers would yield any fruit. We drove through the city and crossed over the canal into South Boston.

Beckerman had taken the Congress Street Bridge, which skirted the old mills and row homes to the right and the expanding commercial buildings to the left. He banged a right onto A Street and drove beneath an overpass.

We entered a gentrified part of South Boston, where new apartment buildings were going up amidst the decaying backdrop of broken city streets and ramshackle triple-deckers.

He turned and soon we were driving through an industrial area. Large brick mill buildings lined both sides of the streets. A few showed signs of current use, with shiny rollup warehouse doors reflecting off the headlight beams. Other buildings had broken windows. Vacant dwellings cast eerie shadows on the roadway. Graffiti covered some of the buildings and street signs, while weeds sprouted between the cracked driveways. The place was desolate, and few cars passed in the opposite direction. Even fewer people walked along the dilapidated sidewalks.

Eventually, he slowed and pulled over a low, disintegrating curb, onto a gravel area in front of a deserted building. Beckerman shifted into park and got out of the car.

He headed across the street towards a seedy bar, which was wedged between an old apartment building with asbestos siding and a brick mill building. The tavern was a faded light green with a neon Miller Beer sign in the window.

"Why are you going in there?" I said, trying to keep up.

He opened the door and we traipsed across a slanted floor towards the bar. The place smelled like stale beer and rank cigarette smoke, worn into the paneling from bygone days.

The bartender approached. He looked us over disapprovingly.

I took it that we weren't his usual clientele. He had a round face with ruddy cheeks, thinning hair, and wore a tattered flannel shirt.

Glancing around the bar, a few regulars were gathered on stools taking in the game. They were dressed in work clothes and had the tired appearance of laboring long hours over decades. The sort of fatigue you don't shake off by sleeping in on a weekend. Most ignored us. A few stared at us suspiciously.

Beckerman dropped a fifty note down on the bar.

The bartender raised his eyebrows. "What do you want?"

"The next round is on me," Beckerman said.

The bartender frowned. "What gives?"

"Just taking care of you." Beckerman shrugged. "Treat others how I'd like to be treated. You know the saying."

"Twelve years of Catholic school. I know the drill."

"Great."

The bartender grabbed the money, then he wiped down the counter in front of us. "What are you having?"

"We'll each have a Sam Adams on draft. You can ring up the bill now."

The bartender looked us over.

"We're stepping out for a smoke. Might take a few minutes, but we'll be back." Beckerman smiled. "You take care of us, there could be a couple more rounds on the house. Plus a good tip."

"Sure thing." The bartender grinned.

As we headed for the door, the bartender called down the line. "The next round is on that fella," he said, pointing at Beckerman.

They hoisted their glasses. "Cheers," someone called to us.

Outside, we headed across the street and walked down a narrow driveway, leading behind another old mill building. There was a crumbled parking area covered with sand. Across the parking lot, there was another ramshackle building. Both buildings had loading docks bumped against the spacious parking lot.

Beckerman headed for the distant building. I followed him. We climbed up onto the loading dock and found a door ajar. He shoved it open. Then, we stepped inside. It was pitch black. I couldn't see a thing.

He pulled a flashlight from his trench coat pocket, and I used the light from my cellphone.

The place stank like urine. Beckman's large foot kicked a can, and something scurried along the far wall. A ship rat. Moonlight filtered through the broken factory windows.

"How are we ever going to find Evers in this place?" I griped.

"There's supposed to be a jog in the building, where the homeless bed down at night. Once we find it, the goal is to roust everyone until we get him."

THIRTY

KARA AND CHANDLER rolled into a parking area separating two mill buildings. A cruiser with two uniformed patrolman were already there. The place looked abandoned.

"You sure this is the place?" she asked Chandler.

"This is it," he said, opening a car door. "Whether Evers is here right now is another story altogether."

Carefully opening her door, Kara climbed out of the unmarked car, then eased the door shut. Chandler shut his with a slight click. They walked over to the cruiser and the patrolmen quietly alighted from the vehicle. One was young and athletic. The other was husky and a few years older.

"This way," said the husky officer.

He led them past the loading dock and jimmied a door open, located directly off the parking area. They climbed a rickety set of metal stairs, then walked onto an abandoned factory floor. An expansive room lay before them.

Kara gripped her Maglite tightly. The others also clutched flashlights, except the younger officer held his pistol in his right hand, while scoping the area with his flashlight in the left. The place was cold, and she could see puffy clouds from her breath.

In the distance, a flashlight beam bobbed off the far wall. Another light jounced back and forth as it shined on the floor.

"Somebody's in here," she whispered to Chandler.

"Yeah. Like I've told you… this place is frequented by a lot of homeless people."

The movements appeared swift and surefooted.

Kara didn't get the feeling these two were wandering homeless people, squatting in the vacant building.

Who the hell was in here? Kara wondered.

THIRTY-ONE

BECKERMAN TURNED A CORNER, and we entered a narrow wing of the building. At one time, business offices for the factory were probably located here.

Light reflected through broken windows along the far wall. A few people stood around a barrel outside, with flames wavering into the night. Smoke whisked into the building through the deteriorating façade. Metal desks and filing cabinets were jammed together with heaps of discarded supplies piled around them.

Someone groaned and we both turned, alarmed.

Lying in the rubble, an older man was bedded down with a few thick blankets. We scanned our flashlights about the place. There were a few others sleeping in nooks. A couple vagrants were perched against an old desk, nursing bottles of cheap whiskey.

We treaded across broken bricks and chunks of mortar, strewn on the floor from the decaying levels above. We studied each person we came across. Most were older than Keith Evers. Almost everyone had unkempt hair and a beard. I wondered if Evers still resembled the youthful person depicted in the photographs we carried.

Rounding the jumble of office equipment, we both froze.

A man knelt by someone on the ground. Something about the dark silhouette caused me to shudder. His movements were too careful, smooth; he incited apprehension.

We eased forward slowly. Adrenaline raced through my body.

Beckerman's foot kicked a bottle. It skittered across the floor, clanging into debris.

The man stood and stared at us. His face was opaque in the shadows.

He raised an arm. A muzzle flashed.

A gunshot resounded through the mill building, then I heard the bullet dinging as it ricocheted off the metal office equipment.

Beckerman reached into his coat and withdrew a .357 Colt Python revolver from a shoulder holster. Light reflected off the 8-inch nickel barrel. The man turned and ran.

We started for him.

Rounding the debris, I glanced towards the spot where the assailant had been kneeling, trying to discern what he'd been doing. A body lay on the floor, writhing in agony.

I stepped over and crouched beside him, while Beckerman kept up the chase.

Shining my light, the person on the floor was Keith Evers. He was unshaven and looked banged up from drugs and street living, but it was unmistakably him. The dark eyes had the same penetrating look as in his mug shot.

Evers foamed at the mouth. A rubber band was tied around his left arm. His sleeve was rolled up, and a syringe lay on the floor.

Then, his eyes rolled back, and he stopped convulsing. He quit breathing.

I wedged my phone against a brick, shining light on the body. Pressing his chest, I began to perform CPR.

Metal stairs near the outside wall clanged as Beckerman raced down to ground level in pursuit of our attacker. A door squeaked opened, smacking brick.

Footfalls resounded from the interior, as a group of people advanced upon the scene. I peered over the debris and saw multiple flashlights bobbing in various directions. They'd heard the shot but were uncertain of the exact location.

My pulse raced, worrying that I'd be found at the scene of a possible murder.

I reached for my phone and turned off the flashlight. Then, I slowly made for the stairs, remaining stooped over as I trod through the shadows.

Clearing the decrepit office space, I stepped onto the metal staircase. The landing jounced and creaked under my weight. A few of the newcomers broke in my direction. Pale moonlight filtered through broken glass, reflecting off their badges.

Policemen, I thought. Then, I doubled my efforts.

The police were in pursuit. And I was fleeing the scene of a crime.

THIRTY-TWO

KARA WATCHED CHANDLER and the uniformed officers break after a person absconding from the building. A gunshot had tripped her senses into high gear. She held her pistol in one hand and the flashlight in the other, scanning the area for suspects and clues.

Her father had warned her about situations when other officers chase someone. You can't afford to let your guard down. Another fugitive could be hiding, lying in wait.

She came across a person strewn on the floor. He looked in bad shape. Foam trickled from his mouth. Kara stepped closer and didn't think he was breathing. Checking his wrist, the man was cold to the touch. She couldn't detect a pulse. The young man was dead.

She looked him over. There was a rubber band tied around his left bicep. A syringe lay on the floor.

An overdose, she thought. Then, she retraced the flashlight beam over the dead man's face.

He looked familiar. Studying him, she realized it was the person they were seeking to interview; Keith Evers lay before her. And now he was dead and unable to defend himself from accusations by a defense lawyer. She wondered who had snuck out of the building and whether he had anything to do with the young man's death.

Kara called in for back up. She requested a crime scene team, then stepped back to avoid contaminating the area.

Two dead witnesses, she considered. *Can't be a coincidence.*

THIRTY-THREE

OUTSIDE, I found myself standing in a courtyard walled in brick. To the right, it dead ended with buildings in a horseshoe fashion, while my left opened into an expansive parking lot.

Rattling emanated from behind me, as the officers mounted the metal stairs.

They would expect me to head to the left, so I took a chance and broke for the right. Various doorways jutted into the building façade. I found one in the shadows and pressed my back into the corner. Then, I waited.

I breathed slowly through my nose. They wouldn't be able to see me unless they ventured in my direction. I just hoped they didn't split up.

Officers charged over the stairs and burst through the door. It slammed against the brick entryway. Then, footsteps treaded over the gravel and sand, seeming to linger.

"Which way?" one of the officers said.

"He must have gone towards the parking lot."

Feet scampered, and they all broke for the open area.

I exhaled, relieved.

It sounded like two or three officers had run in the other direction. The pattering of their boots and shoes faded as they turned a corner.

My concern was someone else might pop through the doorway and spot me if I stepped out from the niche. I waited. And I wondered how long it would be before it was safe to leave.

Suddenly, I heard footsteps approaching my hiding spot. I took a deep breath.

A hand reached in from the shadows and clamped onto my shoulder. I was thrust forward. Then, the moonlight revealed my assailant. It was Beckerman.

He held an index finger to his lips, shushing me to keep quiet.

"Come this way," he whispered. "There's a door open."

Beckerman led me to the next doorway, inset into the building face. He gently opened a door partway, and we both squeezed through. Inside, there was a metal staircase leading up to the main floor. We took the stairs as quietly as possible. Then, we made our way towards the far side of the building, away from where Evers was located.

When we got to the other side, we scanned for the officers. The coast was clear, so we headed outside into the wintry night.

***

WE HURRIED along the deteriorated sidewalk and made our way for the bar.

Gathering ourselves, we stepped inside and found our seats. We slipped off our coats and draped them over the stools. Beckerman wore a suit jacket beneath his trench coat. He kept it on to conceal the big pistol.

The bartender approached. "Took you guys a while."

"He got a call," Beckerman said, indicating towards me.

"Always the case. The fancy guys are all business." The bartender laughed, then poured two Samuel Adams – Boston Lagers from the tap. He slid the pints in front of us, then nodded and headed to the other end of the bar.

Beckerman drank half of his down in one gulp.

I took a sip and put my beer on the bar.

"You better catch up. Make it look like we've been here."

Guzzling a third of mine, I set my pint jar on the bar. Then, the door swung open. A plain clothes officer walked inside. Sirens from first responders bellowed in the distance.

The officer walked up to us. "You see anybody come in here."

We both shrugged.

"What did he look like?" Beckerman said.

"Not sure. Would have come through a few minutes ago."

"Sorry, can't help you," Beckerman said.

The officer walked down the line. I took a deep breath, wondering what the regulars would say about the timing of when we came in. Anxiety fueled me with energy. I was ready to bolt if necessary.

As the officer approached the other end of the bar, the bartender eyeballed me. I worried the bartender understood the police were searching for us. Perhaps he'd mention we were outside for a long time or that we just came in. I didn't like the way this was shaping up. On the other hand, only one officer had come into the bar, which told me they were just running out balls and didn't have a strong suspicion the person they were trying to find had come into the tavern. The police were likely searching for one man and wouldn't think there were two people, either. But you never know.

The officer spoke to the bartender and the regulars. We couldn't hear what was being said, but a few of the regulars had shrugged and the bartender shook his head.

A moment later, the officer headed back our way. He walked directly toward us.

He reached to his vest and clicked on his mic, which had a cord running to a radio strapped to his belt. Leaning his head to speak over the police line, he kept his eyes on us. I figured he was calling for backup. The jig was up.

I was ready to make a break for it.

Beckerman nudged me. "Easy," he said.

"All clear," the officer said into the microphone.

He stopped by us.

Beckerman nodded a kind greeting.

"If a guy wanders in here looking suspicious, please give us a call. Ask for Detective Sergeant Malloy."

"Will do," Beckerman said, lifting his glass in salute.

The officer pushed the door open. A cool breeze whipped into the bar. Then he stepped into the night, continuing the search for an unidentified suspect.

"How did you know they wouldn't rat us out," I said to Beckerman.

"This is Southie." He shrugged. "Nobody around here likes a rat."

We laughed at the comment. Some things never change. Then, I wondered who had taken a shot at us, and whether Evers had been murdered.

THIRTY-FOUR

ENTERING HER NORTH END CONDOMINIUM, Kara found her partner clacking at a keyboard. Sandra was finishing up a PhD in psychology and tended to work late into the evenings.

The place was small but updated with a modern kitchen. The living room was adjacent to the kitchen area, and a granite counter with stools separated the two spaces. Windows overlooked Richmond Street. They were located on the second floor of an old brick building, directly above an Italian bakery.

"There's a pizza on the counter and wine in the fridge," Sandra said.

Kara stepped towards the kitchen area. "Great."

She grabbed a plate from the cupboard, then slid on a slice. After pouring a small glass of wine, Kara walked into the living room and sat on the sofa. She ate a few bites to settle her stomach, then took a long sip of Merlot.

"Long day?" Sandra said. She sat at a small desk in the living area.

"Yeah." Kara ate more pizza and tried to relax. It felt good to get off her feet.

"Saw you on the news today. Appears like this is a really big deal."

The comment caused Kara to pause. She breathed deeply, trying to settle herself. "How much airtime did the story get?"

"A lot." Sandra grinned. "It's been running all day."

Kara had picked up bits during the course of the day, but she'd just considered them as highlights. Now, she realized the story had traction. It could even hit the national news.

The arrest came too fast, she thought. Two dead bodies had recently stacked up and one while Bradford Wallace was in jail.

He couldn't have done that one. She didn't think he had an opportunity for someone else to arrange it, either.

"Something on your mind?" Sandra said, rising from the chair.

Kara shook her head, not wanting to trouble Sandra.

Sandra had a tall lean build, with shoulder length brown hair. Taking a seat on the sofa, she glanced at Kara with penetrating blue eyes. "You can tell me. I'll keep it confidential."

Her background allowed Kara comfort in divulging certain things about work. It wasn't a desire to keep the situation privileged as much as she didn't want to burden Sandra with worry, especially if Kara's concerns never came to fruition. "Look, it's been a long day," Kara finally said. "I have some concerns about how the prosecutor is handling this. But I've done everything by the book, so there's nothing to worry about."

"Yet, you're still worried."

Kara nodded. "Yeah, I'm worried."

THIRTY-FIVE

THE NEXT MORNING, I pushed through a mob gathered at the Boston Municipal Courthouse. My briefcase got caught up on people's bags, as folks swarmed around me. News vans were pulled to the curb and a couple police cruisers were parked across the street. Uniformed officers worked the crowd, but the turnout was immense. They couldn't hold everyone back.

Courthouse gadflies had taken up positions along the sidewalk, spilling into the roadway. People trying to enter the courthouse for legitimate business purposes were stymied by the throng. Activists held signs and screamed at me. They had taken a position that Brad was abusive to subordinates and killed them to cover wrongdoing. The scene was utter chaos.

Reporters approached me with microphones extended. "Mr. Dwyer, do you care to comment on Senator Wallace's arrest?"

"No comment," I said, waving them off.

I kept to the standard protocol: keep your eyes focused on your destination, and don't respond to questions. Communications with the press hardly ever show up in print correctly. The comments by a criminal defense attorney outside the courthouse often get spliced and recast to follow the message the news outlet wants to deliver.

Entering the building, I finagled my way through security, then stood with a pack of people waiting for the elevator. This was just a routine bail hearing and arraignment, where not much could go wrong. Yet, stress pulsated through my veins.

An elevator door opened. One person got off and a cluster of people boarded it. They crammed inside, shoulder to shoulder, leaving little room. I contemplated taking the next elevator, but I needed to get upstairs and assess the situation.

Stepping forward, I meant to join them. A stout woman shook her head. She didn't want me to enter. I watched the doors close, then turned to see if the other was available. Across the elevator bank, a light dinged. Newcomers flocked for the next elevator. I was too late. Now, I had to wait for the first one to return, or venture across the courthouse lobby to the stairs.

The BMC is the central district courthouse for Boston. It has a multistory lobby with balconies and railings on each floor. Courtrooms are located on many levels. A light illuminated and the first elevator dinged, signaling a return to ground level.

Finally, the elevator doors opened, and I was the closest person to it. I climbed inside. People piled in after me; I got pushed to the back. I was concerned about not being able to alight at my floor before the doors closed and the lift moved to the next level. It happened on occasion that people just stand there blocking your way.

The pressure was getting to me. Cramped in the elevator, I felt lightheaded. The walls were closing in on me, and I found it hard to breathe. People unloaded onto floors along the way upward, which eased the tension. My concerns lessened about exiting at my floor.

When the elevator doors finally opened, I departed with a surge of confidence. I was ten minutes early and had time to regroup.

Walking along the open corridor, my heels clacked on the polished floor. I glanced at the tiers below and found the usual activities taking place. Lawyers chatted with clients near the railings, and unrepresented criminal defendants lingered with family and friends who accompanied them for support.

I found the courtroom. Only a few people stood outside. It was a good sign that most of the press were out on the sidewalk. I relaxed and opened one of the double doors.

Stepping inside, I found the entire courtroom jam-packed, and the judge had already taken the bench. Alyson stood at the prosecutor's table with a colleague. I figured she was there for various matters.

Then, I noted Courtney at the other table. She glanced over her shoulder and frowned at me.

Scanning the rest of the courtroom, I noticed Nate in the first row, and Brad standing at a side entrance with a bailiff. He wasn't wearing a jumpsuit. They had let Brad wear the suit he had on at the time of his arrest, sans the tie. This was an approach they often permitted, especially with high-profile defendants. I knew Alyson was going to contest bail.

Rushing to the table, I tried not to delay things any longer. I dropped my bag on the table and looked up.

The judge smirked. "Glad you could make it Mr. Dwyer."

THIRTY-SIX

STANDING ALONGSIDE Courtney, my pulse raced. I quickly pulled out a notepad and pen from my briefcase and set the bag on the floor.

The BMC is a fairly new courthouse. Named after Edward W. Brooke, the first black United States Senator, the courthouse was built in 1996. It was fairly well-maintained.

I glanced at the nameplate on the bench and gathered that Judge Camile Sanders had the case. I'd never been before her, but I had a few civil cases pending under her purview over the years. Many civil actions get filed and settled without a trial or even counsel appearing in court. I recalled she had a background as a general practitioner before taking the bench. She didn't lean heavily towards the prosecution.

"Are you ready? Judge Sanders asked. She was attractive, with short blonde hair.

"Yes, Your Honor."

"Let's get started," the judge said. She glanced around at the crammed gallery. "Seems we have attracted quite a bit of interest in this case."

"Your Honor," Alyson began.

The judge held up her hand, cutting off the prosecution. "I am not going to enter a gag order at this time. But I suggest that counsel keep their arguments in the courtroom. Any conduct by counsel to disrupt this proceeding through the press may cause me to revisit my decision. Am I making myself clear?"

"Yes, Your Honor," Alyson and I responded in unison.

"I understand we are here on a couple of issues. An arraignment and a bail hearing." The judge paused and looked at both lead attorneys for confirmation.

I nodded. But Alyson shook her head.

"Ms. Sheehan, do you have something to add?" asked the judge.

"Your Honor, we would like to add additional charges."

This was the ambush that I anticipated. I interjected, "Your Honor—"

"Let her finish," Judge Sanders snapped.

"We have a criminal complaint for first-degree murder," Alyson said in a somber tone. She paused for dramatic effect. "This involves the death of Audrey Martin."

The gallery erupted with commotion. A few press correspondents scrambled from the courtroom, eager to contact their colleagues about the new murder charge in order to get a jump on the breaking story. Others held on for more information. A few clacked at keyboards on small laptops.

Judge Sanders appeared as surprised by the development as everyone else. The clamor persisted, while she registered what the prosecution had disclosed.

Judge Sanders adjusted her robe, then told everyone to settle down.

"Are you saying the defendant is being charged in connection with *two* murders?" The judge pointed toward Brad.

"Absolutely," Alyson said.

"Your Honor," I said. "This is just grandstanding for the press. We should get an offer of proof before those charges are added here."

Judge Sanders shook her head. "While I can understand your concern, counselor… I'm afraid that I cannot control what charges the DA's Office brings. The offer of proof will be provided in consideration of bail."

Alyson took the comment as a cue to proceed. She handed a charge sheet to me, then she asked to approach and brought one to the clerk seated near the bench. The clerk handed it over to the judge.

"Do we have a plea for these charges?" the judge asked me.

"Your Honor, I haven't been able to consult with my client about the first charge, never mind the latest one."

She raised her eyebrows and looked at Alyson. "Is this true?"

Alyson nodded. "The timing of the arrest prevented—"

Judge Sanders held up her hand, then she turned to me. "Were you available to see your client after the arrest?"

"Yes, I went to the precinct, and they wouldn't allow me to see him."

The judge looked at Alyson. "Explain."

Alyson shrugged. "The defendant had already been taken to Nashua Street."

"Did you permit counsel to see him there?"

"The prisoner didn't get settled until after visiting hours."

"After visiting hours?" the judge repeated. "This is a double murder case. You need to make the defendant available to his counsel. This type of grandstanding disrupts the court system. Now, we need to pause to allow counsel and client to confer."

"Sorry, Your Honor. It wasn't an attempt to grandstand."

The judge canted her head. "Come now."

"Your Honor, may I speak," Brad called from the sidelines. "The prosecutor tried to interrogate me after I asked to speak to my counsel, then she told me that I wouldn't be permitted to see him before this hearing."

The judge looked at Brad. "I'm going to stop you right there. You have counsel, so please let him speak for you."

"Sure thing, Your Honor," Brad said.

I figured this was only one of a few times Brad had ever spoken to a judge in the last ten years. His approach reminded me that he had worked as a prosecutor for a year or two out of law school. I'm not even sure how many cases he'd handled during that time. His public service as a prosecutor was undertaken merely to put the job on his political resume.

"Bailiff," the judge said. "Please escort the defendant over to his counsel's table, so the two can confer."

The bailiff led Brad over to our table. Brad looked smart in his suit without a tie and a four o'clock shadow. Aside from appearing without a jumpsuit, he wasn't shackled, either. Brad stepped between me and Courtney.

Leaning toward him, I just said, "You plead not guilty on both. And keep quiet."

He nodded, understanding. "Okay."

"Are you all set, counselor?" asked the judge.

"Yes, Your Honor."

She went through all the preliminaries with us on the first charge. Then, she asked Brad, "How do you plead?"

"Not guilty," he said.

Judge Sanders went through the same approach for the new case. Brad pled not guilty again. When the arraignment was concluded, the judge turned to Alyson. "What is the Commonwealth's position on bail?"

Alyson straightened herself. "We seek denial of bail altogether."

The judge blanched. "Does this defendant have a criminal record?"

"None, Your Honor."

"Do you have probable cause for these charges?"

"We do, Your Honor."

"I've perused the file, and what I've seen to date appears quite thin." The judge shook her head. "Now, you're asking me to keep this man incarcerated."

"We merely request that you hold him over until after the probable cause hearing," Alyson explained. "That way the trial judge can hear the evidence against Mr. Wallace and make a decision on bail."

"So, you do not plan an offer of proof now?"

"We feel that would be premature."

"Mr. Dwyer," the judge said. "What do you have to say."

"This is highly unusual. If they aren't going to make an offer of proof, then they should at least provide the factors considered for bail."

Judge Sanders turned back to Alyson. "Please do."

Alyson glanced at her legal pad. Then, she looked up and ran a hand through her hair. "Mr. Wallace is charged with two heinous crimes. There is compelling evidence connecting him to both murders. Further, he is a man of tremendous means. We estimate that he's worth at least ten million dollars. His family and his wife's family have even more. Mr. Wallace even has access to a family home in Bermuda."

The judge glanced at me. "I doubt you have much to say in response."

"Your Honor, I would like to respond."

"Please do."

"The prosecution overstates my client's affluence. In addition, he did not commit these crimes. The prosecution hasn't offered any direct evidence connecting Mr. Wallace to these crimes. He stands prepared to defend and clear his name."

The judge nodded. "Your position is well taken by the court."

I glanced at Alyson and smiled. She looked at me with daggers in her eyes.

"Don't relax, yet," Judge Sanders said.

"Your Honor," I complained.

"These are serious crimes. Your client does have means."

"But—"

"Let me finish."

"Okay."

"This is what I am going to do. We'll hold him over until the probable cause hearing, then the trial judge assigned to the case in Superior Court can make the decision."

"You're going to let him rot in a cell?" I objected.

"I'm not through." The judge adjusted her robe. "The probable cause hearing is going to be set for tomorrow. No extensions."

Brad leaned over. "You can't let me sit in there."

"Your Honor. My client doesn't have a criminal record."

She shook her head. "That's how I'm ruling."

This was a high-profile case with a lot of media attention. She had done the savvy move and punted the decision on bail to another judge. Still, the thought of Brad in the county jail was unsettling. I had further concerns. Judge Sander's comments about leaving the decision on bail to the Superior Court judge made it seem like she considered thc probable cause hearing a forgone conclusion.

"How am I supposed to prepare under these circumstances?"

"Lawyers do it all the time," the judge replied.

Her comment was a dig at me for handling mostly private paying clients, who could typically afford bail. We got to prepare in a conference room, with coffee and doughnuts. Attorneys who handle court assigned cases often represent the indigent and people who cannot afford a lawyer or bail. They were accustomed to meetings at metal tables in jailhouses.

Alyson did not respond to the requirement of an immediate probable cause hearing. However, I got a sense that her grandstanding moves to arrest Brad quickly and without a warrant had backfired. Now, she had to streamline her case and wouldn't have much further opportunity to investigate.

The judge looked at Alyson. "Are you all set?"

"Yes, Your Honor," Alyson said, beginning to pack her things.

"Now, you can put up, or shut up," the judge said to her.

Alyson paused and looked up. She appeared like a deer in headlights.

They don't have much, I concluded.

Courtney led the way out of the courthouse. We stood on the steps with Courtney flanking my right and Nate on the left. The reporters gathered around us.

"Do you have anything to say about the recent charges?" A reporter asked.

Another pushed in front of me. "What do you have to say about today's events?"

Cameras were rolling, and various flashbulbs stunned me.

Then, I gathered myself and looked sternly into a camera. "My client is innocent of these charges." And with that comment, I became fiercely committed to vindicate him.

PART FOUR

PROBABLE CAUSE

THIRTY-SEVEN

BACK IN THE FINANCIAL DISTRICT, we had to push through more press to get into our building. This was turning into a media frenzy without any sign of letting up.

After dropping my bag and overcoat in my office, I grabbed a notepad and headed to the conference room. Joey and Courtney were already there. I took a seat at the head of the table and Nate walked in with a glass of water.

"Emily stepped out for coffee from Dunkins," Joey said.

She was our office administrator. Emily had graduated from Northeastern University and started as an administrative assistant. After only a few years, she'd proven her value and I promoted her to Office Manager. She kept tabs on the attorneys and got their timesheets in and the bills out to clients, among other things like paying our rent.

"Let's trace out what we think they have for each case," I said, reaching for a pen in my shirt pocket.

"This is going to be hard without the client." Courtney shook her head.

"Tell me about it," I said.

A rap on the door made us all pause and look. Jack Delaney poked his head in. "Joey told me you'd all be meeting, so I thought I'd join you."

"Jack, this is a strategy session." I shook my head. "We cannot divulge attorney/client privileged information."

He stepped into the room and eased the door closed behind him. "Okay, but we need to go over how things went down today."

Jack took a seat beside Joey, and everyone looked him over.

This was getting to be more aggravation than the case was worth. Dealing with other parties comes with the territory in a case where the defendant has a lot of visibility. However, we seemed to get stymied by them at every turn. And I questioned whether we got full disclosure of all the facts. People had spoken to the police without informing us. Someone was jerking us around, and I occasionally wondered if it was Jack.

"Listen, I heard on the news Brad didn't get bail," Jack said.

I nodded. "They ambushed us with charges in the Audrey Martin case, too."

"Yeah. I heard about that as well." Jack appeared somber, but an intensity flickered in his eyes. He wasn't used to things unraveling.

Civil cases provide for discovery and time to respond to developments. There wasn't the same level of thinking on your feet as found in criminal matters. As a civil litigator and political consultant, he didn't have the experience to properly assess what had gone down. Now, he was likely frustrated and running Monday morning quarterback scenarios through his head.

"We have to focus on what needs to be done going forward," I said.

"Sure. But from my end, I need a better understanding than what's on the news."

Courtney shook her head. "Why didn't you come to court today?"

It was a good question and we all seemed eager to hear the response.

Jack shrugged. "Just thought it was a routine event. Never thought they'd torpedo us."

His comment reflected what I'd been thinking all along. Jack didn't have the experience to anticipate moves the prosecution might make in a case like this. Alyson intended to play dirty and pull every trick in the book.

We all sat there, flabbergasted by his naivete.

"Look, I'm just trying to get a handle on what's gone on, so I can report to Brad and Harper." His voice had elevated and sounded defensive.

I wondered how he thought this could blow back on him. "Okay, let's just ease up."

"Don't tell me to ease up," he snapped. "This is a complete shitshow."

Finally, we were addressing the elephant in the room. He blamed me for the charges brought against Brad. "How so?" I asked.

"This wasn't ever supposed to get to an arraignment. *You* should have gotten the case kicked first." He pointed at me. Veins bulged from his temples. "I asked you to let the police interview him, so—"

"And they didn't respond."

Jack looked surprised.

"You assumed that I hadn't called?"

He nodded, chagrinned.

"Well, I called the prosecutor three times. And I texted her. I even mentioned bringing Brad in for an interview, so there wouldn't be any confusion about why I was contacting her. No response."

Jack looked confused. "Why wouldn't they want free discovery?"

"Beats me," I said, shaking my head.

"I thought you almost married her," Jack said. "If you don't know, then none of us have any chance of figuring her out."

Even to this day, I really didn't know why Alyson had broken off our engagement. We had even gotten together a few times since then. I could never figure her out. And I didn't have a clue as to her intentions with this case. She remained a mystery to me. The circumstances of this case weren't any better.

Joey looked at Courtney. "You're friends with her."

Everyone turned to her, waiting to see if she could shed any light on the subject.

Courtney looked us over, while contemplating her response. Then, she hiked her right shoulder and said, "Alyson screwed up. She moved too fast."

THIRTY-EIGHT

KARA SAT IN A CONFERENCE ROOM at the DA's Office with Alyson Sheehan across from her. A younger prosecutor accompanied them. He scribbled notes as Alyson worked off a prepared outline.

Although she'd testified in court countless times, Kara felt nervous. She wondered if they had enough to allow the case to go forward. The defense wouldn't know about Keith Evers's fingerprint on the front door yet. But they might think of him as a scapegoat anyway. He had a negative history with the family.

"Relax," Alyson said. "You're doing just fine."

"Guess, I'm just worried about the case. That's all."

Alyson canted her head in a motherly way, despite being only a few years older than Kara. "You let me worry about the case. Remember, you only have a certain role in a probable cause hearing. Just focus on your role. I'll do the rest."

"Okay, sure."

They went over the typical rules. Give a brief pause before responding, appear polite, even on cross-examination, and just answer the question asked. Don't volunteer information. Let the questioning unfold with a lot of back and forth, like a tennis match. This avoids lengthy narratives, which are not permitted, unless a witness is not represented by counsel, because such testimony does not respond to a question. It also leads to lack of control and divulging facts you don't want to reveal right now. And most importantly, it's harder for the judge to follow.

Going over some practice questions, Alyson shook her head. "You still seem distracted. I need you to focus on getting your testimony right."

They went through a practice run of Kara's testimony, taking it from the top.

She noticed that Alyson appeared extremely relaxed, like this hearing was just a formality. The prosecutor didn't have the same level of concern Kara had witnessed in her previously. Considering the difference between this preparation session and a couple of their prior discussions, Kara figured it out.

Alyson's got a ringer.

THIRTY-NINE

WHILE WE DIGESTED the statement Courtney had floated to the group, Emily arrived with a Box O' Joe from Dunkins. She set the cardboard box of coffee down on the table, then she placed a bag next to it, filled with cups and napkins.

"Anything else?" she asked.

"No munchkins?" Joey said, disappointedly.

Emily shook her head; the aroma of coffee drifted through the room. "Not this time," she said. "You can't afford to get sluggish during such a big case."

Joey's face turned red. The rest of us laughed at Emily's comment.

She left and closed the door behind her.

Jack cleared his throat. "Aren't you worried about not having enough time to prepare for this hearing? Shouldn't we have requested an extension?"

He was thinking like a civil litigator again. "No," I said.

"Why not?"

"Listen, Jack. I understand that you have good intentions, but this is distracting us."

"Just answer the question."

"We deal with *Jenkins* hearings all the time," I explained. "The Commonwealth is required to present at a probable cause hearing within twenty-four hours of a warrantless arrest. You see, part of the goal is to make the prosecution show that it had probable cause for the arrest. Mostly it concerns having enough evidence to bind the defendant over for trial. It prevents them from making an arrest, then ginning up more evidence to justify the charge. However, the prosecution can present evidence obtained *after* an arrest to support its position that binding the defendant over for trial is justified. So, you never want to delay these hearings."

"That applies to the prosecution, but we could ask for an extension."

"You're still not getting it. More time only helps the prosecution." I shrugged. "We're used to functioning under these timeframes. In fact, we're likely going to request an immediate trial date."

Jack blanched. "Do you really think it will go to trial?"

"Probable cause is a rather low threshold." I nodded. "We're likely going to have to defend this if you want Brad acquitted. I expect any plea deal would include prison time."

"This goes against everything I believe," Jack said. "Get a case kicked quickly. If you can't get a dismissal, drag it out and prepare like hell."

"Such an approach works in defending civil cases. We rarely have opportunities for motions to dismiss. And more time allows the prosecution to shore up their case."

"Guess I'd better leave you to prepare." He rose from his chair.

This came as a welcomed relief. We had a tight schedule and Jack had turned into a distraction. "Good," I said. "You need to check in with Harper anyway."

Jack stared at me, blankly.

"What?" I said.

"That raises another issue," Jack replied. Then, he filled us in on the problem.

FORTY

WALKING INTO THE Nashua Street jailhouse, Courtney and I checked in at a large desk. The place smelled like a day-old salami sandwich left in the sun. We flashed our credentials to a corrections officer and signed a visitor's logbook.

The guard on duty smirked at us, like he anticipated our defense would be an exercise in futility. Everyone around town already knew about the case and were forming opinions early. Usually, you just checked into a jail and received a perfunctory welcome.

We had to leave our bags and phones in a locker near the desk. The guard let me take a notepad and pen for the meeting with Brad. A few guards walked by and ogled Courtney.

Given the desk guard's smug behavior, I pondered whether anyone might try to listen in on our discussion. It happened on occasion that you met with a client at a jailhouse or corrections facility and certain guards had their ears peeled the entire time.

Thinking about the case, Alyson's actions reflected a hint of desperation. I was beginning to suspect Courtney was right about Alyson jumping the gun with a quick arrest. This made me consider treading carefully going forward. You don't want to overplay a case when the prosecution held a weak hand of playing cards.

The front desk guard led us across the lobby area. A steel door with a window on the top half rattled open, and we were directed to a transition room. It was rectangular and only slightly wider than the door we'd just walked through. The room had cinderblock walls on two sides and a long window overlooking a hallway. The windows had crosshatching, reflecting safety glass. A similar door led into the hallway.

Our guard turned away, and the door from the lobby shut behind us with a metallic clang. Then, another guard traipsed down the hallway. He stood by the interior door, and it clanged open. He motioned for us to step into the corridor.

We entered a narrow hallway with cinderblock walls, and the door from the sally port jangled shut. The guard led us down the corridor.

Passing a few metal doors, he finally stopped and motioned to a door. "You can go in," he said, pointing to a small interview room.

I opened it. Brad was wearing an orange jumpsuit. He was seated on a metal stool fastened to the floor. Stale air drifted from the room.

We stepped inside and Brad looked despondent.

The guard nodded to us, touching the brim of his hat. "You've got twenty minutes," he said, closing the door.

Brad stood up and hugged me. "Ken, you don't know how glad I am to see you."

After we greeted him, he shook Courtney's hand.

There was a metal table affixed to the floor and another shiny stool.

"You can have it," I said to Courtney, motioning to the stool.

She took a seat and Brad sat back down.

Handing over the notepad and pen to Courtney, I felt better just pacing around the small room. There was a lot to cover in a short meeting. So, I organized my thoughts, and considered where to begin.

Brad stared at me expectantly. "Any news?"

His question was vague. I figured he was hoping the prosecutor would suddenly change her mind. This made me think he understood the evidence against him was weak.

"How you holding up?" I said, changing the topic. I wanted to follow an agenda without getting sidetracked by the client.

"This place is a zoo, with actual criminals." He shook his head.

"Any concerns? I could try to get you sequestered."

Brad shook his head. "So far, they think I'm getting railroaded, and nobody's made a play at me. I think I'm good to go until the hearing. But you'll get me out of here then? Right?"

I couldn't promise anything, but I had to reassure him. "Sure."

He forced a smile. "You've got to get me out of here."

"We'll do our best," Courtney said. She scratched some notes on her pad.

Brad looked us both over. He appeared out of place in a jumpsuit. Some of our clients were well-suited for jailhouse attire. I decided to walk him through the procedural events to date. Even though he understood what had transpired, I preferred to get a client acquainted with the system based upon their current knowledge.

"The process from here," I explained, "involves a probable cause hearing. The Commonwealth must present evidence to establish it had probable cause for binding you over for trial."

"I don't see how they can," Brad said. "I'm innocent."

"Look, you need to understand two things. First, probable cause is an extremely low standard. It's not anything like the reasonable doubt standard they need to convict. They just need to show there is evidence to support a reasonable belief that you may have committed a crime."

"And the other point?"

"Second, we don't want to give them free discovery."

"Meaning?"

"You're not going to testify at this hearing. If I can't beat down their case, I do not want to risk digging you in deeper."

Brad shook his head. "I'm not one of your criminal defendants for Pete's sake. I'm an attorney and a politician. You know I can talk my way out of anything."

"Listen, this is not the time for you to start talking. The prosecution is not required to turn over their entire case before this hearing. We simply don't know what they have, and I don't want to feed them information to use against us."

"But—"

"You're not listening. You have a timeline issue," I said. "Which they *can* expose."

"I just think you should hear me out."

I shook my head, objecting to his approach. "No criminal defense lawyer would ever have the client testify at a probable cause hearing under these circumstances."

"But you're not just any defense lawyer. That's why I hired you."

Now, he was taking us back to their original goal of me helping to get the prosecution off his back. They'd wanted the case dropped against him without an arraignment. Although I've worked a few miracles in the past, this matter didn't afford such an opportunity. Brad's whereabouts at the time of the death were an issue.

"Under the present circumstances, I simply cannot let you testify. We'll surprise the prosecution at trial. You'll have the opportunity to explain at that time. When the standard is reasonable doubt."

Courtney leaned forward. "This approach makes the most sense."

Brad nodded, conceding. "Okay, I'll go with your judgment."

His comment allowed me to relax a bit. Sometimes convincing a client to take the right strategic approach is harder than cross-examining a hostile witness. I smiled and patted Brad on the shoulder. "Don't worry, I have your back."

He smiled. "I know."

I canted my head, puzzled.

"We get news updates in here. Your comment on the courthouse steps came with conviction." He shrugged. "I think that's partly why they're leaving me alone in here."

Courtney stood up. "We're going to need to get going. There's still a lot to do."

"Wait a minute," I said, motioning for her to sit back down. "We have a couple more things to cover."

"Shoot," Brad said.

"First, tell me what the hell is going on with the unions." I explained the situation to him with the Teamster's boss at the bar, the threats, and the person who followed us.

"You have to understand… those guys are basically gangsters."

"Should we be worried?" This from Courtney.

Brad shook his head. "I seriously doubt they would commit a major crime over my political positions. They may threaten you. Keep tabs on you. But I can't see them doing anything serious."

"Then who killed Danforth?" I'd pinned it on them.

"I don't have the faintest idea," Brad said. He sounded sincere.

Then, I told him about Keith Evers dying. I didn't tell him how we had found him, but rather made it seem like a leak from the police department. He didn't have the faintest idea who killed Evers, and we didn't know for certain if it was a murder or overdose.

His comments reinforced my belief in his innocence. "That's good to know," I said, chuckling. "Especially when you're facing a conspiracy to murder charge."

"Anything else?" Brad said. "I know you like to bullet these things out. You began with a first, so there's got to be another issue you wanted to discuss."

"Yeah. About that…" I didn't know how to begin.

"Just say it."

"We may have a little problem with Harper."

***

THE GUARD RETURNED and led us to the sally port. I could see the other guard working the front desk through the windows. He looked over and pressed a button. The interior door shook open, and we stepped into the transition room.

As the door started to close behind us, the hallway guard raised a hand to his visor and gave a mock salute, then he pivoted and disappeared down the corridor.

I stepped to the door leading to the lobby. It didn't open.

The guard at the front desk stepped away. He didn't glance back at us.

We remained trapped in the sally port, without any means to call for help. There wasn't an intercom on any of the walls and our cellphones were in a locker. Somehow, I figured this was against protocols for the guard working the front desk to leave his post until he was relieved. Anyone could just walk into the jailhouse right now and there was nobody around.

"Can you believe this?" Courtney griped.

"Alyson did this. I just know it."

"Why?"

"To harass us. Maybe cause us to lose time, get distracted."

We waited and waited, but the guard did not return to the front desk.

At least thirty minutes had elapsed without anyone coming through the lobby. The space was cramped, and the walls seemed to close in on me. Air quality got worse. It was musty and the oxygen level seemed to dip. Within time, the room started getting warmer. I loosened my tie. It grew harder to breathe.

"Ken, are you all right?" Courtney stepped closer and looked me in the eyes.

"Just getting warm in here. That's all."

"You're claustrophobic," she said.

"A little," I reluctantly admitted.

She dropped the notepad on the floor, then gently cupped her hands around my face. "You need something to distract you," Courtney said, pulling me towards her.

Courtney kissed me. A long and passionate embrace ensued.

Wrapping my arms around her, I pulled her close and returned the favor. Her tongue darted around in my mouth. Emotions aroused, I totally forgot about the confined space.

The door clinked and started to open; we straightened up.

We stepped into the lobby area, then walked over to the locker and retrieved our belongings. A different guard manned the desk. "Hope you weren't waiting long," he said, feigning concern. "Just underwent a shift change."

"Your predecessor could have easily let us out before leaving," Courtney snapped. She wasn't going to let them off easy.

"Just a shift change hang-up," the guard said.

She wouldn't let it go. "He buzzed us into the transition room. So, he could have let us out. This is total bullshit."

To the guard's credit, he didn't try to rationalize the situation further. He just stood there looking dumbfounded and took the lashing she'd handed him.

Outside, we stepped onto the sidewalk. The temperature had dropped. Courtney called for an Uber. While perusing the street for our driver, I noticed a Chevy sedan parked at the curb across the street. A thug sat behind the wheel, watching us. They weren't even trying to hide it anymore.

"That's it," I said, crossing the street.

"Ken…" Courtney called after me, trying to dissuade me.

"Hey, you!" I accosted the man, as I neared the car.

The driver did a double take, and then he shifted into drive and hit the gas. Apparently, he sought to avoid a confrontation. He pulled away fast. They weren't ready to move on us.

FORTY-ONE

RETURNING TO THE BMC the next morning, I was anxious to learn about the prosecution's case. We really didn't have much information on either charge brought against Brad. This time we planned our arrival together, with Nate and Courtney by my side.

We encountered the same media circus and angry protestors. Shoving our way towards the door, we walked over to a security officer. We flashed our IDs and he let us pass.

I opted for the stairs, and we quickly ascended them to our floor.

A pack of people gathered outside the courtroom. We walked to the doors and a few reporters jumped in front of us. I declined to comment, then entered the battlefield.

The courtroom was crammed with spectators. All the pews were filled, and people stood crowding the lane. We had to meander through them. Pushing the gate open, I held it for Courtney and Nate to pass.

Alyson and her team were setting up at the prosecution table.

I took the first chair, closest to opposing counsel. Courtney sat beside me in the second chair, and Nate took the third. We unloaded our bags and slid them under the table. Then, I peered at the gallery, trying to identify the witnesses. I especially checked to see if the people that I'd put on standby had arrived.

The bailiff called: "All rise!"

Everyone came to attention and the room fell silent.

A door in the back of the courtroom opened, and the judge entered. Her robe flowed behind her as she took the bench.

The bailiff then opened the proceeding: "Hear ye, hear ye. The court of the Commonwealth of Massachusetts is now in session. The Honorable Judge Sanders is presiding."

Judge Camile Sanders glanced around and smiled. "You may be seated."

People in the pews sat down, while others were forced to remain standing. Others crouched, trying to use a knee to support a notepad.

"Do we have the defendant?" Judge Sanders asked the bailiff.

"He's on his way," a husky bailiff said.

A moment later, the doors to the side of the room opened. Brad stood wearing the same suit as the last appearance. It was wrinkled and his hair was unkempt. He didn't look as prim and proper as the day before.

"Let's bring him over and have him sit with counsel," the judge said.

The bailiff directed Brad to our table. Courtney grabbed another chair, and we made room for him to sit between us. He leaned toward me and whispered, "I'm nervous as hell."

I gave him a pat on the arm and smiled reassuringly.

The judge looked at Alyson. "Counselor, your first witness."

Alyson rose and called Detective Sergeant Kara Malloy. Malloy took the stand, and the judge swore her in. Malloy looked a little tired, but she appeared composed. I wondered if she had been at the scene of the Keith Evers debacle a couple nights beforehand. The fact the police had been looking into Evers made me think they might have something in their file linking him to the scene of the crime. We wouldn't get their file until after the hearing. The deck was always stacked in the prosecution's favor.

Alyson moved to a podium located between our tables, lugging a binder over. She set it down before her. They went over Malloy's education and experience, then turned to the investigation.

"How did you learn of this matter?" Alyson asked.

"I was on duty, and we got a call at 11:34 P.M."

"Who called?"

"The defendant, Bradford Wallace."

"What did he say?"

"Someone had died at his house."

"What did you do then?"

"We dispatched a unit to the house, then I went over there."

"Explain what happened upon your arrival."

"The defendant met us at the front door," Malloy said. "He walked us to the living room. His wife was seated in there."

"What did he say?"

"He told me that his aide, Audrey Martin, was on the patio. I asked him to show me where." Malloy paused; she poured a glass of water. Then, she took a sip.

The court keeps a small pitcher of water and plastic cups in a corner of the witness box. She drew this response out, almost for dramatic effect. Malloy finally looked up.

"What happened from there?" Alyson asked, poised.

"The defendant led me through the house into the kitchen. Then, he flipped on an outside light and pointed at the body on the patio."

"What happened from there?"

"Stepping outside, I examined the body. Ms. Martin had clearly suffered a blunt force trauma to the head, typically associated with a fall from a high place. I examined the area and concluded she had fallen from the balcony above. The spot where she landed wasn't a straight drop from the balcony, so I determined that she was likely pushed."

"Tell us what you did from there?"

"At that point, I took the defendant back to the living room. I asked him what she was doing there. He explained that his aides utilized the study on the second floor. I asked him to show us around. He showed us the study and we noted the computer. I asked him to show us the balcony. He took us to the master bedroom on the third floor. A set of French doors led out to the balcony."

"Did you notice anything?"

"I noticed the balcony had snow along the edges. There were small footprints near the railing. Later, I noticed the bed seemed disturbed, like someone had used it and tucked it in quickly."

This testimony was well rehearsed. Malloy used the term defendant repeatedly to cement a connotation of Brad's guilt.

This also helped dehumanize him by not referring to his name. They were careful to call Audrey Martin by name to humanize her. I expected they'd shift to calling her the victim to garner sympathy. A skilled examination, the lawyer does all the work on the front end and practices the examination with the witness. So, when the live testimony occurs in court, it appears natural and unrehearsed. You also cannot lead a witness on a direct examination. Thus far, they were doing a spectacular job.

They had also revealed a few points that weren't known to me. Brad had failed to inform me of everything he told the police that night.

Alyson continued. "What happened next?"

"My partner, Detective Chandler arranged for a search warrant, while I called the crime scene investigators. Then, we went through the three primary areas of inquiry: the patio, balcony, and study. We took photographs of each location to document the crime scene prior to the search. Then, we underwent the search, bagging all items that could be evidence in the case."

"Did you question the defendant further?"

"No. I'm afraid he called his lawyer and refused to give further comment."

"Did you speak with the defendant's lawyer?"

Malloy nodded. "He arrived at the crime scene and refused to let—"

"Objection!" I bellowed.

"Sustained." The judge shook her head. "Counsel, please keep this to the salient facts."

"My apologies, Your Honor," Alyson said.

"Did you investigate further?"

"Yes. I met with the Medical Examiner and observed Ms. Martin's body."

"What did you find?"

"There were bruises on the front of her thighs, scrapes on her shins, and scratches along the side of her left leg." Malloy adjusted in her seat. "This is evidence that someone had pushed her off the balcony. Examination of the skull fracture confirmed a fall from a high place."

Alyson raised a stack of photographs. "May I approach the witness, Your Honor?"

Judge Sanders nodded. "Yes."

Stepping to the witness, Alyson dropped copies of the photographs on our table. I grabbed them and sifted through the photographs. They depicted a horrible death of a once vibrant young woman.

After handing the original photographs to Malloy, Alyson returned to the podium. "Please look though them carefully."

Malloy perused the pictures like I had done. "Okay, I'm ready."

"Are those fair and accurate photographs of the victim's body taken at the scene of the crime?" asked Alyson.

"Yes, they are."

"Your Honor, we request these photographs be marked as exhibits," Alyson said.

The judge looked at me. "Any objections?"

I shook my head. "None."

"Okay," the judge said to the clerk. "Let's get these marked."

The clerk rose from her table next to the judge's bench. Malloy handed over the photographs. Then, the clerk placed exhibit stickers on each one and marked them with a pen. "These are the Commonwealth's exhibits 1 through 9," she said.

"Thank you," Alyson said to the clerk. "Now, Detective Sergeant Malloy, please tell us whether you undertook any further investigation."

"Yes, we did."

"What did you do?"

"We examined the security system at the defendant's home. And we were able to determine that the victim entered at 10:00 P.M."

"Anything else?"

"We undertook forensics on her computer and cellphone, which revealed she stopped using them around 10:30 P.M."

"Anything else?"

"I met with the Medical Examiner, and I reviewed her final report prior to the arrest."

They went over physical evidence found on the body and covered a few other aspects of the investigation in detail. None of this examination included ruling out other suspects. It's like they focused on Brad from the beginning with blinders on and didn't consider anyone else. Police often do this. The approach got me thinking Brad just might be innocent. Yet, there I was sitting beside him at counsel table while the Commonwealth sought to take away his liberty.

"Did you conclude anything from all of this?" Alyson said.

"Yes. We determined that the victim died between 10:30 and 11:30 P.M."

"Did you find anything to link the defendant to the crime?"

"We found an inordinate number of phone calls and text messages sent between the defendant and the victim. This was a vastly higher amount of communication than the defendant had with his other aide, who was far more experienced than the victim. Some text messages reflected digital usage associated with pictures being sent. From my experience—"

"Objection." I said, rising from my chair. "Calls for speculation."

"Sustained."

Alyson inhaled, frustrated. "Did you conclude anything from this for your investigation?"

"Objection. Same grounds."

"Now, let's hold on counselor," the judge said to me, raising a hand. "This is a slightly different inquiry. It deals with the officer's mental impressions, rather than those of another."

"But it deals with conjecture and not something based on direct evidence."

"Understood. But I think they are entitled to go there." The judge turned to Alyson. "You may proceed, but I plan to keep you on a tight leash."

Alyson smiled. "Thank you, Your Honor."

"We determined the defendant had a personal relationship with the victim that exceeded their employer and employee arrangement."

"Did you find anything else?"

"We found certain campaign information on the victim's computer, which reflects some potential impropriety."

"Anything else from your investigation?"

"We interviewed Phillip Danforth."

"Objection. Hearsay."

Judge Sanders looked at Alyson. "Will he be here to testify?"

Alyson shook her head. "Afraid not. He's the other victim."

"I see." The judge looked at Malloy. "You cannot repeat what he said. Counsel is correct. That would be hearsay."

Alyson breathed deeply. Stymied again. "Did you conclude anything from your interview with Mr. Danforth for your investigation?"

"Objection!" I stood. "This is just an end run around the hearsay ruling."

"I tend to agree," Judge Sanders said. "Sustained."

"Did your interview with Danforth cause you to take any further steps?"

"Yes. We sought evidence to show the defendant was in the vicinity of the crime and unaccounted for at the time of the victim's death."

"Did you find such evidence?"

"We most certainly did."

The comment hit me like being hit by a dump truck.

"What did you find?"

"We found CCTV footage of the defendant not far from his home at 10:50 P.M."

The statement came as a complete surprise. All the air went out of the room. Brad grabbed my hand, panicked. "What do they have?" he asked.

"Just stay calm and hold the line," I said. "We don't know yet."

Alyson walked over to a flatscreen television, which was set up on a stand with wheels. She slid a CD into a disc player and picked up the remote. "May I present this, Your Honor?"

"You need to authenticate it further," Judge Sanders replied.

Alyson went through the formalities with Malloy, showing the chain of custody.

Then, the judge allowed her to show the video. It contained clear footage of Brad walking up to an ATM machine, which was lodged into the side of the building diagonal to the State House. The location was also across the street from Scollay Square, which was the restaurant Brad had visited on the night of Audrey Martin's death. This wasn't far from Brad's house.

There was a timestamp of 10:50 P.M., just as Malloy had testified. It demonstrated that Brad had access to the scene of the crime around the time the murder had occurred.

It was damning evidence. And we'd been totally blindsided.

FORTY-TWO

I WATCHED AS KARA MALLOY remained collected in the witness box. She carefully walked everyone through the video sequence. Then, Alyson hit the stop button and turned off the video.

Alyson faced the court with a satisfied grin.

The gallery was silent, as people absorbed the monumental development. News stories would break about Brad having committed a heinous crime. Legal analysts would have a field day explaining the implications of the video.

"Do you have anything else?" the judge finally asked.

"A few more questions."

The judge nodded. "You may proceed."

Alyson walked Malloy through a few other aspects of the investigation. They quickly covered procedures and investigation techniques.

"Were there any other events that impacted your investigation?" Alyson asked.

"Shortly after Audrey Martin was killed, the other aide, Phillip Danforth was run down by a van." Malloy blurted the answer so it came out before I could object.

"Did you find any corroborating evidence to link the two deaths?" Alyson asked.

"Objection!" I thundered, rising from my chair.

Judge Sanders calmly looked my way. "Basis?"

"This is entirely speculation."

The judge nodded. "You may be right. But I haven't heard enough to know for certain. The witness can answer."

I sat down, ready for another bomb to drop.

Malloy took a sip of water. "The van used to kill Mr. Danforth was tied to the defendant, Bradford Wallace's campaign."

The courtroom erupted with murmurings. People were shocked.

"Objection!" I stood. "Foundation. Move to strike."

"Sustained." Judge Sanders perused the gallery, providing them a cue to settle down.

"Very well," Alyson muttered. "What evidence did you find relative to the Danforth murder?"

Malloy nodded. "The van that ran Phillip Danforth over was owned by the defendant's political campaign. He or someone working for him would have had access to the van."

Another volley of gasps erupted from behind me.

Fortunately, this testimony didn't come as a surprise. I didn't care for the reaction from the bystanders, however. Courtney glanced over at me. She looked downtrodden. Her face said it all. This wasn't going well for us. I suspected the judge had bought into the theory of a double murder hook, line, and sinker.

When the ruckus continued, the judge banged her gavel. "Quiet!"

The courtroom fell into a buzz, then people stopped talking altogether.

Alyson let the gallery simmer down for a moment before continuing. "Did you reach any conclusions in your investigation?"

"We determined the defendant had the motive and opportunity to kill the victim. And he did in fact kill Audrey Martin. We also determined that the defendant had motive to kill Phillip Danforth to conceal his relationship with Audrey Martin."

"Did you have any other evidence to support your decision to arrest the defendant for Audrey Martin's murder?"

Malloy smiled. "Yes. We had the defendant's confession."

"Objection," I yelled, jumping from my chair.

The judge looked over at me. "Basis?"

"He never gave a confession." I pointed at Brad.

The judge looked at Alyson. "Is this true?"

"He confessed to an inmate while being held at Nashua Street," Alyson said, stepping over to her counsel table to fetch a document.

A jailhouse snitch, I concluded.

The judge frowned.

Alyson seemed to relish this development, but Malloy now looked like a deer in headlights. I suspected that she didn't trust the jailhouse snitch. This was something Alyson had set up to bring in a ringer to ensure the case went to trial.

"Move to strike," I said. "That's hearsay."

"Sustained."

"This is just a dirty trick—" I griped.

The judge smiled. "And I'm sure you'll attack his credibility at trial."

"*Trial?*" I stammered. We haven't even presented yet, and she was shutting us down.

"Well, counselor… you are entitled to present evidence." Judge Sanders stared at me in earnest. "It's your call."

Alyson cleared her throat. "The Commonwealth rests."

She hadn't even offered an argument summarizing her position. Relying on a dirty trick, slipping hearsay into the equation, she hadn't offered the snitch as a witness. Alyson had read the judge as leaning her way. She sought to wrap up quickly, while momentum was on her side.

I shrugged. "Your Honor…"

Judge Sanders held up a hand and looked my way. "Counselor, I am prepared to make a preliminary ruling. You can then decide whether you wish to proceed or not."

I didn't like this one bit. But my experience told me the judge was trying to do us a favor. She was flagging which way she would rule, so we could move on from this hearing without divulging our defense. Avoiding a cross-examination at a preliminary hearing makes the other side less prepared at trial. Now, I was forced to make a key decision on the fly.

"Okay," I said, nodding with deference. "The defense rests, Your Honor."

Judge Sanders straightened up and turned to face everyone. "My preliminary finding is that the Commonwealth has probable cause to bind the defendant over for trial in the Audrey Martin matter. I find the Commonwealth has not met its burden in the Phillip Danforth matter, relative to a conspiracy to commit murder charge."

The gallery burst into a flutter of activity. Several reporters bolted to get a jump on the big scoop. Judge Sanders waited a moment and things settled down.

"Very well," Judge Sanders continued. "The defendant is bound over for trial in Superior Court on the count of First-degree murder in relation to Audrey Martin's death. The charge of conspiracy to commit murder in connection to Phillip Danforth is hereby dismissed without prejudice. The Commonwealth can refile if it obtains further evidence to support the charge."

A flutter of activity erupted in the gallery as reporters jotted down the result.

The judge looked from counsel table to counsel table and smiled. "The bail order will remain in place. You can revisit it with the trial judge."

"But—" I pled.

"That will be all." She smacked her gavel. "This court is now in recess."

The bailiff called: "All rise!"

Judge Sanders stepped off the bench and headed through the rear door of the courtroom before most people could even get to their feet. She was likely happy to put this behind her, and I couldn't blame her.

Brad looked at me. He appeared dazed and chagrinned. "So, that's it?"

"Afraid so."

Then, he shook his head. "Sorry."

He was apologizing to me for not having prepared us. He'd tried to keep his activities quiet, likely to protect his political career. Now, that career was in the gutter, and he was facing a murder trial with compelling evidence against him.

FORTY-THREE

FOLLOWING the probable cause hearing, I needed to gather my thoughts and consider next steps. We grabbed an Uber and headed back over towards the office.

When the driver stopped at the corner of Broad and State Street, I handed my briefcase to Courtney. "Can you take this upstairs?" I asked.

"Sure." Courtney canted her head. "Where are you going?"

"Got up early. It's about lunchtime, so I plan to grab a bite."

"You don't want any company?" she asked.

"No," I said, shaking my head. And I didn't. I just wanted to be alone.

She looked me over, as if reading my emotions. "Ken, you handled that as well as possible. We were all surprised…"

"That's the problem. I shouldn't have been surprised."

She hiked her shoulders, conceding to the point. "Okay. See you when you get back."

I nodded to her and Nate, then I climbed from the car and walked through the breezy city streets towards Joshua's Deli, located on Batterymarch Street.

Stepping under a crimson awning with the words Breakfast & Lunch embroidered on the front, I walked inside and approached the counter. An aroma of fresh brewed coffee and fried eggs hung in the air. Joshua's was the perfect place for an attorney working downtown. You often run off to court in the morning with nothing more than a cup of coffee in your belly. Sometimes you don't have time to eat, and often you simply can't eat due to nerves. When you finally get out of court in the late morning, you need a place that can handle both meals, depending upon how you're feeling.

I ordered a pastrami sandwich and a large coffee. Then, I paid at the cash register, took the slip and my beverage and grabbed a table by the window. I slid out of my overcoat.

Waiting for my order, I considered the brief discussion with Courtney. Brad should have clued us in on his whereabouts when we had interviewed him at Jack's office prior to his arrest. But eventually, Jack had come clean about Brad's gap in time. I should have probed the client for more details. Sometimes you put a client through a thorough examination to ferret out all the facts to avoid surprises. You'd be amazed what a client will forget to tell a lawyer.

I'd let down my guard because Brad was an attorney and we had been assisted by Jack. Relying on them to provide me with all the facts was a huge mistake.

My number was called, and I fetched the sandwich. Steam rose from the meat and cheese. I treaded across the worn tile floor and sat down. I took a few bites, then washed it down with coffee. The sandwich hit the spot. I sipped more coffee, trying to relax.

Then, I reached for my cellphone and called Beckerman. He didn't have any news on the Keith Evers development. I wondered if he would ever learn anything more about our case from his contacts at the police station. Everyone was keeping a tight lid on the matter. Beckerman didn't have any new information whatsoever. It looked as though I'd remain in the dark about the police investigation until we got the prosecution's case files.

We needed to flesh out more details about Brad's whereabouts on the night of Audrey Martin's murder. I scheduled a meeting with Jack and Harper. They were available. This time, I decided to meet with them by myself.

I finished my brunch and walked back to the office and grabbed the file. Shoving it into my briefcase, I updated Courtney on my plans. Then, I took an Uber over to the Seaport District.

Stepping into reception at Jack's fancy office, I noticed them sitting in the large boardroom. It seemed odd that Jack hadn't opted for the more private conference room we'd used previously. Then, I figured maybe a senior partner had grabbed it. But my hackles were up.

Jack strode out to greet me. We shook hands. "This way," he said, pointing to the big conference room.

I walked in and took a seat across from Harper.

She smiled and said, "Hello." It was a rather perfunctory salutation.

Jack sat down at the head of the table. Neither of them had notepads and their general demeanor was cool. I set my briefcase down and slid out of my overcoat. Then, I grabbed a notepad and pen, expecting another shoe to drop.

"Glad you decided to come by," Jack said, leaning back in his chair.

"I know this is difficult," I said to Harper, indicating we needed to cover some ground. "When I met with Jack previously, he'd mentioned Brad had a little problem. That problem might turn out to be his alibi. He had sought to keep it quiet, hoping this would go away without the issue coming out. I'm sure you've heard about the developments in court today…"

"That's actually what we wanted to discuss," Jack cut in.

"Well, if the two of you had been in court this morning," I chided them. "You would already know how it went down. A wife needs to stand behind her husband in times like these. Even if you are upset with him, the public and the prospective jury need to see Harper seated in the gallery."

Jack waved a hand, trying to shut me down.

"What?" I was confused.

"Afraid we can't get into this right now."

Glancing them over one at a time, they appeared stone-faced; bureaucratic. "What's going on here?"

"Kenny," Harper said.

Jack leaned towards her. "Let me explain."

She nodded. "Okay."

"I'm listening," I said.

"There's no real good place to begin."

"You need to start somewhere."

"Probably makes sense to address the pressing legal issue," Jack said, gesticulating. "Brad and Harper signed a joint defense agreement at the start of this."

"I remember."

"The agreement called for joint representation by my firm. And it had the standard waiver of any conflicts. It also stated that in the event the agreement was terminated, one party could go forward with our firm's services."

"You're going to end the joint defense agreement," I snapped.

"Look, it's not personal."

"The hell it's not!"

Jack glanced through the glass walls of the conference room to make sure nobody passing by had seen my outburst. He was all image.

Harper tried to placate me. "Kenny, this has been coming for quite some time."

"What?" I sat back, perplexed. *She's filing for divorce*, I realized.

"First, so we are perfectly clear," Jack said. "Harper is terminating the joint defense agreement. She is going forward with our services. We are terminating Brad as a client, effective immediately."

"You're going to let Brad hang in the wind?" I was exasperated.

"Brad has been unfaithful the entire marriage," Harper said.

"Why not file for divorce sooner? Why now? Why not after trial?"

"Those are perfectly good questions," Jack said. "But we're not at liberty to say."

"Why not?"

"You represent Brad," said Jack.

"There's a prenup?" I questioned.

Harper nodded.

"With a morality clause?"

She nodded again.

This revealed a lot. Being young when they got married, the prenuptial agreement probably didn't have a provision for infidelity. Young people are either naïve and don't think they'll need it, or they both worry that it could impact them and don't want it. I suspected the prenup included a provision with penalties for committing a serious crime. An indictment could trigger it. The probable cause hearing had set this in motion. It explained why the two of them hadn't been in court for the arraignment or the probable cause hearing. The cat was out of the bag.

Jack had been balancing on a fence. His major client was likely headed downhill, so he waited to see how it would unfold. Then, he decided to cut bait when things looked bad. Brad was a sinking ship, so Jack jumped aboard Harper's vessel to salvage what he could.

"You must understand," Harper said. "At our level…"

And there it was. *At our level*, I thought.

She must have caught the disappointment in my eyes. Harper stopped talking and turned away. I really couldn't fathom how they operated, or how they lived with themselves.

I had a case to prepare, and I wasn't going to get anything productive from them.

"We've sent the termination letter to the jailhouse," Jack said. "The divorce papers will be served there as well."

"Then, I guess we're through." I stood up and shoved the notepad into my briefcase.

"Kenny…" Harper cried.

"This isn't how decent people act," I said, grabbing my coat.

I headed for the door and didn't look back. Another major blow to my case and the prosecution hadn't even gotten started.

FORTY-FOUR

ON THE WAY to the jailhouse, I called Courtney and asked her to meet me there. I planned to go straight over in hope of updating Brad before he got served with the divorce.

Riding in an Uber through the Seaport District, I couldn't wait to get back into the older part of town. The glitzy high-rises, covered in glass facades, wore on you after a while. I preferred the older limestone buildings downtown. Smeared in decades of grime, the buildings resonated history and the bustle of city life as it's meant to be. The streets in the Financial District were narrow and took sharp turns, occasionally bending up a hill. The Seaport District was relatively flat and laid out on a grid. Once you got past the harbor views, it felt like being in a younger city.

We crossed Atlantic Avenue and fell under the shadows of the buildings downtown. Meandering through the city, we drove along Congress Street, then we popped over to Merrimack Street and cut around North Station. A train station that serviced points north of the city, North Station also housed the TD Garden where the Celtics and Bruins play home games. A bronze statue of Bobby Orr stands in front of the entrance. It depicts him jumping through the air after scoring a historic Stanley Cup goal.

The driver pulled up to the jailhouse and parked at the curb. Courtney stood near the entrance; she had gotten there first. The jail was much closer to our office.

She waited impatiently, tapping a foot on the walkway. I'd updated her during a call on the way over. Her reaction to the news was harsh. I'd heard an earful during the call and expected to get more of the same through trial.

"These people are cheeky," she said, as we approached the building.

I shrugged. "Sometimes managing client issues is more work than tackling the case itself."

"That doesn't make it any less disturbing," she replied.

"Sure. But it comes with the territory. That's all I'm saying."

Courtney frowned as we stepped inside.

We walked to the front desk and met with the same guard as last time. He tried to avoid eye contact and perfunctorily went through the motions. Once we were settled, he pointed to the door leading to the sally port. "You know the routine," he said.

"Don't get any ideas of locking us in there," Courtney said. "If you do, I'll press a criminal charge for false imprisonment and sue you civilly. You got that?"

"Yes, ma'am." He drooped his head and perused some paperwork.

Walking across the lobby, the door rattled open. We stepped inside. It smelled musty. The door closed, then the one to the hallway opened. A guard ambled down the corridor. Brad trundled behind him wearing chains.

"Is that necessary?" I said, pointing at the shackles.

"Afraid so. He's been indicted for murder."

We went into the meeting room. Brad sat down on a metal stool. His chains gently rattled as he adjusted himself. I took a seat across from him. He appeared dejected. I'd never seen him resonate such lack of confidence.

"You got the news?" he asked. Brad evidently had been served.

I nodded. "Yup," I said, explaining the situation.

"Harper's leaving me. After all these years."

Courtney stood leaning against a wall with her arms crossed. She didn't care for the power play Harper and Jack had put into motion. But she also detested Brad's proclivities.

I leaned forward to comfort him. "Hang in there."

"My life's falling apart."

"The case is circumstantial. You have to remember that."

"What's the use?" He shook his head, full of emotion. He seemed ready to cry. "Everything that I've worked for is gone in the blink of an eye."

"So, what are you going to do?" I snapped. "Give up?"

He considered me for a moment. "I don't deserve a friend like you."

"You keep talking like that and you'll start believing it."

Brad cracked a smile. "You're a fighter, Ken."

"That's right. And we need to get down to business."

Courtney took notes, while I grilled Brad about his activities on the night of Audrey Martin's murder. We learned he'd been using an escort service. He'd met a girl named Vanesa through the service, and he occasionally saw her on an independent basis. There were others, but he claims to have been with Vanesa at the approximate time of Audrey Martin's death. He hadn't wanted to disclose any of this, unless it was necessary. Now, it absolutely had to be done.

The use of an escort as an alibi had its downside, regardless of the political fallout. A call girl wasn't a highly credible witness. People sitting on a jury figure a prostitute's testimony can be bought. Further, escort agencies weren't inclined to cooperate. They kept things extremely confidential. And this circumstance was even worse, because he'd met Vanesa that night without going through the agency. Heck, even I had my doubts about his alibi.

Wanting to probe into as many details as possible, I asked Brad whether he really believed Danforth and Martin were dating. He confessed that he knew Danforth was gay when he hired him. After some cajoling, Brad admitted he'd been hitting on Audrey Martin. This explained the high level of communications between them. Brad swore she never reciprocated his advances. They'd never had an affair.

I then sought to ascertain more details on his whereabouts at the time of Phillip Danforth's death. Leaving any stones unturned just wasn't going to happen again.

"What does any of that even matter?" he asked. "I'm not being charged with it anymore."

"I think it can help if we show you weren't involved. So, where were you precisely?"

"I've told you that I was on my way to meet with you. I haven't got an alibi."

"Just think about it further."

Brad asked me the exact time of the hit and run, then he ran it through his mind. "I was planning to meet you about that time. I had worked in the dining room at my brownstone. Ran a few minutes late. When I was preparing to leave, you called with the news." He grimaced. "Someone likely tried to catch me without an alibi. They had to have known about Phillip heading that way in order to run him down, so they probably knew I'd be en route to meet with you at that time. Except, I was running late as usual."

His comments left me with concerns. It seemed like someone had inside information on his whereabouts. They likely knew Danforth's activities as well. Harper came to mind.

Given the driver of the van hadn't been identified, the police and prosecution might claim Brad was driving the van. Failure to establish him in the van didn't preclude the possibility they might come back with a renewed charge for conspiracy to commit murder. However, they needed something else to tie him to Danforth's death before they could reinstate the charge.

"Guess we'll have to see how the Danforth angle plays out," I finally said.

"Why is Harper doing this now?" Brad muttered, as if talking to himself.

The question hung in the room like an ominous cloud. We all pondered her motives.

Most high-profile couples stick together during an event like this. After the dust settles, they quietly get divorced. "Maybe she can't stomach coming to court," I offered. "The media hype."

Brad shook his head. "She could bow out and file later. There's an ulterior motive to this."

I tended to agree. And I wondered just what her game plan was and how it would impact the case.

***

LEAVING THE OFFICE for the evening, I ran into Courtney on the way to the elevators. We stood for a moment waiting for the lift. Neither of us had spoken about the kiss from when we were stranded in the sally port at the jailhouse.

"Long day," she said, as the elevator doors jounced open.

"Yeah," I replied, letting her step in first. I moved in beside her.

"Are you headed home?" she asked coyly.

I got the feeling she wanted to grab a drink, maybe notch up the relationship to something a little more serious. The thought had crossed my mind as well, but I worried where things would lead after a few cocktails. Large cases like this are all-consuming, and you can't afford to get distracted. Everything gets pushed off, including obligations you have around the office. Attorneys have to fend for themselves without my supervision, and bills pile up. Relationships suffer. The only thing you do is work the case and make payroll.

"Just planning to go home," I finally said. The lift jounced as it descended.

"Sure you don't want to grab a drink?" Courtney edged closer, trying to appear hopeful so I wouldn't disappoint her.

"Not tonight. Sorry."

Courtney looked discouraged.

The doors shook open, and we stepped into the lobby.

Starting for the door, I stopped. I wanted to explain. She kept walking away. Her heels smacked the tiles and resounded her displeasure with me.

"Courtney!" I called, almost pleading for her to stop and listen.

She halted at the door, then turned to face me. I stared at her.

"What?" Her eyes revealed sadness.

"This isn't what you think."

"And what do I think?" Her tone turned sharp.

"I'm not brushing you off."

Placing a hand on her hip, she smirked. "You most certainly are."

"Maybe," I said, stepping towards her.

"And…"

"It's just this case."

Just as I reached her, she shook her head, flabbergasted. Then, she turned and pushed through the door. She stepped outside into the cold night.

I stepped after her, hoping to clear things up.

She marched up the sidewalk, spreading the distance between us. I wanted to call out and say that I was sorry. Every fiber in my being ached for the same thing she sought. My pulse raced with passion. Yet, I stood there and watched her race away from me.

Emotions bottled up inside me, I couldn't bring myself to declare my affection.

Paralysis muzzled my voice. I stood mute, watching her leave. I hoped there would be another day to sort things out. Yet, I anticipated she didn't plan to let that happen.

FORTY-FIVE

BACK IN COURT counsel sat at their respective tables, while the trial judge sifted through the file. The gallery held various members of the press, but it wasn't packed like before.

We were in the upper level of Suffolk Superior Court. It was an older courthouse with three-story ceilings and a worn oak judge's bench. The pews were solid hardwood. Oak railings separated the gallery and jury box from the well of the courtroom. A musty smell hung in the air, possibly from an aging air-conditioning system.

Judge Cornelius Mathers sat perched at the bench, rooting through the file. He was an old-school judge, who had been on the bench for decades. He'd been a prosecutor before becoming a judge. But he did everything by the book. His balding pate had a few gray hairs, combed over, and held in place with some old-fashioned barbershop gel. He wore glasses with black, acetate frames and thick lenses.

Alyson and I stood at our tables, ready to address the court. Courtney sat beside me, and a slick young prosecutor accompanied Alyson. I wondered when he'd gotten involved in the case. Probably much sooner than when he had filed an appearance. They seemed loaded for bear.

When the judge finally got through perusing the court file, he looked up at us. "You're here for a status conference and a bail hearing, right?"

We answered in unison. "Yes, Your Honor."

Judge Mathers turned toward Alyson. "Are you still opposing bail?"

"We are, Your Honor. I believe—"

The judge shook his head. "You're a chatty Cathy. We'll have none of that here. We have a busy schedule to keep.

You've got a rather thin case. Bail is set at $250,000 cash." He looked at me. "Your client will be required to wear an ankle bracelet monitor."

"Sure," I said, surprised he hadn't let the prosecution present argument.

"Your Honor," Alyson interjected. "We'd ask the defendant be restricted to his home."

"No." He frowned. "Your case is quite thin. He doesn't pose a flight risk."

"How can you say that?" Alyson quipped.

"I'm sure he just wants to get this over with." The judge waved his hands at her.

I suspected the judge had followed the media enough to determine there wasn't any direct evidence pointing to Brad. If there had been a witness or strong piece of physical evidence, they would have mentioned it in the newspapers. The press had just focused on the sensational aspects of the matter. His demeanor reflected a possible belief the case was merely a political stunt.

"The Commonwealth requests to be heard." Alyson kept at him.

"Denied."

She glanced over at me for support.

I hiked my shoulders.

This wasn't going as she'd expected. Alyson had come into the courtroom planning to put on a dog and pony show for the press. Now, the headlines could swing the other way. Most of the papers had printed scathing articles about Brad's involvement with the deaths of two aides. They had taken the sensational route. I imaged a few outlets might go against the grain and offer stories about his possible innocence. Certain newspapers sometimes ran a contrarian story to stand out from the others.

"Let's turn to scheduling," the judge said. "Shall we?"

"Yes, Your Honor," we replied.

Alyson flipped open a day planner. I grabbed my phone and clicked on an app that connected with the software my office used for calendaring, document retention, and billing. We both looked up.

"Ready?" asked Judge Mathers.

"Yes, Your Honor." We both stood poised.

"Good. We're setting this for trial in two weeks." He glanced over at the clerk. "Is that right?"

She nodded, "Yes, sir."

"Okay then." He pointed at Alyson. "You get your file to him," Judge Mathers said, pointing at me. "I'll give you one week to do so."

"But… Your Honor," Alyson quibbled.

The judge looked at me. "Does that work for you?"

"It does, Your Honor."

"Good."

"But—" Alyson couldn't let it go.

"You listen, here. Ms. Cathy," the judge said, pointing a finger at her. "We've got a schedule to keep. The pre-trial order is in. Good-bye."

She stood there dumbfounded.

Courtney and I began packing our bags.

The judge and Alyson stared at each other for a moment. She seemed like she was going to speak again. He shook his head; the judge made a shooing gesture with both hands. "Go," he said to her. Then, he set the file aside and started reviewing another one.

Leaving the courtroom, we ran into Alyson. "Can you believe him?" she said.

"He's an old-school judge," I replied. "The last of a breed."

"Well, I don't particularly care for it."

"You're just lucky he had a busy schedule. Else, you might have gotten the 'when I was a prosecutor speech.'"

Alyson chuckled. Her eyes sparkled. It was the first time I had seen her happy since this case began. This caused me to relax.

Listen," I said. "You're not planning to go through with that jailhouse snitch testimony?"

"What's the matter, Kenny?" She smirked. "Afraid you won't eviscerate this one."

"You know damn well Brad never confessed to anyone," I snapped. "You have an obligation as an officer of the court to only put on credible evidence."

"Don't lecture me on the law." Her eyes turned to daggers.

"Somebody obviously has to remind you." I shook my head in dismay.

Alyson scowled, then turned and marched off.

Their intent to use a jailhouse snitch to support a confession had me concerned. Some jurors are naïve and would never expect the prosecution to put on false testimony. Our plan was to rely upon the Commonwealth's failure to show guilt beyond a reasonable doubt.

Now, I had grave concerns as to whether that would be enough.

FORTY-SIX

KARA WALKED into the war room and took a seat near the lieutenant. Everyone on the team was there except Alyson Sheehan. Detectives Davis and Nguyen sat on one side of the table, and Chandler was next to Kara, while Lieutenant Johnson commanded the meeting from the head of the table.

"Care to get started," Lieutenant Johnson said to her.

"Are we still waiting on anyone?" Kara looked to the empty chair where Alyson usual sat, wondering if the prosecutor was running late. Something told her that wasn't the case, though.

"We're all here," the lieutenant said.

Kara looked at her perplexed. "Doesn't it make sense to include her?"

Lieutenant Johnson shook her head. "This is a police force only meeting. It was ordered by the deputy chief."

"Okay," Kara said, sheepishly.

She stood and walked over to the white board and cork boards. A photograph of Keith Evers taken in the coroner's office was added to a board.

The room smelled of coffee and doughnuts. She wished she'd grabbed a cup before entering the room. This case was beginning to wear her down. Lack of sleep was catching up to her.

"As some of you may know, we sought a statement from Keith Evers." Kara pointed at a mugshot of Evers. "He has a history of violent crimes. Nothing too serious, but the kid has a temper and issues with substance abuse. His fingerprint was found on the Wallace's front door. No telling when it was put there. No trace of him in the house."

"So, can't we rule him out?" This from Nguyen.

"We wanted to get a statement from him to show we had investigated him as a suspect and properly ruled him out. We found him dead. A gun was fired right before we found him."

"Cause of death?" asked Johnson.

"There wasn't a bullet wound. He died from an overdose of heroin."

"Any signs of foul play?" Davis asked in a gravelly voice.

"We secured the scene. The M.E. has ruled out murder." Kara pointed to the death pic. "There's no way to connect this to murder. No signs of struggle or impacts to his body. Evers either shot himself up, or else he let someone do it for him."

"How do we know someone didn't O.D. him on purpose?" Davis said. "Keep him quiet. We've got one murdered witness already. Why not two?"

Kara nodded, acceding to the point. "We thought the same. But it turns out the heroin he'd injected was cut with a dangerous level of fentanyl. There were two other deaths in the vicinity with similar findings. We think a bad mix had gotten out on the street."

Davis shook his head. "What about the gun shot?"

"Maybe we startled someone. The fact is… we'll never know for certain."

Johnson appeared to have heard enough. "Okay. What else?"

"We compared the DNA under Audrey Martin's fingernail and compared it to Keith Evers." Kara glanced around the room, and everyone seemed interested.

"Match?" asked Johnson.

Kara shook her head. "Nope."

"What about Wallace?"

"We ran tests against his DNA obtained after his arrest—"

"Wait. Don't tell me," Davis interrupted. "No match."

"Bingo."

Davis shook his head and his jowls swayed back and forth. He looked at Lieutenant Johnson. "This is why *she* isn't here," he said, pointing to the empty chair.

"You said it, not me." Johnson hiked one shoulder.

"We do have the final Medical Examiner report on Martin," Kara offered.

"Continue," Johnson said.

"It concludes that Martin died as a result of the fall from the balcony. The M.E. determined the death was likely a murder. This is based on a few physical findings. One is the distance from the balcony to the location of the body on the patio, which demonstrates Martin was pitched over the railing, rather than a fall."

"That's not entirely scientific," Johnson said, taking a sip of water from her Hydro Flask.

"The M.E. also found bruises on the front of the victim's thighs, scrapes along the shins, and scratches along the side of one thigh, which support the theory of Martin being hurled over the railing."

People around the room were inattentive, glancing at phones and the screens to their laptops. Nobody seemed interested in hearing her rehash old findings.

"Anything new?" Johnson didn't seem impressed.

Kara nodded.

"What?"

"She'd had sex before she was killed."

The room fell silent. Everyone looked up at her.

They finally had proof of an affair.

FORTY-SEVEN

THE DAYS FOLLOWING the probable cause hearing blew by rather quickly without many developments.

We reached out to Joey's cousin without any success. Checking in with Beckerman didn't fare much better. Officers at the precinct were tight-lipped about the case, even the ones that occasionally talked out of school.

Every few days I put my feelers out, hoping for a glimpse into the prosecution's case.

Sitting at my desk discussing an appellate brief with Joey in another matter, my cellphone buzzed. It was Beckerman reaching out to me.

"Ken Dwyer," I said, leaning back in my chair.

"Hey, it's Paul Beckerman here."

"What have you got?"

"You get right to business. I like that."

"Anything good?"

"Yes. But it's not solid."

"Okay, shoot."

"There's talk around the station that the prosecution might have a weak case." He paused to let the comment simmer. "They're saying you might be able to pull this one off."

"Did you get any details?" He had my interest piqued.

"Afraid not. Nobody's talking."

This information was interesting, but I couldn't trust it. Coming from the police, it could be officers talking about a juicy case. There could also be a play at hand. Alyson might have intentionally leaked this in order to make me overconfident going into trial. A lawyer thinking a case is a slam dunk can let his or her guard down, causing mistakes. You could even walk into a slaughter.

"Has anyone said something to the contrary?" I finally asked.

"Funny that you ask. There are some bets going down at the precinct. They've got a pool. Officers are betting on you and the odds are in your favor. But one guy has bet against you, and he's put a great deal of money into it. Thing is… he should know best."

"Chandler!" I snapped.

Joey sat up in his chair, alarmed.

"That's it," Beckerman said.

"What's his story?" I asked.

"A couple divorces cleaned him out. Gets into trouble on the force from time to time. People say he's a decent cop, though."

"What else?"

"He told a friend they have a surprise to knock you off your feet at trial."

FORTY-EIGHT

LATER THAT EVENING, I cut around the reception desk after grabbing a file Anne had left for me. Barbara and Courtney stood by the elevators. They were chatting quietly.

"What's happening?" I said, greeting them.

"Hello," Barbara said, with a polite nod.

Courtney forced a smile. "Ken."

"Hi," I replied, meekly.

Then, I walked down to my office and started gathering materials to bring home for the evening.

Courtney had been standoffish since the night she stormed away from me. My expectation was she'd cool off over time, but I began to wonder if a reconciliation might not happen. She was a valuable member of the firm, and I worried she might leave due to the friction. Smaller firms have a lot of turnover. Attorneys get experience and go to larger firms; they go in-house; they get government jobs with pensions; and, sometimes they leave to open their own firms.

All this ran through my mind as I packed up to leave the office.

Stepping into the elevator, I knew things that had gone wrong in my relationships were mostly my fault. I had issues from my childhood, which caused me to be reserved. This prevented me from communicating effectively. At times, my reticence has been mistaken for aloofness. People think I don't care when I actually do.

Outside, a cold gust of wind smacked into my cheeks, turning them raw. I pulled up the collar to my overcoat, then traipsed down the sidewalk with my chin down.

Approaching the alley that led behind the building, I started to turn and head for my car parked out back. Something caught my attention. An unusual movement further down the sidewalk.

I stopped, but I could only see the corner of the next building.

Then, somebody stumbled into view. The coat looked familiar. *Barbara!*

Darting back to the sidewalk, a melee came into view. A few men stood on the opposite corner of Merchants Row near Starbucks. They were shoving two women: Barbara and Courtney.

Two of the men held Courtney by the arms.

Barbara tried to assist, grabbing one.

Another yanked Barbara's hair and tossed her to the ground. Her head smacked the brick walkway. She scrambled to get to her feet, as bystanders called the police.

I ran towards the fracas, dropping my briefcase as I closed in on the scene.

A thug spotted me. Then, the crew broke down the sidewalk.

Nearing my colleagues, I grabbed Courtney's shoulder to get her attention. "Are you all right?" I asked.

She was disoriented. Courtney took a moment to recognize me. "Yeah," she said, nodding and gasping for air.

Then, I turned to Barbara. She was floundering on the ground, trying desperately to get up. Reaching out with a hand, I offered to assist her. Barbara glanced up at me. Fear resonated in her eyes, then relief as she registered me. Blood oozed from a cut on her temple.

I pulled her up to her feet.

"Are you guys okay?" I said.

Barbara nodded.

I did a hasty scan to see if anyone else lurked in the area. Nothing.

Facing Courtney, I said, "I'll be back."

Then, I ran up the sidewalk in pursuit of the attackers.

I looked way up ahead, and they weren't in sight. Running to the corner of Congress Street, I glanced around. They weren't anywhere to be found.

Retracing my steps, I headed back down the sidewalk. I trotted past the high-rise at 60 State Street. There is a narrow walkway leading to a plaza behind the building. In warmer months, a restaurant on the lower level opens an outdoor bar there.

I walked down the dark passageway, checking nooks in the building. Along the side of the building, there were numerous picture windows inset into the façade. They could have darted down the alley and stopped in an alcove to catch their breath.

All was quiet, and I didn't happen upon them.

Climbing a set of stairs, I continued down the walkway, then I ascended another small set of stairs. The plaza lay before me. It was an open brick area with planters located along the edges. A steep staircase led down to the cobblestone courtyard of Faneuil Hall Marketplace.

I ambled over and scanned the marketplace; I spotted them below. The three men jogged towards the edge of the market. They slowed to a brisk walk as a car on Congress Street pulled to the curb. Watching them pile into the vehicle, one of them checked to see if they were being followed.

He spotted me.

The glow from a nearby streetlight caught on his hard features. It was the man that had warned me to withdraw from the case. He climbed into the car, and it sped away.

***

RETURNING TO THE STREET CORNER where the incident occurred, I found Courtney and Barbara inside Starbucks. Courtney was patting down Barbara's gashed head with a napkin. My briefcase sat on the floor next to the table.

"That hurts," Barbara said, with a laugh.

"Almost done." Courtney kept at it.

She apparently had gotten a few napkins and either asked a server to run them under the faucet, or she'd gone into the restroom and done it herself. I was glad to see neither of them had serious injuries. And they seemed to be handling the situation well.

The place was dead. I took a seat at the next table. "How you guys holding up?"

Courtney glanced over her shoulder at me. "Don't ask."

"What?" She seemed upset with me. I didn't know why.

She frowned and shook her head, ignoring me. Once she finished cleaning Barbara's wound, Courtney turned to face me. "You're on my shit list right now. And I'm not sure if you're ever getting off."

"I understand you're upset—"

"Upset!" She stood up and stared me in the eyes.

"Why are you so mad at me?"

"You knew."

"Knew what?"

"They might come after me." She crossed her arms. "The thugs told us they had warned you that we might get hurt. And you did nothing. You didn't tell us."

"I'm sorry." I shrugged. "Never thought they would do anything."

"You could have at least told us."

"I didn't want you to worry."

"Worry?" she said. "If we had some warning, we might have seen it coming."

Courtney's point made sense. "You're right," I said, holding up my hands in surrender. "I should have told you. I'm really sorry."

"Don't give me that puppy dog look. I'm pissed at you."

A lull fell over the discussion. Courtney stood there, eyeballing me. I didn't know what to say or do. Finally, Barbara broke the silence. "Ken, you really should have withdrawn from the case, like they demanded."

I truly felt awful about what happened to Barbara, but her comment was inappropriate. I had an obligation as Brad's counsel. There was a trial in a couple weeks. If I withdrew, it could have a negative impact on his defense. It would be prejudicial to the client.

Rather than argue, I sat quiet and waited for the hostile tide to ebb. Eventually, emotions would simmer, and we could discuss the issue intelligently.

A cruiser rolled up to the curb with blue lights flashing.

I stood up and stepped to the plate-glass window. Waving to an officer, I tried to let him know we were inside. Two uniformed patrolmen headed for the door to the coffee shop.

"Remember to keep this to exactly what you saw and heard tonight," I said to Barbara and Courtney. "We can't slip and divulge any attorney/client information."

They both nodded, understanding. Barbara and Courtney looked somber.

I suspected they figured from my comments that a withdrawal wouldn't be forthcoming. Courtney took a seat next to Barbara. Sliding into an empty chair, I joined them at the same table. An aroma of dark coffee floated through the café.

The officers pushed the heavy door open. One was young and muscular, while the other was older with a potbelly. They approached and stood near the table.

"We can tell you what happened," I said, looking up.

The younger officer shrugged. "Actually, we've got a detective on the way."

"A detective?" I said. "For a routine street crime?"

"Yup." The younger officer shrugged.

A few minutes later, Detective Chandler strolled through the door. He wore a trench coat and walked briskly, so the bottom of the coat fanned behind him. "Well, well," he said, smiling. "Look who we've got here."

"How did you get in on this?" I said, shaking my head.

Courtney sat up and looked at me. "I called the police, too. And I mentioned you were chasing the assailants."

This made sense as to how Chandler knew we were involved, but it didn't explain why he'd come over to check on a routine street crime. He was a homicide detective in the middle of a case that was getting ready for trial.

"Let me rephrase," I said. "What's your interest in this?"

"You have a way of stirring up trouble." He grinned. "Just checking all the angles."

"What angles?" Now, I was really confused.

"So, was this a random act of violence? Or does it have something to do with you?"

"Interesting you'd say something like that," I said. "Who would harass us, if our client was guilty?"

"Can't say." Chandler shook his head. "You probably piss a lot of people off."

"We'll give statements to the uniformed officers, who are supposed to be covering this," I said. "Not you."

"Hey," Chandler griped. "I'm here to get the statements."

"You have a conflict," I replied.

"This is where you clam up," he said, shaking his head, dismayed. "Like the last time, when I found you in a hospital bed. Your old man would really be proud."

"You leave him out of this," I snapped.

Courtney grabbed my arm. "What's he talking about?"

"Nothing," I said, dodging the question.

She looked at Chandler.

He smiled. "What? Hasn't he ever told you?" Chandler looked amused. "His old man was on the job."

"No. His parents own a baking supply company."

"Maybe," Chandler said. "I don't know any of that. But his *real* father… he was a cop."

She pulled me to face her. "Is this true? How could you not tell me?"

"Let's talk about it later," I said, turning back to Chandler.

Courtney stood up and marched towards the door.

"Where are you going?" I called to her.

"I've had enough of this. I'm going home."

"What about the incident?"

"I'll stop by the precinct on my way to work in the morning and give a statement." Without another word, she stepped outside, and a frigid breeze tossed her blonde hair. She hustled down the sidewalk and disappeared into the shadows.

Barbara gave the officers a detailed statement. Thugs had approached and told Courtney they had warned me to withdraw from the case. Chandler smiled with glee at the revelation. Then, she described the scuffle and my pursuit. She went on to explain how nice it was for Courtney to help her clean up.

The potbellied officer told Barbara she should go a hospital and get checked out. I expressed it was a good idea. Chandler scribbled some notes, then closed his pad. He ended up just listening in and let the uniformed officers handle the call.

The younger officer collected our written statements. "We'll look into this and let you know if we find anything."

Both patrolmen headed for the door. They stepped outside and climbed into the cruiser.

I wasn't very hopeful they'd find anything. We hadn't divulged much.

Any connection between the assailants and the unions wasn't revealed. I couldn't trust why Chandler was at this call, or who he might report to outside of the police force. Heads of the unions were politically connected, and I wondered what we were mixed up in.

Chandler watched me suspiciously. "You're holding something back," he said.

I shrugged. "We told you about this incident."

"Yeah, it's what you haven't told me that's troubling."

"Maybe you know more than you're telling us," I said flatly.

"What's that supposed to mean?" he snapped.

"You get my drift." I stood to leave.

The police cruiser pulled away from the curb and rolled down the street. I helped Barbara get to her feet. We made it to the door and Chandler just sat there.

Stepping outside, I walked Barbara to the corner. The bleeding had stopped, and the wound was superficial. She didn't want to go to a hospital or urgent care. I ordered an Uber and paid for her ride home. Then, I started walking down Merchants Row, which cut behind my building. My car was parked in the lot out back.

Glancing over my shoulder, I looked into the coffee shop. Chandler was on his phone reporting to someone. I wondered if it was the prosecutor or a union boss.

FORTY-NINE

BACK IN THE WAR ROOM, Kara glanced around the table and checked to see if everyone was present. Alyson shifted in her seat uncomfortably. The prosecutor focused on reading pages in a binder set in front of her. She avoided eye contact with the officers.

A palpable tension had divided the police and prosecution. Many had come to believe Wallace's arrest was premature. They blamed Alyson for grandstanding. Kara worried about an eventual lawsuit if the politician were acquitted. This meeting came as a pleasant surprise. Davis and Nguyen had discovered some new evidence.

"Detective Davis, why don't you start," Lieutenant Johnson said. "You called this meeting."

"Sure." He smiled and stood up. Davis's heavy jowls shook as he trundled to the front of the room. He carried a laptop under his beefy arm.

Pushing a tripod mounted with a diagram out of the way, he cleared the view to a flatscreen television. Then, he set the laptop on a podium. Davis took a moment to get the computer in sync with the television.

A moment later, a black and white still photograph of an intersection came into view. There were vehicles entering and leaving the intersection.

"What are we looking at?" Johnson said.

Davis pointed to a van on the screen. "This is the vehicle that struck Danforth," he said as if that explained it all.

Kara took a sip of coffee. This development was immediately clear to her.

Stepping closer to the screen, Davis pointed to an elbow that was visible through the driver's side window. "Here," he said. It showed the driver wore a dress shirt.

"Looks like a man's arm," Johnson said. "Got any footage of the face."

"Afraid not," Davis said, shaking his head like a bulldog.

"Can we even get this in?" Johnson asked Alyson.

Alyson sat up and shrugged. "Defense counsel in the Audrey Martin case filed a motion *in limine* to preclude argument and evidence related to the Danforth murder. It was granted without oral argument. The only way to get this into evidence would be to backdoor it."

"Do you think that could happen?" the lieutenant said.

"Probably not." Alyson nodded. "We should bury this in discovery."

"What do you need from us?"

"About fifty other intersections videoed around the scene of the hit and run, with hours and hours of footage."

"Will do," Davis said.

Kara figured this was just the type of tactic that could backfire later. It could be used to show police misconduct and wrongful prosecution if Wallace was acquitted.

FIFTY

A WEEK AFTER the judge ordered production of the prosecution's file, we received a delivery at the office. Alyson sent over twelve Bankers Boxes full of materials. She provided a witness list a mile long. I suspected the key elements of her case were scattered among the various boxes.

We all stood in the conference room, staring at the boxes piled on the table and around the room. "How are we going to get through all of this?" Joey griped.

"I have an idea," I said, stepping closer to the table.

"Hope so," Nate said. "Because this is nuts."

"You have to be careful not to miss anything important," I said. "This is what you all need to do. Get a new box and take one of the prosecutor's boxes. You go through the box and anything you think is of value, you place in your new box. Return the less important items to the original box."

This approach was simpler than what I usually require. Most of the time, you want to keep track as to how the documents were produced, so anything going in the new box required you to stop and make a copy. Alyson had likely created these boxes without much rhyme or reason, so I didn't worry about keeping the original production in check. Our approach for this case made it more streamlined. Time was of the essence.

"This is still going to be a pain in the neck," Courtney said, grabbing a box.

"Yeah. But it keeps everything organized. Law is drudgery."

She shook her head and frowned. "It's not always glamorous. I agree."

"When you get done with a box," I said, "place the new one and the original on the conference room table."

They got going with their assignments, working from their offices. I started digging through my first box. Planning to have each of them focus closely on three or four boxes, I sought to quickly peruse them all. Somehow, I was born with an audio/visual memory. Few people have this type of brain function. It allows me to record what I see and hear in my mind. The approach is not quite the same as a photographic memory, but it allows for capturing conversations and observations. Someone with an audio/visual brain can basically take a mental video with sound of an event and store it in their head, with the ability to replay it later. Much of my success as a lawyer can be attributed to this trait.

So, I began the arduous task of flipping through each document in every box. Whenever something appeared like it could have some significance, I stopped to review it carefully. I let the images sink in, whether or not I thought the evidence had any probative value.

The day dragged on as we all churned through box after box. Sounds of crinkled paper echoed through the office. Each of them would lug boxes into the conference room, and I'd run through a second review. We uncovered a bunch of video of intersections from around town. None of it seemed relevant to Audrey Martin's death. Eventually, nighttime set in and streetlights illuminated into the office.

As people slowly left for the day, I remained vigilant. I kept doublechecking the boxes and pulled together various discovery items that appeared relevant to the case. We couldn't find a final Medical Examiner's report. I wondered if they had dropped a ball.

Finally, everything was paired down into one Bankers Box. We had located what we needed to begin our defense strategy: scene photographs of Brad's house; DNA test results, fingerprints; text message and cellphone data usage; emails; two M.E. reports; photographs of the victim; and a few witness statements. We found these items in various boxes. The two M.E. reports weren't even in the same box. Usually, there are two sets of pictures of the scene. One taken before their search, and one taken after. We located the various sets in different boxes.

I carefully set them on the table, planning to look at the date stamps. An envelope had photographs of the crime scene shortly after the police got there on the day of Audrey Martin's death. There was another set with date stamping from later that evening. A third set was dated a week later, well after Brad's arrest.

They'd returned to the crime scene, I thought. *Why?*

***

THE NEXT MORNING our trial team met in the conference room. I revealed my discovery from the night before. Everyone seemed surprised at finding three sets of photographs, but Joey didn't think it was a meaningful development.

"This doesn't say a lot," Joey reasoned. "Police often go back to the scene."

"You need to check the dates for some of their forensics." I grinned.

"What are you getting at?" Courtney sought an explanation.

"I think they found something on the night of the murder, which they anticipated would lead to a suspect. Something that would connect Brad to the crime."

"And?" Courtney was getting anxious.

"It clearly didn't pan out. So, they went back."

"How do you know this?" Joey said.

"The date of the follow-up visit is the day after a forensics report was filed."

Nate pressed to the table. "What didn't pan out the first time?"

I shrugged and held up my hands. "Beats me. Whatever it is, the item is located in one of these boxes. They tried to bury it because it probably points to someone else."

"Who?" asked Nate.

"Perhaps the actual murderer," I said.

FIFTY-ONE

THE FOLLOWING WEEK raced by as we prepared for trial. Beckerman ran out a few more leads, and the trial team worked on lining up witnesses. This included subpoenas to people who were reluctant to appear.

One of the biggest stressors in trial work concerns anxiety over whether all the witnesses will appear as scheduled. You tend to organize witnesses like book ends, starting your portion of a case with a strong witness and closing with a solid witness. This allows the jury to get a favorable glimpse into your case at the beginning and leaves them on a high note when they step out to deliberate. Any difficult witnesses you sandwich between the strong witnesses, so they are less memorable if things do not go exactly as planned with the difficult witnesses.

We met with Brad daily, discussing our findings relative to the prosecution's file. He was holding up better than when we'd visited him at the jailhouse. Brad helped contribute to the defense strategy. He also replenished the retainer for a second time.

He stayed at the brownstone, while Harper lived at their house on the cape with the couple's young daughter. At one point, I contacted Jack and tried to play the middleman. I explained we had developed solid defenses, and it was quite possible Brad could get acquitted. Jack put a damper on any hopes of reconciliation. Apparently, Harper felt Brad had brought this all on himself. She was certain he had an affair with Audrey Martin, which gave the police and prosecution a reason to go after him. We still hadn't found any concrete evidence of an affair. Harper felt Brad should have put his family first. Now, their daughter Hailey was going through a terrible time.

Hailey had been displaced from school and tutors weren't able to keep her from falling behind. I couldn't argue with Harper's reasoning. So, I just focused on the case.

Sometimes you have to keep clients focused on each step in the process to prevent them from getting overwhelmed. This includes avoiding tendencies of client's preoccupation with a bad result. You have to prevent them from contemplating the disastrous impact a criminal case can have on a person's life.

The approach also kept me from worrying too much about what might happen to Brad when the matter concluded. Even a defense verdict left him in a pickle. I just focused on trying to win the case. Contemplating failure can lead to failure. Yet, a nagging image of Brad in a prison cell haunted me.

PART FIVE

TRIAL

FIFTY-TWO

WE APPEARED for the first day of trial in Suffolk Superior Court. The pre-trial order required us to appear at 10:00 A.M. Counsel stood at their respective tables waiting for Judge Cornelius Mathers to enter the courtroom. Brad stood between me and Courtney, looking anxious.

The place was packed with press correspondents. They sat behind the worn oak railing, separating the gallery from the courtroom. I wasn't as worried about the media coverage, however. Apparently, the judge's comments at the scheduling conference had caught wind in the press. Some media outlets continued to run with guilty politician headlines, while a couple newspapers had infused a question of potential innocence into the reporting. Those articles suggested this could all be a political stunt. A more level playing field was preferrable to the defense.

A major goal in a criminal case is to keep everyone guessing. If the matter fails to reach the difficult threshold of beyond a reasonable doubt, the defendant is acquitted. Many jurors would have heard about this case in the media, but they might deny having seen the news in order to get on the jury. Balanced reporting helped us tremendously. It kept potential jurors wondering about Brad's innocence.

Unlike a lot of criminal matters, this case didn't have many pre-trial motions. You often file motions to suppress evidence the police obtained through improper means. Such motions include evidence seized without a warrant or proper consent. The police had rummaged through the entire house on the day of Audrey Martin's death. They had exceeded the scope of the warrant, but they had only confiscated items from the three rooms noted in the search warrant. Hence, we didn't have any evidence to preclude from their unlawful conduct.

We had filed a motion *in limine* to preclude evidence or argument about the Phillip Danforth and Keith Evers deaths. The motion was based on such evidence being more prejudicial than probative, and we argued there wasn't sufficient evidence to connect Brad to either death. In fact, Keith Evers's death had been ruled an accidental overdose. The judge granted the motion without a hearing. We had filed another motion to preclude evidence that hadn't been decided. It concerned evidence of the video footage of the van, which we found hidden in the prosecution's discovery.

After a few minutes, the judge entered the courtroom from a side door. He walked hunched over towards the bench, carrying a file. The judge's black robe hung loosely on his boney frame and appeared slightly crooked. His gray hair was unkempt, and his thick glasses were askew. I wondered if he'd had a restless night.

The bailiff to the side of the courtroom jumped to her feet. "All rise," she called.

Everyone became silent and whooshed to attention.

"Hear ye, hear ye, hear ye," the Bailiff said. "The Court of the Commonwealth of Massachusetts is now in session."

The judge took the bench and set the file down in front of him. "Sit down," he said, waving at everyone dismissively.

We all sat down and waited for him to continue.

He glanced around the courtroom and adjusted his glasses. "Well, it seems we have a full house." Then, he looked at Alyson and then me. "Counselors, are you all set to go?"

We both stood to respond, individually.

"Yes, Your Honor," I said. "We're ready to get started."

"Your Honor," Alyson said. "The Commonwealth is ready to proceed."

"Anything outstanding before we pick the jury?" Judge Mathers said.

"Yes, Your Honor," I said. "We have a motion *in limine*…"

Judge Mathers nodded, seeming to recall the issue. He motioned for me to sit down.

I took a seat, wondering if he would even let me argue the issue.

"The motion is denied," said Judge Mathers.

Jumping to my feet, I bellowed, "Your Honor!"

The judge looked at me perplexed. "What are you bickering about? You won."

"Your Honor, it was my motion to preclude evidence. And you just denied it."

Judge Mathers really looked confused. Then, he seemed to collect himself. "Granted," he finally said. "The motion is granted. This death business is precluded. The van video is precluded."

Now, Alyson was at him. "Your Honor, the Commonwealth wishes to be heard."

"What for?" He shooed her away with both hands.

"There is evidence to connect this defendant with another death," Alyson said, seizing the opening to speak. "He may have killed a witness to cover up the crime in this matter."

"Does he have any charges pending in the other matter?"

He clearly had waited to see if the Commonwealth was bringing new charges relative to the Danforth murder prior to issuing this ruling on the van. If they had more evidence, it could cause him to revisit submission of evidence as to Danforth's death. I waited anxiously to see if Alyson would surprise us with another lastminute stunt.

"No, Your Honor," Alyson said. "But—"

Judge Mathers shook his head, frustrated. "Then it's quite simple," he snapped. "Allowing evidence of another crime, when you don't even have charges pending… Well, that's the definition of prejudicial evidence. I'm sorry, you're not permitted to mention the other death or get into evidence about the van that caused the death."

The judge's comments were cogent and well stated. At times, he seemed like an addled jurist who should consider retirement. His comments and behavior sometimes made me nervous about him presiding over this trial. But his ultimate rulings were fair, and the reasoning was sound. So, I decided to move ahead without seeking a recusal.

"Anything else?" asked Judge Mathers.

"No, Your Honor," we replied in unison.

"Let's get started," he said to us.

Judge Mathers glanced toward the gallery. "I'm afraid we are going to need that space for the jury panel. You'll all have to step out until the jury is selected." He shrugged. "Sorry. But we simply do not have the room. You'll be able to return once the jury is seated."

A couple bailiffs started clearing the gallery.

Reporters trundled out, peeved. Several courthouse gadflies looked confused, but they followed the others. There were spectators who appeared to be law students, likely sent to watch a real trial.

After the gallery was empty, another bailiff appeared in the main doorway of the courtroom. Behind him stood a gaggle of potential jurors. Everyone at counsel tables stood to address the jury panel. We waited for the judge's instructions.

"Bailiff, you may bring the panel in," said Judge Mathers.

Then, the bailiffs ushered the jury panel into the gallery, pointing at pews. As the procession of prospective jurors walked inside, some glanced around, taking in the mystique of the storied courtroom. They stared in awe at the oak bench, wooden railings, and plush leather chairs.

A tinge of anxiety rippled through my body, as I watched them file into the room.

It remained cold outside. The older courthouse had an outdated heating and cooling system. An occasional rattle of pipes from steam running through them echoed into the courtroom. The temperature rose as the morning wore on.

"Let's move it along," a bailiff said to the stragglers.

We all faced the jury panel as they entered the room. Some were dressed professionally, taking their role as jurors quite seriously. Others were casually dressed, but they looked attentive. Still, a number of them moped along, displeased with being there.

All the lawyers were dressed in their finest suits. Brad remained beside me. He wore a decent suit and had a fresh haircut. Somehow, he'd managed to restore a little of his charisma, despite the circumstances. Being released on bail had served a great benefit in getting him presentable for trial.

Once the panel of jurors entered the room, the judge told them to sit down. The pews were quickly filled and many of them were forced to stand.

Selecting a jury is an arduous process in any case. But when you pick a jury in a murder case, you have to be especially careful. We categorized potential favorable jurors into three categories. The first being people who may be suspicious of the police. Anyone from a poorer neighborhood would fit this. Next, we wanted people who are genuinely sympathetic to those who get caught in unfortunate circumstances. Social workers, psychologists, and nurses would do. Lastly, we wanted people who might be analytical, but we didn't want anyone overly conservative. This would include college professors, teachers, non-profit executives, and employees in larger corporations.

We eschewed anyone who we felt might be overly conservative or supportive of the police. Military veterans, police officers, and family members of these groups of people. We also were concerned about financial planners and engineers, especially engineers. They tend to favor the prosecution.

Once the jury panel was situated, a bailiff walked over and dropped a stack of juror questionnaires on each counsel table. Courtney snatched them off our table and began to review them. Our method was to highlight the potential jurors we preferred in green, and we marked the ones we didn't like in red. All the others were checked off in yellow.

The judge went over the general *voir dire* with the jury panel. He began by introducing all counsel and the defendant. Anyone who had a personal relationship with any of us was asked to come forward. Most panels have one or two people excused on that basis.

A few people raised their hands. The judge asked a young man to come forward. Counselors are required to approach the bench and stand at sidebar while the judge undertakes an inquiry. This young man smiled at me pleasantly as he walked towards the bench.

Judge Mathers asked him to explain the conflict. He worked for a document retention company that did business with my firm. He'd been to the office a few times. The judge excused him from this case and told him to go back and sit in the gallery.

Three other people came forward, explaining they had knowledge of the defendant. Judge Mathers asked if they personally knew Bradford Wallace. All three denied having a personal relationship with him. Then, the judge asked if they had any bias towards Mr. Wallace. Two said they did not have an opinion of him either way. But one potential juror explained that she disagreed with Bradford Wallace's political opinions, and she could not maintain objectivity due to this. The judge excused her, but not the other two.

The judge went through the same procedure for all the witnesses in the case. He read off each name and nobody raised a hand. Thereafter, he asked if anyone claimed a hardship from standing jury duty. Several people raised their hands.

Counsel approached the bench, and each one was called in turn. A woman worked as a teacher and didn't have after school care for her child. She was excused. A doctor wanted off jury duty, claiming that he had patients lined up and no way to direct them to other treatment.

The judge covered the microphone to the court's audio system. "I think his excuse is hogwash," Judge Mathers said. "But do any of you want him on this jury?"

Alyson shook her head. I followed suit.

The doctor was dismissed.

Then, a young man approached wearing a t-shirt stating he was angry and planned to get even. A potential conspiracy theorist, he might side against the police. But I figured such an angry man might be envious of Brad's wealth. The young man complained jury duty was a hardship. The judge didn't buy his rationale. So, then the man complained that jury duty was an act of a fascist government. This ordinarily wouldn't work either. But with Brad being a politician, the judge suggested we excuse the man from this case. I didn't object to him not serving on the jury. Alyson didn't fight the issue.

We went through a few others, whittling down the jury pool.

Finally, the judge finished his *voir dire* and suggested that we take a lunch break. It took half a day just to get though the first aspect of jury selection.

FIFTY-THREE

RETURNING FROM LUNCH, the court clerk drew twenty-one names from a tumbler. Then, the judge sat most of them in the jury box. Several were seated in chairs in front of the box. Each juror was assigned a number when seated.

This process required selecting more than the number needed for the actual trial. In the event some of them were removed, there would typically be enough who sat through the process to serve on the jury.

Now, the lawyers began their *voir dire* of the potential jurors.

Alyson directed her inquiry into bias against the police. She kept it simple.

Our side had a bit more of a challenge. We had to rule out any prejudice against someone accused of a crime, and we needed to remove anyone with animosity against a person of wealth. Given Brad's status as a politician, I asked questions to ferret out any bias against him or his political party.

Throughout this process, a few jurors raised their hands, affirmatively responding to certain questions. This allowed counsel an opportunity for follow-up questions, which were not previously scripted.

Judge Mathers had sat quietly while Alyson asked questions. But he interrupted me a few times. We eventually cut the panel down by two prospective jurors during this process.

A potential jury with a couple alternates sat before us. More would have to go.

We then went through the process where each side had the opportunity to strike a juror for any reason. This is known as a preemptory challenge. Courtney stood beside me with our list. A few people selected were marked in red.

There was an engineer seated in the third chair, a wife of a police officer in the tenth seat, and the fifteenth seat was occupied by a financial planner.

Once a juror is stricken, he or she is asked to return to the gallery. Then, the next person in line moves up. You typically seat twelve jurors and a few alternates. Most of the time, the parties do not use all three of their preemptory challenges out of fear of seating someone worse than who is being removed. This can be the case if you run out of jurors seated before you and need to pull one from the gallery. When that occurs, the person selected is done at random.

Each side takes a turn removing a juror. Occasionally, the other side will remove someone you do not like. Most of the time, they remove someone you prefer.

Alyson culled the jurors, using all of her challenges. We lost a couple of people we wanted on the jury. I struck two of the three people we had concerns about. The engineer and the police officer's wife were gone. We left a financial planner on the jury. There were people in the gallery who definitely were worse options.

Finally, after an entire day in court, the judge called us to sidebar. "Are you satisfied with the jury?" Judge Mathers said.

Alyson leaned towards the microphone. "The Commonwealth is satisfied."

"The defense is satisfied," I said, nodding.

We finally had a jury selected for our murder trial. And I was incredibly pleased with the result.

Judge Mathers recessed for the day, stating we would begin with opening statements in the morning. My stomach turned. The real performance would begin the next morning.

FIFTY-FOUR

WE BROKE THROUGH an onslaught of reporters and found an attorney/client conference room. I stepped inside and felt a wave of relief cast over me. The room was ten degrees cooler than the courtroom.

Brad rushed in after me, followed by Courtney. She closed the door, shutting out the clamor in the hallway. A moment later Nate and Joey entered the room.

I turned to the team and smiled. "That went fairly well."

"You think we got a decent jury?" Brad said, facing all of us.

"As well as can be expected," I said, motioning with my hands. "We didn't seat any police, military, or engineers. There are a few defendant-oriented types: a social worker, a teacher, and a delivery truck driver with a dismissed theft charge in his past. Many others would fall into the neutral category. Such people can be persuaded. The only one that leans towards the prosecution is a financial planner, which isn't nearly as bad as other options on the jury pool."

A lull fell over the conversation as Brad considered my explanation.

"Should we have struck the financial planner?" Brad finally said.

Courtney cleared her throat, like she was about to answer. I shook my head and waited a moment to respond.

An attorney has to be careful about explaining judgment calls made during a trial. The client will start thinking of every possible mistake if the case doesn't go his way. Brad would come back to this one day and blame a loss on keeping the financial planner on the jury. If we had struck him, the replacement could have easily been an engineer or a relative of a police officer.

"It was the right call," I said after a moment. "We had run out of options from the pool lined up by the box. Striking him would have meant the court would have selected someone random from the larger pool. We were out of challenges. So, we'd be stuck with whoever replaced the financial planner. There were a couple engineers and a few people related to police officers who could have taken his place. It was too risky. Besides, he might come in handy when we attack the technical issues in the case."

"Okay," Brad said, appeased by my explanation.

We waited for the place to quiet down, then headed for the elevators.

Everyone was quiet as the lift jounced down to the lobby. When the doors shook open, we filed out and walked across the tile floors towards the center door.

Outside, a cool breeze blew across the brick plaza and the glow from an afternoon sun reflected off patches of snow. I slid my overcoat on. A news van was pulled up to the building, and the crew was filming a reporter with the courthouse in the background.

Grabbing Brad's arm, I ushered him across the plaza towards a staircase leading beneath an office building to the street a level below.

We moved quickly enough to avoid the press. They had spotted us, but we were out of earshot and a good distance away before they recognized Brad. It was too late to chase us down. Once we reached the steps, we headed down single file.

At the bottom of the stairs, we gathered around to discuss next steps. Cars whipped past us, heading downhill along Tremont Street.

I needed time to further prepare my opening statement. That was the next big event in the case. In reality, criminal trials settle down a bit after opening statements. It's the prosecution's case and their burden. You have to be prepared with cross-examinations, but more pressure is placed on the other side.

Also, I wanted to figure out a way to divide up the cross-examinations with Courtney. Many first chair trial lawyers like to handle all the witnesses. However, the approach of dividing up witnesses helps take the pressure off and allows for you to be rested and focused during your witness examinations. Younger lawyers can perform quite well and feel confident just because a senior lawyer is there to help. I tend to opt for splitting up the responsibilities.

"Courtney and I need to focus on the opening and the cross-examinations," I said to the team.

Joey nodded, understanding. "Sure thing."

"We aren't sure if Brad will testify, but I think the two of you," I said, pointing to Joey and Nate, "need to work on preparing him. Start with digging into further background information. Take good notes."

They both nodded.

"Go over the rules for witness examinations. Then walk him through some practice direct and cross-examination."

"Okay, we'll get on it," Joey said.

They turned away and headed for the crosswalk with brad in tow.

"Joey," I called.

He looked back.

"Use the conference rooms at Suffolk Law," I said, pointing down Tremont Street towards the law school.

Joey nodded, understanding.

We waited for them to get ahead of us, then we crossed the street.

They turned right and we stood at the intersection of Court Street, waiting to cross to the other side.

"Coffee?" I said, indicating to the Starbucks across the street with the tea pot hanging above the doorway.

"Sure."

The walk sign changed, and we headed over.

"What was all that about?" Courtney said.

"There's no way we can focus on this murder trial with Brad in the office."

FIFTY-FIVE

STEPPING INTO THE COFFEE SHOP, we found it busy for late afternoon. Being located near a courthouse, the café tended to attract lawyers needing a caffeine boost to get through the rest of the day.

We waited while attorneys fumbled through their orders and took time trying to dig out their wallets. The aroma of coffee beans wafted through the shop. A complete lack of urgency accompanied their actions. I could appreciate the respite they were feeling from trekking to court last minute and motions deadlines.

Eventually, we placed our orders. Courtney got a latte, which took time to prepare; I just asked for a cup of black coffee.

Grabbing two stools by the windows, we sat overlooking City Plaza. We sipped our javas and enjoyed a short break from the pressure. Neither of us talked for a bit. This was a regular routine and we both appreciated the quiet.

"So, how do you want to proceed?" Courtney eventually said, breaking the silence.

"I'll do the opening," I said. "We'll decide who does the closing, depending upon how the trial goes."

"Okay." She nodded.

"They will likely lead with Malloy. You'll handle the cross."

Courtney blanched. "Kenny, that's a key witness. I seriously doubt Brad would agree to having me handle her."

"Precisely why he's not here right now."

"Still, I'm not sure that I feel comfortable…"

"You're more than capable," I said, touching her shoulder.

"This isn't about us?"

I was taken aback. "What? Do you really think I would use strategy in a murder trial to get on your good side?"

She nodded. "The thought did occur to me."

"Well, erase it from your mind," I snorted. "This is a good strategy. Alyson is expecting me to handle the cross, when you get up it will come as a huge surprise. They will prepare the witness for my approach. Not yours."

Courtney smiled. "Okay, I see the point."

"Heck, I'd have you do the opening, but it could clue them in that you'd be taking a bigger role in the case, so the Malloy cross-examination might not come as a surprise."

"The opening? Really?" She canted her head, questioningly.

"You're still not seeing this. Brad is accused of killing an attractive young woman. What could be more convincing than another beautiful woman defending him?"

"So, now I'm gorgeous?" Courtney smirked.

"You do sort of look like Blake Lively."

She'd begun to sip her latte through a straw and laughed. Foam blew out of the hole in the cup. Courtney giggled and patted down the sides with a napkin. "I'd prefer to handle the expert."

"I'd rather have you handle the detective. She's a woman. You're a woman."

"The M.E. is a woman, too."

"Yeah. But she's older," I said. "And besides. I've got a feeling that I can wrap her around an axle."

Courtney laughed again and shook her head. We were really having a light moment, while in the thick of a major trial. Sometimes the pressure builds, and lawyers use humor to take the edge off. More often, they rely on cocktails.

"Okay, I'll handle Malloy. You take the expert. What about the others?"

Shaking my head, I grinned. "I have no idea."

"That's not reassuring."

"We have to handle this intuitively. Take it one step at a time."

And with that comment, I indicated to Courtney that I wasn't entirely sure how this trial would play out. The roadmap for our case wasn't even written and we were headed into day two of trial the next morning.

***

LATER, I walked into my condominium on Revere Street and set my briefcase near the mid-century sofa. I took off my overcoat and shoes. Steampipes rattled as the heat came on.

I'd brought a portion of the file home, so I could work on my opening and go directly to the courthouse in the morning. Joey and Nate would lug a handcart piled with a few Bankers Boxes to and from the courthouse every day until the end of the trial. A burden of being third and fourth chair trial lawyers.

Stepping to the kitchen, I poured myself a gin and tonic and slid the green bottle of Tanqueray against the backsplash. Then, I cut up a lime and dropped a couple wedges into the glass, pushing them beneath the ice with the knife.

The drink was close to overflowing, so I took a sip. And then, I took a long swig. The drink went directly to my head. I felt an immediate buzz. Long hours and caffeine had set this in motion.

I walked into the living room and clicked on the evening news. There were reports of a shooting in Dorchester, and segments covering a major traffic accident on Route 93. They touched on Brad's case briefly. I slipped out of my suit jacket and took a seat on the sofa.

Reaching for my briefcase, I pulled out my notepad and reviewed the opening statement. It had a number of scratch outs, corrections, and additions. I decided to rewrite it. The opening was broken down into several sections. Going over the process slowly, I pictured myself in front of the jury and ran through my mind exactly what I planned to say. Then, I jotted down each section with tight language. They say you only have two to three minutes to grab a jury's attention.

My phone vibrated. I really didn't feel like taking a call. Fielding an issue on the case was the last thing I needed to be doing. A lead attorney needs a solid opening and rest for a trial like this.

Glancing at my phone, it was my sister, Catherine.

She was an equestrian, who divided her time between Chester County, Pennsylvania and Aiken, South Carolina. Eventing is a demanding and risky sport. They compete in dressage, show jumping, then cross-country, which is basically jumping over huge jumps laid out through fields and wooded terrain. They trained and competed in South Carolina during the winter. She was calling from a horse farm in Aiken.

"Hey," I said, answering.

"It's Catherine. How are you doing?"

"Good. How about you?"

"Same old grind," she said.

Catherine worked six to seven days a week. Eventing didn't pay as much as other professional sports, so riders do other things to make ends meet. She rented a farm in each state and boarded other people's horses. She also trained horses for competition and sold them to younger riders. Occasionally, she taught clinics and gave riding lessons. I knew the routine.

"Are you staying healthy?"

"No injuries."

"What about the horses?"

She had three horses she competed with. The sport is difficult because you needed a healthy rider and horse to compete. At any given time, a horse can get sick or have an injury.

"Bosch is solid. Finn threw a shoe, but he hasn't come up lame. And Willie is still recovering from sore hocks."

I shook my head and laughed. "In my business, I always worry about the key witnesses showing up for trial. You have to worry about getting your horses to a show."

"Every profession has it's downsides."

"You can say that again."

"Every profession has it's downsides."

We both laughed.

"How are you coming with the present case?" she asked.

The question caught me off guard. "Did Mom tell you about it?"

"No."

"Then—"

"Kenny, it made the national news. They're even talking about it at the pub down here. Seems like a big deal."

"You didn't mention that you're my sister."

"Heavens no. I can't let the other riders think we have any dough."

We both chuckled. Most professional eventers just scrape by.

"But really… how's it going?"

I had wanted to call her after the Keith Evers incident, unload about the situation. Him dying and us getting shot at. The police search afterward. But I didn't want to burden her; she had enough to contend with in her business.

"Good," I finally said. "We're looking pretty good on this one."

"So, he's innocent?"

"Probably."

Then it hit me. I'd missed something for my opening.

"You sound fairly sure," she said.

"It's looking like he's innocent." I paused. "I've got to run. More work to do. But let's plan to catch up soon."

"Sure. Great talking to you."

We ended the call. Then, I ripped the pages I'd written for my opening off the notepad and tossed them on the floor. I'd come up with a new angle.

FIFTY-SIX

ALYSON STOOD to present her opening statement in a packed courtroom. Press swarmed all over the place. After jury selection was completed, Judge Mathers had made the gallery available to the public. I was still unsure exactly what she'd say.

She gently pushed back her chair and walked around the counsel table, stacked with binders and notepads. Alyson didn't reach for anything.

Approaching the jury box, she didn't opt for a podium. The courtroom was silent and all eyes where upon her. Alyson wore a short black suit jacket and skirt. The collar of a cream-colored blouse protruded slightly over the lapels on her jacket. Her long, black hair was pulled back in a ponytail. She looked like the girl next door. Trustworthy.

Many lawyers hide behind a podium and read from a script during opening argument. I'd tried several cases against Alyson. Even when she was well-prepared, she often carried a notepad and perused it during her opening statements. I suspected she diligently planned her arguments and sought the security of having an outline in hand. Today marked a stark contrast. Alyson stood before the jury and looked them directly in the eyes. She'd spent a lot of time preparing for this. Alyson was loaded for bear.

"Ladies and gentlemen of the jury," she said. "My name is Alyson Sheehan. And I am a prosecutor for the Commonwealth of Massachusetts."

Several jurors nodded to her. The prosecution usually comes to the table with a certain level of clout and credibility.

"Here with me today is my colleague, Jeremiah Faircloth." Alyson pointed toward the young lawyer at her counsel table. "Also, here with me today are the parents of a vibrant young professional woman. The relatives of our *murder* victim."

She pointed to the front row of the gallery at a couple seated behind the prosecution table. "Roger and Sally Martin."

The jurors followed the trace of Alyson's finger. Audrey Marin's parents truly looked crestfallen. A couple jurors then glanced at Brad and shook their heads in dismay.

"We thank you for your time and consideration. Jury duty comes with a certain level of burden, impacting your personal and professional lives due to the time you have to be here. My hope is that you will give this matter your full attention. Audrey Martin and her parents deserve no less."

Several jurors nodded, indicating a willingness to pay close attention.

"The evidence will show that the defendant, Bradford Wallace, had an illicit relationship with the victim." Alyson motioned towards Brad. "There was an abundance of communications between them, which demonstrates more than a work relationship. In fact, the two had sexual relations on the day of the murder."

The comment caught me off guard. There was nothing in the Medical Examiner's reports about sex. And there certainly wasn't any DNA evidence connecting Brad to the death.

Sounds of notebook pages flipping emanated from the gallery; keyboards clacked behind me.

Brad grabbed my shoulder. "What's she talking about?" he griped.

"Calm down," I whispered. "You need to maintain control in front of the jury."

"She can just make stuff like that up?" Brad said.

"We'll deal with it. Now, stop talking."

Alyson spun on a high heel, eyeballing Brad for a moment. Evidently, she'd heard the carping at our counsel table and probably wanted the jury to see Brad losing control.

He met her gaze and sat up straight. Regaining composure, he stared back, pokerfaced.

She turned back towards the jury. The movement accentuated her lean figure and chiseled calves. Alyson projected an image of someone completely pulled together: athletic, well-groomed, focused, and highly intelligent.

Pausing for a moment longer, she looked them over.

"You will also see video taken from a bank near the defendant's home," she continued. "It shows the defendant near the scene of the crime. He was a high-powered political figure in an affair that likely had gone wrong. He was in the vicinity of the crime. He had motive and opportunity."

She walked over to her counsel table and glanced down at a sheet of paper. The jurors followed her every move. Everyone in the courtroom was glued to her.

Alyson turned back to them, stepping into the well. "Ladies and gentlemen of the jury, the evidence will also show the murder occurred at the defendant's house. That's correct. Audrey Martin worked as a political aide for the defendant. They were having an affair. He was nearby at the time of the murder. And she was murdered at his house. Tossed off a balcony leading from his bedroom. Expert evidence will establish he brutishly grabbed her and threw her over the railing of a third story balcony. Where she plummeted downward towards a brick patio, fracturing her skull."

Somehow, the courtroom appeared even quieter than before.

Everyone in the jury box stared at Alyson wide-eyed and hungry for justice.

"At the close of this case, I am going to come back here after showing all of this evidence to you. The Commonwealth of Massachusetts will have proven its case beyond a reasonable doubt. And we are going to ask that you return a verdict of guilty. Thank you again for your time and consideration."

She flashed a polite smile, then marched back toward her counsel table. Her movements were swift and graceful. Alyson commanded the room. Taking her seat, she appeared like a victor returning from a war and the battle had just begun.

FIFTY-SEVEN

KARA SAT IN THE GALLERY behind counsel table watching the trial unfold. She wasn't as optimistic as the prosecutors after jury selection. There simply weren't any juror profiles leaning towards the police and prosecution.

After observing Alyson's opening statement, Kara was impressed with the presentation. Several jurors appeared to connect with the prosecutor. A few had even scowled at the defendant. The case had opened with momentum on their side. Kara wondered whether they could keep it going throughout the trial. Some of the evidence was thin.

The point about an affair and sexual relations between the victim and defendant on the day of the murder wasn't strongly established. Wallace had reacted indignantly to the assertion that he'd had relations with Audrey Martin the day she died. Even Kara wasn't sure if that had been the case. The only way to pull this off would be for the defense attorneys to blunder during trial.

Once Alyson was seated, the trial judge glanced over at the defense table. "Mr. Dwyer, do you plan to open now?"

Judge Mathers was referring to the option defense lawyers have in reserving their opening statement until after the prosecution rests its case. Kara had seen it done many times.

Ken Dwyer glanced at his co-counsel and client. They nodded.

"Yes, we do, Your Honor," Ken Dwyer said, standing. "Thank you."

He fastened the top button of his suit coat. Then, he walked across the courtroom, taking long strides, while keeping his back straight. The military background left him with an air of formality that many criminal defense lawyers lack.

Ken Dwyer didn't opt for fancy dress, either. He took a position before the jury and stood with his feet at shoulder-width apart. The defense lawyer wore a gray suit, tailored after the look of John F. Kennedy. He also wore a blue rep-tie with maroon stripes. His shoes were black, with a conservative cap toe.

"Ladies and Gentlemen of the jury," Dwyer said. "We also thank you for your time and consideration. While I understand and appreciate the sacrifice you are all making by being here, please be reminded that jury duty is a civil obligation in this country. A country where many brave men and women, and their families, have given the ultimate sacrifice, so that we may participate in this trial."

A few jurors glanced at his 82nd Airborne lapel pin and nodded. At least one smiled.

Dwyer wore his black hair cut short. His eyes were a sparkling blue. Kara watched the jury respond to him. He presented like anything but a sleezy defense attorney. The man looked the part of a prior military officer. His service gave him credibility. In fact, he resembled the insurance defense lawyers she'd sometimes see in court rather than a criminal lawyer.

"With me today is my colleague, Courtney Richardson." He motioned to her.

She stood and partly bowed at the jurors. A couple of them smiled kindly. Richardson was extremely attractive.

"Also with us, seated at counsel table is our client, Bradford Wallace."

Wallace flashed a cool politician smile at them and nodded to the jurors, like he was out on the campaign trail. Most of the jurors nodded in return. He resembled Tom Brady.

Kara had never seen anything like it. Wallace had disarmed them with a smile.

Dwyer turned back to the jury. "Bradford Wallace is a pillar of the community. He has served his country in the military, he has served in lay positions with his church, and he serves as a State Senator in the Commonwealth of Massachusetts. In fact, he holds the Minority Leader position in the State Senate."

All the jurors were highly focused on everything Dwyer was saying.

"We're going to ask you to carefully review the evidence the prosecution presents in this case. The evidence is flimsy," he said, voice cracking. Dwyer stepped closer and paused, letting the last point sink in.

His last comment seemed to resonate with the jury. Jurors projected countenances that reflected suspicion. Suspicion with the prosecution.

This isn't going well, Kara thought. *He's shifting the tide.*

"You're going to hear about an affair. However, you will not see evidence of an affair. You will not see racy text messages or emails demonstrating an affair. The prosecution has nothing to prove an affair. You have two people working together and communicating. Nothing more."

He hesitated for a moment. They were on the edge of their seats.

"There is nothing to show an affair took place. And nothing to connect Bradford Wallace with a sexual encounter on the day Audrey Martin died."

Again, he waited for the comment to stick.

"We do not have any hard evidence connecting Bradford Wallace to a crime. I'll say that again. You will not see any real evidence connecting Bradford Wallace to a crime. His DNA was not found on the victim."

Watching them carefully, Dwyer moved a little closer to the jury box.

"They don't have a real motive. They don't have hard forensics," he said, lowering his voice slightly. Dwyer bent towards them.

He drew them in. A few jurors actually leaned towards him, making sure they heard everything. They were buying it hook, line, and sinker.

"The biggest issue with this case, you are going to find… it's not clear if Audrey Martin was *even* murdered. This could have been a tragic accident."

Dwyer straightened up. He glanced to the pews behind the prosecution table.

"My heart goes out for the loss of Audrey Martin, taken from this world at too young an age. We also feel deeply for her family's grief and suffering."

The defense lawyer casually brushed his left shoulder, as if scratching an itch. His hand rubbed the lapel pin, a reminder that he'd likely suffered loss and grief himself. Fallen comrades in arms. Kara wondered if it was a natural reaction, or whether it was a practiced and deceptive move.

"The Medical Examiner's report is not entirely clear on the cause of death. Audrey Martin could have fallen over the railing." He stepped back. "If she was murdered, it wasn't Bradford Wallace."

Ken Dwyer turned at an angle, so the jury could catch a glimpse of Bradford Wallace. Then, the lawyer pointed at the defendant. "This man has not demonstrated a single act of guilt…"

He spun back to the jury and moved closer. "This is the man who called the police!"

A couple jurors sat back in their seats, aghast. Most were wide-eyed. Only a few remained stone-faced. Still, they were hard to read. Kara couldn't tell if they were for the prosecution or just in shock. Reporters seated all around Kara were scribbling notes on pads. A few banged away on laptops. The case was getting juicy.

"At the close of this case, we are going to ask you to return a swift verdict in favor of the defendant," Dwyer said. "Not guilty."

"Thank you, again." He slowly turned and started walking back to his table.

A few jurors shook their heads, seeming dismayed. One juror glanced at Alyson; the juror was an older woman, and she looked peeved.

Kara watched Dwyer exhale, relieved the opening performance was behind him. When he came around to his chair, he inhaled and collected himself. Dwyer then turned into the viewpoint of the jurors, appearing highly confident. He nodded to the judge, then sat down.

Dwyer's behavior reflected someone under tremendous pressure. He might feel stress because it's a friend in the defendant's chair. It could relate to the media attention on a highly public trial. Kara suspected it was much simpler than any of this.

He thinks Wallace is innocent, she thought.

FIFTY-EIGHT

JUDGE MATHERS glanced at Alyson. "You ready to call your first witness?" he said. The judge adjusted his glasses, waiting for her response.

I took a deep breath while nobody was watching and settled deeper into my chair. A notepad and pen were set on the table before me. Her direct examination would take some time. The pressure was on the prosecution right now.

There are aspects of every trial where a lawyer completes a task and desires a reprieve from the tension. Often judges take a break between opening statements and the first witness, allowing the jury an opportunity to stretch their legs and counsel a moment to gather themselves. Judge Mathers was the type to plow ahead at every moment to assure time wasn't wasted. The openings were relatively short, so he'd decided to get started with the first witness. He likely didn't want this trial clogging up his courtroom longer than necessary.

Rising to her feet, Alyson fetched a binder and notepad. "The Commonwealth calls Detective Sergeant Kara Malloy as our first witness."

"Very well," Judge Mathers replied. He motioned for the witness to come forward.

Alyson inhaled, gathering herself. Then, marched to the podium, which was situated near the far corner of the jury box.

While Alyson organized her materials, Malloy stood up and walked from the pews towards the witness box. She wore a black pantsuit. Her hair was also pulled back in a ponytail, resembling a kid sister of the prosecutor. Crossing the well of the courtroom, Kara Malloy appeared nervous.

She walked past the jurors and approached the witness stand.

The jurors watched her closely. People in the pews observed every movement.

When Malloy reached the witness box, she stepped up and stood by the chair. Some witnesses sit down and settle into the chair, often staring wide-eyed at the spectators in the gallery. Malloy was seasoned and waited for the judge to swear her in before sitting down.

Judge Mathers swung towards her. Malloy raised her right hand. The judge swore her in and told her to take a seat. Malloy nodded, then she sat in the chair.

She poured herself a cup of water from a pitcher nestled in a corner of the witness box. Then, she glanced up and looked directly at Alyson. Malloy still looked a little nervous, and I wondered if she had ever testified in such a packed courtroom.

Alyson smiled kindly at her, trying to loosen her up. "Are you all set?"

Malloy nodded and said, "Yes, ma'am."

They went over the detective's background, working in the fact that she grew up in the area and came from a family of police officers. We learned Malloy had obtained a degree in criminal justice from Saint Anslem's College, up in New Hampshire. A few jurors smiled at this. In the end, Malloy presented as the Irish girl next door, who went on to follow in her family's footsteps.

Once Alyson got rolling with the softball questioning on Malloy's background, the detective settled in. Her jitters subsided.

Much of the material testimony went in similar to the probable cause hearing. They went through how Malloy had first learned of Audrey Martin's death, explaining how she had arrived on the scene. The detective walked the jury through the steps taken to secure the scene, efforts to obtain a search warrant, and the gathering of evidence.

Alyson sought to cement the jury's minds with visons of a grisly death. She grabbed a stack of photographs blown up on foamboards. "May I approach the witness, Your Honor?"

Judge Mathers nodded. "You may."

She walked across the well holding the foamboards in both hands. Then, she stepped alongside the witness box and showed each photograph to Malloy without letting the jury see them before the evidence was properly authenticated.

"Are these all photographs of the crime scene?" Alyson said.

"Yes," Malloy replied.

"Are these photographs fair and accurate copies of the ones you previously explained having taken while you supervised the scene?"

"They are."

"You explained the process for the chain of custody?"

"Yes, I have."

"Did these photographs follow that chain of custody?"

"They most certainly did."

Alyson turned to the judge. "You Honor, I would like these photographs marked as evidence for the Commonwealth."

The judge looked over at me. "Any objections."

I half stood at my table. "No, Your Honor."

"Very well." Judge Mathers glanced at the clerk. "These can be marked as exhibits for the plaintiff… or rather the prosecution."

The clerk smiled and looked towards Alyson.

Alyson walked over to the clerk's table, and the clerk placed exhibit tabs in the corner of each foamboard. "There you are," she said, handing the stack back to Alyson.

Alyson walked around to the middle of the well; she stood in front of the judge's bench. "Your Honor, I would like permission to publish these exhibits to the jury."

"You may," Judge Mathers said, "but make it quick."

He was trying to interrupt the common process of passing each photograph around the jury box. An attorney hands over a foamboard to the first juror, who studies it closely. Then, the juror passes it to the next juror. Eventually, the photograph gets passed around to everyone on the jury. This is done with each exhibit, so for a period of time, many jurors are left holding the various photographs.

Alyson handed the first photograph over to a juror. It had the most shocking and horrific picture in the stack. It showed

Audrey Martin dead on the patio with a pool of blood congealing around her face.

The juror looked the photograph over, then passed it along.

Alyson handed him another, and they repeated the process. She handed over another and another. Once several photographs were circulating around the jury, she pulled a tripod over to the corner of the jury box near the witness stand, not too far from the door the jurors enter and leave the courtroom for breaks.

She waited until the foamboards circulating around the jury were returned to her. Then, she placed a photograph that hadn't been circulated on the tripod. Alyson waited for the jury to take in a picture of the balcony.

Alyson took it down and placed another on the tripod. This one was taken from the balcony and depicted Audrey Martin on the ground below. It distorted her location and made it seem like she lay further away from the balcony. Alyson repeated the process until all the photographs had been shown. Then, she bundled them together except for one.

She grabbed the lone foamboard and returned it to the tripod.

Then, Alyson walked over to the clerk's table and leaned the rest of them against a leg to the clerk's table. She swiftly walked back to the podium; a hint of a proud smile cracked at the edges of her mouth. Alyson had pulled this off smoothly.

She turned and faced the witness. Alyson smiled. "What did you do after completing the scene investigation?"

"We tried to obtain a statement from Bradford Wallace."

"Objection!" I bellowed, rising to my feet.

"Sustained." The judge looked to the jury. "The defendant has a 5th Amendment right to remain silent. His silence shall not be used against him. You must disregard the question."

I sat down and the judge motioned for Alyson to continue.

"What else did you do?" said Alyson.

"The next step was a statement from Philip Danforth."

"Objection," I said.

"Basis?" the judge asked.

"Hearsay."

Judge Mathers turned to Alyson. "Will this man be testifying?"

"No, but—"

"There's a motion *in limine* dealing with this," I interrupted.

"May we approach, Your Honor," Alyson said.

The judge shook his head. "Sustained. The witness shall not get into statements from people who won't be coming into court to testify."

While the judge's ruling was favorable, he didn't afford the prosecution an opportunity to explain their position. A witness shouldn't be able to testify as to what a non-party stated, unless it fit squarely within an exception to the hearsay rule. I anticipated Alyson would use a dying declaration exception to try to get around the rule, but Danforth had no idea he'd die at the time he'd given the statement. I feared the judge's ruling prevented us from fully exploring the issue on the record.

They then went over the investigation of emails and text messages, without putting the details of the investigation into evidence. I anticipated Detective Chandler would serve that purpose.

Malloy testified briefly as to other evidence gathered from the investigation, including evidence the victim had sexual relations on the day she died. Specifics were punted to the Medical Examiner's testimony.

"Did your investigation eventually settle on a suspect?" Alyson said.

"Yes."

"Who was your suspect?"

"The defendant, Bradford Wallace."

"Can you identify him?"

Malloy pointed at my client. "That's him there, seated at the defense table."

"Did you eventually make an arrest?"

"Yes."

"Was there anything in your investigation leading to the arrest?"

Malloy straightened up. "Our investigation pointed to the defendant. He had an enormous volume of communications with the victim. More than would be expected for a work relationship. There was also another major development."

"What was it?"

"We obtained video footage from a nearby bank."

They walked through the process to authenticate the CCTV video near a local bank. Alyson strutted over to a flatscreen television, which was situated on a cart with wheels. She rolled it into the well.

Clicking a remote, the screen buzzed with static. Then, an image of Brad standing by an ATM machine came into view. He looked a little creepy as he pulled out his wallet and made a withdrawal. The segment showed him shoving cash into the wallet. Then, he stepped out of sight. It wasn't clear which direction he'd taken.

"Is this the video you discovered?" Alyson asked.

Malloy nodded. "Yes."

"Where is this bank?"

"Right near the corner of Beacon and Park Streets."

"How far away was this from the crime scene?"

"About three blocks."

"Did your investigation determine an approximate time of death?"

"Yes."

"What was it?"

"The death occurred between 10:30 and 11:30 P.M."

"What time was this video taken?"

"You can see from the time stamp in the corner that it was taken at 10:50 P.M." Malloy took a sip of water, letting the point sink. "This was within the window the death had occurred."

"Did this lead to an arrest?"

"This video along with the strength of our investigation led to an arrest of the defendant, Braford Wallace."

"Thank you," Alyson said with a perfunctory smile. "That's all I have for now."

She walked back to her table and glanced at me. I nodded to her.

"Your witness," she said, then smirked.

Judge Mathers leaned towards her. “I’ll orchestrate this courtroom young lady,” he grumbled.

“Sorry, Your Honor.” Alyson said.

She peeked at the jury to see if any had gotten perturbed. I noticed a few shaking their heads. I let the moment pass, then I stood and slowly buttoned my suit jacket. I planned to address the court, advising that Courtney would handle Malloy’s cross-examination.

Although the prosecution had put on a nice presentation, the evidence wasn’t particularly damning. However, juries can sometimes get confused by the initial evidence.

Judge Mathers sat up and looked at the clock. “Afraid it’s gotten a little late. We’ll break for lunch. Return in an hour.”

A bailiff stood. “All rise. This court of the Commonwealth of Massachusetts is now in recess.”

Everyone came to attention, while the judge exited the courtroom.

Another bailiff led the jurors out through a side door. Some glanced at the photograph of Audrey Martin’s dead body on the way out. Others peeked over at Brad with disdainful eyes.

We had the answer. Jurors had been persuaded by the opening witness.

FIFTY-NINE

THE JURORS FILED out the side door, as press in the gallery broke for the hallway. I started packing up a few things, so I could get work done over the break.

Brad grabbed my arm. "What was that?" he griped.

Turning, I met his fierce eyes. Brad looked like he could kill.

"Relax. Not here," I said.

He let go of me. Regaining composure, he glanced around the room as if checking to see if anyone had noticed his outburst.

I looked over for a reaction from the jury. Most had already stepped out of the courtroom. The ones that were left appeared focused on navigating down from the jury box and getting through the exit door.

There had been a lot of clamor in the courtroom, so I doubted the jurors had heard Brad's comment. But I couldn't be certain. It was an ill-advised move for someone on trial for murder.

Courtney quickly gathered her things; Joey and Nate approached our table.

"Take that thing down," I said to Joey, pointing at the picture of Audrey Martin on the tripod.

He hustled over to take care of it.

"Nice move," I called over to Alyson.

She smirked in triumph.

"Makes me think you're worried about losing when stooping to such antics."

"You'll be the one pulling desperate moves before this is over." She focused on packing up and didn't look over. Her words reflected confidence, but her tone sounded doubtful.

"We'll see," I said, closing my briefcase.

I headed for the gate. "Let's go guys," I called back to the team.

Holding the gate open for our team, Brad stepped past me, followed by Courtney. I called to Joey, "Grab our box of the prosecution's discovery."

Nate waited for Joey to catch up and held the gate, while Joey hefted the Bankers Box onto a file cart. They caught up with us at the double doors leading into the hallway. Pushing an oak door open, a mob of reporters and camera crews blocked the way to the attorney and client meeting rooms.

Flashbulbs popped as the crowd converged on us. The place suddenly got hotter, and it became difficult to breathe. I inhaled, leveling myself.

"Mr. Dwyer, did your client have an affair with the victim?" a reporter asked.

"No comment," I said, pressing through them.

Another reported grabbed my arm. "Any comment about the bank video?"

"No." I yanked my arm free, continuing on.

Brad followed on my heels. A female reporter ducked between us and shoved a microphone under his nose. I recognized her as a short, perky anchor of a local news station. "Did you sleep with the victim on the day of her murder?"

Brad shook his head. "No."

I grabbed his arm and dragged him through the throng. Nate and Courtney fought to position themselves on either side of him. Now, we moved towards the meeting room like a presidential motorcade, with Joey bringing up the rear.

As we turned a corner, the press remained behind; some lingered in the hallway outside the courtroom, while others headed for the elevators to film and take photographs outside the courthouse.

Opening the heavy wooden door to a meeting room, I was relieved to find it unoccupied. Most of the time when you desperately need space for a conference, other attorneys and clients are already bogged down in the rooms.

We stepped inside. Brad took a seat in an oak chair, and Courtney sat next to him. Then, Nate sat down. I held the door open, as Joey wheeled the cart into the room.

"What the hell was that all about?" Brad snapped. "Sex on the day she died? I never had sex with her. Ever."

"Easy," I said, holding my hands up.

His face turned red, but he nodded, acquiescing to my request to calm down.

"Let's all just take a breather here," I said.

Joey took a seat at the table. I remained standing.

"What next?" asked Courtney.

"I'd like to run this out by the numbers." I turned to Brad. "We usually get a break after opening statements, which we use to discuss how they went. Judge Mathers wanted to start with a witness. So, this is our first opportunity to rehash the openings. We'll start there."

Brad nodded. "Makes sense."

"Any surprises?" I put the question to the group.

"The part about sexual relations on the day Audrey Martin died," Courtney said.

Joey interjected. "Maybe they're just throwing that at the wall, hoping it will stick."

"Alyson doesn't work that way," I said, shaking my head.

"What do you mean?" asked Brad.

"She wouldn't offer a point in an opening without having a piece of evidence to support her position. There has to be something we're missing."

"Like what?" Nate asked.

"Something like this would come from the Medical Examiner's report," Joey explained. "But we've been through the preliminary report and final report. There's nothing about sex."

"Where else could they get it?" Brad said.

"Nowhere," Joey replied. "That's the point. You'd have to have an examination of the body. Only the M.E. examines the corpse. It should be in the reports. But it's not. This is hinky."

"He's right," Courtney said, pulling out a notepad.

Thinking over the way the prosecution's file was delivered to our office, I got a keen sense they were trying to bury something. We'd found the video footage of Brad at the ATM machine, so that's what I figured they were trying to hide. We also found the footage of the van. Now, I came to believe they might have shoved other evidence in their file out of order.

"I'd bet my car there's a supplemental M.E. report," I said.

"Your car is getting some miles on it," Courtney chimed in.

Everyone chuckled at the moment of comic relief. I laughed and it felt good.

"Seriously, Joey and Nate, I want you both to go through that box with a fine-tooth comb." I pointed at the Bankers Box.

Joey sat back and shook his head. "We've been over everything. Plus, there's eleven more boxes back at the office. This is just what we've culled down."

"My guess is a supplemental M.E. report is stuck to the back of another document. If it's not in here, then we'll have to look for it when we get back to the office."

Courtney was following along, taking notes for the group. "Maybe we should send Nate or Joey back to the office. One can look through this box, while the other starts looking through the other boxes. We shouldn't wait until tonight. I've got to cross-examine the detective after lunch. And we don't need any surprises."

"Don't worry about it," I said.

"How can you say that?" she griped.

"Easily. They didn't bring it up during Malloy's direct examination. Joey's right. The evidence isn't something they found at the scene. The evidence comes from the M.E. There wouldn't be the proper foundation for it to come in under Malloy. So, we probably have until late tomorrow morning to find it."

"Sounds good," Brad said, agreeing with the plan.

"Anything else from their opening?"

They all shook their heads.

"What about Malloy's direct examination?"

"Came across about how we expected," Courtney said. "A couple areas we might want to hit differently on cross, but the gameplan doesn't change."

"Okay, you two get started," I said, to Joey and Nate, motioning to the box. "The three of us are going to grab lunch and work on Malloy's cross-examination."

They nodded, then rolled up their sleeves and dug into the box.

We stepped into the corridor and circulated around a back hallway, avoiding the circus in front of our courtroom. Then, we climbed into a packed elevator and headed down to the lobby.

Outside, a gaggle of press was gathered at the bottom of the stairs. We took a walkway leading towards the appeals courthouse, rather than the staircase in front to avoid a confrontation with reporters.

Walking over to a local sandwich shop, I'd already devised a few new points to hit on the cross-examination.

SIXTY

RETURNING FROM LUNCH, we settled into our chairs behind the defense counsel table and waited for the judge. We were ready to go. But I had some anxiety about turning over the reins at such an early stage in the trial.

Members of the press trickled in behind us, along with the family of the victim, interested parties, and the usual courthouse gadflies. Some of them bumped around in the pews, getting situated with laptops and notepads. The din of their movements was less frantic than when the trial had begun. They were more subdued, appearing less anxious, as they developed a comfort with the surroundings. Experienced reporters covering the crime beat likely didn't expect us to score many points on Malloy's cross-examination.

Alyson frantically flipped through her trial binder, trying to get a last-minute review of her materials. It seemed like she'd been at her table as soon as the bailiff had unlocked the courtroom doors. This was a sign that she'd gone out to lunch and returned early to further prepare.

"Make your cross as quickly as possible," I whispered to Courtney.

"What?" she asked, looking perplexed.

With a thumb, I indicated towards Alyson.

Courtney glanced over and smiled. "She's not prepared for the next witness?"

"Bingo. They spent all their time on Malloy, hoping her examination would take us through the end of the—."

"All rise." The bailiff at the side of the courtroom stepped forward, as the judge entered from a side door.

Everyone stood and waited for him.

The bailiff continued, "The Court of the Commonwealth of Massachusetts is now in session."

Judge Mathers took the bench. "You may be seated," he said, motioning with his hand.

He sat on a lofty oak perch and scanned the courtroom. Then, he turned to another bailiff on the far side of the room. "Let's bring the jury back in."

The bailiff nodded, then opened a rear door located near the jury box.

Jurors walked through the doorway and took their respective seats. None of them glanced over at Brad, which was a good sign for us. Similar to the press corps, they were beginning to grow accustomed to the process. This possibly meant they were listening to the evidence with a certain level of skepticism, keeping an open mind until they heard everything from both sides. But you could never know what they were thinking for sure.

Once they were settled, the judge looked over at me. Then, he turned to Alyson. "Where were we?" asked Judge Mathers.

"Detective Sergeant Kara Malloy was on the stand," Alyson replied.

"Well, let's get her back up here."

Malloy stood and walked towards the witness box. Her movements were swift and assured, reflecting more confidence than the last time she'd crossed the well. It had only been a few hours since she sat for her direct examination; however, it seemed like days.

She took a seat and looked at the judge expectantly.

"You are still under oath," he said. Then, he turned toward me. "You may procced."

I stood up. "Your Honor, my colleague, Courtney Richardson, will handle this examination."

"Very well." Judge Mathers looked over to Malloy. "You're still under oath."

The jury chuckled at his comment.

He looked at them quizzically. Then, he grinned. "Proceed," he said to Courtney after a moment.

She stood up and gathered a trial binder, notepad and pen. Courtney gracefully walked to the podium. Her three-inch heels did not disrupt her cadence. Wearing a tailored blue suit jacket and skirt, her attire and flowing blonde hair contrasted with the appearances of Alyson and Malloy. They looked like government employees, while Courtney reflected an air of the private sector. Her movements were fluid and projected confidence. She held her head high and took command of the courtroom.

After setting her materials on the podium, Courtney casually walked back to our table and grabbed a plastic cup. She poured water into the cup from the pitcher, located at the front of the table. She took a sip, then walked back to the podium. All eyes were glued to her.

Courtney took another sip of water, then looked at the witness. She observed Malloy like a wolf staring down unsuspecting prey. "Can you repeat your name for the record?"

"Detective Sergeant Kara Malloy."

"You were the lead investigating officer for this case, correct?"

Malloy pondered the question, as though it had never been posed to her before. "Yes. I suppose that is true."

"You would have knowledge of all aspects of the investigation, right?"

Malloy again paused. "That would be a fair statement. But I can't say that I know all the ins and outs of every aspect of the investigation undertaken by other officers."

"You would know the key evidence obtained in this case," Courtney said, raising her voice, showing the jury she was annoyed. This clued them in that Malloy was dodging the question. "Isn't that true?"

"You'd have to be more specific. I'm afraid that I cannot respond to generalities."

Glancing over at Alyson, I found her smirking.

A few members of the jury appeared peeved with Malloy. The rest seemed like they were anxiously awaiting substantive questioning.

You only have a few minutes to really capture the interest of jurors. Malloy was dodging simple background questions to use up time. The problem was if Courtney skipped ahead, Alyson would jump from her chair objecting to lack of foundation.

"You have knowledge about the key suspects?"

"That is correct."

"You have knowledge of the evidence gathered at the scene?"

"Correct."

"You have knowledge about the forensic tests and reports?"

Malloy nodded. "Yes."

Courtney then moved away from the podium and stepped into the well, prepared to ask a series of questions without any notes. "Detective Sergeant Malloy, you do not have any witnesses to place Mr. Wallace at the scene of the crime at the time Ms. Martin died, correct?"

"No. Unfortunately, we do not."

"You did not discover any of Mr. Wallace's DNA on Ms. Martin, right?"

"No. We did not."

"You found a scrap of skin under Ms. Martin's fingernail?"

"Yes."

"It did *not* belong to Mr. Wallace, correct?"

"Correct."

"Did that skin belong to Ms. Martin?"

"No."

Malloy was a well-controlled witness. Many witnesses try to fight the obvious and lose credibility with the jury. She knew to keep her answers short and avoid arguing with counsel. I found her highly intelligent and extremely well-prepared. This approach, however, was exactly what we had anticipated.

"You didn't find any of Ms. Martin's DNA on Mr. Wallace, right?"

"No. But we did not arrest him on the day of the murder."

"Nobody will testify for the prosecution that they witnessed Ms. Martin being pushed over the railing, correct?"

"That is correct."

"You deduced that she was murdered in part due to bruises on her thighs?"

"That is correct."

Courtney walked over to the far side of our counsel table, where the jury had a direct line of sight to her. "The bruises could be explained by Ms. Martin leaning against the railing and then falling over?"

Courtney pressed her thighs against the table, so the jury could get a visualization.

"Yes. But we also found scratches on her left leg."

"So, you agree the bruises could have occurred from Ms. Martin falling over on her own accord?"

"Objection." Alyson shot up from her chair.

"Basis," Judge Mathers asked.

"This calls for expert testimony. Such cross-examination is better suited for the Medical Examiner."

Judge Mathers looked at Alyson perplexed. "You had her testify as to her experience and qualifications. Then you asked her how the victim died. She commented on the bruises during your direct examination." He shook his head as though Alyson had launched a trivial objection. "No. No." He waved a hand at Alyson, dismissively. "Overruled."

Courtney waited a moment to make sure the judge was through. "You can answer," she said to Malloy.

"Well, yes. That is possible. But it's not highly probable."

"You put much evidential weight on the scratches on Ms. Martin's leg, right?"

"They are certainly part of the analysis."

"May I approach, Your Honor?" Courtney asked.

Judge Mathers waved for her to proceed. "Heavens yes."

Courtney walked up to the clerk's table and flipped through the prosecution's exhibits used on Malloy's direct examination. She pulled a foamboard from the stack. Placing the photograph of Martin's scratched thigh on the tripod, she used a pointer and tapped on the photograph. "These striations appear rather deep."

"You could say that."

"The scratches are fairly close together."

Malloy shrugged. "You could say so."

"The indentations are rather small, reflecting smaller hands, right?"

"Not necessarily."

"Well, the indentations are not from large hands, right?"

"You're getting into generalizations." Malloy sat up. "I can only comment on the evidence. That's a photograph of scratches."

"You don't know for certain who caused these scratches, right?"

"No. I don't."

"They could have been caused by a woman, right?"

"Possibly, but not likely."

"Heck, they could have been caused by Ms. Martin?"

"Possibly, but not likely."

"Did you take measurements of Ms. Martin's nails and make a comparison to these photographs?"

"No. We did not."

"You are capable of scaling the photographs?"

"We are."

"But you didn't bother to do so?"

"No. We did not think it necessary."

"Determining the skin under Ms. Martin's fingernail wasn't her DNA does not rule out that she could have scratched her thigh, right?"

"Correct."

"In fact, you cannot say for certain the scratches were made at the time of Ms. Martin's death?"

"No. We can't."

"Isn't it true that you didn't review Ms. Martin's fingernails to see if they were the source of the scratches because you were dead set on pinning this death on Mr. Wallace?"

"No. That's not true at all. But we did have a confession."

"Objection!" I bellowed. "Move to strike."

Judge Mathers looked at me confused. "Who's handling this examination anyway?" He shook his head. "Only one lawyer at a time."

"We object to this hearsay statement," Courtney said. "And ask for it to be stricken."

Judge Mathers nodded. "Sustained." He looked at the jury. "You will disregard the last comment by the witness."

Many of the jurors nodded, as though understanding the reasoning for the instruction.

"You and the prosecutor were after headlines?" Courtney continued. "And you got them?"

"Objection!" Alyson bellowed. "Argumentative."

Judge Mathers shook his head. "Miss, all cross-examination is argumentative. But it was a compound question. Miss Richardson, please ask one question at a time."

"I'll strike the questions," Courtney said, walking back to the podium.

"Very well," He nodded, satisfied.

"You only really considered Mr. Wallace as a suspect, right?"

"All evidence pointed to him. We considered all leads, but the investigation pointed to him as the primary suspect."

"Did you consider Keith Evers?"

Alyson had been fishing through a binder and froze when hearing the question. She was surprised we'd found Evers's fingerprint in the heap of documents she'd sent to our office. We honestly might have missed it, except Beckerman had previously clued us in. We'd deliberately looked for information about Evers.

"Excuse me?" asked Malloy.

Judge Mathers frantically waved his hands at Malloy. "You. You… let her ask the questions," he said, motioning towards Courtney.

"Evers was a person of interest, but he was never really a suspect," Malloy finally said.

"You found his fingerprint on the front door, right?"

"Sure."

"Did you ever question him?"

"No. We ruled him out."

"Mr. Wallace doesn't have a criminal history, but Evers has committed assault and battery and other crimes, right?"

Alyson sprung from her chair. "Objection."

"That's another compound question," the judge said. "I'll let you have it. But don't do it again." He looked at Malloy. "Go ahead and answer about this fella."

"We didn't think he had motive as to the victim."

"The Wallaces had previously taken out a restraining order on Evers, right?"

"Yes, that is correct."

A reporter in the gallery gasped at this development. Others were frantically scratching notes or clacking on keyboards. Some of the jurors had begun to nod off. Now, they all sat up in their chairs, anxious to see where this was going.

"A 209A restraining order concerns matters where the person is believed to be violent?" Courtney said, moving alongside the jury box.

"I'm afraid that's more of a legal conclusion," said Malloy.

Judge Mathers slammed his gavel on the bench. "Miss, you're a police officer and you'll answer the question about restraining orders."

Several jurors flinched when the gavel came down. A couple of them scowled at Malloy, like they felt she was holding back, possibly hiding something.

"Yes. They tend to deal with fear of violence."

"They are issued… from your experience as a police officer, under a reasonable belief standard and not a subjective standard, correct?"

"Correct."

"You don't know where Evers was on the night of Ms. Martin's death," Courtney said, moving closer to the witness box.

"That's correct."

"You had blinders on, focusing on Mr. Wallace?" Courtney stood four feet from Malloy.

"No. We did not."

"You focused on Mr. Wallace after finding him at an ATM machine located near his home and near where he works?" Courtney asked, raising her voice.

"We obtained CCTV footage of him near the scenc of the crime around the time the crime was committed."

"Do murderers usually go banking before committing a crime?" Courtney quipped.

"Objection," Alyson called, standing up. "Calls for speculation."

Judge Mathers canted his head, trying to follow. "She's not asking about what was in the defendant's mind," he said, pointing to Courtney. "She's asking about the witness's experience as a police officer," he said, motioning to Malloy. "I'm afraid you opened the door for this."

Alyson sat down. Then, she nodded, instructing Malloy to answer.

Malloy said, "I cannot get into the minds of murderers and criminal conduct. We find that people act in strange and bizarre ways before and after committing a crime. And when dealing with crimes of passion… Well, it's possible the defendant didn't plan to kill the victim until after he left the bank."

I was on my feet. "Move to strike. That was unresponsive."

The judge shook his head. "She answered the question. It was responsive. You just don't like the answer."

Sitting down, I shook my head, dismayed with the ruling.

Judge Mathers stared at me. "Counselor, please… One lawyer at a time."

I nodded. "Yes, sir."

Courtney had discreetly moved away from the witness box during my colloquy with the trial judge. Now, she stood next to the podium, located at the far corner of the witness box. All eyes were upon her. Jurors appeared anxious to hear the next question.

"You don't have any direct evidence placing Mr. Wallace at the scene around the time Ms. Martin died, correct?"

All the jurors spun their heads, like watching a tennis match. They eagerly awaited Malloy's response.

"Yes," Malloy said after a moment.

"In fact, you have evidence placing Mr. Wallace at a bank around the time of the death?"

The jury stared at Malloy even harder than the last question.

Malloy pondered her response. "We have CCTV footage of the defendant at a bank, which was located near the scene of the crime. And the time stamp on the video is within a window of opportunity that we estimate the time of death."

"Who reported the death to the police?"

"The defendant."

"So, other than Mr. Wallace calling the police and providing comments to officers, you would not have had any evidence that he'd even been in the house that evening, right?"

Malloy sat up and looked towards Alyson. Glancing over at the prosecution table, I watched Alyson shake her head. She was instructing the witness not to unload with her response. Clearly, Malloy was thinking of saying: *Other than the dead body*.

Such an answer would inflame the jury in this case. It would debase the loss of life.

"Unfortunately, we do not have a witness seeing him enter the house or CCTV footage of the front door."

Courtney marched to the halfway point between the podium and the witness box. A few jurors in the front row glanced up at her. "Yes or no," Courtney snapped. "Other than Mr. Wallace's comments to the police, you do not have any evidence that he was even in the house on the evening that Audrey Martin died?"

"No. We do not."

"That's all I have at this time," Courtney said to Judge Mathers.

"Very well," he replied.

She grabbed her materials and walked back to our table. Courtney sat down, and she exhaled.

"Any redirect?" Judge Mathers asked Alyson.

She appeared to consider the question carefully. "I have a few questions," Alyson finally said.

He nodded. "Go ahead."

Alyson stood behind her table and leaned slightly towards the witness. "You were asked on direct examination whether you have information as to whether the defendant was in the house where the crime was committed. Do you recall that question?"

Malloy nodded. "Yes."

"Did you have any evidence that the defendant was in the house around the time the murder was committed?" Her question was meant to cast dispersion upon the defense, making it seem like we had merely harangued with syntax.

"I most certainly do."

"What is that evidence?"

"The defendant told us that he found the victim. And we determined the time of death to have occurred shortly before he found her."

"So, he was in the house around the time Audrey Martin was murdered?"

I nudged Courtney.

"Objection!" she said, rising to her feet.

Judge Mathers looked at her confused. "Basis?"

"Leading," Courtney said.

The perplexed look never left the judge's face.

"This is a redirect. The witness is the prosecution's witness."

Judge Mathers nodded, finally understanding. "Sustained. You can't go around leading your own witnesses. Rephrase the question."

"Sure." Alyson stepped around her table and stood directly in front of it. "What time did you get the call from the defendant that Audrey Martin was dead?"

"It was 11:30 P.M."

"And what time did your investigation place the time of death?"

"Between 10:30 and 11:30 P.M."

Alyson smiled triumphantly. "I've completed my examination of this witness."

Judge Mathers did not intend to allow us further questions. He didn't even look our way. Instead, he kept his eyes trained on Alyson. She did not notice because she was returning to her seat, while he watched her sashay towards her chair.

Alyson looked at her co-counsel and smiled. She whispered something, and it sounded like she asked how she'd done. The junior lawyer looked nervous and pointed towards the judge.

She looked towards the bench and realized the judge was watching her. The jury and all the courtroom spectators were watching her. "What?" she muttered.

"Please call your next witness," Judge Mathers said.

Alyson glanced at the clock. Panic registered in her eyes. She shot upright. "You Honor, the Commonwealth asks for a short recess before starting the next witness."

"Do you have the witness in the courtroom?"

She glanced back into the gallery. "Yes," she said, turning to the judge.

"Why don't we get started then?"

"Your Honor, I think we can all use a short restroom break," Alyson said, with her voice quivering.

Judge Mathers studied her keenly, as if trying to decide whether she had a legitimate reason for taking a break. Sitting there with pursed lips, he seemed to doubt it was about use of the facilities. "Very well," he finally said.

A bailiff stepped forward. He went through the preamble for vacating the courtroom.

The judge stepped from the bench, and the jury funneled out a side door. Before the last jurors exited the courtroom, Alyson had already bolted for the door.

SIXTY-ONE

WATCHING ALYSON exit the courtroom, I tried to ascertain the dilemma emanating from the prosecution's camp. We'd jabbed them with a few points, but Malloy had stood up as a witness. I couldn't discern what they thought might have gone wrong.

Both teams stepped into the hallway and were met with reporters blocking the way to the meeting rooms.

Someone shoved a recorder under Alyson's nose. "Is the case against Wallace thin?" the reporter asked.

Alyson shook her head. "Our case is quite strong."

We plied our way through the mob, and I couldn't hear anything else. It seemed Alyson had stopped and continued speaking with the press.

Damage control, I thought.

Seasoned spectators of criminal trials, certain members of the press were probably shocked at the lack of evidence presented by the Commonwealth's opening witness. This made me wonder how the jury was digesting the case. Jurors aren't experienced in watching trials like the press, so I couldn't place much weight on reactions from reporters.

Entering a conference room, we all took our respective positions. I stood pacing before the group, trying to decide what to say.

"That went well," Joey said, smiling.

Courtney didn't look convinced. "I'm not so sure."

"You were in the heat of things," Joey said, attempting to mollify her.

Brad shook his head, and said, "I can't be sure, either."

Everyone turned to me, waiting for my input. At times, people think because you have a lot of experience, you can read the development of a trial better. Yet, no matter how many trials you've undertaken, it's always a bit of a guessing game. Often you read the jury correctly. However, there are times when you get blindsided by a result.

"This is a tough call," I finally said. "From the commotion outside…" I pointed at the door towards the corridor. "The press corps appears surprised by the lack of any meaningful direct evidence."

"Isn't that a good thing?" asked Brad.

"Yeah. But the jury isn't as experienced. We can't assume things are so clear to them. This case is circumstantial. But people sometimes get convicted based upon slight evidence."

"But those cases have a clear motive," Courtney said. "We don't."

She was right. The prosecution had scant evidence to argue an affair. But they didn't have anything to explain a murder. Without direct evidence there was an affair, they couldn't show with any level of credibility that an affair went sour.

"We need to keep her comment in mind," I said, indicating to Courtney.

They all nodded, following my point.

"What's got them nervous?" Brad said.

"They think they're losing," Joey said.

Brad looked at him. Joey sounded credible. He had a bird's eye seat in the gallery, with an opportunity to observe opposing counsel and the jury. I wasn't certain.

"My thought," I said, shaking my head. "They simply weren't prepared for us to accelerate Malloy's testimony." I directed my attention to Brad. "When lawyers prepare for a case, they focus on what happens first and what is most important. Malloy was first, and she was the lead investigator. While her testimony might have been a wash to some extent, she held up quite well. They spent a lot of time with her. Any shortcomings related to the evidence and not her."

"So, where does this leave us?" Nate finally chimed in.

"They might not be prepared for the next witness," I said.

"Who will it be?" asked Joey.

"The Medical Examiner was in the courtroom. They'll probably call her."

Courtney grinned. "Who's going to do the cross?"

"I'll handle it. This could get ugly."

"We've got to get back in there," she said. "This was supposed to be a five-minute break."

SIXTY-TWO

THE HALLWAY WAS QUIET, so I knew we were late returning to the courtroom. Stepping inside, the judge was already on the bench.

Joey and Nate found seats in the gallery, while the rest of us hustled to our table.

All eyes were on us as we got situated. You could hear a pin drop.

I got my notepad and pen ready.

"Glad you could make it," Judge Mathers said.

Looking up, we locked glances. He stared at me through thick lenses. I smiled, trying to disarm him. He didn't smile back. The hostility caused me to gulp. The judge continued the stare-down for a moment, as if quietly admonishing me in front of everyone.

Judge Mathers turned his attention to Alyson. "Your next witness?"

"The Commonwealth calls Detective Aron Chandler," Alyson said standing up.

As Chandler walked to the witness box, she casually stepped over to the podium. It was still located at the far corner of the jury box. Her demeanor was calm and collected. All the prior histrionics had slipped away.

I got the feeling they weren't planning to accomplish much with this witness, so the pressure was low. They wanted to kill time to work on the M.E.'s testimony during the evening. Steampipes rattled and hissed. The temperature in the courtroom had risen. I started feeling the heat.

They merely went through Chandler's involvement with the investigation. He commented on the chain of custody, and they entered emails and text messages into evidence. This included communications between Brad and Phillip Danforth, as well as between Brad and Audrey Martin.

I didn't object to the questions, even when they were leading. We did not object to entering the communications and data, either. This seemed to curry some favor with the trial judge. He appreciated a streamlined process.

The testimony and exhibits were merely foundation for a later question.

Alyson developed some line of questioning around the fact that Danforth had considerably more experience than Martin. Danforth had worked on several high-profile campaigns. He would have been the go-to aide.

Eventually, Alyson got to the salient point; she moved into the well. "Detective Chandler, did you find anything unusual about the communications you obtained in your investigation?"

"Yes."

"What did you find?"

"There were considerably more communications occurring between the defendant and the victim than the amount between the defendant and the senior aide."

"Anything else?"

"Many of the communications between the defendant and the victim were at night," he said, smiling. Chandler gloated for a moment, and members of the jury shook their heads.

Alyson stepped closer to the jury box. "Did you arrive at any conclusions—"

"Objection!" I bellowed, standing up.

Judge Mathers glanced at me and started nodding, as if he agreed with me.

"Side bar?" Alyson stammered.

The judge took each of us in, then he motioned for us to approach.

"State the basis of the objection on the record," Judge Mathers said to me.

"Calls for speculation."

"I tend to agree," the judge said.

"The witness is commenting on his own conclusions from the investigation," Alyson said, shoving her way closer to the bench.

"But he's speculating about what this evidence means," the judge replied.

"He's allowed..."

Judge Mathers waved a hand at her. "Not on thin evidence like this." He shook his head. "The objection is sustained. You can rephrase the question."

Alyson inhaled. She was pissed off.

The judge shooed us away.

We walked back to our tables, and I grinned at Courtney, showing the jury we had prevailed on the dispute. This also was a play to the jury, demonstrating to them we thought the issue and the case was going our way. In reality, Alyson had made some good points and there was a compelling argument to say she was correct.

Returning to the podium, Alyson faced the witness. "Can you tell us what you did after obtaining and reviewing the evidence we just discussed?"

Chandler looked perplexed for a moment. He paused and mulled it over. "We arrested the defendant?" he finally said.

"Did any of the evidence we discussed contribute to your decision to make an arrest?"

"Yes."

"Explain how?"

"We believed the number and extent of communications with the junior aide reflected a personal relationship beyond the level of work-related communications."

"Was the evidence we discussed the only reason you arrested the defendant?"

Chandler smiled and shook his head. "No. We had all the evidence that Detective Sergeant Malloy has testified to as well."

Alyson smiled proudly, as though Chandler had hit a triple and was rounding second base. Then, she turned to the judge. "That concludes my examination for now," she said, and headed for her seat.

The direct examination was over soon after it began.

"Any cross?" the judge asked me.

The question suggested we didn't need to bother cross-examining the witness. The judge likely hadn't attributed much weight to Chandler's testimony. It was all conjecture based upon scant evidence.

"Yes," I said, standing up.

"Make it quick," the judge said. "It's now getting late."

We couldn't trust the jury to come to the same conclusion as the judge. But his point was well taken. This needed to be short and to the point.

Stepping into the well without a notepad or any documents, I faced the witness and stared him down. Chandler sat there with a hard look on his face. I continued to stalk him. He finally got uncomfortable and smirked.

"What's this?" he said. "Gonna ask any questions?"

Judge Mathers smacked the bench with his hand. He looked at Chandler. "Son, you'll let him ask the questions," he said, pointing at me.

"Yes, sir," Chandler replied.

"And you," Judge Mathers said, "you hurry it along."

"Very well, Your Honor," I said.

Then, I moved a little closer to the witness. "You completed forensics on the emails and the text messages, right?"

"Sure," Chandler said, shrugging.

"You didn't find a single communication expressly demonstrating an affair, right?"

"Well, ahh," Chandler fumbled. "We… found a high volume of—"

"Objection!" I barked. "Move to strike, the question is non-responsive."

"Sustained," Judge Mathers said.

"Yes or no, sir. You did not find any evidence expressly demonstrating an affair."

"No, we did not."

"Thank you." I moved a little closer. "You found a higher volume of communications between the decedent and Bradford Wallace than with the other aide, right? That's your evidence?"

"Yes. But also more communications at night."

"Couldn't that be explained by the two of them working on a project that did not involve the other aide?"

"Sure. But in these cases…"

"Thank you," I said, stepping back from the witness. "You answered the question."

"That's all I have, Your Honor." I turned and walked back to my table.

Sitting down, Brad grabbed my arm. "You nailed it," he said.

Courtney couldn't restrain her grin. I glanced at the jury. A couple of them looked me directly in the eyes and shook their heads in amazement.

They're not buying the prosecution's theory, I thought.

The judge looked at Alyson. "Re-direct?"

She seemed to muddle it over. "No," she said after a moment.

"The court is now in recess," Judge Mathers said, exiting the bench.

SIXTY-THREE

WE SAT HUNKERED down at a local watering hole, trying to recap the day of trial. Our team ended up at the posh bar, located across the street from my office. We hadn't even stopped to unload our trial bags.

After the jury had left the courtroom, I decided we needed to clear out and find someplace to regroup. We'd dodged the press, then trekked down Court Street. A frigid wind blew through the corridor of high-rises. Stopping in a coffee shop wasn't in the cards. The stress pulsating through my veins required a cocktail to take the edge off. Maybe two.

We sat on leather barstools. Brad sat to my left and Courtney was on the right. Joey and Nate huddled around her, giving the client space. Our bags were piled on the floor behind us. The file cart was surrounded by briefcases, making the area resemble a hotel lobby. An empty stool was heaped with our overcoats.

The place was quiet. It was still early, and professionals were just beginning to trickle in from nearby office buildings. We had a decent amount of space as a buffer to talk shop.

Nobody had begun to order meals. Familiar scents of seafood and burgers didn't emanate from the kitchen. This was a cocktail crowd. Dinner patrons wouldn't arrive for another hour. A flatscreen above the bar broadcasted a sports talk show. The hosts were discussing the latest trades around the NBA.

Thankfully, none of the televisions in the restaurant were broadcasting the local news. Given the amount of press coverage at the courthouse, I expected our case would consume a lot of airtime.

Even with the amount of publicity to date, we didn't attract much attention at the bar. A few people pointed to us. Most appeared preoccupied with their own shop talk.

Aside from murmurings about office politics, we could only hear the occasional din of silverware clattering against glass as the staff prepared for the dinner crowd. We didn't have to worry about being overheard.

"How do you think it went today?" I said, looking at Joey.

"As well as it could go," he replied. "But overall it was a wash."

"What do you mean?" asked Brad.

"He means," I cut in. "We countered anything presented by the prosecution."

"But that's good, right?" Brad said.

"It's good when defending a case on circumstantial evidence. We left the jury with a lot of doubt. But—"

"What?" Brad insisted.

"Nothing dramatic happened today to knock back their case."

"Do we need to do that?"

"No. But it's nice when it happens."

A bartender walked over. He wore a professional outfit with a vest. "Can I help you?" he asked.

"I'll have a gin and tonic," I said.

"Gin. Always gin," he said with a smile.

"David?" I asked the bartender.

"Right." He grinned. "I've waited on you guys a few times."

"Then you know the deal?"

He nodded. "Shrimp cocktail, potato skins, a cosmopolitan for the lady…" He pointed at Courtney. Then, he looked at Nate. "A Kettle One." He glanced over to Joey. "Sam Adams on draft."

Everyone laughed.

"Are we that obvious?" Courtney said.

"Pretty consistent," David said. "I like that."

"How so?" asked Joey.

"Solid decision makers. Don't waste any time." He looked at Brad. "You're the only mystery here."

Brad hiked his shoulders. "I'll have a Tanqueray as well."

"You've got it." David turned away to prepare our orders.

"Okay, so that's a thirty-thousand-foot level viewpoint," I said. "Nate, how we coming with the jurors?"

We had assigned Nate to focus on the jury, while Joey was to watch opposing counsel and the jury. Courtney and I would keep an eye on the judge, switching it up depending upon who wasn't taking a witness.

"Most of the jurors seem to be paying attention," Nate said. "They are watching every detail, not tuning out." He paused. "Some of them have shaken their heads, dissatisfied with the prosecution's evidence. But they are hard to read as a group."

"How do they react to us?" I said.

"I've seen jurors nod at times, like they understand a point you've tried to make."

"Yeah. I've seen that too," Joey said. "Like they think it's a good point."

"Let's not get ahead of ourselves. I think we have a long way to go before we convince them Brad's innocent." I shrugged. "People tend to think when someone is arrested, the person did something wrong, despite how many news shows run stories about innocent people being convicted of crimes."

"So, what do we need to work on?" Brad said.

"There's still a document likely missing," I replied. "Joey and Nate are going to have to work steadily combing through the prosecution's discovery file until they find it. If they don't locate it tonight, they're going to have to stay back at the office tomorrow and keep digging through the file. We'll need Emily to step in and watch the trial if they're not able."

Everyone nodded and understood the gameplan.

David returned and placed our drink orders on the bar. Then, he brought over the appetizers. "Anything else?" he said.

I glanced around. Everyone shrugged or shook their heads.

"We're all set for now," I replied. "Thanks."

We then spent a considerable amount of time talking about various points made and how to approach the next day of trial. A key witness would testify, and I needed to have a sharp cross-examination to push the jury in our direction.

The bustle of patrons filling the restaurant sent a cacophony of noise throughout the place. Scents from the grill wafted into the dining area, as the dinner crowd geared up. People filled the stools around us, and we had to give up the extra stool and drape our overcoats over the backs of our chairs. We could no longer strategize for fear of being overhead.

Polishing off my drink, I contemplated another. I wondered if we should call it a night. There was more work to do.

A smack on my shoulder brought me out of thought.

Turning, I found the big union boss standing behind me.

He forced a smile. "Mr. Dwyer," he said, speaking in a gruff Boston accent, "Mr. Flannigan would like to speak with you."

I glanced over and saw Michael Flannigan holding court at a nearby table.

Flannigan looked my way. Then, he waved for me to join him.

I got up and plodded over to his table.

Michael Flannigan sat at the head of the table. He was flanked by businesspeople, lawyers, and politicians. Every seat was taken along both sides of the table.

A gentleman seated next to Flannigan got up and grabbed a chair from another table. Then, he squeezed in at the far side of the table, near a female partner from Flannigan's firm.

"Sit down," Flannigan said, motioning to the empty seat.

He had a full head of gray hair. It was thin and longer than most corporate types would grow their hair. Flannigan resembled the talk show host Donahue, sans the outdated glasses. A partner at a mid-sized firm, he served on Boston's City Counsel. He had an unsuccessful run for mayor. Flannigan always wore a suit and sat there with the jacket hung over the back of his chair. His belly stretched his dress shirt at the waist.

I took a seat. "What's up?"

Flannigan shook his head and waved his hand dismissively. "What are you drinking?"

"Tanqueray and tonic," I replied.

"Okay." He raised a hand and indicated towards me with two fingers.

A waiter rushed over. "May I help you?"

"He'll have a T&T," Flannigan said.

The waiter nodded, then he hurried towards the bar.

Everyone at the table remained engaged in conversation, like the two of us didn't exist. It felt as though we were in a bubble, without a care of the rest of the world. Flannigan did not make a lot of money, but he wielded tremendous power in Boston. He was a personification of the axiom that power and influence weren't necessarily driven by wealth.

A moment later, the waiter returned with my drink. "Sorry for the wait," he said, apologetically.

"That's fine," I said. It was the fastest service I'd ever received in my life.

"Anything else?" asked the waiter, clasping his hands together.

"No. That will be all," I said.

He walked off and Flannigan watched him leave. Then, he turned to me and said, "I heard you did well in court today."

The comment came as a surprise. I couldn't believe he'd gotten intelligence on the trial that fast. "I cannot comment on an ongoing matter," I finally said.

"Sure. But I already know this to be the case."

We both sipped our cocktails for a moment. Mine was stronger than usual.

"Your client isn't very popular in this town right now," Flannigan said.

"My concern is with defending a client. Regardless of how he's perceived by others."

"There are *important* people who would like to see him derailed from this trial. Whether he gets convicted, or just neutralized, it doesn't really matter. So long as he's no longer a factor."

Flannigan was a powerful local politician, connected to some well-heeled people, but I couldn't place who exactly he was talking about. The unions didn't care for Brad, and I wondered if there could be others.

"You don't need to know who I'm talking about," he said, as if reading my thoughts.

"I'm not sure what you're getting at," I said.

"You do a good job with this case. Wallace gets neutralized as a political factor, and your firm will be added to the list of firms representing the city."

I blanched. The statement came out of left field.

"You know the city gets sued all the time for trip and falls in the wintertime. Icy sidewalks, roads, public parking lots. We also see lawsuits arising from accidents in city vehicles and falls on public property, like Boston Common."

He was talking about a franchise client. The type of steady work that can keep a small firm afloat in hard times. You wouldn't need a line of credit to make payroll. I simply didn't know what to say.

"How's a file a month sound?" he continued.

That amount of work could potentially cover our overhead. All the other files would be gravy.

"You choke on a bone?" he asked, then laughed.

"Well, I have a job to do. I can't compromise a client."

"Figured you'd say that." He nodded. "You're known around town as an honest player. Old-fashioned hard work and honesty. I like that. But you must understand, people get ahead in this world by trading chips. You've got a chip to play."

"Sure. But my duty is to my client. I can't just phone it in."

"You thought about it when I first put it out there." Flannigan smiled, then he sat back in his chair. Took a sip of his drink. "I suggest you keep thinking about it."

"Sure." I stood up. "I've got to get back to my group."

He nodded. "Enjoy the drink."

Walking back over to the bar, I took a long swig of my drink. Then, I set the half empty glass down. "Let's wrap this up," I said.

"What did *he* want?" Courtney said.

"Nothing. He was just fishing for intel on the case."

"What did you say?"

"Just that I couldn't talk about an ongoing matter," I said, digging out the firm credit card from my wallet, tucked away in a pocket of my overcoat.

"Okay, I'm ready to go," Joey said, hopping down from his stool.

"Me too," Brad said.

We wriggled into our coats, then grabbed our bags and headed for the door.

Courtney and Nate stayed behind to pay the tab.

Outside, the cold night bit into my exposed skin. I gave instructions to Brad about meeting the next morning at the Starbucks with the copper teapot hanging above the door, so we could regroup and shield him from the press on the way into court.

We bid our farewells, then I trotted across State Street with Joey pulling the file cart behind him.

When we reached the other side of the street, I turned back and helped him jockey the cart over the frozen ruts running in front of the curb cut. Brad stood on the opposite side of the street at the corner, waiting for a car service. He looked like a lame duck. Vulnerable.

I grabbed hold of the handle to the cart and yanked it over the dirty mound of ice. Then, I turned up the sidewalk before Brad could exchange glances with me.

Hastening towards the office, Flannigan's proposal ran through my mind like an illicit offer made while you're in an exclusive relationship. One you must refuse, but it haunts your mind, even after you've declined the overture.

SIXTY-FOUR

RETURNING TO COURT the next morning at nine o'clock, Judge Mathers took the bench appearing more disheveled than usual. We waited at our counsel tables while he shifted through folders on his desk. The gallery was hushed, and reporters were slumped in the pews.

He finally looked at Alyson and said, "Call your next witness."

"The Commonwealth calls Dr. Elizabeth Chenoweth," Alyson said, standing.

"Very well," Judge Mathers said.

A slender woman conservatively dressed rose from a bench seat located behind the prosecution table. Her hair was gray and fine, cut at shoulder-length. She pushed through the gate and stepped past the oak railing, which separated the gallery from the rest of the courtroom.

Dr. Chenoweth gracefully walked across the well of the courtroom. She took a position alongside the witness stand and waited for the judge to swear her in. Afterward, she sat down in the box. A seasoned witness, she knew exactly what to do. I figured she'd probably testified countless times and felt comfortable in court.

Alyson grabbed a binder and moved to the podium, located near the end of the jury box.

The Medical Examiner waited for the prosecutor to get situated. Dr. Chenoweth wore spectacles with platinum wiring, which sat comfortably on the bridge of her long, beakish nose.

Glancing up, Alyson began her direct examination. She had the M.E. state her full name for the record, then she went into the doctor's credentials.

Dr. Chenoweth had gone to Williams College and Harvard University Medical School. She'd completed her residency at

Massachusetts General Hospital. She had undergone further training in pathology and eventually became a Medical Examiner. Now, she had over two decades of experience.

Thereafter, Dr. Chenoweth explained how she had become involved in the matter. She testified as to when she first saw the body of Audrey Martin. Then, Dr. Chenoweth walked through her medical examination in detail. This expended a lot of time. Alyson covered the minutiae to provide for all the factual findings, which would support the witness's opinions. I noticed several of the jurors tuning out. One juror seemed to be nodding off.

They covered the bruising on the front of Audrey Martin's thighs, the scrapes along the left thigh, and a skull fracture. Dr. Chenoweth stated the skull fracture was the cause of death.

All of this was merely foundation for a crucial opinion the witness would provide. Namely, that Audrey Martin died from a homicide rather than an accidental death. Sitting anxiously at the edge of my chair, I took copious notes. I wondered how they would handle the opinion.

Eventually, Alyson walked over to the clerk's table. She pulled out the foamboards of crime scene photographs and shuffled through them. She selected one to use in her examination.

A photograph depicted Audrey Martin on the patio, with a tape measure running alongside the body; it extended to the vertical plane where the balcony lined up with the patio below. Then, she grabbed another blowup of the scene where the picture was taken from the balcony above.

The latter photograph distorted the scene slightly, making it appear as though Audrey Martin was further away from the terrace. Her head faced towards the balcony, making it seem as though she'd been hurled over the railing.

Alyson casually set up the foamboards in front of the witness.

She put the one with a measuring tape on the tripod, while resting the other photograph on the floor by leaning it against the legs of the easel.

Then, she stepped a few feet away and looked at the witness.

"During the course of your examination, did you consider factors other than the examination of the body to arrive at your conclusion?" asked Alyson.

"Yes."

"Why is that?"

"Many times, as in a case like this, the manner of the death is not readily discernible from the cause of death," Dr. Chenoweth said with authority.

"Meaning?"

"When you have a gunshot wound, you know there has been a homicide. A fall from a balcony needs to be reviewed with consideration as to an examination of the body in connection with physical evidence at the scene."

"Did you find any evidence at the scene, which you found useful in reaching your conclusions?"

"Yes," Dr. Chenoweth said, nodding.

"Care to explain?"

"The body was found with the head facing the balcony, suggesting the victim had been tossed head-over-heels. You can see this in both photographs." She pointed at the foamboards. "There was also an appreciable distance from the balcony to where the victim was found, suggesting that she had been thrown over the railing, rather than a straight shot downward."

Alyson nodded, as though indicating the points made sense. "Did you arrive at an opinion in this matter?"

"Yes, I did."

"What was the basis of your opinion?"

"Considering all of the facts we have discussed here, including, but not limited to, the location of the body from the balcony, the direction of the body on the patio, the scratches on the victim's leg, the forcible bruising on the victim's thighs, I arrived at an opinion."

"Kindly tell us your opinion," asked Alyson.

"I determined Audrey Martin suffered from a homicide. She was thrown over the railing of the balcony."

Alyson smiled coyly. "Can you state your opinion to a reasonable degree of certainty?"

"I most certainly can," Dr. Chenoweth said, "and I do."

"Do you have any other opinions?" Alyson asked.

"Yes. During my examination, we found traces of lubricant in her vagina," Dr. Chenoweth said. "This led me to opine the victim had sexual relations prior to her death."

"That's all the questions I have at this time," Alyson said, suavely.

Alyson clearly felt the witness had nailed the examination. She started towards the foamboards, intending to collect them. There was a spring in her step.

"Cross?" Judge Mathers said to me.

Standing, I briskly stepped into the well. "You can leave those," I said to Alyson.

Alyson straightened up and headed back to her table.

"Dr. Chenoweth," I said, kindly. "There was a piece of skin found under Audrey Marin's fingernail, correct?"

"I believe so."

"You didn't account for that in your testimony."

"It wasn't a factor that I relied upon."

"Well, couldn't the scratches on her leg have been made from the victim?"

"That's possible, but unlikely."

I moved closer to the witness box. "Do you arrive at that position because the skin under her nail didn't belong to Ms. Martin?"

"In part."

"The skin under Ms. Martin's fingernail didn't belong to the defendant, either?"

"That is correct."

Suddenly, the gallery came to life. A cacophony of activity emanated from the pews as soon as the last point was made. Jurors snapped to attention. The point wasn't missed. DNA evidence found on the victim could mean somebody else killed her.

"So, someone else might have scratched her leg?"

"Possibly."

"The DNA under the fingernail didn't necessarily come from the scratch on Ms. Martin's leg, right?"

"True."

"And Ms. Martin might have scratched her own leg, correct?"

"Possibly, but—"

"Thank you," I said, sternly. "You answered my question."

Reporters in the gallery heated up their interest further, scribbling notes, flipping pages in notepads, and clacking on keyboards to laptops. The jury locked on the witness.

"You ruled this as a murder?" I said.

"I concluded the victim died as a result of a homicide," Dr. Chenoweth said, poised.

Stepping to the foamboard on the easel, I pointed to Audrey Martin's head. "The direction of her fall could have been caused by her teetering over the railing without being pushed, right?"

"Possibly."

"The vertical line, from the edge of the balcony to where her head rested, was measured at two and a half feet, correct?"

"That sounds about right."

"Doctor, it's possible that distance could be covered from her falling without being pushed?"

"Yes, that is possible."

"Dr. Chenoweth," I said, intensely. "You reviewed the police report?"

"Yes, I did."

"There wasn't any sign of a struggle in the adjacent room?"

"No there was not."

"You cannot say for certain when the scratches appeared on her leg?"

"No, I cannot." She shrugged. "It was likely within twenty-four hours of her death."

"Bruising on the front of the thighs would be consistent with her teetering over the railing without being pushed, right?" I said, raising my voice slightly.

"Possibly."

"Doctor, you didn't undertake any accident re-creation efforts?" I insisted.

"No. That wouldn't be in my area of specialty."

"You do not have *any* qualifications as to the amount of force that would be necessary for someone of Ms. Martin's weight and size to land where she did?"

"No. I would not."

"You've testified that it's possible Ms. Martin fell over the balcony, did you not?"

"Objection," Alyson called. "Mischaracterizes her prior testimony."

Judge Mathers shook his head. "I think the question is asking her to characterize her prior testimony." He looked at the witness. "You may answer."

"I suppose my responses could lead to that conclusion."

"And your opinion that she was pushed is not based on any biomechanics study or report, right?"

"That is correct."

"So, you can't say with any reasonable certainty that she was pushed?"

"Objection!" Alyson bellowed.

"Basis?" asked the judge.

"Argumentative. He's badgering the witness."

"That's what lawyers do during cross-examination," Judge Mathers said, shaking his head. "Overruled. The witness will answer."

Dr. Chenoweth frowned. "I seriously doubt this young woman simply fell over the railing."

"You do not have a scientific study to support your opinion, right?" I said calmly.

"Not as to biomechanics. No."

"It's possible she fell," I said, lowering my tone.

"I believe we've covered this already. But yes, it is possible."

"You think she was pushed?"

"I believe so."

"Doctor, isn't it true the evidence you are relying upon could equally speak to her falling as her being pushed?"

"You could look at it that way. But I do not believe it to be the case."

"This is a fifty-fifty likelihood of a fall verse a push, right?"

"Without a biomechanics study, you make a valid point. However, I simply do not believe that to be the case."

"Your belief is not based upon any physical evidence tipping the scale, right?"

"No. It's based upon my decades of experience."

"But none of that experience is in biomechanics, correct?"

"That is correct."

Turning to the judge, I said, "Your Honor, may we approach?"

Judge Mathers nodded. "You may."

All the attorneys from both sides hustled to a sidebar. I made it there first and waited for the others. My pulse raced from exhilaration due to the prospects of a pivotal development.

Judge Mathers sat high on the oak bench with his gray hair unkempt. His glasses sat slightly askew. Yet, his eyes appeared more focused and coherent than at any time during the trial. "Let's have it," he said.

"The witness has recanted her opinion," I said. "The defense moves to strike her testimony in its entirety. She has not stated her opinion to the threshold of more likely than not. She has qualified her opinion at a fifty-fifty probability. As such, it cannot stand as an expert opinion under Massachusetts law. We also move for a directed verdict."

The judge turned to Alyson. "Your response?"

She looked like a deer in headlights. I suspected she was blindsided by my approach. It was more often used in products liability matters, and not often taken in a criminal case. The judge surely had ample experience in civil matters and understood my point.

"Your Honor," Alyson said. "The witness has provided an opinion to a reasonable degree of certainty. The cross-examination merely raised possibilities, but it did not rescind the witness's opinion."

"Very well," Judge Mathers said. "I am going to allow the prosecution an opportunity for a redirect. I am going to reserve my ruling on the motion to strike and motion for a directed verdict until the close of the prosecution's case. In the meantime, I suggest both sides seriously consider resolving this matter with a plea bargain."

"Your Honor…" I griped.

He shook his head in dismay. "Let's move it along."

Returning to the podium, I addressed the witness. "You testified the victim had sexual relations prior to her death, correct?"

"Yes, that is correct."

"This wasn't forced sexual intercourse, right?"

"No. I believe it was consensual. There was no sign of force."

"You didn't find any DNA from the sexual encounter?"

"No. I believe the man wore a contraceptive."

"You don't know when the sexual activity took place."

"I would estimate between an hour and a day before her death."

"So, she could have met with a boyfriend a day before her death? Right?"

"That is possible."

Walking to the corner of my counsel table, I addressed the court. "Your Honor, I have completed my examination of this witness at this time."

"Redirect?" Judge Mathers said to Alyson.

She stood and strode into the well, projecting an air of confidence. "Dr. Chenoweth, you testified an opinion during your direct examination, did you not?"

"I most certainly did," Dr. Chenoweth said, straightening up.

"Was anything said during your cross-examination that caused you to change your opinion?"

"No. My opinion as not changed," Dr. Chenoweth said with a tone of condescension.

"And you maintain that opinion to a reasonable degree of certainty?"

"I most certainly do." Dr. Chenoweth nodded for effect.

"That concludes my questioning at this time," Alyson said, smugly.

Rising from my chair, I planned to rehash some of my earlier points.

The judge's forehead wrinkled in dismay. He clearly wanted to move this along and preferred that I skip the re-cross. Then, he seemed to glance over my shoulder, intently. I turned and found Nate standing at the railing. He held a sheet of paper in his hand. Stepping over, I grabbed it and gave it a quick review, then I returned to my table.

"Your Honor, I have just a few more questions," I said.

"Very well," he griped. "But make it quick."

Moving into the well, I stood before Dr. Chenoweth and looked her in the eyes. "You just stated that you did not change your opinion, right?"

She paused, as if suspicious of being led into a trap. "Yes," she said meekly.

"But you have changed your opinion previously?" I asked kindly.

"I'm afraid I don't quite follow."

"Objection," Alyson called from her table. "This is beyond the scope of the redirect."

Judge Mathers thought it over. "I believe this falls within the line of questioning you left off with. Besides, I'd like to hear the answer. Overruled."

"I'll clarify," I said. "You completed an initial report in this matter, correct?"

"Yes."

"And that report did not include an opinion on the cause of death?"

"That is correct."

"You later completed a finalized report?"

"Correct."

"And that report noted a cause of death, as possibly being a fall or a shove from the balcony?" I asked.

"I believe it noted the cause of death as either a fall or a shove from the balcony."

She had tried to soften the blow of the question by omitting the word possibly, but her answer still boxed the opinion in as one that is fifty-fifty either way, which does not reach the threshold of the standard for an expert opinion. And the prosecution was utilizing the M.E.'s testimony as one of expert opinion.

"Those reports were written just a few days apart, right?" I continued.

"I believe so."

"Then a week later, you wrote a supplemental finding," I said, waving the document Nate had handed to me. "Isn't that true?"

"Yes,"

"You changed your opinion from a fifty-fifty opinion, of a fall or a push, to one of just a push, right?" I coaxed her.

"Yes."

"Were you provided any additional information between the time that you completed the initial reports and the time you completed this supplemental report?" I again waved the document.

"No. I'm afraid not," Dr. Chenoweth said. "I was just—"

"Thank you," I interrupted. "You answered my question."

"But…"

"That will be all." I turned to the judge. "Your Honor, I renew my motions to strike and for a directed verdict."

He shook his head, agitated. My request should have been spoken at a side bar. "Rulings are reserved until after the Commonwealth's case," Judge Mathers said.

"I've concluded my examination of this witness," I said, returning to my table.

Alyson launched from her chair. "I just have one question."

Judge Mathers looked at her and shook his head. "That's enough with this witness. We'll take our lunch break now. Be back here in an hour."

As I packed up a few things to go over during lunch, Courtney and Brad headed through the gate. I shoved a notepad into my briefcase, then turned and was met by Joey.

"Nice work finding the supplemental report," I said, smiling.

"Can I talk to you for a minute?" he said, looking serious.

Joey usually responds to praise, so he had my interest piqued. "Sure. What's up?"

"Your job is to focus on putting the case in, so you probably haven't noticed something…"

"What is it?"

Joey paused and inhaled. "It's Brad."

"What about him?"

Brad had been fairly quiet during trial, which is a good thing. Many clients make a scene whenever they hear testimony they don't like or find untruthful. I had no idea where Joey was going with this.

A somber countenance clouded his being. Joey had me concerned.

Joey finally said, "He had a maniacal look in his eyes during the M.E.'s testimony."

"Are you sure?" I couldn't believe it.

"Positive. He looked like he could kill her."

"Christ!" I shook my head, alarmed.

"And it gets worse. I think a couple jurors noticed."

SIXTY-FIVE

KARA SAT IN THE GALLERY behind the prosecution table after watching the defense attorney cross-examine the Medical Examiner. Ken Dwyer argued during his opening statement that it wasn't clear Audrey Martin had been murdered, and now the prosecution's own expert didn't seem sure. The case wasn't going well.

The judge cleared the courtroom and the jury filed out a side door. Members of the press rushed out to report on the story. Kara waited for the rest of her team.

After the prosecutors packed up for lunch, they pushed through the gate. Alyson motioned for Kara to join them. She got up and followed them through a throng of reporters waiting in the hallway. Chandler joined up with them.

Alyson didn't stop to grandstand for the reporters. Kara wasn't sure whether it was due to lack of time during the lunch break or because the M.E. hadn't stood up well on cross. They piled into an elevator jampacked with people going to lunch, so Alyson didn't address the situation until they got outside.

"We need to seriously think of a plea deal," she said, walking across the brick plaza towards a luncheonette on the corner of Tremont and Beacon Streets.

They entered the restaurant and the place buzzed with chatter of busy professionals grabbing a quick lunch. Clanging silverware and plates resounded throughout the luncheonette. Plate-glass windows overlooked Tremont Street, and a counter ran along the back wall. There was a line for takeout orders. Most of the tables were taken, but there were a couple open along a sidewall.

Once settled at a table, they ordered sandwiches and soft drinks.

"You aren't serious about a plea deal?" Chandler eventually griped.

"Detective, you haven't been in court the whole time," Alyson said. "This case is based on circumstantial evidence, and it hasn't been going well. The defendant is a polished speaker, so he could sway the jury into an acquittal based upon reasonable doubt."

Kara leaned forward. "But if we make an offer now, they'll think we're caving."

Everyone sat quietly for a while, contemplating Kara's comment.

The waitress approached and placed soft drinks on the table. A worker from out back brought out their sandwiches. "Anything else?" the waitress said.

"No, that will be all," Alyson replied.

"This place is fast," Chandler commented, biting into his ham on rye.

Alyson pulled out a credit card and placed it by the ticket. "I'll get this," she said.

"Great," Chandler said, sipping his drink.

The rest of them hadn't started eating yet. Fear of a dismal outcome had them reticent. Nobody seemed ready to offer an action plan.

Finally, the young lawyer sitting next to Alyson cleared his throat. "We'll make the offer at the end of the day after we're finished with the next witness."

Alyson's eyes lit up. "That's better than offering it now."

"What if the judge grants a dismissal at the close of our case?" Kara said.

"Not likely," Alyson said, biting into a sandwich.

Kara started on her lunch and left the decision making on the plea to the prosecutors. Still, she had her reservations about the case. It was brought too soon.

"You think he'll get off," Chandler said to Kara.

"He might," Alyson interjected. "That's why we'll offer a favorable plea."

"What are you thinking?" Chandler asked.

"Manslaughter," Alyson said.

"Really?" He shook his head, disgruntled.

"We need a conviction on this."

"He won't serve much time," Chandler kept at it.

"Perhaps," Alyson said. "But a conviction means he doesn't get off Scott-Free with an acquittal. And a conviction would prevent him from suing us later."

There it was. Finally, the brash prosecutor had put the real concern on the table. Kara wondered how deep the apprehension went. Bradford Wallace had connections and wealth. It wouldn't take much for him to turn an acquittal into a crusade against them.

"I'll tell you how we'd have dealt with this in the old days," Chandler said. "Someone would meet up with Ken Dwyer in a dark alley with a lead pipe."

SIXTY-SIX

RETURING FROM LUNCH the judge took the bench and instructed a bailiff to fetch the jury. The jury filed into the courtroom and took their seats.

"Do you have any more witnesses?" Judge Mathers said to Alyson.

"The Commonwealth calls Eric Novak," she said. A self-satisfied gleam consumed her.

A man with wavy brown hair and a slick dress shirt stood up. He strutted through the gate and approached the witness stand. Novak was about forty and probably single or divorced. He resembled the type of guy that hung out in nightclubs, never growing up. I expected he was in the shady side of sales, vinyl siding and windows. Probably got into scrapes from time to time because he was short on cash from lack of commissions.

The judge swore him in. Then, he took a seat, dropping into the chair with a thud. Novak smiled like a schoolboy from the commotion he'd just made. He glanced around the courtroom looking for a response. Nobody laughed. No one smiled.

Alyson inhaled, as though registering the witness wasn't making a good impression.

She walked over to the podium and took a sip of water, trying to place some distance between her witness's antics and his testimony.

"Please state your full name for the record," she finally said.

Novak testified as to his background, growing up in the area, attending college for a couple years, then leaving to sell cars in Florida. He moved back to the area and worked in a variety of sales positions. Novak was divorced with a daughter.

"Did you come to spend any time in the Nashua Street jail recently?"

"Yes," Novak said, nodding. He supplied the dates.

"How did you come to be there?" she asked.

"Basically, I was picked up for drinking one too many and getting behind the wheel." He shrugged, like saying it could happen to anyone.

A few of the jurors nodded, as if they agreed.

"Was that your first offense?"

"Yes. And it will be my last."

"Did you encounter the defendant when you were in the Nashua Street jail?" Alyson said, pointing to Brad.

Novak nodded. "I did."

"Where?"

"He was in the holding cell when I was brought in."

"Did the two of you speak?"

"Yes," Novak said.

"How did you come to speak?"

"When I was brought in, I saw him seated on a bench. There were street thugs all around. He looked nervous. He was like a clean-cut guy. Given we were both professionals, I thought I'd hang out with him to pass the time. I walked over and sat down next to him."

"Did the two of you talk?"

"We did."

"Did he say anything about his charges?"

"He did."

"What did he say?"

"He said the girl had it coming," Novak said, shaking his head, as if dismayed by the thought of such a heinous crime.

"Did he admit to killing her?"

"Objection!" I shouted. "The question is leading and lacks foundation because it assumes facts not in evidence."

"Sustained," Judge Mathers snapped.

"Did he say anything else about his charges?"

"No, that's about it," said Novak. "'She had it coming.'"

"What did you take this to mean?"

"Objection," I said, standing up.

"Approach," the judge commanded.

All the lawyers hurried across the well and encroached upon the bench.

"Basis?" Judge Mathers asked me, not following.

"Speculation."

The judge shook his head. "She's asking about *his* thoughts," Judge Mathers said, pointing to the witness. "And not his thoughts." He pointed over at Brad.

"But the question does not deal with direct evidence of what the witness saw or heard," I pled. "It's more prejudicial than probative."

"That's a different objection." Judge Mathers looked at Alyson. "Response?"

"The witness is entitled to state what he thought a comment meant."

"But only if it explains some action or conduct undertaken as a result of the impression," the judge lectured. "Do you have an offer of proof?"

Alyson looked like a deer in headlights. "No, Your Honor."

"Very well," he replied. "The objection is sustained."

We returned to our positions and Alyson commented that she had completed her direct examination of the witness.

Judge Mathers glanced over at the defense table. "Cross?"

Standing, I walked into the well of the courtroom. Novak stared at me with a maniacal gleam in his eye. He seemed to be taunting me, hoping for me to come out with guns blazing, so he could shoot me down. I suspected a trap.

"You were arrested for DUI, correct?" I said with an even tone.

"That's what I said already." He smirked like it was a stupid question.

"Did the prosecution offer you some consideration for your testimony today?"

"They didn't promise me anything," he snapped.

"That wasn't the question," I said stepping closer to the witness stand.

Anticipating a trick, I hadn't come out strong and accused him of getting a better deal for his testimony. Rather, I just asked a broad, opened-ended question. I waited for a response. The judge waited. The jury waited, too.

Novak looked me over, considering. "Yeah. They said they'd consider a more lenient deal… but they didn't guarantee anything."

"And so you came in here and testified, hoping for a more lenient deal, right?"

"Hey," Novak griped. "What I said here was the truth." And there it was.

"Do you always do the truthful and honest thing?" I asked, walking over to my table and grabbing a manilla folder. Beckerman investigated everyone on the prosecution's witness list and prepared a file for each one. I headed back to the well and stood before the witness.

Novak's jaw dropped open. "I… Well, I guess so."

"You guess so?" I stepped closer and looked him directly in the eyes.

He appeared nervous. Novak nodded.

"You have to speak up for the record," Judge Mathers quipped.

"Sure," he said. "I try to." He'd qualified the response.

"You do or you don't?" I demanded. "I remind you that you're under the pains and penalties of perjury."

"I'll remind you as well," Judge Mathers said, sternly.

Novak looked at the judge, then back at me. He shrugged. "Not always."

"You don't always tell the truth, right?" I said.

"No, I don't."

"You're dishonest at times."

"I've done some dishonest things."

"You've been convicted of crimes related to dishonesty."

"Objection!" Alyson bellowed.

Judge Mathers glanced over to her and furrowed his eyebrows. "Basis?"

"This is unfair character evidence that wasn't broached on direct. Prior bad acts."

"Your witness opened the door to this," the judge said, shaking his head. "He walked right into this one. Besides, I want to hear the answer."

Novak drooped his head. "Yes."

"In fact, you've been convicted three times of crimes of dishonesty, right?" I said, waiving the folder around to show the jury and court that I had a good faith basis for my question.

"A few times, I guess," he said.

Rattling off his rap sheet, I listed each crime and the date of sentencing. He admitted to them all. Several jurors shook their heads. I noticed a couple of them looking over at the prosecution table, as if miffed by such an underhanded trick.

After I sat down, Alyson got up and tried to rehabilitate him. "Have you learned your lesson from those days?"

"Certainly."

"In fact, you haven't committed a crime of dishonesty in a few years?"

Her question was leading, but I let it go.

"That's correct," Novak replied. "I haven't written any bad checks, or nothing like that in quite some time."

Alyson frowned. "You were in jail for a DUI when you heard the defendant?"

"That's correct," Novak said proudly, as though he'd done a good thing by not being in lockup due to a crime of dishonesty.

"Have you testified truthfully in this trial?"

"I most certainly have." Novak nodded for effect.

Alyson turned to the judge. "That completes my examination."

Bolting upright, I grabbed the judge's attention. "Just one question, Your Honor."

He nodded. "Very well."

"And you hope to get favorable consideration for your testimony, correct?"

"Sure. But that don't mean I ain't telling the truth," Novak said.

"That's all I have, Your Honor." I sat down.

The judge smiled, then he looked at the clock. "Let's call it a day."

A bailiff stood and announced, "All rise!"

The judge whisked off the bench, and the jury filed out a side door.

We packed up as people in the gallery funneled out of the courtroom. My colleagues appeared elated, and the prosecution table looked grim. Caught in the middle of the strife, I wasn't able to digest the result of the day. I still had my concerns.

SIXTY-SEVEN

WE GATHERED FOR A DRINK at The Last Hurrah. It was near the courthouse and most of the team felt we had something to celebrate after a productive day in court.

Brad got us a table in the back of the famed restaurant, so we could talk shop. The place was relatively quiet because it was early, but we wanted to be careful when the happy hour crowd started rolling in. Joey and Nate piled the file materials by a window. Then, Courtney ordered a Cosmopolitan, while Brad and Nate opted for Manhattans. Joey kept to his usual beer.

Once we were all settled, the chitchat waned into silence. Nobody appeared ready to broach the subject about next steps.

"That went well today, Ken," Brad finally said, holding up a toast.

Everyone clinked glasses. Then, Joey waged into war stories about the cross-examinations of the Medical Examiner and Novak. He thought we had done a tremendous job.

"You should have seen the look on Novak's face when you asked him about his criminal record," Joey said, laughing.

Others chuckled at the comment, confirming his viewpoint.

"I really think they thought you'd take the bait," Courtney added, "and expected you would jump in and ask about a plea deal that never happened. When you didn't, Novak fell apart. He really didn't hold up. Neither did the M.E."

"So, what happens next?" asked Brad. He looked better than he had in days past.

"I think they are out of witnesses," I replied. "The Commonwealth will likely come in and rest in the morning."

"What then?" Brad said.

"Then we'll renew our motion to strike the Medical Examiner's testimony and move for a directed verdict after the close of the Commonwealth's case."

"Any chance either of those will be successful?"

I shook my head. "Doubtful."

"The M.E. really didn't hold up," Courtney said.

"Sure, but the judge will think it comes down to credibility rather than striking her testimony. The problem is she did not entirely recant her opinion. On redirect, she stated that she maintained her opinion. The same issue goes to Novak. It comes down to credibility. I expect the judge to either deny or reserve both motions."

Joey edged closer to the table. "What about arguing a reasonable jury couldn't convict based upon the evidence?"

"The judge would deny it," I said, shaking my head. "He'll want to hear our case."

"What about after our case?" Joey pressed.

"He'd wait until after the jury deliberates, then he'd decide whether to take the case away from them and enter a directed verdict."

"Why?" This from Brad.

"Because if the jury comes back with an acquittal, the burden is taken off the judge."

Brad nodded, understanding the point.

"So, what are we going to do with our part of the case?" Nate asked the million-dollar question.

"We need to make a fundamental strategic decision," I said.

"And that is… " Nate said.

"Whether or not Brad testifies."

"Don't you think we have reasonable doubt?" Brad asked, looking around at the group.

"That depends," Joey said. "If the jury questions whether or not she was murdered, then we have established a solid defense based upon reasonable doubt."

"What if they think she was murdered?" Nate said.

"Then I seriously doubt we would win by resting and then arguing reasonable doubt at closing." Joey took a sip of beer. "If they think she was murdered, they'll assume it was Brad because he was arrested and he had accessibility to the crime scene. He'd have to testify to explain he was somewhere else."

"That makes sense," Courtney said. "If I was on the jury, I would want the defendant to tell me where he was at the time of the murder."

"But if I take the stand," Brad lamented, "it will ruin my political career."

Brad was talking about the fact he'd spent time that night with a high-priced call girl. We contemplated the implications of this previously, but we'd gone ahead and listed her as a defense witness. But we'd never made a final decision as to whether we would call either of them. Often, you wait and see how the prosecution's case presents before making final decisions of how to put on the defense case.

"If you don't," Joey said. "It could ruin your life."

A lull fell over the conversation.

"What are the chances the jury questions she was murdered?" I said after a moment.

"Some do and some don't," Joey said flatly.

"What does that mean?" asked Brad.

"It means that some jurors might acquit based upon reasonable doubt because they aren't even sure Audrey Martin was murdered," I said. "Others believe she was murdered and want to hear it wasn't you."

"Well, isn't that good for us?" Brad said. "Don't they need a unanimous vote."

I shook my head. "The trouble is when the jury goes back to deliberate, some will think there was a murder and others won't. Then they get to talking and stronger personalities try to push others their way."

"Maybe they'll push to acquit," Courtney offered.

"We can't know for certain. But I would guess the stronger personalities will think there was a murder. I'm leaning towards having Brad testify."

"You haven't made up your mind?" Brad said.

"No. And quite frankly, I'd like to see how the jury presents tomorrow."

"So, what's the game plan?" Brad asked.

"Courtney and Joey will prepare you for direct and cross. Given it was a younger woman that died, it makes sense for Courtney to handle your cross. You folks can head back to the office and get started."

"Sounds like a plan," Joey said, rising to leave.

"What are you two going to do?" asked Courtney.

"Unwind and have another."

Everyone laughed, then the three of them headed out a side door leading to School Street. A cold gust of air whipped inside the restaurant. It sent a chill down my spine. I hoped it wasn't an indication of how things were headed.

SIXTY-EIGHT

AFTER POLISHING OFF OUR DRINKS, I headed over to the bar to order a second round for each of us. Nate checked emails on his phone, while he waited at the table. Leaning my elbows on the bar, I waited for the bartender to come around.

The afterwork crowd had begun trickling into the posh whiskey bar. A din of clanging glasses and office banter emanated about the place. Despite the bar and tables quickly crowding, I sensed someone staring at me.

Glancing around, I spotted Jack Delaney seated in a deep leather sofa. He was surrounded by a few other suits, who I took for lawyers rather than clients. Two sofas were set across from each other with a coffee table in between them. Situated low to the ground, they all sat conversing about some exciting matter.

He smiled and waved for me to come over. I decided to see what he had to say.

"Ken," Jack said, standing to shake my hand.

"Jack," I replied, then I glanced at the others.

"Don't let me be rude," Jack said. "This is Ken Dwyer. We were tight in law school. And this is Margo, Tim, and Chuck. They're all attorneys at my firm."

Everyone greeted me kindly. Margo mentioned she'd heard of me.

Then, Jack pointed to a spot on the opposite sofa.

"How are you?" I said, taking a seat. I sunk into the soft cushion.

"Good as can be expected." Jack forced a smile.

"I guess you'll undergo some changes now."

"Most certainly. But this business with Brad shouldn't come between us."

The comment caught me off guard. Jack took his conduct as a dispute with Brad and didn't appear to understand he'd affronted me professionally. Rather than create a further riff, I just smiled and nodded, reflecting a desire to move past our grievance.

"Listen, you did quite well today," Jack said.

"Thanks," I replied. "I'd seen you in the courtroom a few times, but I didn't notice you in there today."

"I was huddled in the back and caught part of your cross of the M.E., and the entire examination of the jailhouse snitch." Jack sat back and laughed. "You really nailed both of them. I wouldn't be surprised if Brad gets acquitted."

A waiter walked over and addressed Jack for an order.

"We'll take a bottle of MacCallum 25," Jack said. "And could you bring five glasses."

"Sure thing," the waiter said, then departed.

"Kind of an expensive drink," Margo said. "It better be on you."

"Relax," Jack said, motioning to her. "I've got it."

"I really should be getting back to Nate," I said, politely declining the offer.

"Oh, I didn't realize you were here with anyone. I figured your team had all headed back to the shop to prepare for tomorrow."

"That's about it. Except for Nate."

"You should invite him over," Jack offered.

"I was thinking of heading back. We've got some strategy to discuss."

The waiter returned carrying a tray, balancing a bottle of scotch and five glasses. He stepped alongside the coffee table. Then, he carefully unloaded the tray, setting items down one at a time. "There you are," he said. "Anything else?"

Jack glanced at all of us. Everyone shook their heads.

"No. That will be all," Jack said.

Sliding forward on the puffy sofa, I intended to get up and leave.

Jack leaned forward and gently grabbed my arm. "Have you ever tried this?" he said, pointing at the scotch. His tone was kind and not condescending.

"Can't say that I have," I replied.

"You should at least try some. I made the order to celebrate a deal we closed, but I was also thinking about your stellar performance today. Please have a small glass."

"Sure," I said, sitting back.

Jack smiled and let go of my arm. He cracked the bottle open, then poured a little scotch into an old-fashioned glass. After setting the bottle down, he handed the glass to me. Jack waited for me to take a sip before serving the others.

Taking the drink, I lifted it to my nose. Inhaling, the scent whisked up my nostrils.

"Nice. Right?" Jack said, grinning.

I took a sip, sloshing the liquor around in my mouth. Scents of dried fruits and a hint of chocolate and orange mixed with the whiskey. Then, I swallowed. It had a slightly smoky aftertaste. The scotch was good stuff.

"Like it?" Jack said.

"Definitely."

"Good. It will grow on you."

Jack poured scotch into the other glasses and handed them out.

His colleagues each took their glasses and followed my lead; they sniffed the whiskey, then worked it around their mouths. Finally, they swallowed.

Each one of them smiled, satisfied.

I took another drink. "It's smooth," I said.

"Yeah, for sure," Margo replied.

The display grew old. Professionals often go out for a drink and engage in upmanship. Jack was trying to impress his colleagues. I'd known him too long to fall for the uppity exposition. He had grown up in a decent town, but his family wasn't wealthy. Jack didn't have any cause for pretentiousness.

Sitting back, I began to run the trial through my mind. I considered the prosecution's discovery and tried to figure out what we might have missed. What else could be utilized to sway the jury remained a key consideration for the defense.

During the lull in our conversation, an overlooked item sifted to the forefront of my mind.

"What do you have planned for tomorrow?" Jack asked, interrupting my thoughts.

"You know I can't get into it." I shrugged.

He cracked a smile. "Just trying to decide if I should stop by in the morning."

Jack's comment got me thinking about our next steps. "You should definitely plan to be there. I expect it to be more dramatic than today."

"More dramatic than today?" Jack repeated. "How could that even be possible?"

"Just come by and see," I said, smirking.

He perked up. "Can't wait."

I wondered if he'd contact anyone in the press. Attendance in the gallery had dropped off a little each day of trial. Reporters popped in and out, but few remained watching the trial for the entire time. Jack's eagerness had me wondering if the morning would see a bigger turnout. He was known to talk out of school.

Polishing off the drink, I set the glass down. Then, I stood up and looked at Jack.

"Brad's going to testify, right?" Jack said, with a wild gleam in his eyes.

"You know I can't comment."

"Sure." He raised his glass, as if toasting me.

"Take care, Jack." I gave him a pat on the shoulder. I bid adieu to the others. Then, I walked back to rejoin Nate and debrief on my latest thoughts.

SIXTY-NINE

AFTER A FEW COCKTAILS, Nate and I ventured out into the wintry night. I kept my collar up and head down, trying to ward off frigid wind gusts. We trucked down School Street then meandered our way to a corner near the office. Traffic inched past us as commuters made their way out of town.

"Come on," I said. "I'll give you a ride home."

"Don't you want to go up and check in on them?" asked Nate.

"No," I said, shaking my head. "They'll be just fine. We'll head home and get some rest. Tomorrow is going to be a big day."

Nate looked at me skeptically. He hiked his shoulders. "Okay."

He had devotion to our team from his years of playing sports. I could tell he wanted to head up to the office and plow ahead with the case. The truth is trials are extremely draining and every once in a while, you are better off recharging yourself rather than expending more time and effort with continued preparation. Appearing fresh and focused helps with the presentation.

Clapping him on the shoulder, I said, "Come on. Let's get you home."

"Sure," Nate said. Then, we turned down Merchants Row.

We cut across the street and walked past a pub. Then, we rounded a corner and headed down the rickety sidewalk, running along the industrial road that curved behind the office. We chatted about the day in court, and I praised Nate for his keen observations. He had the common sense and gut instincts that helped foster the growth of a trial lawyer.

My aging Porsche sat in the near-empty parking lot with a couple other cars. The lot was surrounded on three sides by the brick-and-mortar backsides of office buildings, with an alley leading out to State Street. All the buildings were old, and the brick was darkened by soot.

Approaching the car from the industrial road, we walked into the open space.

Just as I reached for the key fob, a dilapidated van raced into the lot. It came to an abrupt halt and the rear doors banged open. Men jumped out.

The sliding door drew back, and more men piled out of the van.

Stepping between Nate and the assailants, I raised my left hand and ordered them to stop. The men broke off their approach, work boots scraping the macadam. They stood four feet away; wild eyes reflected in the glow from a nearby streetlamp.

The men parted, and someone stepped through the gauntlet.

A familiar face jeered at me. "Counselor, we told you to *withdraw*."

"What's the meaning of this?" I demanded.

He snickered. "You are not in position to question us."

Glancing around, we were alone. It wasn't like when he had accosted me on a main street. This time there weren't any witnesses.

Then, his face contorted into a vile countenance. "Take them," he said.

Two of the men stepped past me, headed for Nate.

A surge of rage pulsated through me. The thought of them hurting him spurred me to fight. I shoved my foot between the boots of the one closest to me.

He tripped, and I drove my fist into the side of his head, accelerating the fall.

His head cracked into the pavement and blood sprayed everywhere.

A scent of copper wafted upward. Then, I tore after the other thug. Punching him in the face repeatedly, he lost balance and staggered. He stepped back, dazed, swinging wildly.

I pursued him and landed a solid punch into his cheekbone. Something cracked. A bone.

He dropped to the ground like a load of bricks.

"Run!" I called to Nate.

Footfalls scampered, as he fled the scene.

Turning to face the others, I heard a boot scrape on the ground behind me. I threw back an elbow, but it swiped air.

Then, a blow conked my head, something heavy and metallic.

My vision blurred.

I dropped to my knees.

Blackness.

SEVENTY

JOUNCING STIRRED ME AWAKE, but I was too groggy to immediately discern my surroundings. It was dark and smelled of dirt, electrical equipment, rubber wires and grease.

My body shifted and a worn suspension creaked. I was in the back of the van.

Frigid air caused me to shiver. They had removed my overcoat and the cargo area wasn't heated. I wondered what they had in store for me.

Fear pinpricked at the base of my skull.

Light occasionally flickered into the space. Men sat on wooden benches running along each side of the van. I lay on the floor with boots near my face. Trying to lift my chin to see if they'd grabbed Nate, the back of my head ached, and my vision swirled.

Then, I fell in and out of consciousness. Mostly, I was passed out.

Later, boots smacking wooden planks roused me. Men gripped my arms and legs. They were carrying me up a set of stairs.

One of the men kicked open a door. They carried me into an attic space.

They let go of me all at once. My body dropped onto the hard, plank floor. Pain shot into my knees and elbows.

Moonlight shined through a window lodged at the gable end of the house.

Exposed rafters ran along the slanted ceiling and the flooring wasn't finished. The place stank of urine and feces. Chains and shackles were bolted to a lower wall, but there weren't any padlocks for the bindings.

Iron bars were bolted to the window.

What kind of place is this? I wondered. Panic pulsated through my extremities.

Lifting my head, I tried to scan the room for a better understanding of the chamber. Nate was strewn on the floor. A man was crouched beside him. Something about the silhouette seemed familiar. His shape. The movements.

"You killed Keith Evers," I called to the man.

He turned towards me. "No. That was a misfortunate death. He really did overdose. Died before I could question him."

"You shot at me."

"Only to spook you." The man stood and walked towards me.

He stood above. Light reflecting through the window revealed him to be the hired gun that had been conducting surveillance on us.

"You," I said. "The private detective."

The man nodded. "You'll never know my identity."

He cackled. Then, he turned and walked towards the door.

"What are you going to do with us?"

"Afraid that it's not up to me." He shrugged, then turned and stepped out.

The heavy door closed, and I heard a bolt being latched into place.

Considering the window and the sealed door, it seemed we couldn't escape. I pushed off the floor with my hands, trying to get to my feet. My head whirled from dizziness. Then, I lost balance and my face smacked the floor. It felt like a drunken stupor.

Later, I awoke to find Nate sitting by my side. "How long was I out?"

"Quite a while. No telling for sure," he said. The comment was an indicator of our predicament.

I sat up and bright light hurt my eyes.

Daylight shined through the window at the end of the attic space. After a moment, my eyes adjusted. I realized we'd miss court in the middle of a murder trial. Nobody would know our whereabouts, and the judge might likely conclude I'd done something wrong.

The thought of being trapped in the attic caused all the air to leave the room. I found it difficult to breath. Taking a deep breath, I tried to get oxygen into my lungs. My effort abated a panic attack.

"Any way to break out?" I asked Nate.

He shook his head. "Nope. I've checked everything. The door is solid and deadbolted, likely with a metal bar securing it from the outside. The window is barred with the bolts running into the framing. You can't access them. Judging by those shackles, I'd bet the place has been used for human trafficking."

"Doesn't seem like it's been used in a while," I said, looking around.

"Probably not. Otherwise, they'd have chained us to the walls."

"This was a last minute, uncalculated move," I said. "How many people do you think are in the house?"

"None. There was some noise downstairs, then I heard a storm door slam. It's been quiet ever since. I think they left us here. I'd bet nobody wants to be around if we're found."

"They just want to keep us out of court. It would lead to a mistrial."

"How does that help anyone but the defense?" asked Nate.

"The prosecution gets a new trial to put on a smoother case after getting a preview of our cross-examinations. They will do a better job, and everyone knows it. I'd expect a favorable plea deal before the new trial. They'd get a conviction, but something with minimal jail time. So, Brad might be inclined to take it."

Nate nodded, understanding.

I gingerly rose to my feet. Then, I walked over to the window.

The bars were tight and couldn't be pulled loose, not even with a crowbar. The heads of the bolts were countersunk into openings in the bars, likely drilled through the entire wall and affixed with nuts screwed on from the outside.

My hand ached. I realized the crack I'd heard was a fractured bone in my hand.

Walking over to the door, I tried the handle. It was locked.

There were bolts leading to the outside, likely a deadbolt as Nate suspected.

I shook the doorknob, and the door didn't rattle one bit. He was right again. There surely was a metal bar on the other side, latching the heavy wooden door in place.

"Told you," Nate said, shaking his head in dismay.

My mind raced with thoughts of missing court. Visions of the judge inquiring as to the reason for my absence. Courtney and Joey not being able to explain our disappearance. The fact that Nate was missing as well might cause them alarm. We'd had threats and even an attack on lawyers in the office over the case.

The walls started closing in. I couldn't breathe.

Placing my back to the wall, I slid to the floor and my chest constricted. I rapidly began inhaling and exhaling. The room turned dark in my mind's eye, as a vision from combat returned to me. My team had been buried in a tunnel. It took hours to dig us out.

Thoughts of being trapped in the attic indefinitely consumed me.

A bunch of goons hurting the firm's reputation by keeping us from court, infuriated me. But contemplating the strain placed on Courtney and Joey flipped a switch inside my body. Taking Nate wasn't necessary. It ignited something within me.

Panic transformed to rage. "They can't do this to us!" I screamed.

"What can we do?" Nate muttered. But his words only registered as a murmur.

Rising to my feet, I took a deep breath. Then, I began kicking the wall up near the deadbolt. Kicking and kicking with all my might, an effort fueled by anxiety and rage.

Chunks of plaster broke off and dropped to the floor. White dust clouded my vision.

If people were downstairs, they'd likely ascend the stairs with a firearm ready.

The thought of an armed assailant didn't discourage me. It caused me to redouble my efforts. Time was essential. Kicking away the plaster, the wooden lathe beneath split and broke apart. Soon, I had broken through, and daylight shined into the room.

Punching into the demolished wall with my fist, I broke through and debris crashed onto the hallway floor outside the room. I reached my hand through the opening and drew back the deadbolt. Then, I began fiddling with the iron bar, trying to wriggle it free.

Just as I budged the bar upward, the sound of a storm door slamming shut echoed throughout the house. Then, boots quickly ascended the staircase.

SEVENTY-ONE

THE METAL BAR CRASHED to the floor and Nate pushed the door open. I stepped outside behind him.

As a billow of dust settled to the floor, a burly man appeared on the landing holding a pistol pointed right at me.

"You pull the trigger and neighbors will hear it," I said.

The man stood there, eyes locked on mine, considering the situation.

"We both know this wasn't meant to get serious. No killing."

He tightened his hold on the pistol grip. "Get back in the room," he said, motioning with the gun.

"No. You're going to have to shoot us," I said, calling his bluff.

The tip of the barrel began to tremble. "Move!"

We stood there with our feet planted, determined not to obey. If they had any dire intentions, this would likely be our only chance of escape. The thug's eyes darted about; he grew nervous at not being able to control the situation.

"You can tell them we broke out before you got back," Nate offered. "Nobody will ever know we got past you."

"I'll know," the man said, turning kind for a moment.

"You're going to need to stand down," I said.

"Or what?" His voice crackled.

"You're either going to have to shoot us, or we're coming past you," I replied.

Bending down, I grabbed the metal bar from the floor. It was heavy, with straight edges. A blunt object.

"You win," the man said, easing down the stairs.

We stepped down after him.

Reaching the bottom, the man turned and headed out of the house. The storm door slammed shut behind him. He obviously planned to replay his arrival and come back later.

We stepped outside into a side yard with a driveway leading past the house to a detached garage. A frigid wind smacked into my exposed skin and turned it raw. Snow flurries danced in the air, whisking back and forth.

"Let's go," I said to Nate, heading towards the street.

Wandering out to the sidewalk, we were in a typical working-class neighborhood, similar to many towns outside of Boston. The surroundings were all too familiar, but I didn't have the slightest clue of which town we were in.

I patted my pockets, searching for my phone. Nothing.

Glancing at Nate, he shrugged. "They took our coats, phones, and wallets."

"How the hell are we going to get back?" I muttered.

The thought of being stranded anywhere had totally escaped me these last few years. You were always a couple minutes from an Uber or had a credit card for a cab.

"Come on," I said, briskly heading up the sidewalk.

"Where are we going?" asked Nate.

"These towns have a superette on a corner in every neighborhood like this," I said. "We'll find a phone and I'll call Joey. He can send a cab to get us."

I wondered if we were too late to stop a mistrial.

SEVENTY-TWO

ENTERING THE COURTROOM, the place was dead silent. You could hear a pin drop. All eyes were upon us, except the judge. He was busy speaking to the sessions clerk.

We had taken a moment while waiting for the cab to brush off the dust and straighten our ties. But spending the night in the same clothes couldn't be masked. Even after another quick cleanup in the courthouse restroom, I felt disheveled and embarrassed of my appearance.

Nate took a seat in the gallery and slipped out of view. I remained the sole focal point of attention, as I stepped through the gate. Making my way towards the defense table, pain spiked throughout my body. Courtney stared at me with anguish in her eyes.

"Glad you could join us, Mr. Dwyer," Judge Mathers said, catching my appearance out of the corner of his eye.

"Sorry, Your Honor."

He finally glanced over at me and did a double take. "Approach!"

All the trial lawyers in the case converged at a sidebar.

"What is the meaning of this?" Judge Mathers asked. "Nobody knew where you were. We thought you'd been in an accident."

"Your Honor—" I pled.

Judge Mathers shook his head. "You apparently went out and celebrated after a successful day in court. Well, I won't stand for that kind of bravura. You kept us waiting for twenty minutes. I should fine you."

"But, Your Honor…."

"You've wasted enough time," he said, waving a hand in admonishment.

Judge Mathers looked at Alyson. "Anymore witnesses."

"No, Your Honor. The Commonwealth rests."

"Aren't you going to hear from me?" I said.

"No." He shook his head. "Now get back to your tables."

The other lawyers started to turn away. I remained, so they lingered nearby.

"What?" Judge Mathers snapped.

Stepping closer, I spoke with a lower tone to help defuse him. "While we are here, I'd like to renew my motion to strike the Medical Examiner's testimony, and I am making a motion for a directed verdict following the close of the Commonwealth's case."

"Denied!" He shooed us away.

"I'd like to put the basis of the motion on the record."

"Also denied," he said, derisively.

"Your Honor," I continued.

"Did you even go home last night?" he said, glancing me over.

"I was…"

"You were, what?"

"I'm afraid, I was injured."

Judge Mathers sat back, contemplating. "You look like hell. Here's what we're going to do. The Commonwealth is going to rest, so it's on the record for everyone to hear. Then we're going to take a recess. We'll get the jury some snacks and coffee. The two of you will discuss a plea deal. Got it?"

"Yes, Your Honor," we replied in unison.

Returning to our tables, I gingerly took a seat and Alyson remained standing.

A few of the jurors were glancing my way. No doubt they suspected I had been reprimanded for being late. I expected a few reporters would take some potshots at me in upcoming articles.

"The Commonwealth rests, Your Honor," Alyson said.

"Very well," Judge Mathers said, adjusting his thick eyeglass frames. "We'll adjourn for a recess. Please return in thirty minutes."

The judge whisked off the bench and exited the courtroom, then a bailiff led the jury out. As people began to leave the gallery, the sessions clerk called out a reminder to keep cellphones off when everyone returned to the courtroom.

Standing up, I stretched out my back. My ribs hurt, the back of my head ached, and the fracture in my hand throbbed. It was beginning to swell. "Have you got something to offer?" I said to Alyson.

"Give me a minute. I'll come find you."

"Okay," I said. But her response didn't leave me with any feelings of comfort.

If they understood the implications of what happened in court the day before, they would have come to court prepared to make an offer. Instead, they needed to discuss the prospect like it had never even occurred to them.

I couldn't be sure if this was an act, or whether they never planned to make a proposal.

SEVENTY-THREE

WE BROKE FOR a meeting room, while the police and prosecution huddled around their table discussing next steps.

Entering the hallway, a reporter approached me. A cameraman lingered behind him, shooting film as the reporter spoke.

"Mr. Dwyer, can you tell us why you were late to court today?"

"No comment," I replied, trying to step past him.

"You appear to have some bruising. Can you tell us what happened?"

Ignoring the reporter, we pushed ahead. The camera kept filming as we walked away. We found the attorney/client meeting room occupied. Then, we headed to another room. Same result. A lawyer seated at the table glanced up, miffed at the intrusion.

Joey shut the door. "Where to?" he asked.

We meandered down the hallway, moving away from the press near the courtroom. Then we circled around and found an empty conference room on the opposite side of the building.

Settling in the room, we fell into our usual positions, except this time I slid into a chair. Exhaustion consumed me. Joey and Courtney bombarded me with questions about what happened. When I explained, they asked if we should withdraw. We were in the middle of a trial, and I owed Brad; there really wasn't any way out of it. The best we could hope for was a police security detail if we reported the crime.

Nate must have picked up on the dire look in Brad's eyes and told them we needed to address the client's options first. I tended to agree with him.

"What do you think they'll offer?" Courtney said to the group.

"Second degree murder," Joey replied flatly.

The comment caused us all to sit back and think. It made perfect sense.

A charge of first-degree murder involves planning and a premeditation, like bringing a gun to a neighbor's house after suspecting him of sleeping with your wife. You plan to kill the guy when you leave your house with the gun. On the other hand, second-degree murder concerns a situation where you intend to kill someone, but you never planned it. A fight breaks out and you get so angry that you grab a rock and cave the other person's skull in. Manslaughter is when you kill someone, but you never planned or intended a death to result.

The prosecution had gone after Brad for first-degree murder, believing he had planned to kill Audrey Martin because she was going to end an affair, reveal the affair, or possibly expose him relative to campaign finance irregularities. However, it was possible, if he did in fact kill her, the incident was happenstance. She confronted him at the house, and he threw her over the railing to silence her. One could never know for sure which scenario went down, or if he even killed her.

"How much time would I get?" Brad said, breaking the lull in our discussion.

"It's a life sentence with an opportunity for parole," I said. "You could be out in fifteen years."

"You can't get something better than that?" Brad asked, sheepishly.

"No." I shook my head. "There is a statutory fifteen year minimum, so the judge only has discretion to set it between fifteen and twenty-five years. We can't get you less in a plea for second-degree murder."

This was all speculation. I just wanted to hear what Alyson actually had to offer.

A few minutes later, there was a knock on the door. I stood up and opened it. Alyson stood in the threshold with Detective Sergeant Kara Malloy behind her.

"Can we have a moment?" Alyson said.

"Sure." I stepped outside and closed the door behind me.

We found a corner near a doorway and huddled to discuss a potential deal. Many cases are resolved in the nooks and crannies of courthouses.

Alyson stared at me with a somber look in her eyes.

"What?" I snapped, defensively.

"Just wondering if you're okay," she replied.

"I'm fine. Now, can we get on with it?"

She placed her hand on my shoulder. "Are you sure you're all right? I've never seen you like this. It isn't like you to go on a bender in the middle—"

"A bender?" I repeated, peeved.

She was taken aback. "What?"

"Alyson, we were taken hostage and held all night."

She looked astonished. "I'm so sorry."

"Yeah. I'm sure…"

"Listen," she said, moving closer. "You don't think we had anything to do with it? This is a serious crime, Kenny. You need to report it to the judge and the police. We can take a recess."

"That's exactly what they want," I said, shaking my head. "I'll report it later."

"Okay, if that's what you want." She let her hand drop away from my shoulder.

"What's the offer?" I demanded, getting back to business.

"Manslaughter. He's got fifteen minutes to decide, then it's off the table."

All the air left the room. I couldn't believe they'd made such a lenient proposal. Glancing at Alyson, I searched her eyes to make sure I'd heard it correctly. Then, I looked at Malloy to see if it was a joke.

Kara Malloy looked at me in earnest. Then, she nodded.

"I'll talk to my client and get back to you."

They turned and headed down the hallway towards the congested area by the courtroom. I headed inside the meeting room.

Standing before the team, I explained the proposal.

Joey and Courtney looked shocked. Nate seemed interested. However, the response from Brad was anything but delight. He sat there mulling it over, like it was a horrible development. Maybe the reality of a conviction was taking hold.

"How much time would I serve," Brad finally said.

"You would likely serve ten to fifteen months," I replied.

Brad looked at the floor, contemplating. Then, he glanced back up at me, staring with an ardent gleam in his eyes. "Would I have to say that I killed her?"

"Admission of the crime is part of any plea."

"How can I stand up there under oath and lie?" asked Brad, disheartened.

"People do it all the time," Joey cut in. "You just say what you have to say in order to take the deal. It's just risk management."

"If I could take the deal without admitting I killed her, I might be willing to consider it. But I can't live with everyone thinking I did it." Brad shook his head, dismayed. "Like you were saying, people plead to avoid the risk of trial. I'm willing to consider it, but I can't get up there and say I killed her."

This is how things often turn out in situations like this. You have a client seriously contemplating second-degree murder and fifteen years to life in prison. Then a sweet deal comes to you unexpectedly, and the client decides to turn it down. In the past, I would try to persuade a client to take the deal, pressure him to see the light. Now that I'm older and seen a lot more cases, I leave the decision up to the client. It's better practice to just explain the options. Otherwise, they resent you after taking the deal. Buyer's remorse.

"I'm afraid you have to confess to the crime in order to cop to a plea," I said, taking a seat beside Brad.

He stared at the floor again. After a moment, Brad looked up and shook his head. "I can't do it."

"Okay," I said, clapping him on the shoulder. "Looks like we have a case to finish."

"What are we going to do next?" asked Courtney.

"I'm not sure," I said, spreading my hands.

"When are you going to be sure?" Joey snapped, exasperated.

Joey likely felt we should cram the plea deal down Brad's throat. I didn't take offense to his outburst. "Let's settle down," I said. "We need to figure this out."

"Isn't putting Brad on the stand next our best approach?" Courtney said.

"Did you write out his examination?" I asked her.

"I've got it right here." She nodded and patted her handbag.

"Can I see it?" I said, reaching for the outline.

She pulled a yellow-lined legal pad from her bag and handed it over.

Perusing the examination, I knew putting Brad on the stand next was the sound tactical thing to do. But something in my gut told me we had another card to play.

"Come on," I said. "We need to get back there."

"So, what are we going to do?" Joey said.

"You'll know… when I know."

We left the meeting room and headed back to the courtroom. I felt like a boxer getting back into the ring after being knocked to the mat.

And I truly didn't know what to do next.

SEVENTY-FOUR

GETTING SITUATED AT OUR respective counsel tables, the courtroom was a flutter with activity, as the judge took the bench and people in the gallery got settled.

Alyson glanced over at me expectantly. "*Well?*" She mouthed the word.

I shook my head. "No deal," I muttered in response.

She frowned. Then, she shrugged, suggesting our rejection of the plea was foolhardy.

Judge Mathers seemed to observe our communications. "Do either of you have anything to report to the court?" he asked.

Alyson stood and addressed the court. "The parties were not able to reach an agreement."

The judge looked over at me. "Is this the case?"

"Yes, Your Honor," I said, standing up.

"Very well." Judge Mathers turned to a bailiff. "Let's bring the jury back in."

A moment later, the jury filed into the courtroom and took their respective seats.

"Mr. Dwyer," Judge Mathers said. "Do you plan to call any witnesses?"

The comment made me pause. Judge Mathers used a tonc reflecting he anticipated the answer might be no. He may have figured we could put on a strong reasonable doubt argument at closing. I stood there for a bit, considering my options.

I perused the jurors. Each one stared at me pokerfaced.

Glancing around the courtroom, I watched the reporters in the gallery. None of them revealed a viewpoint of innocence or guilt. Kara Malloy and other people interested in the case sat peppered around the pews. They didn't divulge any indication of the possible outcome.

After a moment, I looked down at Brad. He started to rise from his chair.

Rapidly running the evidence through my mind, I considered recent developments. I hesitated. Then, instinct kicked in.

"The defense calls John Delany," I finally said.

"Objection!" Alyson bolted upright.

Judge Mathers looked at her, bewildered. "What's the matter?"

"This is a surprise witness," she said.

"You can't call surprise witnesses," the judge said to me.

"He's on our witness list," I retorted.

"That so?" He looked at Alyson. "Response?"

"This witness is at the end of the list. It comes as a surprise."

Judge Mathers shook his head, dismissively. "If he's on their list, then it cannot come as a surprise. Overruled."

"But, Your Honor?"

He shrugged. "Missy, you'll likely get the lunch break to prepare. I'll let you have an hour. Tell me that's not fair."

"Thank you, Your Honor." Alyson sat down, understanding when to quit.

Jack Delany stood up and walked through the gate.

We gazed at each other, as he approached the witness stand. Scorn registered in his eyes. He clearly resented being brought into the matter. It was a public trial where his former client was accused of murder.

I headed to the podium. The judge swore him under oath, then Jack sat down in the witness box.

My examination took him through various softball questions. The approach was to show he knew the defendant, had been friends with him since law school. Jack Delany admitted he represented Bradford Wallace. Then, he stated he'd been to Brad's house countless times. He even candidly stated he knew the decedent, but he qualified his response by stating he had only met her a few times in passing.

The clock slowly ticked away towards the lunch hour. My practice with a witness like this was to chew up the time with background and foundation questions. Then, the team circles up at lunch to develop some poignant questions before turning him over to the prosecution.

Alyson sat on her hands so to speak, biding her time. She didn't object to slightly leading questions, and she held back objecting to the relevance of my questions.

Many lawyers would have been at sidebar arguing what the witness or the testimony had to do with the case. Knowing me well, she understood I would respond by stating the questions related to the location of the crime, affiliation with the main players, and that I was laying foundation. Hence, the objections would have been overruled, and she would look poorly in front of the jury near the end of the trial. Nevertheless, she couldn't help herself, and maybe she had a plan. This was exactly what I was counting on.

"Mr. Delany, when were you last in the Wallace's house prior to Audrey Martin's death?" I asked.

"Objection," Alyson said, standing up. "May we approach?"

Judge Mathers didn't look thrilled, but he agreed to hear her out. "Come up here."

We walked over and stood by the oak bench for a sidebar.

The judge leaned forward. "What is it you would like to say?"

"You Honor, this entire line of questioning is irrelevant," Alyson said. "We simply do not need to hear about the defendant's friends and house guests."

Judge Mathers turned to me. "I tend to agree."

"This is the classic example," I retorted, "of an attorney laying a foundation and the opposing lawyer saying that it's not relevant. And if you jump to the salient testimony, they object stating that there wasn't a foundation."

"I also agree," Judge Mathers muttered. "But you've been going at it for some time now."

"Just give me a few more minutes and the relevance will become clear."

Alyson rolled her eyes. "He's just trying to distract the jury."

I gently touched her arm. "You'll want to hear this. I promise you."

She searched my eyes for a moment. "Okay, then."

"Very well," Judge Mathers concluded. "Now, back to your stations."

We returned to our positions, and I couldn't help wondering what branch of the military the judge had served in. Maybe the army. He was old-school and didn't address female attorneys properly. In fact, he had a blunt way of dealing with all lawyers.

Once situated at the podium, I smiled at Jack Delaney. He returned the favor, but a nervousness consumed him.

"Mr. Delany, when had you last seen Audrey Martin prior to her death?" I finally asked.

He sat there looking like a deer in headlights. Delany seemed to have realized the danger in my question. "I'm not entirely sure," he said, trying to buy some time. "I'd have to check my calendar."

"Do you have your calendar on your phone?"

"Sure," he said, shrugging. "But come to think of it, my calendar wouldn't shed any light on it. I'd never made an appointment to see her."

"Approach, Your Honor," I said, turning to the judge.

Judge Mathers motioned for us to take up a sidebar.

When Alyson stepped alongside me, I leaned closer to the bench. "Your Honor, I would like to treat Mr. Delaney as a hostile witness. He's clearly evading the answer here."

"Response?" Judge Mathers said to Alyson.

"This is too early in the examination to determine how the witness is performing. Counsel is just seeking a reason to ask leading questions."

Judge Mathers thought it over. "I'm going to allow the request. The witness was evasive, and I'd like to move this along."

Alyson walked back to her table, and I returned to the well and faced Delaney. "But you have met her?" I said, continuing my examination.

"Yes, that's true."

"Had you seen her the day she died?"

"No, I did not."

"What about in the few days before she died?"

"Unlikely."

"How about the few weeks before she died?"

"Quite possible."

"Would you have taken a shower in that time?" I said, stepping into the well.

Jack Delany's eyebrows furrowed. He paused, as he tried to determine where I was going with this line of questioning. A moment passed, then another.

"Could you instruct the witness to answer, Your Honor?"

The judge seemed to have drifted off for a moment himself. "Ah, the witness will answer the question," Judge Mathers finally said.

"Yes. I would have taken a shower," Delaney barked.

"Audrey Martin would have taken a shower as well," I said.

Delany sat there for a moment, as if waiting for the prosecution to object. Eventually, he glanced over at Alyson.

She stayed planted.

"Aren't you going to object?" Delany scolded her.

Judge Mathers snapped out of his stupor. He cracked the gavel, then turned to Delaney. "You will not address the lawyers in this case. I will address them. Only I will speak to them."

"Yes, sir," Delaney replied.

"Are you going to object?" the judge asked Alyson.

"No," she said, shaking her head. "Let's hear the answer."

The breakup in the questioning gave Delaney time to think. "I'm afraid that I cannot speculate upon her bathing habits," he said, jeering at me.

"You've met her," I said, moving closer to the witness box.

"Sure. I think we covered that," he quipped.

"Audrey Martin didn't present as someone who would go three days without a shower, correct?"

"I can't speculate," Delaney said, turning to the judge.

"The question is based on his personal knowledge and experience with the witness."

"On that basis, the witness will answer," said Judge Mathers.

"Fine," Delaney said, irritated. "I guess you can say she presented like someone who would have showered or bathed regularly."

His anger had gotten the best of him. I grinned.

This line of questioning laid the groundwork for showing that certain physical evidence found at the scene would have been put there around the time of her death, as compared to days or weeks beforehand. It could be used to direct the juror's attention to other potential suspects during my closing argument.

"Can you tell us why you called Audrey Martin on the day she died?" I said.

Delany looked at me confused. "What?"

"You don't remember calling her?" I said.

Delaney shrugged. "No."

Stepping to my table, I fetched a bound copy of Audrey Martin's phone records from the defense table. It was put into evidence during Detective Chandler's examination. I showed it to Alyson.

Then, I faced the judge. "May I approach the witness?"

"You most certainly may," Judge Mathers said.

I walked up to the witness box and placed the bound document down on the edge. Flipping the pages, I stopped at one where a phone number was highlighted in orange. Then, I pointed to the number for Delaney to see it.

He looked down at the document.

"Does this document refresh your recollection that you called Audrey Martin on the day of her death?" I asked in a level tone.

He leaned forward and stared at the document. Delaney ran a hand over his blading head, then he began rubbing his chin.

"Well?" I said, pointing to the highlighted phone call.

"That's my phone number, but I don't remember calling her. In fact, I wouldn't even recognize her number. There was no reason for me to call her." He sat back and exhaled. "I question whether this is authentic."

Turning from the witness, I peeked at the jury. Ever juror was glued to Delaney, and a few were glowering at him. People in the gallery had similar expressions. Malloy looked astonished. They all anticipated another question, like on television.

I didn't have a good faith basis to ask if he had killed Audrey Martin. We had to conclude the questioning with subtle inferences.

"That's all I have at this time," I said, walking towards the defense table.

Judge Mathers glanced at the clock. "We'll break for lunch. Everyone return in an hour. That will give you time to prepare," he added, speaking to Alyson.

We broke for lunch. I dropped the last exhibit on Alyson's table and flashed a sly grin. Then, I pushed through the gate and gathered with our team, planning to head to the luncheonette near Tremont and Beacon Street.

I knew they'd have a barrage of questions of what went down. And I didn't know how to explain it.

***

KARA MALLOY stood up and waited for the defense team to clear the courtroom. Then, she headed through the gate and walked up to the prosecution table.

"How are we going to handle that?" Kara said, referring to the Delaney examination.

"Never mind," Alyson said. "I'll take care of it."

"Dwyer made it seem like Jack Delaney had something to do with the death," Kara griped. "The jury is going to be confused as hell."

"Like I said, I'll take care of it. Find Chandler and look into this." Alyson handed her the document that defense counsel had just used on Delaney.

"Right," Kara said. Then, she left to find Chandler, thinking Bradford Wallace might just get an acquittal. They'd all get sued.

SEVENTY-FIVE

RETURNING FROM LUNCH, our team huddled near the defense table. Joey and Nate stood on the other side of the bar, while Brad and Courtney circled around me. We were still weighing the options of Brad's testimony.

The rest of the courtroom was deserted, except for a couple of bailiffs chatting about local sports. We were a few minutes early, but the place seemed dead for a murder trial.

Eventually, we made a joint decision to put Brad on the stand next.

"Where is everyone?" Joey said, breaking a lull in the discussion.

I glanced over at the prosecution table. Empty.

"Maybe people got tied up with the extended lunch break," Courtney offered. Sometimes having a little extra time will cause you to do more and run late."

"Sounds like you're talking from personal experience," Brad said, chuckling.

It was the first time Brad had shown any buoyancy since Audrey Martin had died. This was a good sign. He likely felt confident in the case and would testify better.

Clapping him on the shoulder, I said, "She's been known to push the envelope on late arrivals."

"Look who's talking," Courtney jibed.

Everyone laughed, signaling we'd reached a highpoint. The trial was going well.

Several reporters entered the courtroom and took up their seats in the gallery. A few of them watched us and took measure of our high spirits.

Jack Delaney walked in. He scowled at me, still riled at being called as a witness.

Glancing at the witness box, he seemed unsure about approaching it while the court was in recess. He lingered by the gate for a moment. Then, more people started filling up the pews. Jack walked into the well of the courtroom and leaned against the jury box.

"Come on," I said. "We're about to get started."

Joey and Nate sat down in the front pew, while the rest of us took our seats at the defense table. It was a couple minutes before the hour and the judge would likely take the bench. Taking a deep breath, I readied myself for the turbulent handling of Delany's cross-examination. I anticipated having to object a lot. I also wondered if the prosecution had gotten the gist of my actions undertaken right before the lunch break.

A moment later, six uniformed Boston police officers rushed into the courtroom. Malloy and Chandler trailed behind them, while Alyson brought up the rear.

They rushed into the well and circled Jack Delaney. He looked dumbfounded.

Just as an officer snatched a pair of handcuffs from his belt, the judge stepped into the courtroom.

He looked bewildered. "What is the meaning of this?"

"Your Honor, my apologies for the intrusion," Alyson said. "But we wanted to take care of this before the jury returned."

"Take care of what?" Judge Mathers said.

Kara Malloy stepped between two officers. "Mr. Delaney. We are with the Boston police. Please turn around and place your hands on your head."

"What's this about?" Delaney demanded.

"You are under arrest. Please comply with my commands."

Delaney tried to make a break for it. He charged Malloy, knocking her backward.

She pivoted and grabbed his hand, twisting it. Then, she raised his wrist and arm. He dropped to a knee. The other officers pinned him to the floor and snapped handcuffs on him.

They lifted him to his feet.

"John Delaney," Malloy said. "You are under arrest for the murders of Audrey Martin and Phillip Danforth."

Delany looked dumbfounded as he was escorted from the courtroom.

EPILOGUE

A FEW DAYS LATER, I walked into the office and plopped down in the chair behind my desk. My body ached from tussling with the thugs, and my hand was in a splint. I'd suffered a non-displaced fracture. Luckily, the doctor thought it would heal quickly.

Alyson had withdrawn the charges against Brad and the case was dismissed. People around town credited me for Jack Delaney's arrest. The story got a lot of press, and it was a big win for the firm. Yet, I wasn't satisfied. The attacks on members of the firm and holding us captive didn't sit well.

We had reported the incident to the police, but they were slow to act on the complaint. Beckerman had run out some leads and identified the guy who'd done most of the talking. This didn't result in an arrest. I wasn't sure whether someone with connections had put the hooligans into play. I still wondered if Detective Chandler had some involvement in the mess.

After considering the situation further, I called a former client and he showed up at the office around the time staff and attorneys were arriving for work. Pat led him into my office.

"How you been?" Lou Katsaros said, standing before my desk.

"We're doing well," I replied. Then, I got up and closed the door.

"So, what do ya' need?" Lou eyed me.

He didn't sit down, and I didn't offer him a chair. Instead, I walked behind my desk and pulled a set of keys from my pocket. Unlocking a drawer, I reached in and grabbed a bundle of cash. "I need a favor," I said.

"What kind of favor?" he grinned, taking the money.

Explaining the situation, I asked him to plant drugs in the head union honcho's car. Then, I wanted him to have someone dime the thug out to the police.

"No problem," Lou said, hefting the cash. "We've got a guy who's sort of a double-agent. He works as a CI for the BPD. We feed him information about our competitors, and they make arrests. In return, he picks up bits of information. He can call it in. When do you want it done?"

"Let's wait a couple of weeks, then bring him down."

"You got it." Lou laughed. Then, he headed for the door.

"Take care," I said.

"Sure thing."

Lou opened the door and shoved the cash into his coat pocket, almost bumping into Courtney on his way out of my office.

She walked in with a perplexed look on her face. "That what I think it was?"

"Don't worry about it," I said. "It's fine."

"Kenny, it's not fine. If you do something to retaliate, then you're no better—"

"Save me the lecture," I snapped. "They came at you and Barbara. And they took Nate hostage for Christ's sake!" I shook my head. "We have to hit them back, or else there will be a never-ending line of people trying to coerce us."

Courtney's face contorted into a crestfallen expression. She turned and marched away.

The manner of her egress announced she was through with the discussion. And I wondered if she was done with me.

***

TWO WEEKS AFTER THE TRIAL, a bunch of us got together for cocktails at the swanky restaurant near my office. Brad couldn't make it and Courtney was out on a blind date.

Everyone launched into war stories, making jokes about Novak's testimony and Jack Delany's arrest. We laughed and had a good time reliving the trial. I nursed a gin and tonic and kept a low profile, enjoying the banter.

The union worker set-up had resulted in an arrest. I started having second thoughts about it. My reaction was emotional. If I had waited, I probably would have just let things go.

As the night wore on, I moved to the edge of the crowd. I hunkered down at a corner of the bar and caught glimpses of the Celtics game. The place began filling up and the cacophony of bargoers drowned out the joking from our crew.

Eventually, Alyson ventured over and took a seat on the stool beside me. "How's it going?" she said, smiling.

"Good. I guess." I shrugged.

"You guess?" she repeated. "This was a great result for you."

"I might be talking more about my nonexistent personal life, rather than my professional life at the moment."

Alyson blanched. She had been the one who broke off our engagement.

"Sorry," I said. "I didn't mean to put you on the spot."

"What made you think it was Delaney?" she asked, changing the subject.

"A couple of things," I said, turning to face her.

"Like what?"

"I ran into him at The Last Hurrah," I explained. "He was drinking the same expensive scotch that was found at the crime scene."

She nodded. "And you remembered that little detail from all the files we sent over?"

"Not at first. But it eventually clicked."

"What else?" she asked, taking a sip of wine.

"Brad had an alibi for Audrey Martin's death. And he was supposed to meet me around the time Phillip Danforth was killed. I had a call with him not long beforehand, and it didn't sound like he was in a car. I figured the same person was behind both deaths, and the second death couldn't have been Brad."

Alyson smiled. "You had good instincts."

"How did you pick Delaney up for both murders?" I said.

"When you handed over the bound phone records to me in the courtroom, we took a strand of Delaney's hair, which had fallen into it during your examination, and ran it for a DNA test. It matched the piece of skin found under Audrey Martin's fingernail. Which I expect is what you hoped for."

"That's what I wanted you to do," I said. "But I was surprised you jumped to arrest him so quickly, and you agreed to dismiss Brad's charges. Arresting Delaney for Danforth's murder shocked me."

"We had found a hair in the van used to kill Danforth. It was a match with the sample you got from Delaney during his testimony at trial."

"Anything else?"

"Well…" Alyson said, running her fingers around the stem to her wine glass.

"Come on," I coaxed. "The suspense is killing me."

"Kara Malloy had a concern about an empty cup of coffee. The timing of Audrey Martin's entrance into the brownstone and her death… it really wouldn't account for time to drink a cup of coffee and engage in a tryst."

"You could have concluded the coffee was consumed another day."

"Harper Wallace kept that place as tidy as I've ever seen a house. No way."

"So, you doubted Brad's guilt all along?"

"Not me. I prosecuted in good faith. I just figured they met up soon before she died and had an argument. They didn't need to have slept together right before she died."

"But Malloy wasn't as convinced?"

Alyson shook her head. "Nope. She found the bed slightly unkempt, a bottle of expensive booze, and an attractive aide. She figured someone had hooked up and it turned ugly. We took the logical path. But sometimes the truth has more twists and turns."

A lull fell over our discussion as we nursed our drinks.

"I never thought my approach would lead to lead to an arrest for both murders," I finally said, talking about the hair sample taken from the van. "Just comes to show you guys often have more evidence than we realize."

Alyson grinned mischievously.

"So, what's going happen next?" I asked.

"You know I cannot comment on an ongoing investigation."

"Come on. I helped you nail this prick."

Alyson laughed. "Harper Wallace is going to flip on him."

"What?" I shook my head in disbelief.

"She was there," Alyson said.

"There?" I asked.

"At the crime scene. We've offered her immunity for an obstruction of justice charge in exchange for her testimony."

"So, what happened?" I said.

"Apparently, she was having an affair with Jack Delaney. They had been fooling around, thinking Brad would be out for the night. Jack didn't know about Brad's plans to work that evening from the house. Audrey Martin was working in the study and eventually heard something upstairs. She went to check it out and caught them in the act."

Sitting back in my chair, I couldn't believe it. "And?"

"Audrey was loyal to Brad. She told them she had to squeal. Harper and Jack tried to persuade her to keep quiet. But she wouldn't listen. She was young and grew hysterical. Jack and Audrey stepped onto the balcony, so she could get some air. After she calmed down, she told Jack she was resolved to speak to Brad about what she'd seen. Jack snapped and hurled her over the balcony."

"Who scratched her thigh?" I was thinking about the narrow nails. "Harper?"

Alyson shrugged. "Maybe Harper Wallace had some involvement. Could be Audrey had scratched herself at some point. Harper stated she had suspected Audrey Martin was having an affair with Brad, and maybe he'd gouged her. You can never know the entire truth in a case like this."

"Why did Jack Delaney kill the other aide?" I had plenty of questions.

"Harper Wallace told us Delaney was worried you'd get Brad acquitted for the Audrey Martin murder. Remember Harper and Brad had a prenup. Delaney sought to show a pattern of illegal conduct by Brad Wallace. His approach worked, too. We really had pegged Brad for both deaths. Killing

Danforth made it seem more probable that Audrey Martin had been murdered."

"How did he do it?" I shook my head. "Getting Danforth where he could be hit?"

"We aren't entirely sure. But Danforth had a few phone calls from a phone paid for by Brad's campaign. Our thought is that Delaney lured the aide to the scene by sending him on an errand, then telling him to meet Brad at The Last Hurrah."

Her comment made sense. I thought back to the meeting at Jack Delany's office after Brad was arrested. The arrest was later in the afternoon after Danforth had been killed. I'd noticed that Jack's suit appeared wrinkled, like he'd been out during the snowstorm.

Lawyers are often left with unanswered questions. I eventually nodded in agreement. Then, I polished off my glass. "I'm ready to call it quits," I said.

A hand clapped me on the shoulder. Turning, it was Michael Flannigan.

"Look, it's the man of the hour," Flannigan said.

"The police and prosecution deserve all the credit. I just helped feed them some evidence."

"Don't be so humble," he said, grinning. "You solved both cases."

"Just glad that it's over. To be honest with you.'

Flannigan nodded. "I'm sure."

His last comment should have been the end of our discussion. Yet, he lingered there, holding the grin longer than a genuine response. I wondered about his angle.

"You did us a favor with Brad Wallace," he finally said.

"I'm not sure I follow. He got acquitted. That doesn't help you at all."

Flannigan exhaled with a slight laugh. "A contact I've got in the press plans to run a story tomorrow morning. Brad Wallace is through."

"What story?"

"The one you set up for us,' he said, smacking my back.

I looked at him, baffled.

"You listed a woman as a witness. We investigated and tracked the girl down." Flannigan couldn't stop smiling. "It's getting out that he was dating call girls."

The comment took me aback. I wondered if I'd been careless.

Alyson sat quiet, with her mouth agape.

"You really did us a big favor," Flannigan said.

"Were you guys really that worried over his stance on unions?" I asked.

"No." He gesticulated. "This was about keeping *him* from getting into office. This state runs better with a governor from our party sitting on top of Beacon Hill."

"Just bushwhacking a rival candidate," I concluded.

"Politics has always been rough and tumble in this town. Just think back to the days of Michael Curley." He laughed.

"Isn't he the one who went to jail?"

"That's my point." Flannigan started to leave. Then, he turned back to me. "You had a good case going on reasonable doubt. You could have left her out of it. In fact, you could have left her off the witness list and called her as a rebuttal witness if you needed her. But you deliberately put her on the list. It was easy for us to track down, despite your efforts in not divulging her background."

"I didn't mean to—"

"Relax." He held up his hand. "You did good by us. We're putting your firm on the list, so you should expect to start receiving some cases filed against the city."

Flannigan walked away. I sat there dumbfounded, considering whether I had subconsciously brought about Brad's demise.

Ordering another drink, I tried to tell myself it was just a belt and suspenders approach to list the call girl as a witness. Ensuring a witness can testify, it is a better practice to list the witness than call her as a rebuttal witness. Some judges will not let a witness testify unless she is listed, even though the rules allow for unnamed rebuttal testimony. It was my practice to list everyone, rather than hope the rules for rebuttal witnesses get followed.

Made in the USA
Las Vegas, NV
05 March 2022